To Barb–
Get away with
a good book!

BW
5/22

Getaway

MOUNTAIN

PennWoods Mystery – Book 1

Blessings !

Michele Huey

Michele Huey

Zephaniah 3:17

S0-BZM-940

5-14-22

Getaway Mountain
PennWoods Mystery Book 1
Copyright © 2016 by Michele Huey

Cover design by Lynnette Bonner of Indie Cover Design
images ©
      www.bigstock.com, File: #90898190
      www.peopleimages.com, File: #ID1188164

Scripture taken from the HOLY BIBLE, NEW INTERNATIONAL VERSION®. NIV®. Copyright © 1973, 1978, 1984 by International Bible Society. Used by permission of Zondervan. All rights reserved worldwide.

All rights reserved. No part of this publication may be reproduced, stored in a retrieval system, or transmitted in any form or by any means—electronic, mechanical, photocopying, recording, or otherwise—without the prior permission of the author. The only exception is brief quotations in printed reviews, as provided by USA.

This book is a work of fiction. Names, characters, places, and incidents are either products of the author's imagination or have been used fictitiously. Any similarity to actual events, organizations, and/or persons, living or dead, is coincidental.

Michele Huey
121 Homestead Lane
Glen Campbell, PA 15742
www.michelehuey.wordpress.com

First Edition

ISBN-13: 978-1523302062

ISBN-10: 1523302062

Book Layout © 2014 BookDesignTemplates.com

Printed in the United States of America

Dedicated to the memory of my parents,

Peter and Mary Maddock, who ignited in me a love for the mountains

AUTHOR'S NOTE

I fell in love with the western Pennsylvania mountains when I was nine years old and my parents bought a one-room, rustic cabin with no running water, electricity, or foundation—the building rested on piers. For the next several years our family vacations were spent at Camp St. Jude, which my mother named for the saint of impossible cases. Whether the "impossible case" was the cabin, which Dad was remodeling, or my dad himself, Mom never divulged.

It quickly became my special place. I spent countless hours nestled in the limbs of a tall pine tree, dreaming of someday. So, yes, I had a dreaming tree, just like Melody did. It was at camp one summer evening on the swing beneath the pines I received my first kiss from my first boyfriend, the son of a reclusive man who lived in the middle of the forest in a log cabin he built himself—hence the inspiration for the mysterious mountain man of this book.

When my father died, we found a yellowed newspaper clipping in Dad's wallet: "High up in the lofty mountains is a cabin small but grand/Where I go when things perplex me, where I seek to understand . . ." I don't remember the rest of the poem, but it ended with the poet saying that when he came down from his mountain cabin and returned to real life, he saw more clearly and experienced a peace he couldn't find elsewhere.

It was a sad day when we decided to sell it, but close friends bought it, and my husband and I still have access to it.

There are times when I need camp time, and if I can't go physically to my special place, I go there in my mind and spirit.

So it only seems right to include my parents, Peter and Mary Maddock, who have long since passed on to their heavenly cabin, on my list of people to acknowledge. Thank you, Dad, for talking Mom into buying the cabin on the mountain near Cook Forest, and thank you, Mom, for going along with it. I know you both loved it as much as I do and had dreams to retire there.

Thanks also go out to Phil and Kathie Tubin, our dear, lifelong friends who bought the cabin and, recognizing its healing powers, generously put out the welcome mat to us and many others.

Special thanks also to my Christian Writers Guild mentor, Sandra Byrd, for her guidance, wisdom, instruction, and encouragement as I wrote the first chapters of this book as my assignment for the Craftsman course. Thank you, Jerry Jenkins and the staff of the former Christian Writers Guild, for the excellent resources you offered Christian writers. I wouldn't be pursuing my dream of writing fiction without you. And I can't forget the members of the Craftsman Class X, whose suggestions and encouragement helped to get this project off the ground: Bria Arline, Christy Brunke, Christine Eimers, Bonnie Lafitte, Neladene Middleton, Jan Olmstead, Eldon Reed, Erica Smiley, Elizabeth Van Tassel, Sammy Tippet, Brittany Valentine, and Jodie Wolfe, as well as the faculty of the three-day Craftsman residence: Dennis Hensley, Jeff Vankooten, and Julie Neils.

Thank you to my critique partners for your sharp eyes that caught what mine did not and for your suggestions and encouragement: Kathy Bolduc, Kay Clark, Virelle Kidder, Patty Krylach, Melanie Rigney, Jan Sady, Cass Wessel, and Robyn Whitlock. Thank you to my friend and mentor, Karen O'Connor, who graciously took the time to read through the manuscript and write a review.

Also special thanks to Lynnette Bonner, the talented woman who caught the vision of this story and designed the cover; Barbara J. Scott of Heartland Editorial Services for your suggestions and advice that made this manuscript shine; and to Linda M. Au, proofreader extraordinaire, for patiently answering all my questions and being available to help with formatting and walking me through the steps of indie publishing.

And finally, thank you to my brother, Pete Maddock; my best friend, Sharon Cessna; and my husband, Dean, for your unfailing faith in me and your steadfast support and encouragement.

CHAPTER ONE

"Melody Harmon," I told the headwaiter when I arrived at the Italian restaurant fifteen minutes late. "I'm with Cassie Stiles."

I didn't want to meet with my literary agent any more than I wanted to meet with the bank manager this afternoon to explain why I hadn't made a mortgage payment in three months. But Cassie had insisted, so I agreed.

I followed the waiter as he weaved through the sea of red-linen tablecloths, the aromas of garlic, basil, and tomato sauce reminding my stomach it hadn't been fed since my supper of yogurt and granola yesterday.

"Hi." I slipped into the booth across from Cassie, fighting the urge to run my fingers through my hair. I always felt underdressed around her. Her classy attire and perfect makeup reflected her success as a literary agent.

Today a V-neck, purple cashmere sweater hugged her generous curves, and a matching silk scarf draped gracefully around her shoulders, setting off the blonde highlights in her hair. A heart-shaped gold locket glinted against her tanned skin in the late morning sun. Perfect. Everything about Cassie was perfect.

Finally, she lowered the menu and looked at me, a hint of disapproval in her hazel eyes. "You look good in rust. That wide-boned corduroy vest is a good choice."

"But?" I snapped open the cloth napkin and laid it across my lap.

"Why do you think there's a 'but'?"

"There's always a 'but.'"

"Let's order," she said, turning her attention back to the menu.

I reached over and pulled it down so I could see her eyes. "Not yet. You issue your queenly summons, totally ignoring the fact that I had plans—important plans—for this morning. I rush to get here, and you're more interested in the food choices than me. Not even a 'Hello, Mel, glad you could make it on such short notice.' When you finally do acknowledge me . . ."

I realized the hum of conversation around us had lowered a decibel or two. When I get excited, I tend to get loud.

"How can I think of eating," I whispered, leaning toward her, "when I feel like there's something hanging over my head?"

Cassie's expression remained stoic as she stared at her menu.

She glanced up. "It's the way you look."

"What's wrong with the way I look?"

A patronizing smile warped her face as she placed her manicured hand over my nail-bitten one. "I've known you for twenty years and negotiated contracts for all ten of your romance novels. Believe me when I say I have your best interests at heart."

I pulled my hand away. "Mine? Or yours?" *Did I just say that?*

Her red glossy lips curved into a pout. "Have you looked at yourself in a mirror lately? A full-length mirror? You look like a frump. Every time I see you, you're wearing those baggy black pants. With cat hairs sticking to them. You've got a decent figure for your age. You're what? Fifty-five?"

"Fifty-one." As discreetly as possible, I brushed cat hair off my slacks.

"It's been over a year since Paul died, Mel. Time to get out of your widow's weeds."

Sudden hot tears pressed against my eyelids.

"First, black goes with everything." I swallowed hard. "Second, all my pants are baggy. My appetite went AWOL a year and a half ago. Third, Paul left me with a ton of debt and I can't afford—" I slammed the menu on the table. "Do we have to talk about this?"

The conversation around us hushed.

"Lower your voice. You're making a scene." She gave me a forced smile. "Yes, we have to talk about it. That's part of my job."

"Your job is to sell my manuscripts, not give me a fashion makeover."

"My job is to sell *you*. People are celebrity-hungry these days. So readers, naturally, want to know all about their favorite authors. You've hidden behind a pen name long enough. Time to break out the real you. But with a few modifications."

"Romance novels by Melanie Joy are still on the bookshelves, so I don't see what the problem is."

"The problem *is*, my friend—"

The waiter appeared at the table, a pencil poised above his tablet. "Are you ready to order, ladies? The specials are—"

Cassie shoved her menu at him. "Skip the specials. I'll have the baked Italian sub."

Where were my glasses? No wonder I couldn't read the menu. I fumbled through my bag and then patted my neckline.

"On top of your head."

"Huh?"

"Your reading glasses are stuck in that crazy hair of yours. Look, I know a great hairdresser—"

"Stop." I untangled the frames from my frizz and slid them on my nose. "Please, just stop." A lump lodged in my throat as I scanned the lunch selections. I had to blink away the tears to see the prices. Yikes! I could eat for a week with what the tab for the two of us would be. Toast, yogurt, and ramen noodles, however, weren't offered on the menu.

"Order what you want. I'm buying," Cassie said.

Then it's bad news. I folded the menu and handed it to the waiter. "I'll have the wedding soup, please."

Cassie held up her empty coffee cup. "Refill, please. And add a big bowl of salad with your special homemade dressing. Bring two salad plates."

"I'll have hot tea," I said. "Please."

I waited until the young man had rounded the corner and then looked Cassie straight in the eye.

"I sent my manuscript in four months ago. It doesn't take this long. And why the sudden interest in my looks?"

Cassie grinned, reached into her briefcase, and pulled out two books. "Here's some reading material for you."

I scanned the covers. "Don Bridges. I don't read guy books."

"You do now."

"I don't like mysteries."

"No, you like sappy love stories because . . . Look, Mel, I'll give it to you straight. Your manuscript was a no-go. They want you and Don to team up and coauthor a romantic suspense. If the first one's any good, we'll see about a series."

"I write romance, not sappy love stories. There's a difference. And I write alone."

"Yeah, yeah, in that mountaintop shack in redneck country."

"It's not a shack, it's a cottage. And I've spent quite a bit of time and money modernizing it."

"I still don't see why you didn't buy that old farmhouse up the road you told me about when it went up for sale. At least you'd have central heat."

I glanced out the window. "My place is . . . special. Has been since I was a kid."

She shrugged. "Loyalty won't keep you warm or save you unnecessary work, like cutting firewood."

We watched, an awkward silence between us, as the waiter poured steaming coffee into Cassie's cup and left.

Where's my tea?

"Is the farmhouse still available?" Cassie added cream to her coffee.

"I don't know. Why? Are you thinking of snapping it up?"

Cassie snorted. "You know better. But I know someone who might be interested in renting it for a time. Where exactly is this getaway mountain of yours anyway?"

"Near Seneca Forest."

"Nearest town?"

"Clarington is the name of the little village down the mountain, but I think the realtor's from Marysville."

Cassie tapped the information into her smart phone. She was up to something. She was suddenly much too interested in the property I'd told her about months ago.

"And just who might be interested?" I tried to read her phone, but she turned it face down on the table and then attempted to hide her sheepish grin behind her linen napkin. "You aren't trying to fix me up with anyone again, are you?"

"No, no. Nothing like that. Since you and Don are going to be working together, don't you think it would be a good idea for him to be just up the road from your writing getaway?"

"No. I. Write. Alone. Period."

"Oh, stop being such a prig."

"I'm not being a prig. I just don't want a writing partner."

The waiter appeared, plunking down our salad and a basket of steaming breadsticks on the table between us. The tangy aroma of the homemade dressing mingled with the sweet smell of freshly baked bread. My mouth watered. Cassie served us both with generous portions of greens and slathered two breadsticks with soft butter, dropping one on my bread plate.

"Why did they reject my manuscript?" I plucked out the onions and hot peppers from the salad and dropped them on the paper placemat. "I thought they liked the proposal."

Cassie sighed. "They're looking at numbers, and your last two books didn't sell as well as they'd hoped. They think Don's suspense will blend with your romance for a nice balance. You'll complement each other."

"I don't need anybody to complement me."

"Well, according to your publisher—soon to be *former* publisher if you don't get your act together—you need something to boost sales."

"I don't understand. My last royalty check wasn't as big as it has been in the past, but my e-books are selling well."

"Not as well as they want."

"What about my fans? I get at least a hundred hits a day on my website and at least that many on my blog."

I stabbed a tomato, dripping with dressing, and shoved it into my mouth, barely chewing it before I swallowed. It almost stuck in my throat. This was not the conversation I'd expected.

I watched an older couple follow the headwaiter to a table near ours. A familiar ache wrapped around my heart as the man held the chair for the woman and then smiled at her with a tenderness I only wrote about. When was the last time Paul had smiled at me like that? Or held the chair for me?

Cassie's voice broke into my longings. "Listen, I tried, but they said your plots are too predictable."

I tore my eyes away from the couple. "Maybe I could write under another pen name."

"I tried that angle, too, but they said the writing is bland. And I agree. Sorry, Mel. But I think collaborating with Don will be just the boost your writing career needs right now. Who knows? Maybe a little passion in your real life will ignite the fire that's been missing in your romances."

She *was* up to her matchmaking again.

"Don't even think it. I'm perfectly content being single."

She cocked one eyebrow. "You're not fooling me. If you ask me, you've been single for a lot longer than eighteen months."

I shot her my best withering look. "Don't even go there."

"All right, all right. But think about it. I have your best—"

"Interests at heart. I know. What about a woman coauthor?"

"They want Don."

"What's so special about him?"

A seductive smile deepened her dimples. "That's for you to discover."

"Or not. How do you know him anyway?" Her smile widened. "Oh, I get it. He's another client of yours. Don't want to share your 15 percent with another agent, huh?"

"Why are you always so defensive? Don't you trust me?" She took a sip of coffee.

I shifted in my seat and avoided her eyes. Trust is a lot like Humpty Dumpty. Once it's broken, you can't put it back together.

The golden flecks in her hazel eyes ignited. "Our relationship has to be built on trust. Without it, we have no relationship."

Cassie had always steered me true. She'd believed in me when no one else did.

"You have to stop second guessing everyone's motives. Just because—"

"Okay, I trust you. I'm sorry." I looked around for the waiter who had forgotten to bring my tea. That's me. Good ole Mel. Forgettable and forsaken. "Do I have any other options?"

"Not if you want to publish with Deagan Press."

"What about another publisher?"

Cassie shook her head. "Mel, the publishing industry isn't what it was when you first started. They want big names—and I mean *big* names. The ones who produce big numbers. And they want authors who are more visible. Why don't you teach a workshop at a writers' conference or accept some speaking engagements? I know you've been asked." She picked up her phone again. "In fact, I have a contact—"

"No." I dropped my fork and stared out the window at the white vapor trails crisscrossing the vivid blue sky above the shopping mall. "I'm a writer. Not a teacher or a speaker."

"Stop being so stubborn. At least give writing with Don a try."

"And if I don't?"

"Then I hope you have a good retirement plan."

The waiter brought our entrees. Conversation was stilted the rest of the meal. I couldn't believe this could be the end of my writing career. I stirred my soup and sipped a couple of spoonfuls, but when the server came to take our dessert order, my bowl was still full. Cassie ordered two slices of cherry cheesecake to go and told the waiter to box up my soup and the remaining breadsticks. When he returned with the to-go bag and the check, Cassie removed one of the cheesecake boxes and put the Don Bridges books in the bag, which she slid across the table.

"Read them," she said. "It'll be good for you to break out and try something new. Call me when you're done. Then we'll talk."

I never did get my tea.

At five minutes after two, I pulled my aging Explorer into the bank parking lot and wheeled into a stall. Pulling down the sun visor, I ran my fingers through my frizzy dark hair. I'd stopped taming it long ago, opting instead for what I called a "windblown, wild look." Paul bought a flat iron for me one year for Christmas, but it just made things worse. Why couldn't he have just accepted me the way I was?

I pulled the foreclosure notice out of my tote bag to check for the hundredth time the name of the bank manager. "Stephen Morley, 2 p.m.," I'd scribbled across the top along with the date. Not the friendly loan officer who'd approved our mortgage twenty years ago. That guy was long gone, along with the hometown atmosphere that had made me feel like a person, not just an account number. These days there was a drive-up window and online banking and maddening telephone menus and other methods of not meeting customers face-to-face. I stared at the September sky.

"Hey, God. Are You up there? Somewhere beyond the blue? I know I haven't talked to You in a long time, but just this once—"

A gleaming black luxury car pulled into the parking space beside me, and a slim young blonde, dressed in the kind of clothes Cassie wanted me to wear, stepped out, slung a black, expensive-looking purse over her shoulder, and disappeared into the bank. Suddenly, I felt frumpy. Old. Poor. Alone. Hopeless.

"Oh, never mind," I muttered to the silent sky. "You don't care anyway."

Shoving the notice into my purse, I grabbed the file folder from the passenger seat, took a deep breath, and followed Miss Class Act into the bank, hoping to keep my house, but doubting very much I would.

CHAPTER TWO

At 2:15 the door to the branch manager's office opened and Miss Class Act stepped out.

Not her. Please, God, no.

"Mrs. Harmon?" she said in a crisp, professional voice. A charcoal-gray suit draped her lithe frame. Black-framed glasses hanging from a gold chain rested on the loose bow of her royal blue silk blouse. I wondered if my sticky roller brush had picked up all the cat hairs on my slacks.

"This way, please."

Maybe she's the mortgage guy's secretary.

I followed her honey-gold chignon into the office. But no. She settled herself into the leather executive chair behind a much-too-clean-and-organized-to-be-busy desk and casually waved to the pair of matching black box armchairs meant to intimidate begging clients like me.

"What can I do for you today?" She flashed me an assured smile.

"There must be some mistake," I stammered, clutching my file folder. "My appointment is with Mr. Morley. Stephen Morley."

She pointed to the nameplate on the desk that identified her as "Stephanie Morley, Branch Manager." *Oh.*

"I must have misheard," I mumbled, glad that my frizz hid my flaming ears.

A quick smile softened her porcelain features. "Don't worry about it. It happens all the time."

I lowered myself onto the upholstered seat.

"I received this yesterday." I handed her the foreclosure notice. "My husband and I took out a home equity loan to build a garage.

Then he died suddenly. We didn't have life insurance on the loan. I was able to make the payments until July. I'm a freelance writer, but my last royalty check was . . . uh . . . less than I'd expected."

She slipped on her eyeglasses and examined the notice.

"Have you been getting any phone calls about this? We turn over outstanding debts to a collection agency before starting the foreclosure process."

I squirmed in the chair. "I don't know. Maybe. Probably."

Her arched eyebrows begged for an explanation of my multiple-choice answer.

"I usually let my calls go to voice mail. I don't like interruptions when I'm writing." I took a breath and smoothed back my hair. I felt a nervous babble coming on. "If they did call and leave a message, I deleted it before I even listened to it. Most of my messages are from telemarketers, and they always lie. They tell me it'll only take a minute, but it takes fifteen. They say all they want to do is thank me for my patronage, but they try to sell me something and follow a script that has an answer to everything I say. They have no shame. Or they leave long messages. And I just hate robo-calls. I can always tell if it's one of those. There's always a two- or three-second delay before it starts."

So much for controlling my nervous babble. I was out of breath.

She folded her hands in front of her, resting her elbows on the sparkling glass desktop.

"You've had a few hard months, I'm sure. I understand."

How could she? She drove a late-model, luxury car; reeked of five-hundred-dollar-an-ounce perfume, and owned a purse that cost more than all the clothes in my entire closet. I doubted if she'd ever had a hard day in her life.

Certainly, her husband wouldn't cheat on her. Or allot her a meager allowance for household expenses and nothing more. She probably never had to ask him for cash for clothes. And she wouldn't have to hide what she made from him.

"If you had come in when you first knew you were going to miss a payment, we could have worked something out." She slid the notice back to me across the shiny glass desktop and shook her head. "As it is, you're three months in arrears, and the foreclosure process has already begun. Is there any way you can make a payment today?"

"If I could, I wouldn't be here." I plucked the notice off her desk, stuffed it in the file folder, and stood. "I'm sorry for bothering you."

A strange look flashed across her face. "Wait." She glanced at her diamond-studded watch. "I have time before my next appointment. Why don't you tell me more about your situation? After all, you and your late husband have been longtime customers of this bank. Maybe I can find a way to buy you some time."

I didn't correct her. *Paul* had his accounts with this bank. I had mine with a credit union through the writers' guild. The mortgage was the only account Paul and I had together with this bank. But if she could help, who was I to keep her from trying? I sat back down.

"Let me see that foreclosure notice again."

"This whole thing has been a shock." I fished the piece of paper back out of the folder and placed it on her desk. "First he falls off a balcony while on a trip to Mexico. Do you know what a nightmare it is when someone dies in a foreign country? The police and autopsy reports were in Spanish—so was the death certificate. And the fees . . . I had to pay that Mexican funeral home five hundred dollars up front. Then another three grand before they'd ship his ashes home. You don't even want to know how much it would have cost—and all the red tape involved—in shipping a body back home. His folks were furious with me for having him cremated, but they weren't offering to help. Personally, I think that Mexican funeral home was on the take, but what could I do?"

Ms. Morley shook her head in apparent sympathy. "I can't imagine. You must have felt so helpless . . . being all by yourself in Playa del Carmen after that horrible accident. Do you speak Spanish?"

I shook my head. "I . . . didn't go with him. I was on deadline."

I hadn't even known Paul had gone to Mexico until I got the call that he was dead. But she didn't need to know that. She did need to know why I hadn't been able to meet my financial obligations. I pushed my hair back from my forehead and continued my tale of woe.

"I finally got things straightened out with the insurance company—they wouldn't accept a Spanish death certificate, and I had to jump through the hoops to get an English Certificate of Death Abroad, which, after consulting with the State Department, they finally accepted. Then I learn my husband borrowed on his life insurance and didn't pay back the loan, leaving me with next to nothing to pay off the three credit cards he maxed out."

It felt as though a giant rubber band tightened around my head. I rubbed my temples and took a deep breath.

"He didn't have traveler's insurance?"

I shook my head. He was too cheap. But, of course, I couldn't say that. I didn't want to sound like a bitter widow.

"It's taken me eighteen months, but I finally paid them off. Without Paul's income or any life insurance benefits, it's been a real struggle to keep up with all the expenses that come with owning a house—utilities, repairs, insurance, taxes."

As she tapped information into her computer, I stared out the window behind her, watching the Japanese maple trees across the parking lot sway in the wind. The property taxes, which had gone up again, were due December 1. I had no idea how I'd pay them. I'd counted on the advance from my publisher to catch up with the mortgage and pay the taxes on time. Last year's taxes, added to the expenses of Paul's funeral, wiped out both my nest egg and my emergency fund. If I were a praying person, I would have been pounding on heaven's doors.

Stephanie Morley studied the screen, deftly maneuvering her purple mouse. After a few minutes, she turned to me.

"Do you have any other banking accounts?"

"I have checking and savings accounts with AWACU—the Artists and Writers Association Credit Union—but there's not much in them."

"Do you have your account numbers with you?"

I squirmed. "Why?"

"So I can access them to see how much you have. So maybe—and that's a big maybe—we can work something out to avoid this foreclosure."

"Can't you just take my word for it?"

Her cotton-candy smile didn't quite reach her steel-gray eyes. "Unfortunately, no. I need documentation."

Why didn't I trust her? Or was it that I just didn't trust anyone these days? Paul hadn't even known my account numbers. Thank God for direct deposit.

"Mrs. Harmon?"

Should I? After all, she was trying to help. But still I paused as I reached into my jumbled purse for my checkbook. I thrust it at her with sweaty palms.

She refocused her attention on the screen, tapping lightly on the keyboard. "I need your password."

"No, you don't," I said, snatching my checkbook from her manicured fingers. I opened the register. "See? There's the balance. Not enough to cover my living expenses until my next royalty check. And here's the savings account balance." I flipped through the savings account register. "Not enough to replace the washer if it goes out on me. Or pay for another repair on my limping SUV. If you don't believe me, you can call the credit union for verification."

I slipped the checkbook into my purse and clutched it to my chest. Her glossy red lips twitched as she regarded me for what seemed an eternity.

She finally blinked. "All right, then. Do you have any assets you could sell to catch up on the payments? An extra car?"

"Paul leased his Mercedes. I just have my sixteen-year-old Explorer, which wouldn't go for much, I'm afraid."

She frowned. "What about property? A beach house? A condo? A getaway place?"

"I have my writing retreat in the mountains, but there's no way I'd sell it."

"Why not?"

Because it's who I am, I wanted to tell her. It's my roots, my heart, and my wings. Instead I said, "It's just not an option."

"All right, then. Any investments you could cash in?"

I shook my head. "Paul cashed in on his . . . our . . . investments the year before he died. He even took out his pension."

She studied me for a moment, the question I'd been asking myself for a year in her eyes. "What did he do with all that money?"

"That, Ms. Morley, is the million-dollar question. I couldn't find it. Couldn't find where he'd bought anything with it or paid any bills with it. My lawyer couldn't find it. My accountant couldn't find it."

"An off-shore account, maybe?"

I shook my head. "Nothing. At least nothing in his name."

We stared at each other, the wall clock behind me ticking away the seconds. Then she folded up the foreclosure notice and slipped it across the desk.

"I'm sorry for your predicament, Mrs. Harmon, but I can't help you—except to advise you to hire an attorney who specializes in bankruptcy and foreclosure—" She raised her eyebrows and cocked her head to one side— "and a good criminal defense lawyer."

I stared at her. "Why a criminal defense lawyer?"

"You refuse to let me see your bank balances, so I wonder—what do you have to hide?"

"You've got to be kidding! I—"

Stephanie Morley stood. "Good afternoon, Mrs. Harmon. And good luck."

Aunt Peg's two-story brick home sat on one hundred acres of former farmland a few miles outside of the city limits. My Explorer spluttered up her poplar-lined driveway as the late afternoon sun played hide-and-seek with the fall sky.

At seventy-five, my mother's youngest sister, Margaret Mary Thompson, still exuded a zest for life that infected all she came in contact with—people, animals, projects—nothing was immune. At fifty-seven, she'd hiked a trail to the top of Mount Whitney with several of her buddies and still enjoyed exploring rugged mountain trails and camping out with her girlfriends. She took her role as my godmother seriously, even though I'd long outgrown any need for her coddling. It was she who'd encouraged me to pursue my lifelong dream to write and to whom I fled when my dreams of happily-ever-after came crashing down.

I found Aunt Peg in the backyard garden, digging up potatoes. She was dressed in what she called her farmer's clothes—faded blue coveralls caked with mud, a red-plaid flannel shirt, and black rubber boots. One petite foot pushed down on the spade as I approached the garden fence. The sweet smell of overturned soil evoked memories of the times I'd worked beside her, my eager fingers plunging into the damp dirt seeking the spuds that would fill her root cellar. I'd always wanted to be like her, to live in the country, grow my own vegetables, and have a half dozen kids. Then I met Paul.

"Hey, stranger," I called, feeling the urge to kick off my loafers, peel down my knee-highs, roll up my pants, and join her.

She peered from under the wide brim of her straw gardening hat and held up her dirt-stained hand to shield her eyes from the sun.

"Melody, what a nice surprise!"

I reached out to balance myself and kick off my shoes to join her when she held up her hand.

"Careful," she called, nodding toward two clothesline wires strung above the chain link fence surrounding the garden. "Those wires have juice."

Puzzled, I stepped back. I didn't see any power lines. "How—"

"Solar-powered fence charger. See that box mounted on the corner post? Butch's idea. Keeps the deer from feasting on our harvest."

Butch was her retired lawyer husband, Clifford David Thompson III.

"Does it work?"

Her small mouth broke out in the wide grin that always made me feel welcome. "Like a dream. So, what brings you here? Not to help me dig potatoes, I'm sure."

"Is Uncle Butch around?"

"I sent him to the grocery store for some Parmesan cheese. He should be back any minute. Unless Mr. Former District Attorney runs into someone he knows. Then it could be hours." Plucking the spuds from the shovel, she placed them in a scarred, red-plastic, five-gallon bucket that leaned on the overturned soil. "Let me finish this row. It won't take long. Why don't you go put the kettle on for some tea?"

An hour later we lazed in a cozy oak booth in the breakfast nook. A blue-flowered teapot sat on a trivet between us. It had taken two mugs of Earl Grey tea to pour out my whole sorry story.

"I can't say I'm surprised," Aunt Peg said. "I never did like Paul. He had shifty eyes."

"Why would that bank woman say I needed a criminal defense lawyer?" Hot tears pressed against my eyelids. I blinked them back. "I didn't do anything wrong."

"What was wrong, my dear niece, was that you trusted Paul with your finances all those years, never questioning him. I know you've always had trouble with numbers—a type of dyslexia, I suppose—and he was an accountant. It's a good thing you hired your own accountant when your novels started to sell and let him think your writing was just a nice little hobby, or he would have gobbled up all your money too."

The back door opened and Uncle Butch stomped in, lugging several grocery sacks, which he deposited on the sunshine-yellow countertop.

Aunt Peg gasped. "Clifford David Thompson the Third, what on earth is all that? All I sent you for was some cheese."

A sheepish grin spread across his tanned face. "Did you know Tuesday is Senior Citizens Day? I got all kinds of discounts, even on the specials."

A sigh escaped Aunt Peg's lips. "Remind me not to send you to the store on Tuesdays." She slipped out of the booth. "I'll put those away. You sit down and have some tea. Melody needs our help."

Uncle Butch took notes on the back of the grocery list as I explained my predicament again.

"I was afraid something like this would happen," he said when I finished.

"Why?" I got up, filled the kettle with tap water, and put it on the stove beside a simmering pot of Aunt Peg's homemade spaghetti sauce. "I didn't see it coming."

He raised a bushy white eyebrow and gave me the look that had withered many an opponent in the courtroom. "My dear, you didn't want to see it coming."

Aunt Peg nodded, her thick white hair framing a concerned face. "That's right, Melody, sweetheart. First you were blinded by love. Then you chose to stay blind. Butch, dear, go get your little black book."

"Don't need to. I know exactly who Mel needs. Give me some paper." Aunt Peg opened a drawer and pulled out a pocket-size, spiral notebook and handed it to him. He scribbled a name and phone number on a sheet, which he slid across the table to me. "Georgina Rosenfield. She's the best."

Aunt Peg nodded. "The only one who ever beat him in court."

After a dinner of spaghetti and meatballs—the sauce prepared with fresh tomatoes from her garden—and a Caesar salad, I helped Aunt

Peg clean up while Uncle Butch made some phone calls. Then we carried our tea into the den. Flames flickered like lazy fingers on the hearth. The scent of wood smoke ignited the longing I'd been fighting all day.

"I'm going to the cottage." I settled onto a plush love seat facing the stone fireplace. "Tomorrow."

"But what about your appointment with Georgina?" Aunt Peg leaned over to place a tray with our dessert on the coffee table, but books and magazines were scattered across the top.

"It can wait until I get back. I need to go." I stacked the magazines and books on the braided rug. "Getaway Mountain is the only place where I can think."

I lifted an open book. Using the back flap as a bookmark, I closed the volume—then gasped. It was one of the two titles Cassie had given me that morning—*The Last Case* by Don Bridges.

"Who's reading this?" I waved the book in the air like a madwoman.

"I am." Aunt Peg's spunky brown eyes widened with surprise. "Why in heaven's name are you so upset?"

"I thought you liked romance," I said. "Not guy books."

She placed a plate of peach pie a la mode in Uncle Butch's hand and set another beside my tea mug on the oak end table.

"Your uncle read it and raved about how good it was—and you know how picky he is about crime and suspense novels. So I started reading it and couldn't put it down. His plots could stand a little sweetening up with some romance, but he's . . . Why do you look like you're ready to puke? Was it the spaghetti? Did I put too much basil in the sauce?"

"No, no," I murmured. I couldn't believe it. Aunt Peg reading Don Bridges. I *was* going to be sick. "I didn't tell you the whole story."

She raised her eyebrows. "There's more?"

"Unfortunately."

"Oh, dear, how much worse can it get?"

"I met with my agent this morning." I wished I'd made some peppermint tea instead of the chocolate hazelnut. Peppermint settles the stomach. "She wants me to team up with Don Bridges to write a romantic suspense novel."

Aunt Peg gasped, obviously delighted. "Oh, how wonderful! It's just what your novels need."

"What do you mean?"

"Oh, dear, how do I say this?" She took a breath. "You know I'm your biggest fan. I've read all your novels and have even used them in the book club. But lately, the past couple of books, something's missing. I can't put my finger on it. They fall flat. I'm not surprised anymore. I can almost predict the storyline."

I bent over and buried my face in my hands. I wanted to weep.

"Melody, dear, I'm sorry." She sat on the love seat next to me and wrapped her arm around my shoulders. "Maybe it's just that you're so . . . well, the past year and a half would send any muse running. It'll come back, you'll see."

I hoped she was right.

CHAPTER THREE

Wilson's General Store, traditionally my last stop of the three-hour drive from home, looked like something out of a Norman Rockwell illustration. A hand-painted wooden sign hung over the white clapboard façade. Red gingham curtains framed the old-fashioned, plate glass display window. A metal shed roof leaned on thick wooden posts, covering a six-foot porch that spanned the front.

I stepped out of my Explorer and stretched the kink out of my shoulders. The late morning sun hadn't yet burned off the autumn mist that hovered in the river valley. Pulling down the sleeves of my hoodie, I drank in the view, basking in the coming-home sensation that filled my soul with my first breath of the pine-scented mountain air.

The village of Clarington was as sleepy now as it had been when my parents bought the cabin that now served as my writing retreat. No more than a dozen houses stood in this riverbank community. Most were well kept. A handful were summer homes. A few needed a good coat of paint and some repairs, but the yards were trim and neat. These proud, stalwart, mountain people got along with the summer people, but they didn't quite respect the outsiders. Behind their backs the villagers called them "summies."

I wasn't a summie. I, like my parents before me, braved Camp St. Jude spring, summer, fall, and winter. My mother named the cottage after the saint of impossible cases. I never knew whether the impossible case was the rustic, one-room cabin or my father, who'd wooed her into buying it. She dreamed of a cozy retirement home. He just wanted to hunt and fish. At least he'd made good on his promise to run electricity and drill a water well, but he died before he could retire. After his funeral, Mom sold the place to me for a dollar.

Shaking off the memories, I strode past the outdated gas pumps and up the wooden steps. A bell jingled as I stepped inside and shut the door behind me. Worn plank floors creaked under my hiking boots as I made my way to the cluttered counter.

"Be right there," called a gravelly voice from the back room. A few seconds later a head of Einstein-like, white hair perched atop a plaid flannel shirt burst through the gingham curtain that separated the store from the office/storage area in the rear. The owner could have doubled for Christopher Lloyd in *Back to the Future*.

"Melody Joyner! Must have a deadline breathing down your neck." Willie Wilson's grin erupted across his wrinkled face and ignited his intense blue eyes. He never could remember my married name and called me by my maiden name. "What can I get for you?"

"The usual. A half-gallon each of white and chocolate milk and a dozen eggs, please."

"Brown or white?"

"Brown."

When we'd first bought the cabin, both the white milk and the eggs were farm fresh. Now only the eggs were. As Willie got my order together, I stared at the age-darkened shelves filled with dusty canned goods, boxes of cereal, and bags of sugar, flour, and coffee that lined the wall behind the counter. Wilson's was the old-fashioned kind of store where you told them what you wanted and the aproned owner filled your order, marking each item on a carbonized sales receipt pad. Some things never changed, I thought, finding comfort in the scene.

"How long you here for?" Willie asked as he placed my order on the counter, taking extra care with the eggs.

"A few days." *Until I figure out what to do.*

"How's that boy of yours? What's his name again?"

"Garrett."

"That's right. Ain't seen him in a while."

"I haven't either. His work keeps him busy."

"Still a photographer?"

"Oh, yes. It's his passion. He travels all over the world for *National Geographic* now. He's out West somewhere—Utah, I think. Or North Dakota." I shrugged. "He calls when he can."

"Married yet?"

"With his hours and travel schedule, he doesn't even have time to date. But I hope he finds someone before too long. I want some grandchildren before I get too old to enjoy them." I eyed a realtor's poster on the crowded bulletin board on the wall to my right. "Has the Campbell place sold yet?"

For some reason, I hoped it hadn't. I'd read Don's bio on the dust jacket of the books Cassie had given me and which I'd begrudgingly packed. A former state trooper with fifteen books published, Don Bridges was a widower who raised three daughters alone and "enjoyed spending time with his four grandchildren." His picture showed a pleasant-looking man with wavy, salt-and-pepper hair, a dimple in his chin, and an easy smile that reached his twinkling blue eyes.

Willie gave me his pooh-pooh look. "Nah. Some city fellers from over in Ohio were looking at it this summer fer a hunting lodge. Wanted it for practically nothing." He finished penciling in my order on the sales pad then punched the keys on the ancient register. The drawer jerked out with a groan, just missing his slight paunch. "But you got a new neighbor."

"Oh?" A mixture of relief that the Campbell farm was still available and annoyance that I wouldn't be alone on my mountain took me by surprise as I handed him a twenty. "Hunter or summie?"

"Neither. Year-round. Bought the cabin a half mile from yours— the red-shingled one. Moved in a couple three weeks ago. Planning to fix it up before winter. Seems to be an okay fella, I guess. His folks must've had a sick sense of humor, though, naming him Jacob Esau. Goes by Jake. Only met him the one time he come in here for a map of the area and some coffee, ready-made, mind you. Told him this weren't no 7-Eleven. I felt sorry for him—a guy's gotta have his cuppa joe, you know—so I poured him a cup from the pot in back." Willie's quick laughter bounced through the store. "Don't like it as strong as I do."

"Is he an older man?" I imagined him as retired. Or unemployed. Maybe he lost his house—like I was about to—and bought the ramshackle cabin away from civilization because it was all he could afford.

Willie scrunched up his face and scratched his whiskered chin. "What do you call older? Me? Now I'm older."

"Retired. In his sixties."

He handed me my change. "Nah, I'd say fifties. His hair—what I could see of it sticking out from under his ball cap, was still dark. A couple days' worth of stubble on his face—but I guess that's the style now. Just about all the fellas who come in here for fishing bait have that five-o'clock shadow look. Couldn't see his eyes, though. Had on them kind of glasses that gets dark when you go outside and lighten up again when you come inside. Eyes tell a lot about a person, you know. But they were bifocals. I seen the line. And if that don't mark you as at least middle-aged, I don't know what does."

After he placed my things in a thick, brown-paper grocery bag, he reached in the glass case below the counter, snatched a candy bar from a box in the display, and dropped it in my bag. It was a tradition he started when I was nine.

"No order for Melody Joyner is complete without some chocolate with almonds."

"William Woodrow Wilson, you spoil me! Thanks for the TLC."

His face suddenly turned serious. "You take care on the mountain, you hear? You're too much of a trusting soul."

Not anymore. I leaned over the counter and gave him a peck on his leathery cheek. "I will. I'll stop by on my way home so you know I'm all right." I smiled at him.

Before I left, I stopped to read the poster advertising the Campbell property. Along the bottom were tags with the realtor's name and phone number. I tore one off and tucked it in my purse. Just in case Cassie needed it.

Fifteen minutes later I turned off the paved road onto the dirt lane leading to my writing retreat. The leaves on the hardwood trees lining the lane were just beginning to turn. Splashes of orange, yellow, red, and the deep green of autumn waved me welcome as I coasted into my parking spot. I shut off the engine and leaned back into the leather seat, letting the familiar pleasure fill me as I admired the cabin set in a clearing. It had been a one-room structure resting on wooden piers when my parents bought it. My carpenter father replaced the piers with a concrete block foundation and expanded it to the current size, thirty feet by twenty, adding a bedroom loft. He rearranged the floor plan to include a cozy kitchen on the back side, which faced east, and a living room with a stone fireplace in the front room. A small bedroom, bathroom, and utility room hugged the north side. When Mom died, the proceeds from her small estate allowed me, her only heir, to hire a local contractor to re-side the cabin with brown vinyl for easy upkeep, install insulated windows and patio doors, add front and back decks, and replace the shingled roof with metal.

A giant pine tree—my "dreaming tree"—arched over the back corner of the yard. As a girl, I spent many an afternoon in its lofty branches, dreaming of a bright and wonderful future. I'd be a writer, of course, and travel the world with my husband. I didn't care if he was rich or poor, an executive or a garbage man. Back in those days I believed in true love. Now I only wrote about it.

Acorns, pinecones, and dried leaves lay scattered throughout the front yard. My mind was already making a to-do list: start refrigerator, turn on water pump and hot water heater, open windows, check mousetraps, vacuum floor and cobwebs, sweep decks, remove sheets from furniture, unpack. I checked the time. Completing my list shouldn't take too long, since I'd been here only a month ago to escape the dog days of summer in the city.

After a late lunch of an egg-salad sandwich and Greek yogurt with granola, I'd have time to rake leaves and mow the overgrown grass on the acre that was my yard. I owned ten acres, but most of it was forest. Unlike back home in the city, work here never seemed like work. I sang, I laughed, I chattered to myself. Here I was a different person. Here I was the real me—a person few people ever saw. Paul had, but he'd just pretended that woman didn't exist. He'd wanted a sophisticated city wife, someone I refused to be.

A faint mewing came from the back of the Explorer.

"I hear you, Rascal." My two-year-old kitty had spent enough time in the animal carrier and was ready to hunt. What the mousetraps didn't catch, she did. I lifted her out of the carrier and held her against my chest, running my cheek over her soft white-and-gray fur before setting her down. As she scooted off into the woods, I climbed up the wooden steps to the front deck, unlocked the patio door, and stepped inside my haven, itching to get to work.

The sun hovered above the treetops by the time I was ready for a shower and a late supper. I was hungry for a grilled hot dog and a bowl of macaroni and cheese. I unloaded the cooler into the refrigerator, which was now cold enough to keep the perishables I brought with me. I was about to remove the cover from the grill on the back deck when I noticed it had been tampered with. I always positioned it so the small tear on the corner was toward the back. Now the tear was on the opposite, front corner.

The hairs on the back of my neck prickled. Had someone used my grill? Maybe some local kids poking around. Unoccupied cabins were prime targets for thieves. I'd have to ask Willie if anyone had reported a break-in or theft. I hadn't noticed anything awry when I unlocked the storage shed to get the lawn mower, but then, I'd been in a hurry to get the "settling in" work done. Daylight was fast fading from the lavender sky. I'd have to wait until tomorrow to inspect for signs of an intruder.

Right now a microwave dinner sounded safer than a hot dog grilled after dark. As I stepped inside the kitchen, Rascal slipped in behind me. I peered into the deepening dark of the woods and shivered. Sliding the glass panel shut, I locked the door and did something I never did at the cottage. I closed the vertical blinds—tight.

A low, gray sky and cold drizzle greeted me when I awoke Thursday morning. The weather forecast had called for a 20 percent chance of rain today. Well, it was 20 percenting now and had the look of an all-day rain. I'd planned on taking a walk through the woods after I'd checked the outside for signs of an intruder, but the leaden sky told me I'd better change my plans.

I pulled on a flannel shirt and jeans and slipped into my moccasins, then treaded down the circular stairway to the kitchen. I opened my laptop on the breakfast bar so I could check an updated forecast and let it boot up while I went to the bathroom. Thankfully, I had Internet service here on top of the mountain. I'd signed up for satellite as soon as it became available. As a full-time writer, I could take the expense as a tax deduction.

While I microwaved my tea, I checked the Doppler radar map online. A green blob covered the entire central-western Pennsylvania area. I clicked on the national map, which showed the blob—dark green in places, meaning heavier rain—covering the entire state of Ohio, the line of rain extending from New York to the Carolinas. Better green than white, which meant snow, or red, which signified ice. And better coming from the west or northwest than from the south or southeast, which meant a nor'easter or a hurricane working its way up the coast. Even this far inland, peripheral bands of tropical storms occasionally flooded the river valley. And September was a prime month for hurricanes. I was safe on top of the mountain, though—unless it snowed. But snow wasn't a concern in mid-September.

I checked my cell phone for messages, but it was showing "no service," typical of the signal on the mountaintop during rainy weather. During sunny weather too. The Internet was a little more dependable, but I often lost its signal during stormy weather. The two things I liked most about living in the city were strong, cell-phone signals and a faster, more reliable Internet connection. I shut off my phone to conserve battery power.

The microwave pinged. I retrieved my hot tea, set it on the bar, and then poured granola in a bowl, sliced some frozen strawberries on top, and added cold milk. Between bites of breakfast, I clicked on the day's forecast for the area. Yep, all-day rain and cool temperatures. A good work day with nothing to distract me except Rascal, who'd want in and out and in and out all day.

Then I realized I had no work-in-progress—no publisher interested in my stuff. I opened a file on my desktop and scanned the list of ideas. Nothing jumped off the screen. Maybe I *was* getting tired of writing the same-old, same-old.

Your manuscript was a no-go. They want you and Don to team up.

A reading day then. Just what I needed to get my mind off my troubles. I powered up my Kindle Fire, but it was showing low battery, and I mean low, and I couldn't find the power cord to recharge it. I hadn't packed any magazines either. Now what?

Here's some reading material for you . . .

No! I would not read Don Bridges, no matter how bored I was or how ruggedly handsome he looked in the photo on the dust jacket. I'd find something else to do.

Cool, rainy days meant crock pot meals. I foraged through the cupboards and fridge and found the makings for an easy crock pot chili—tomato soup, kidney beans, chili powder, dried minced onions, and green pepper flakes. I took the package of ground beef I brought from home out of the freezer and put it in the microwave to defrost.

Most meals for the past ten years had been on the Three-C menu—can, cardboard, or carryout. That was when Garrett had moved out and

Paul had changed jobs, the new position requiring longer hours and business trips that grew lengthier and lengthier. Somewhere along the way, Paul and I stopped talking and lived like strangers. Then about five years before he died, he moved into the guest bedroom, claiming my snoring kept him awake. As if he didn't snore.

After plugging in the crock pot and cleaning up the kitchen, I started a fire in the fireplace and settled in the recliner, tapping my fingers on the arm of the chair. Finally, I picked up the Don Bridges books. Which one first? *The Last Case* or *Murder on the Mountain*? I chose the former.

It was lunchtime before Rascal hopped up in my lap and I returned to the present world. I didn't like guy books, but Don's wasn't the normal macho-guy style—fast-paced and furious. Neither was it slow and rambling, the kind of book that put you to sleep after ten minutes. I surprised myself and kept turning the pages. While the plot drew me in, I thought his characters were a little flat. The storyline could definitely use a feminine touch.

After a lunch of ramen noodles and yogurt with granola, I settled back in the recliner with a cup of tea and a legal pad in my lap. I pored through what I'd read in the morning, jotting down ideas that would put some life into his characters and spice up the narrative with some romance. Then I started reading again—and read right on through the afternoon, stopping only for tea, potty breaks, to let Rascal in or out, or to scribble a few notes.

With Don's book propped in front of me, I sat at the small kitchen table and read chapter after chapter, splattering chili on the pages, a Melody Harmon badge of honor for a good book. By the time I finished the last page at midnight, I could see why Aunt Peg and Uncle Butch were such Don Bridges fans. And I could see where I, reclusive romance novelist Melanie Joy, could fit into his writing life. And maybe even his personal life . . . as a friend.

What I couldn't see was how I would ever trust a man again.

CHAPTER FOUR

Friday morning dawned cool and clear. After a breakfast of scrambled eggs and rye toast, I settled in front of the fireplace with a second cup of tea and my laptop. A good night's sleep had cleared the cerebral cobwebs and sparked an inkling of something that had been missing for a long, long time—hope.

While I planned to make an appointment with the attorney Uncle Butch recommended as soon as I got back home, I needed to do my homework first—something I neglected before meeting with the bank manager. It wasn't any different, really, than getting information for my novels. I'd simply research the foreclosure process online. With my legal pad and favorite gel pen beside me on the sofa, my bare feet propped on the pine coffee table, and the fire in the hearth snapping and popping, I Googled "home foreclosure" and read as many articles and blog posts as I could.

Two hours, three cups of tea, and numerous pages of notes later, my head ached. When Stephanie Morley had told me the foreclosure process had already begun, I'd assumed there was nothing I could do about it. But one website indicated I could sell the house myself and pay off the debt any time before the bank held the foreclosure auction, even having some money left over. But each state handled the process differently. How much of what I'd read applied in Pennsylvania?

I checked the time on my laptop. Eleven o'clock. I didn't have a strong enough cell signal here at the cabin to call the lawyer, but there was a place down by the creek where I could get two bars, sometimes three. I didn't want to wait until next week to call, especially since I didn't know when I'd be able to get an appointment. My last mortgage payment had been due June 1. That meant three missed payments. Time was of the essence.

After pulling on my socks and hiking boots, I threw on my hoodie, and reached for the back doorknob when someone Skyped me on my still-open laptop. I almost ignored it, but maybe it was Garrett calling. I rushed back to the breakfast bar and clicked on the blue "S" symbol. "Incoming call from Cassie Stiles." Seriously? She'd only dropped the Don Bridges bomb on me three days ago. I rarely heard from my agent more than once a month, unless she was negotiating a contract or suggesting revisions to a proposal or manuscript. Maybe she'd found another publisher. I clicked on the "answer call" icon.

"Where in heaven's name are you?" Cassie said, sitting behind her desk. "I've been trying to get you for two days."

As usual, here on the mountaintop, the video lagged behind the audio.

"At the cottage. You know what the cell phone signal is like here, and yesterday's rain washed out the satellite for the day."

"What on earth are you doing up there? You don't have a deadline breathing down your neck."

No publisher in the wings then. I glanced at the lower right-hand corner of the screen: 11:05 a.m. It would take me half an hour to get to the creek. I needed to catch that attorney before she closed her office early for lunch or maybe even the weekend.

"I needed to get away to think." I hadn't told her yet about the foreclosure. "Can you make this fast? There's something I have to do."

"I can see that. You look like you just got out of bed. Have you read Don's books yet?"

"One of them. *The Last Case.*"

"What do you think? Oh, never mind what you think. I'll get to the point since you're in such a big rush out in the middle of nowhere. You're meeting Don for lunch Tuesday at Panera Bread at the East Gate Shopping Village. Eleven o'clock sharp."

Cassie's steamroller tactics didn't surprise me. Her go-getter approach was one of two reasons I'd signed with her, the other being her instinctive knowledge of the publishing world. What did surprise me was that suddenly I felt like a giddy schoolgirl who had just learned she'd landed a date with the hottest guy on campus.

Cassie leaned forward, peering through cyberspace at me. "Are you having a hot flash? Or is that mountain air making your cheeks look like maraschino cherries? Not that they're that plump. Anyway, I told him about that farm for sale up the road from your writing retreat. He's looking for a place for his girl. Which girl, he didn't say, and I didn't ask."

"How many girlfriends does he have?"

Her head shook in stuttered slow motion. Video chats at the cottage were annoying.

"One of his daughters. Don hasn't looked at a woman since Francine died." She glanced down at something below the screen—probably at her perfect manicure. "Listen, I can't be at the meeting. I have an early morning flight to the West Coast, so it'll be just you and Don. Take your notepad. I need some ideas. Hey! I saw you roll your eyes. I'm doing this—"

"For my own good. I know. I'll be there."

"Good. And, Mel?"

"What?"

"Do something with that hair. Call me after your meeting."

She cut the call short without even saying good-bye. What wasn't she telling me?

I made it to the creek by a quarter to twelve. After an overnight recharge, my cell phone showed full battery, but the signal strength was only one bar. It would have to do. Pulling out the slip of paper Uncle Butch gave me, I punched in the number and got a recording: "The office closes for lunch between noon and one. Please call back

during regular business hours. If you know your party's extension . . ."
I didn't. I'd try again at one.

Pulling off my hoodie, I spread it over a patch of moss along the
top of the creek bank and lowered myself to the damp ground.
Sunlight dappled through the trees, dancing on the rain-muddied water
hurrying around partially submerged rocks. The scents of hemlock and
humus mingled in the freshly washed air. I closed my eyes and leaned
back on my elbows, letting the warm rays bathe my face and soak into
my soul. Somewhere chipmunks chattered, a woodpecker tapped for
lunch, and a blue jay cawed its territory. *I could stay here forever.* A
shadow glided across my face. High against the cobalt sky, a turkey
vulture, its finger-like wings spread wide, soared in search of prey.

The spell broken, I sat up and checked my phone messages. There
were multiple texts and missed calls from Cassie. I deleted them all.
One missed call and a text from Garrett: "U must b on deadline. LOL.
Almost done here. Will b home nxt wknd. Luv u."

Home? Next weekend? I'd have to tell him about the foreclosure.
Oh please, God. I'm not ready. Wrapping my arms around my knees, I
pressed my face into my jeans and for the first time since Paul died, I
allowed myself to cry—deep, gut-wrenching sobs that produced real
tears. No one except the forest critters was around to hear, so I just let
loose.

In a strange way, it felt good. Like the pressure of a million gallons
of water unleashed when the cracked dam finally gives way. I wept
until I could weep no more. By then the sun had passed its zenith, and
my sobs had been reduced to sniffles. I checked my pockets for
tissues. None. My sleeve, already wet with tears, would have to do.

I'd answer Garrett's text as if everything were normal—well, as
normal as it had been for the past year and a half. As normal as I'd
pretended it to be. My thumb pressed REPLY.

"Glad to hear from you," I texted. "I should be home Sunday
evening or Monday morning. Looking forward—"

"Don't move."

My head jerked up. A tall man dressed in camouflage from his boots to his wide brimmed hat stood on the other bank, pointing a black, long-barreled pistol right at me. Electric fear shot through every cell in my body. I opened my mouth, but before I could scream, he squeezed the trigger. Flash. Boom. A thud beside me. Then darkness.

I came to, choking, something pressed to my lips, wetness dripping across my cheeks. Blood? My fingers flew to my face and came away wet, but clear. Pushing a plastic water bottle away from my mouth, I looked up into the bearded face of Camo Man, whose concerned blue eyes probed mine. He helped me to a sitting position, one arm around my shoulders. Nothing hurt. I wasn't bleeding anywhere. My head felt woozy, though, and my whole body trembled. He pulled me to him and rubbed my back gently. Something inside me ignited. And scared me more than being shot at.

I pushed him away. "You tried to kill me."

"On the contrary. I saved your life."

"How exactly do you call shooting at me saving my life?"

"Look on the ground beside you."

I glanced down, and my blood turned to ice. Just inches away was the biggest snake I'd ever seen. Over three feet long, as thick as my wrist, and very dead. This was no garter snake.

I swallowed. "What is . . . was . . . it?"

"Timber rattler."

"You mean a *rattlesnake*?" I stared at its body, from the flat, triangular head with cat's eyes to the ebony tail with rattles. "I thought rattlesnakes made a rattling noise before striking."

"Not always."

"Those colors, brown with black bands . . ."A shiver snaked through me. ". . . would be hard to see on the forest floor. How common are these things around here? I've been coming to this mountain since I was a girl and never saw a rattler until now."

He shrugged. "I wouldn't know. I'm new to the area. But timber rattlers can be found throughout the state. Most people aren't aware of them because they would sooner avoid you than attack. This one—" he nodded to the dead snake "must have perceived you as a threat. You may have disturbed its afternoon nap."

A white-and-orange dog came bounding toward us, tags jingling. A pink nose nuzzled my face and a coarse tongue lapped my face. I must look a sight, I thought, pushing my frizz behind my ears—puffy eyes, strawberry nose, tear-blotched cheeks.

"Charlie, sit," Camo Man said in a firm voice.

The dog obeyed.

"Good girl." He caressed the dog's ears and received a quick lick on the lips in return. Chuckling, he pulled his head back.

So this was my new neighbor . . . Jake. Who else would be wandering around on this mountain? I wondered why Willie didn't trust him. "How a man treats an animal says a lot about him," my mother used to say. Too bad I hadn't heeded her advice. Paul avoided our dog, Muttsy, like she was a disease-carrying, mange-infested stray. I could still see him ramrod straight whenever Muttsy came near.

"What breed is he?"

"*She* is a Brittany Spaniel."

Yes, of course. He just called her "girl." If Cassie thought my cheeks looked like maraschino cherries, I was sure they were Detroit Dark Red beets now. Maybe it *was* a hot flash. I plucked my phone from the damp moss beside me and stood. Well, tried to. My limbs felt like deflated airbags. Camo Man's hands steadied me as I slid back to the ground.

"Sit still awhile. Your body needs to warm up." He encircled me with his arms and rubbed my back gently once again. "You've had quite a shock."

I pressed my hands against his muscular chest. "I have to get back."

Not really. There was nothing to get back to. But this ruggedly handsome man unnerved me. Or was it all men lately? First Don Bridges—his picture and his reputation—and now Jake. Perhaps what I thought had been dead had only been hibernating and was now emerging ravenous. I didn't know how to deal with it.

I closed my eyes and took several deep breaths, willing the weak-kneed sensation to fade and imagining strength coursing through my body.

"I'm all right now," I said after a few minutes—a few heart-fluttering minutes in Jake's arms. How long had it been since a man held me? Held me with gentleness and tenderness? Tears threatened once again. I blinked them away and swallowed the lump in my throat. "I need to get back."

Jake stood and held out his broad hands to me. I placed my cold ones in his and let him pull me to a standing position. Charlie watched Jake intently, waiting, I was sure, for the next command. This was a man who was used to giving orders and having them obeyed. Willie hadn't said what he did for a living before moving to the mountain, but my guess was military. It wasn't just his voice. His whole bearing was that of a man in charge. But one who led with compassion and kindness. Not like Paul.

"I'll walk you back." He lifted my hoodie from the ground and gave it a quick shake before draping it over my shoulders.

"No need," I said. "I know my way back."

"I'm sure you do, but you had quite a scare, and Charlie and I want to make sure you're all right."

I was thankful he didn't mention that I might encounter another rattlesnake.

"Why did you name her Charlie?" I asked as he fell in step with me, his handgun couched in a brown-leather shoulder holster.

"She's a gun dog, bred to go on point when she smells a bird, like a grouse, then retrieve it. Because she's purebred, I had to give her a fancy name." He shrugged. "Her full name is Top Gun Charlie."

"Oh, I see." I stopped at a fallen tree branch. It wasn't a snake, so I stepped over it and continued along the trail. "The female lead in the movie *Top Gun* was named Charlie. Clever."

We walked in comfortable silence. The trail wound uphill and was easier to climb without chatting. Besides, I loved listening to the sounds of the woodland. When I was younger—before my brother Sonny died—I pretended to be Maria in *The Sound of Music*, throwing my arms out in sheer joy and waltzing through a meadow, skipping over rocks, and splashing the icy water of the gurgling creek. Why was I thinking of Sonny now? I'd spent the last thirty years suppressing the memories, the disbelief, the denial, the grief. The anger at God. Perhaps it was the military bearing of my escort.

"What branch were you in?" I asked. He looked to be the age my brother would be now.

"Marine Corps. You're pretty observant."

He cocked his head, a question in his eyes.

"Not me." I wanted to ask when and where he served. But this was a room I hadn't opened in three decades, and I wasn't sure I was ready to unlock it now.

We walked out of the woods onto the blacktop road. I turned to Jake. "I'll be okay from here."

Charlie nuzzled next to me. My hand stroked her soft fur. I thought Jake would argue, insist on escorting me the rest of the way, but he just tipped his hat and grinned.

"I'm sure you will," he said, tapping his thigh. Charlie's ears perked up and her stubby tail wagged. She seemed eager to resume chasing critters. "Come on, girl, let's go."

I watched as they disappeared into the fall foliage, a surprising disappointment filling me. And embarrassment. I hadn't even thanked him. As I turned down the driveway to my writing retreat, I remembered the brownie mix I'd brought along for my chocolate fix. Perfect! I'd mix up a quick batch and take them over to his cabin—to show my appreciation. Nothing else.

The brownies were in the oven and I was on the back deck grilling a hot dog for an early supper when a knock sounded at the front door. Maybe Jake had come back to make sure I was all right.

"Out back," I called, wondering whether to put on another hot dog or two. Or three.

But the man who stepped around the cabin and climbed the back steps wasn't the man who'd saved me from a rattler a few hours ago. This guy's beard was scraggly, not well trimmed like Jake's. Of medium height and stocky build, he wore a Boston Red Sox ball cap over shaggy, dark hair. Sunglasses rested on the bridge of a bulbous nose. A black, pocket T-shirt was tucked loosely into his denim jeans. I stared at the large tattoo on his forearm—a coiled snake, poised to strike. A shiver shot up my spine. *Stop over-reacting!* Maybe he was just lost and needed directions.

"Can I help you?" I forced a smile. I wouldn't show the alarm that tingled my nerve endings. I learned that with Paul. Never show fear.

"Actually, I came to see if I could help you." He pulled a business card from his shirt pocket and handed it to me.

"I just retired and moved here this summer." He removed his sunglasses to reveal piercing, dark-brown eyes. "Most folks with cabins don't live here full-time, and I figured I could look out for your place when you're gone, cut firewood for you, fix things—you know, handyman work. Make a few bucks to supplement my pension."

I glanced at the card and froze. "Jake Esau, Handyman." My insides went cold. I gaped at the man standing before me. If he was Jake Esau, who was Camo Man?

CHAPTER FIVE

The next two days were rainy and miserable. I spent the time curled up in front of the fireplace, depleting my stack of firewood as well as my stash of chocolate, and forcing myself to finish *Murder on the Mountain,* which wasn't the best book to read after the scare I'd had on Friday. Nary a scribble on the legal pad this time—unlike the flood of ideas I'd gotten when I'd read *The Last Case.* But try to be creative, let alone think straight, after being on the wrong end of a handgun, then learning your demise at the fangs of a rattlesnake was just inches away. I shivered and pulled the afghan closer.

Willie was tending to another customer when I stopped by the store on my way home Monday morning. I scanned the bulletin board, looking for Jake's business card, as Willie rang up the elderly woman's small order. I recognized her as one of the villagers.

"I tell you, we're going to have one doozy of a winter," she said in a loud voice. "I can feel it in my bones. Literally. Every time we're gonna have a bad winter, my joints hurt something fierce. Early one too."

I waited until she left, then placed a frosty bottle of Diet Dr Pepper and a five-dollar bill on the counter.

"Have there been any problems lately with break-ins on the mountain?" I asked Willie.

He was wearing a white butcher's apron over his usual red-plaid flannel shirt with the sleeves rolled up. "Can't say I've heard anything. Why?"

I told him about the grill cover. "I know I didn't put it on that way. I always put it on so the small tear is toward the back."

"Get yourself a watchdog. That there cat of yours ain't much good when it comes to protection."

"Speaking of protection, I met Jake. He gave me his business card."

Willie's bushy-white eyebrows arched. "Business card?"

"He's starting a handyman-security business. I could use a handyman. I've got a leak in the kitchen faucet, and every now and then the toilet doesn't want to quit running. I have to take the lid off the back and push the stopper down. And firewood—it's already mid-September, and I don't have nearly enough to see me through the winter."

Lower lip curled in thought, Willie scratched his head. "Handyman business, huh? First I heard of it."

"He's just getting started." I twisted the bottle cap just enough for the hiss to escape. "He offered to keep an eye on my place while I'm gone. No charge. I'm surprised he didn't put a business card on your bulletin board. I'm sure the other property owners would appreciate knowing we have a resident security guard on the mountain. His rates are reasonable."

For everyone except a romance writer whose career is on the skids.

"Not a bad idea," Willie said.

"I have another question for you." I told him about Camo Man and how he'd saved me from the rattler. "He couldn't be the mountain man, could he?"

According to local legend, years ago a hot shot from the city got soured on society, chucked it all, and built a log cabin in the thick of the forest on our mountain. And he protected his privacy with a vengeance. No one knew his name, but I'd heard him called "One-Shot Grinch," "Clifton Clowers," or "Mad Man of the Mountain." No one had ever seen him, either, as far as I knew. It was said he had power from the mountain spirits to change into an animal, like a deer or a bear. When he was little, Garrett liked to imagine him as a protective bear.

Willie's words cut into my mind ramblings. "Short, stocky feller with shoulder-length gray hair and a beard down to his chest?"

"No, he was tall—I'd say about six foot three. His beard was brown with streaks of gray and trimmed close to his face. I couldn't see his hair under his wide-brimmed hat, so he must wear it short. Or he's bald. Or maybe it was long and pulled back under his hat. Oh, and he had a Brittany Spaniel—she was really sweet—named Charlie."

And blue eyes that twinkled when he smiled and made my heart stutter.

"Nope. Ain't seen nobody like that. Maybe he was a hunter checking out the area. Archery season comes in at the end of the month, you know, and small game a week after that."

"But isn't all the land on the mountain privately owned? He'd have to have permission from the property owner to hunt."

He snorted. "That don't mean people don't hunt there anyway."

"True. Maybe he was a friend of one of the property owners."

"Could be. Do you want me to ask around?"

Yes. No.

"It doesn't matter," I lied. "I never got a chance to thank him properly and—Willie, now don't you start!"

His weathered face registered mock surprise. "What'd I say?"

"You don't have to say anything. I know what you're thinking. I'm not interested. I like being single."

"You've been *single* for a long time, Sweet Pea. A *long* time. You deserve some happiness."

"You're a hopeless romantic, Willie. You know that?"

"So I'm told." He pointed to my soda. "That all for today?"

I nodded. He reached under the counter for a chocolate-almond bar and handed it to me with my change. "For the road. Safe travels, Melody. God be with you."

Right. Like God really cared about me.

I leaned across the counter and gave the old storeowner a peck on his weathered cheek. "You, too, Willie."

As I backed out of the gravel parking lot, a familiar ache settled in my heart. Leaving Getaway Mountain always made me feel like I'd said good-bye to a dear friend whom I wouldn't see for a long, long time. I eased onto the two-lane highway and crossed the bridge that spanned the river. Drops of sunlight danced on the rushing water, high and muddy after three days of rain. Sodden tree limbs arched over the road, still wet in the shadows, while the tops of the pines tickled the bottom of a cloud-studded sapphire sky. The air was crisp and clean and clear, with none of the mugginess of the city.

I tried to ignore the sick feeling in my stomach as my old Explorer climbed the hill out of the river valley. I felt this way every time I left. You'd think I'd get used to it. I wasn't sure if it was because of what I was leaving or because of what I was going back to. But Paul wasn't there anymore.

As I drove south, my mind reviewed the week ahead. I'd call the attorney today. Hopefully, I could get an appointment this week. Tomorrow I was to meet Don Bridges for lunch. That schoolgirl feeling washed over me. What was it about that guy?

"Silly woman," I mumbled under my breath. "He probably isn't half as handsome in real life as he is in that picture."

Few authors actually looked as good as their publicity photos. Some looked nothing like them. My books, all written under the pseudonym of Melanie Joy, had a kind of generic bio and no photo. I liked the privacy.

Mentally I went through my closet. And my sweater drawers. Yikes! Cassie was right. Black slacks. Dark, somber tops that were at least five years old. Clunky shoes. Unless I wore jeans and sneakers. Why was it that suddenly nothing I had was appropriate? I glanced at the clock on the dashboard. A little before noon. I'd have time to stop at the Glen Valley Mall and see what I could find on the clearance racks. I might even splurge and buy something at regular price. I hadn't done that in years.

"You're being ridiculous," I chided myself. "Your house is going into foreclosure. You can't afford new clothes just because you want to impress a hot guy."

Heat crept up my cheeks. I hadn't considered a guy hot since I met Paul thirty-three years ago. And I didn't even know Don Bridges.

I shook my head and gripped the leather steering wheel. No, I wouldn't get a new outfit. It was just a business meeting. With another over-the-hill author whose career was on the skids. That picture on the dust jacket was probably ten years old. He was probably bald and fat and getting wrinkles around those twinkling blue eyes. Business. That's all it was. Business. Hmm . . . could a new outfit for a business meeting be considered a tax deduction?

"Stop it!"

I'd wear black slacks with a black turtleneck and the burnt orange corduroy vest. No. Blue jeans and my over-sized, beige cable-knit pullover. No. Too many fuzz balls. My Steelers sweatshirt then. No. Too casual. Black slacks. Black turtleneck and orange vest. And my black, clunky nun shoes. I'd smear Vaseline on them to hide the scuffs. I grinned at the woman in the rearview mirror. "That settles that."

Ten miles later I approached the exit for the Glen Valley Mall and, without thinking, flicked on the turn signal.

Turned out it was "Makeover Monday." My first mistake was curiosity about the rather large crowd that gathered outside Hair Heaven. Malls were usually dead on Monday mornings. My second mistake was edging my way to the front of the throng so I could get a better view.

They were just unveiling the morning's makeover. A slide presentation flashed her "before" pictures. She looked to be in her mid-thirties. Long, stringy, mouse-brown hair hung limp past her shoulders. No makeup. Circles under her eyes like she hadn't slept well. Pink baggy sweatshirt over faded jeans that didn't hide the baby fat around her middle. A voice over the speaker identified her as "Tiffany, a busy mother of three who'd dropped off her toddler at the preschool in the mall" to become Victim Number One.

The curtains on the makeshift stage in front of the salon entrance opened. A collective gasp rose from the crowd. This couldn't be the same girl! Blonde hair casually brushed her shoulders, with side-swept bangs that framed her heart-shaped face and subtly highlighted her striking blue eyes and high cheekbones.

"Tiffany, a type-two personality, believes in living life to the fullest," said the commentator, a slim, twenty-fiveish woman with her auburn hair twisted in a French braid. "With three children younger than ten and a husband who works twelve-hour days, Tiffany doesn't have much time for herself. So we styled her hair so that a simple wash and blow-dry would bring out its natural body and accentuate her beautiful eyes."

She went on to describe the clothes that looked best on Tiffany's "A" body shape and how she could draw attention away from her hips and thighs with scarves. A deep purple silk scarf accented the soft periwinkle turtleneck sweater that skimmed her body, which looked ten pounds lighter. Could you do that with just clothes? I wondered, thinking of my own scarecrow-like frame.

"Tiffany's new wardrobe is smart, economical, practical, and comfortable—all important to a busy wife and mother," Ms. Commentator said. "Her new hairstyle is easy to maintain. Both reflect her personality and enable her to have a variety of looks, from romantic to dramatic to simply everyday—and neither takes a lot of maintenance time."

I checked the time on my cell phone. If I wanted to get my hair trimmed at the walk-in place on the other side of the mall and check the clearance racks in Value-Mart for something to wear to tomorrow's meeting with Don Bridges, I'd better get a move on. As I turned to leave, I found the crowd had grown and it would be impossible to edge my way through to the back. I'd have to go around. I turned back to the front to see Ms. Commentator studying me.

"You—the lady with the gray sweatpants and curly hair. How would you like to be this afternoon's Makeover Magic?"

I looked around. No one else with gray sweats. Or frizzy hair. I shook my head.

"Thanks," I said, "but I can't. I have—"

"Ladies and gentlemen won't you give—what's your name, honey?"

"Melody."

"—Melody—some encouragement?" She patted her hands together.

The crowd responded with thunderous applause. Well, maybe it wasn't quite thunderous, but it sure seemed that way to me.

"No, I'm sorry, I can't." I desperately scanned the crowd, looking for an escape. "I have . . ." What? Someone waiting for me at home? Someone expecting me to call? An important appointment to keep? No, no, and no.

"Come on, Melody. This won't cost you a thing but a couple hours of your time. What have you got to lose?"

Don's dust jacket picture flashed through my mind. The next thing I knew, I was standing on the makeshift stage, a microphone thrust in front of my face.

"Tell us about yourself, Melody."

What to say? *I'm the mother of one and the wife of none. A romance writer whose career is going down the tubes. A widow whose husband gambled away their life savings and forced her house into foreclosure.* But I didn't say any of that. All I said was, "I'm a writer. I spend a lot of time alone. Writing."

Her eyes glinted. "Oh, how interesting! What do you write?"

I squirmed. "Romance novels."

A puzzled look shadowed her face.

"I write under a pen name."

Relief washed through her brown eyes. "That's why I couldn't place the name, Melody. What's your pen name?"

I was afraid of this. "I'd rather not say."

The crowd groaned. "Tell us, Melody!" someone shouted. "You might have some fans here!"

"Tell us. Tell us. Tell us." The chant crescendoed.

I help up my hand, palm forward. "I'll tell you." The chanting stopped.

"I write under the name of . . ." I gulped. "Melanie Joy."

All kinds of comments erupted from the crowd.

"Who?"

"Melanie Joy! I love your novels!"

"Never heard of you."

"Melanie Joy," Ms. Commentator cooed. "How exciting to have a real, live author in our midst." She smiled at the crowd. "Now, if you will excuse us, we have a Melody-Melanie makeover to do. Hang around, have some lunch, do some shopping. But be back in two hours sharp for the unveiling of the new Melanie Joy."

Flicking off the microphone, she slipped it into the stand.

"First, let's find out what personality type you are," she said, an arm around my shoulders, leading me inside Hair Heaven. And preventing any chance of escape.

Two hours later I hid behind the black curtain, awaiting my unveiling.

"That's the largest crowd ever!" Ms. Commentator, whose name was Pat, told me. "Word spread throughout the mall we have a famous romance novelist here. Everyone wants to see the new you! Even the bookstore is horning in. They set up a table across the hall with some of your novels. They're hoping you'll autograph some books."

"Of course." Cassie would love this!

"Are you ready?" Pat asked, squaring her shoulders. "Stand straight. Like this. Bosom out. You look terrific, you know."

"Thanks." I thought about how my new picture would look on my dust jacket. That is, if I published any more novels.

Pat winked, gave me a thumbs-up, and stepped between the curtains onto the stage to the applause of a sizable crowd.

After a quick overview of the Makeover Magic program, Pat introduced me.

"Melody Harmon is the mother of a grown son, a widow of less than two years, who has written a dozen romance novels under the pen name of Melanie Joy. Melody's personality test showed she has a Type-one personality. Comfort is the key word for this personality type. She likes to keep a low profile and prefers a relaxed lifestyle. Type-one personalities would rather blend in, not stand out, in a crowd. Therefore, hairstyle and wardrobe must allow this.

"Her hair—" A murmur rose from the crowd. I cringed. They must have flashed my *before* pictures on the screen. "—had a mind of its own, and Melody got tired of fighting with it and let it have its own stubborn way. But thanks to a new technique called the Columbian Calm Curl, we were able to tame her tresses and give her an easy-to-maintain style that makes her look—well, ladies and gentlemen, see for yourself! I present to you the new Melody Harmon, a.k.a. Melanie Joy!"

I stepped out between the curtains and tripped over a microphone cord. The applause abruptly stopped. The silence was deafening as I stared down at my new leather sandals.

I must look horrible! This was a big mistake.

Before I could retreat backstage, what seemed like a thousand hands beat together in a thunderous ovation. Whistles. Catcalls.

"Hey, babe, you free tonight?"

"Awesome!"

Pat waited until the noise died down.

"Melody's body shape—H—doesn't have a definable waistline, so to avoid that straight up-and-down look, we chose a soft burnt orange sweater with moderate shoulder pads to bring out the auburn in her now short hair. To avoid attracting attention to her non-waist, we chose casual slacks the same color as her sweater. Her emerald green silk scarf breaks up the mono-color and brings out the green in her lovely eyes."

When I left the mall an hour later, I'd signed more than two dozen books, turned down five requests for a date, and carried with me three new outfits, all reflecting my "natural" style. I stowed my purchases in the back seat of my Explorer and studied my reflection in the window, which I'd left open an inch or so for Rascal. A stranger stared back at me.

CHAPTER SIX

The cheery musical tone on my cell phone woke me from a sound sleep, and I squinted at the glowing red numbers of my bedside clock. Groaning, I rolled onto my back, jostling Rascal, who was curled up on top of the quilt at my feet, and grunted a hello into the phone.

"How'd it go?"

"Cassie, do you have any idea what time it is?" I snapped on the bedside lamp and closed my eyes against the glare.

"What kind of question is that? Of course I know the time. It's 9:05 p.m."

"That's Pacific Time. Back here in the East, it's after midnight."

"I know that."

"Of course you do. You also know my bedtime was two hours ago."

"Stop grumbling and tell me how the meeting with Don went."

"It didn't."

A beat of silence. Then, "What do you mean, 'It didn't'? You didn't get cold feet, did you? You *do* realize your career is on the line, right?"

"I showed. He didn't."

Rascal stood, stretched, and repositioned herself on the quilt.

"You went to the right place? At the right time?" she pressed.

"Panera Bread at the East Gate Shopping Village at 11:00 a.m."

"What time did you get there?"

"Quarter till."

"Quarter till what? I know your habit of running late."

"Quarter till eleven."

I wasn't going to mention how I'd taken over an hour to get ready. How I tried on all three of my new outfits before settling on the emerald-green silk blouse with matching dress capris. Or how I'd treated myself to an impromptu pedicure as soon as the walk-in salon opened so my matching polish would remain within the bounds of my toenails. Or the shiny black, patent-leather dress sandals I'd bought right after that. Or that I took her advice and did something with my hair.

"That's odd," Cassie said. "If something came up and he had to cancel, he would call me. It's not like Don to just not show. How long did you wait?"

"An hour."

"I was in the air when you two were supposed to meet and had my cell phone turned off, so he couldn't have gotten me if he tried. But I wonder why he didn't leave me a voice mail or text message? I checked my missed calls. Nothing."

Nothing. The story of my life. The balance of my checking account after my makeover madness shopping spree. What was left of the hope I dared to feel. I should have known better.

"Any other bright ideas about jumpstarting my dead career?" I yawned. "If not, good night."

"I'll get back to you."

"Not until . . ." I began, but she'd already hung up. I turned the phone off and shoved it under my pillow. I had bigger things to worry about than being stood up, like an early morning appointment with a foreclosure attorney to see what I could do to save my house. I shut off the light and went back to sleep.

The office of Georgina Rosenfeld, Attorney-At-Law, was located in a restored yellow brick house that would have been considered a mansion in the early 1900s. Located on a quiet, tree-lined street at the edge of the business district, the two-story building also housed the offices of the local Make-A-Wish Foundation on the second floor. I pulled in to the blacktop parking lot in the rear fifteen minutes before my 8:45 a.m. appointment.

"Time is of the essence in these cases," the receptionist had told me when I'd called yesterday and explained my situation. "Mrs. Rosenfeld usually comes in at eight anyway."

I checked the file folder to make sure I had everything she might need, even though I'd gone through it carefully before leaving the house. Pulling down the sun visor, I ran my fingers over my hair, smooth and silky now and much easier to style. The treatment would last ten to twelve weeks. I'd already made an appointment with Hair Heaven for a light trim and shaping in four weeks.

Cassie was right. I'd let myself go for too long. When had I stopped caring what I looked like? When I suspected it wasn't work that kept Paul away until the wee hours of the morning? When I caught him in yet another lie? When I smelled the same expensive perfume on his shirts when I gathered them for the cleaners? When I realized he didn't love me anymore?

As I watched the limbs of a giant oak brush against a leaden sky, I had the urge to pray. But why would God listen to me now after more than three decades of silence? No. I wouldn't trust Him again. His was the betrayal that had hurt the most.

I shoved up the visor and grabbed the file folder and my purse. I could take care of myself. I didn't need God.

"I can help you, but I need some more information," Georgina Rosenfeld said, studying my face over her reading glasses. A ruby-red, cowl-neck sweater set off her snow-white hair that had been cropped short and combed toward her pixie face. She was all of five foot, petite but powerful, according to Uncle Butch. The file folder lay open on the table in front of her beside an empty coffee mug. She'd been poring through the documents and taking notes on a yellow legal pad for fifteen minutes.

The attorney herself, java in hand, had opened the door when I'd rung the bell, and led me to a comfortable consulting room. Apparently, office hours didn't begin until nine.

"What kind of information?" I sat across from her, gripping a cup of spearmint tea—in a real ceramic mug, not a Styrofoam cup—to hide my trembling fingers.

"The purpose for the home equity loan was to build a garage, correct?"

I nodded. "Yes."

"Yet the cost of that garage—fifteen thousand—was much less—*much* less—than what is currently owed. Why?"

I stared at the riot of orange, yellow, red, and white chrysanthemums spilling out of a green vase on the polished mahogany table between us. Much less intimidating than the sterile desk of Stephanie Morley. But still I squirmed in the upholstered chair.

"I never questioned Paul. I should have, I know, but—"

"That's not the point here. Was the extra money used for home repairs?"

"No."

"To pay off another loan or a credit card balance?"

"I don't know. Maybe. Paul took care of the finances."

I'd never paid any attention. Instead, I was happy living in my own fictional world, creating characters who found true love, whose problems worked out in the end, and who lived happily ever after. It was easier than dealing with real life. Real life with Paul, anyway.

"Mrs. Rosenfeld—"

"Gina, please."

"Gina, when Paul died, I inherited his debt—three maxed-out credit cards and the home equity loan. I know of no other loan. He leased his car, so there were no payments once I returned the car. Only his name was on the lease, which expired when he did. I just recently paid off the credit cards, and it wasn't easy with a dwindling royalty check. If there had been any other loans or debt, they would have surfaced by now. Wouldn't they?"

"Who was the attorney who handled the estate?"

"Attorneys." I emphasized the plural. "My attorney, Neil Young, and Paul's, Devon Vane, worked together."

Gina's thin lips pressed into a wry smile. "Ah, the lovely Miss Vane. Brilliant lawyer. Crafty too. But not quite as good as Neil."

She clicked her pen and spoke into it: "Note: Call Neil Young and Devon Vane re: Harmon estate. ASAP." She clicked off the recording device and smiled. "Let's get down to business, shall we?"

She shuffled through the papers from my file, spreading them out, fanlike, across the table between us.

"If there are no other outstanding debts, the only thing you owe is the balance on the home equity loan, correct?"

"Correct."

"I noted Paul took out a loan on his life insurance policy, cashed in his IRA despite the penalty for early withdrawal, and borrowed against the equity in your home, all within the year before he died. How did he die?"

"He fell off an eighth-floor balcony at a resort while on vacation in Mexico."

Gina scribbled on her notepad as I related the details of Paul's death—for the second time in a week.

"You weren't with him on this vacation?" she asked.

"I didn't even know he was in Mexico until I got the call that he'd died. Paul and I had pretty much drifted apart. I suspect he went there with his girlfriend."

Something niggled in my brain—something not quite right. It had to do with the bank woman—Stephanie Morley—but I couldn't put my finger on it.

Gina studied her notes. "Let's get back to the finances. Your house, with the garage, is worth three hundred thousand, and you owe two hundred thousand, plus interest. Say two hundred grand, plus the life insurance, loan pension funds—that's quite a nest egg, plus whatever was in your personal savings account."

"Paul and I had separate accounts. He didn't approve of me writing romance novels. He said it embarrassed him. That's why I use a pen name. He thought it was a nice little hobby, but not appropriate for 'the wife of a man in his position,' to use his words. When my books started to sell, he wanted a joint account again. But by then I knew about his gambling and made sure he couldn't get his hands on my money or my writing retreat."

Her eyebrows arched. "Gambling? That would explain a lot."

She shuffled through the papers again.

"Your husband worked for . . ." She scanned the notes on her legal pad.

"Wellsboro Trucking. He headed up the accounting department."

"That's a pretty big outfit. Ah, here it is. Paul's title was company controller, overseeing payroll, accounts payable and receivable, financial statements—quite a lot of responsibility."

Especially for a man with a gambling addiction.

"He had managers working under him, the accounts payable manager and several others."

"There is no record of this money deposited in his name anywhere, correct?"

"That's right. There was barely enough in his savings and checking accounts to pay the funeral expenses."

"Do you have any assets you can sell to catch up on these payments or even pay off the loan amount?"

"Other than my writing retreat, no."

"Where is this writing retreat?"

"Near Seneca Forest."

"That would raise its value. How much land do you own?"

"I'm not selling it."

"The bank could seize it for nonpayment of the loan."

"Even if they took my house?"

"If they couldn't get enough at the foreclosure auction to pay the debt, yes, they can. But you can sell the house yourself before the auction. You have time. In Pennsylvania the foreclosure process can take up to two years."

Lose my writing retreat? The room spun. "I can't let that happen!"

"What about rich relatives?"

Paul's parents popped in my mind, but they'd sooner see me starve to death than give me a nickel.

I shook my head. "No."

"Not-so-rich relatives or friends who'd loan you some money until your writing income increases?"

Like it would.

"No."

"Do you have anything—besides your property in the north—that you could sell to get caught up on the payments? You'd need—" she scribbled on the legal pad "four months' worth of payments—six thousand."

I mentally went through the house, room by room.

"My furniture is paid off."

"Would it bring in enough?"

Paul had selected every bit of it, and his tastes weren't cheap.

"If I sold all of it, maybe."

"You'd live in an empty house?"

"No." I knew what I had to do—what I *wanted* to do. "Even if I caught up on the payments, I can't afford the house—the payments, the taxes, the utilities, the upkeep. I don't even want that monstrosity. Paul did. It was *his* house. I want to sell the house."

A warm coming-home feeling filled me. "And move into my writing retreat."

"Yoo-hoo! Melody!"

My silver-haired neighbor Bertha Rossi hurried across the street in fuzzy blue slippers, a navy-blue fleece jacket thrown over her thin shoulders. The sun still hid behind heavy, gray clouds, a whisper of winter on the wind.

"Oh," she breathed as she shuffled up my driveway. "I hardly recognized you! You must have a new man in your life."

Don Bridges's picture flashed in my mind.

"No need to blush, dearie. It's perfectly fine to have a love interest. Why, it's been well over a year since your dear Paul passed."

"Is there something you wanted, Mrs. Rossi?"

Bertha knew everything that went on in the neighborhood—even in the wee hours of the morning. Paul used to say he didn't think she ever slept. She once bragged about using her husband's binoculars to see the Thornbills' new baby.

"I couldn't sleep the other night, and I saw someone snooping around your house. I knew you were gone."

The hair on the back of my neck prickled.

"I couldn't see the face clearly. He was almost to your garage door when your motion detector light came on. He left in a hurry. Must have thought you had a home security system. I don't know why you don't."

I did, but I couldn't figure out how to recode the thing after Paul died, so I shut it off and cancelled the service.

"Did you see his car?" I prodded, as if Bertha needed prodding.

"Black SUV. Or was it a truck with a cap? It could have been blue. I'm not sure. It *was* two in the morning on the night of the new moon, and you know what that means—it was black as pitch. He parked on the street under the burned-out streetlight. Oh, did you hear about the Mortons? They're getting a divorce. I'm not surprised . . ."

Bertha's tinny voice droned on, but I wasn't listening.

First the grill cover at my writing retreat had been moved, and now someone was sneaking around my house in the middle of the night. Creepy.

My cell phone rang. I glanced at the caller ID. Cassie.

"I have to take this," I said with what I hoped looked like an apologetic smile. "Thanks for letting me know."

"No problem, dearie. No problem." She pointed to my phone and winked. "It's probably your new man."

She paused, probably hoping I'd answer and she'd get more ammo for her information arsenal. But I waited until she crossed the street before I pressed SEND. By then, as I'd hoped, the call had already gone to voice mail.

Before I called Cassie back a half hour later, I went through every room in the house, looking for signs of an intruder. I'd been gone six days. Maybe whoever it was had returned when Bertha wasn't on guard. But I found nothing amiss. I changed into my sweats, made a cup of tea, and then settled on the love seat in the family room with a fresh legal pad and my favorite pen.

Cassie answered her phone on the first ring. "You are the hardest person to get hold of anymore. I rescheduled the meeting with Don. He had a family emergency. His granddaughter Hannah—she has cystic fibrosis—had another health crisis. Hannah's mother, Don's daughter Anne, is a single mom of two. Anyway, Hannah's back home now, and things have calmed down."

The doorbell chimed. Who could that be?

"Where and when?" I asked, poising my pen above the legal pad. Whoever was at the door could wait.

My agent chuckled. "At your house. Right now. Go answer the door." She hung up on me.

I placed my tea on the coffee table beside the legal pad and considered not answering. But my Explorer was still in the driveway, and I didn't want any more of Cassie's surprises if this meeting didn't pan out. Checking my hair in the hall mirror, I took a deep breath, opened the door—and gasped.

There, on my doorstep with a large boxed pizza in hand, stood Camo Man.

CHAPTER SEVEN

"What did you do to your hair?"

Mouth agape, Don Bridges stared at my hair with horror etched in every crow's foot snaking from his not-twinkling-now blue eyes. I resisted the impulse to run my trembling fingers over my new 'do.

He looked even better in the light-blue oxford shirt and khakis than he did in his mountain man get-up. His shirtsleeves were rolled up to just below his elbows, revealing muscular, bronzed forearms sprouting sun-bleached hair. And he wasn't bald. A thick brown mane was pulled back in a ponytail at the nape of his neck. Streaks of gray, like a lover's fingers, caressed his temples. My heart beat faster than a hummingbird's wings.

It's nice to see you too, Camo Man, the new me would have said.

The new me, however, didn't answer the door. The old me did.

"So, you're, uh, Don Bridges. I didn't recognize you with, uh, your glasses," I said, with none of the grace and aplomb the new me was supposed to possess. Maybe there wasn't a new me after all. Beauty may go skin deep, but stupid runs all the way through. Not that made-over Melody was beautiful, but it sure would be nice to think I was—to *feel* I was. A hot flash crept up my neck through my cheeks to the roots of the hair Don obviously detested.

His gaze shifted from my hair to my tomato sauce-splotched sweatshirt.

"I'm as flummoxed as you." His eyes betrayed a hint of amusement. "I expected to meet Melanie Joy, romance novelist, and who answers the door but my lovely damsel in distress."

"I'm not your—nor anyone's—damsel in distress." I looked around him at the house across the street. The white sheer curtain covering Bertha's front picture window moved ever so slightly. *I'd better get him in before stories of a lovers' spat bore fruit on the afternoon's grapevine.*

"Where are my manners?" I gave him my brightest smile for Bertha's sake and opened the door wider. "Come in, please."

He stepped across the threshold, nudging off his black leather loafers and pushing them under the bench with his bare feet. The aroma of tomato basil sauce and pepperoni wafted from the pizza box in his hands. A sheepish grin tugged at the corners of his mouth.

"Peace offering. Where do you want to indulge?"

Kitchen, dining room, or family room? The remains of last night's failed attempt at cooking dinner still cluttered the kitchen. The dining room was too formal. I led him to the family room.

"Put it there," I said, pointing to the coffee table, which would be on the market by the end of the week. "No, wait. The bottom of the box is sure to be greasy. I'll get a tablecloth. Stay. I mean, stay here. I mean—oh, never mind. I'll be right back."

In the safety of my kitchen, I pulled open the freezer door and thrust my face in, allowing the frigid vapor to put out the wildfire in my cheeks. Stay. I ordered him to stay. Like a dog. Great. What else could go wrong? Across the room behind me, the swinging door that led to the dining room swooshed.

"What in tarnation happened here?"

I spun around. Don stood in the doorway, surveying the disaster. The look on his face told me I managed to horrify him again.

I slammed the freezer door shut and spun around. "What part of 'stay' don't you understand?"

He scanned the cluttered counters, his gaze resting on a burned pot on the ceramic cooktop. "This place looks like a war zone. What *were* you trying to make, soldier?"

Pizza box balanced in the crook of his left arm, he lifted the recipe card from the splattered counter with his right thumb and forefinger and held it out, adjusting his head so he could see the print through his glasses.

"Lasagne Verdi al Forno," he read, then stared at me, repressed laughter in every nook and cranny of his face. "You mean you actually tried to make noodles from scratch?"

I snatched the spattered recipe card from his fingers and tossed it on the counter. "Of course. Don't you?"

He ignored my intended barb. "Are you on Facebook or Pinterest?"

"I'm a published novelist. Of course, I'm on Facebook."

Chalk one up for makeover Melody, I thought, snatching a vinyl tablecloth from a deep drawer and looking around for an unscathed section of countertop. I shoved the tablecloth under my arm.

"I've got lots of good recipes," Don said as I rummaged through a too-full cabinet for paper plates. "They're easy too. I copy and paste the recipes into Word documents. Crock pot recipes are my favorite. I can throw something together in the morning, write all day, then have a tasty supper—with little cleanup. I can e-mail you the recipes."

Write all day. I bristled.

"I don't need any more recipes. Especially easy ones. What do you want to drink? I've got pop—Diet Dr Pepper—raspberry iced tea made from a mix, and bottled water."

"I'll take the soda."

Soda? Where was he from, anyway? He was probably trying to show off his verbal prowess. I pulled two frosty cans from the refrigerator. "Do you want to drink your *pop* from the can or would you prefer a glass with ice?"

The muscles in his cheek twitched with glee. "Whichever is hardest for you."

He followed me to the family room, where I settled on the cushions of the blue flowered sofa, while Don chose the brown leather recliner to the right of the fireplace. When he opened the box, I squealed.

"Pizza Pantry Triple-X! Extra pepperoni, extra cheese, extra thick-stuffed crust—my favorite! Cassie told you, didn't she?"

A blush spread across his cheeks above his beard as he plunked two slices on my plate then served himself.

"Would you mind if I said grace?" he asked just as I was about to sink my teeth into a thick wedge of heaven.

What could I say? I bowed my head. He said a simple prayer, thanking the Lord and asking Him to bless the meal. No big, long discourse covering everything from soup to nuts while the food got cold, as some Christians I knew were wont to do. No special prayer voice either. He spoke like he was talking to a friend.

"Where are you from?" I asked after the amen.

"Erie. Up by the lake."

"I know where Erie is," I snapped, more out of embarrassment than anger. With my comfy old sweats and my messy kitchen, I surely wasn't making a good first impression. And I'd wanted to. Oh, how I'd wanted to. And on top of that, he probably thought I was a geographically challenged woman who couldn't find her way out of a potato sack. So I did what I thought any savvy woman (translation—the new Melody) would do: I went on the offensive. "What were you doing on my mountain, anyway? Oh, I get it. Cassie told you about the Campbell property."

Again he blushed. This time the crimson crept to his ears. "She knew I was looking for a place in the mountains."

"For you or your girlfriend?" Cassie had said "girl," insisting she didn't mean girlfriend, but I wanted to make sure.

"My daughter. Anne needs a place to get away with the girls from time to time, and I've always dreamed of owning a hunting lodge."

"Which one is Anne? I read your bio. You have three daughters, right?"

He nodded. "Carrie, Anne, and Madison. Carrie's the oldest. Married. They live in Arizona. Carrie's a stay-at-home mom. With all the running around she does with the two boys, I don't know how she'd have time for a job outside the home. Anne is the middle child. Divorced. She's an independent computer tech—a real whiz. Works out of her home so she can homeschool her two girls and take care of Hannah, her youngest, who has cystic fibrosis. Maddie—my youngest daughter—teaches kindergarten. Engaged to a state trooper. What about you?"

"Just one son. Garrett. He's a professional photographer who doesn't have a life." I sighed. "You're lucky to have grandchildren."

"Not lucky. Blessed."

I watched a droplet of condensation trickle down my can of Diet Dr Pepper. How could he say he was blessed when his granddaughter had a horrible, incurable disease? I'd read about cystic fibrosis and how thick, sticky mucous could build up and lead to life-threatening health emergencies.

"How old is Hannah?"

"Six."

I'd been lucky—or *blessed* as Don would say. Except for the usual childhood colds and viruses, and an occasional trip to the emergency room, Garrett had always been healthy. And Paul, detached husband that he was, had been a decent father. I panicked when I saw blood. It was level-headed Paul who brought calm and rationality to the crisis.

"What happened to the girls' father? Not that it's any of my business."

Don's lips pressed together. "He bailed out a few months after Hannah was diagnosed. Couldn't take the pressure. They haven't seen him since the divorce." Don's jaw clenched, muscles twitching in his bearded cheeks. "He's remarried."

"Your poor daughter!"

He shook his head. "Actually, Anne's become stronger because of it. She's got a lot of faith."

How could she have faith when her husband had abandoned her, leaving her to deal with a chronically ill child alone? Didn't she blame God?

I wiped my hands on a paper towel and grabbed my legal pad and pen. "Cassie expects us to come up with a list of ideas. We'd better get busy."

After Don left, I researched realtors, poring over their websites, and called a half dozen or so before deciding on the only one that didn't use the recorded menu run-around. I explained about the foreclosure.

"Honey, don't you worry about that!" said Irene something-or-other, one of the five agents employed by Landry Realty. "We move more property than anyone in the Tri-State area. We'll have your house sold and the loan paid off long before the bank can schedule an auction."

She said she'd be by in the morning around tenish to take pictures and get the information for the listing.

I crossed "Find Realtor" off the things-to-do-to-get-house-ready-to-sell list and turned my attention to writing an ad for the furniture, which I posted online, with pictures, on as many free sites as I could find.

I wrote a separate ad for each room—living room, dining room, my bedroom, Paul's bedroom/office, and the game room in the basement. I set the price at a thousand dollars for each room, plus eight hundred for the pool table. I found one online just like the one in the game room, and that's how much the seller was asking.

I wasn't sure what all Paul had stored in the garage, but it probably wouldn't bring in much. Then there were the everyday dishes and the china, the everyday silverware and the real silver, pots and pans. Maybe I could get another thousand or so at a garage sale if I added in Paul's expensive suits and shoes. He never pinched pennies when it came to his clothes.

When Paul died, I stored his things in his walk-in closet and shut the door. I hadn't felt the urge to purge or the nostalgia to save. I had a deadline to meet and wasn't ready to deal with the fact that he'd died while on vacation with his girlfriend. We'd lived on two separate, parallel planes, never intersecting.

Paul's bedroom had been his study before he decided he didn't want to sleep with me anymore. That should have been my first clue. In the original floor plans it had been designated a bedroom. I never darkened his door until he died and I needed financial information when the foreclosure notice came. Who knew what treasures I'd find?

Garrett would be home Saturday, so I'd let him decide what to do with his furniture, as well as all the rest of his stuff that he didn't take when he moved into his apartment in Arlington, Virginia. His room, Paul's, and a second bathroom occupied the second floor, which I called the "dorm" because of the dormer windows.

That evening when I couldn't ignore the rumbling in my stomach any longer, I ate leftover pizza warmed in the microwave while I listed what needed to be done to get the writing retreat ready for winter. By eight o'clock, I was exhausted. After an early shower, I brewed a cup of Dream On tea, settled into my queen-size bed, curled up with Rascal, and called Cassie.

"I was just getting ready to call you." She sounded slightly out of breath. "Don't tell me Don didn't show. Or you refused to answer the door."

"Don showed. I answered the door. But I'm afraid our list of ideas is rather anemic. My mind's on other pressing issues."

I told her about the foreclosure and my decision to sell the house and move into the writing retreat.

"Foreclosure?" she said. "That's awful. I hope you get enough for it to pay off what you owe. Otherwise . . . well, never mind. It'll sell quickly, I'm sure. Just get a good realtor. And work with Don on a proposal for a romantic suspense series. I'm sure I can wangle a nice, sizable advance for you two."

"Aren't you going to say I'm crazy for moving to a deserted mountaintop cabin right before winter?"

She chortled. "I already know you're nuts. That's what makes you such a good writer. Besides, you won't be alone. Don bought that place you told me about."

"I thought you said my writing stunk." *Don bought the place?* I suppressed a smile.

"I never said your writing *stunk*. I said you're stuck in a rut. Professionally and personally. That's why I think this move is a good thing. Upheaval means you're finally leaving behind that god-awful marriage."

Maybe she was right about that last part, but I distinctly recalled her saying my writing was bland and needed some fire, as did my life. But I wasn't going to argue with her. No one argued with Cassie Stiles and won.

"When do you want the proposal?" I ran my fingers over Rascal's soft fur.

"Now, that's what I want to hear. Yesterday, of course."

"Cassie—"

"Okay, a month."

"Three. I have to go through everything in my house and garage, get rid of most of it, get the cottage ready for winter, and move. If I was writing alone, I could probably get it done in two."

"Okay. Six."

"Six months? Oh, Cassie, you're an angel."

"Six *weeks*. I told the publisher there'd be a proposal in her in-box by Halloween."

I groaned. "Cassie, how can you steamroll through my life like this?"

"I'm doing this—"

"I know. For my own good."

"Exactly. Now, have darling Don help you with the move. You two are going to be a writing team. The more time you spend together, the more you'll understand each other and the faster you'll mesh.

Remember, the best teams work together *and* play together. Gotta go. Shalom."

Shalom. I wish.

The For Sale sign went up Thursday around noon. At one o'clock my doorbell rang.

"Bertha, what a surprise. What brings you here?" As if I didn't know.

Shoving a plate at me, she stepped into the foyer. "I made you some cookies," she said, trying but failing to be discreet about gawking at my ring finger.

"Thank you." I slipped my left hand under the paper plate and pulled back the plastic wrap with my right. The sweet aroma of chocolate assailed my sugar-deprived nostrils. "Mmmm. Chocolate chip. My favorite."

"I see you're selling your house."

"Yes, I am." I lifted a still-warm cookie from the stack and bit into it. "Oh, just out of the oven. You're so sweet."

She patted her silver-blue, permed hair. "Oh, nonsense. Just being neighborly. I was wondering, though, with the sign going up so soon after your boyfriend visited the other day, that congratulations might be in order?"

"Whatever for?"

"Are you getting married or something?"

Or *something* meaning am I moving in with my supposed boyfriend. I could imagine what fruit the grapevine would bear today.

The sound of a car pulling in my driveway and an engine shutting off gave me the out I needed. I leaned out the door to see a white Jeep.

"There's Garrett." I smiled. "Thanks again for the cookies."

"No problem, dear. No problem at all." She turned to leave.

"Oh, wait, I almost forgot." She shuffled back to the door. "Your boyfriend's truck? It looked like the same vehicle that was parked on the street the night your prowler came calling."

Alarm bells went off in my head.

CHAPTER EIGHT

"What made you decide to sell?"

Garrett, his long fingers tapping the sides of a mug of strong coffee, sat across from me at the glass patio table on the back deck. The September sun hung above the tree line on the back of the property, resisting its descent behind the grove of maple and oak trees. Between sips of Earl Grey tea and nibbles of my tuna-on-wheat sandwich and potato chips, I told him about the foreclosure.

"Why didn't you tell me?" he said. "I would have sent you the money."

"It doesn't work that way."

"What way?"

"Parents aren't supposed to take money from their children."

"You and Dad certainly helped me out of a few jams. How much do you need?"

I shook my head. "Even if I got caught up with the mortgage payments—and I will when I sell the furniture—there's no way I can afford to keep up with them, plus maintain this place."

"Where there's a will, there's a way. That's what you always told me. If you really wanted to keep this place, you'd find a way. I know you."

I studied this grown-up son of mine. At thirty-two, Garrett was the image of his father at that age—except for his unusual green eyes. Those he got from me. Paul never could deny him, although he'd wanted to when I'd told him I was pregnant.

Garrett's six-foot-four frame, once so lanky his basketball team dubbed him "string bean," had filled out, due to regular visits to the gym and the rugged terrains he'd traveled. Staying in shape meant getting the shot, and Garrett Harmon never failed to get the shot—and he had the prizes to show for it.

Sandy hair curled around his ears and over the collar of his faded blue-denim shirt. He could have been a recent college graduate who turned down several lucrative job offers to pursue his dream, except for his receding hairline and the lines life had etched on his tanned face.

"What about your writing income? I thought you were doing pretty good."

"Times have changed. The industry isn't what it used to be. Publishers are downsizing."

"What aren't you telling me?"

His piercing look dared me to tell the whole truth and nothing but the truth.

"This bread is dry." I bit into my sandwich. "I apologize. I'd planned to go to the store tomorrow morning. You're home a day early."

"Don't change the subject. Answer the question, Mom."

"What makes you think I'm not telling you the whole story?"

"Because you've always been a terrible liar."

"I'm not lying."

"What did you always tell me?"

"I told you lots of things. I'm surprised you remember them."

"A half-truth equals a whole lie. There's more to it than just changes in the industry. Romance is still a popular genre. And with the e-book revolution, your sales should be shooting through the roof. Come on, Mom, what's really going on?"

I took a deep breath and then told him about my declining sales, dwindling spark, and Cassie's ultimatum. If I expected Garrett to commiserate with me and take up the gauntlet on my behalf, I was wrong.

"No way!" His face, travel weary when he walked in, shone with the excitement of a kid who hears the jingle of the ice cream truck on a hot summer day. "I love Don Bridges! I've read every one of his books. And to think my mom is going to collaborate with him!"

A rock settled in my stomach. I held up my hand. "Not so fast. We've met only one time, and I'm not so sure this is going to work." The image of Don bowing his head in prayer flashed through my mind. "In fact, I know it isn't. I can't work with him."

"Why not?"

"He's not married. He's a widower. And Bertha already thinks he's my boyfriend. I wouldn't want people getting the wrong idea."

Bertha also saw what could have been his truck on the street the night my prowler visited. But I wasn't going to tell Garrett that. Besides, it *was* dark. She even said so herself. Bertha might think she knew everything, but she wasn't infallible.

"Mom, you deserve some happiness. Look, Dad was a better father than a husband—I know that. I may have been young, but I wasn't blind. So what if people get 'the wrong idea.' What if it's the right idea?"

"It isn't." I brushed the crumbs off the glass tabletop with my hand.

"You've met the guy one time—"

I held up two fingers. "Twice."

"Twice?"

"I forgot about the time he saved me from a rattlesnake."

Garrett's mouthful of strong coffee spewed from his nostrils.

"Rattlesnake?" he gasped when he stopped choking. "And I thought the places I visit were dangerous. Where were you?"

"At the cottage. Down by the creek. Apparently, the timber rattler population has increased. I was sitting there, enjoying the fall sunshine, when this man dressed in camouflage from head to toe shot at me."

"He *shot* at you?"

"He warned me first. He said, 'Don't move' then aimed this long-barreled handgun at me. I saw a flash, heard a boom, and then passed out. When I came to—" *in his arms* "—he showed me the dead snake beside me." I shuddered. "He walked me back to the cottage with his dog, an adorable Brittany Spaniel named Charlie. We didn't exchange names, so I didn't know it was Don Bridges until he showed up on my doorstep yesterday with a pizza. He didn't look anything like his picture when I met him the first time."

Garrett rubbed the shadow of his beard. "Remind me never to think your life is boring. So you've met Don twice. The first time he came riding in on a white horse. What happened the second time?"

"Cassie set it up." I told him about Don's no-show. "So he brought my favorite pizza as a peace offering, and we worked on novel ideas. But we can't be a writing team." A well of regret opened up in my soul. "He's a Christian."

Clueless was written on Garrett's face. "Why is that a problem?"

"I don't expect you to understand."

"You're right. I don't understand. Why did you let me join the youth group at First Church if you didn't like Christians?"

"Because it was my fight, not yours."

"You were fighting with them?"

"Not them. God." I stared at my half-eaten sandwich. "I don't know if I believe in Him."

"Since when?"

Since He let my brother die.

"It was a long time ago, Garrett. I don't want to talk about it."

He regarded me a long minute, pressing his lips together like he did whenever he knew I wouldn't like what he had to say.

"There's something you should know if you don't like Christians."

"What's that?"

Garrett's gaze bored into mine. "I am one."

Somehow I wasn't surprised. What did surprise me was the sense of a burden being lifted from my shoulders.

"And while we're playing True Confessions here, there's something else I need to tell you."

"You're getting married."

He grinned. "Not yet. I quit my job."

Now I was stunned. There could be only one reason a man of his accomplishments would leave a lucrative job that took him all over the globe.

"You've met someone."

Maybe I shouldn't sell the house. Where would the grandchildren play? That was one of the reasons Paul and I built on this lot—the sprawling backyard that stretched to the trees. The stunning view of the sunset from the back patio. The dazzling display of the leaves in autumn. Those were the times when I almost longed for a relationship again with their Creator.

In the early years Paul and I dreamed of growing old together. He had confidence in himself, in life, in the future, that spilled over on me. Our life together hadn't been all bad. Now he wouldn't be here to watch the grandchildren play on the lawn he so carefully tended.

"I haven't met *the* one, yet," Garrett said, "but I've come to realize that I'm thirty-two and don't have a life other than my job—a job that consumed me—body, mind, and soul."

"Look at all you've accomplished—all your prizes."

"Do you remember *For Love of the Game*?"

I smiled. "My favorite movie. When I wore the videotape out, I bought the DVD. I still watch it at least once a year. What about it?"

"Do you remember the scene when Billy Chapel returns to his hotel room after he pitched the perfect game?"

I nodded, still seeing Kevin Costner's shoulders shake as he puts his face in his hands and weeps.

"He'd accomplished the dream of every pitcher—facing the minimum batters in nine innings with no hits, no walks, no batter he faced getting on base—an achievement so rare less than two dozen pitchers in baseball history have attained it. But it meant nothing to him. Do you remember why?"

The airport scene when Billy runs into his on-again-off-again girlfriend of five years played over in my mind. No matter how many times I've seen it, I still cry when Billy gets down on his knees and tells Jane his greatest achievement was empty "because you weren't there."

A lump lodged in my throat. Garrett's face blurred.

"Yes," I whispered.

We sat in silence, listening to the tree branches swoosh in the wind, watching fiery leaves ride the breeze to the ground.

"What are your plans?" I asked when I trusted my voice not to shake.

"I *had* planned on moving back here until I found a place of my own. I love western Pennsylvania, and this is where I want to raise my family."

"What about your photography?"

"I can still freelance, take short trips, maybe open my own studio."

"Don't box yourself in, Garrett." I pictured him taking shot after shot after shot of graduating seniors, wedding parties, family portraits. He had an eye for nature. He saw what no one else did and captured it in astounding clarity and perspective.

He reached across the table and squeezed my hand. "I won't. As a matter of fact, I've lined up a freelance assignment the first of November. In Alaska. Attu."

"Attu? Is that a city? You know me and geography."

He grinned. "Attu is an uninhabited, godforsaken chunk of lava at the tail end of the Aleutian Islands."

"What could possibly be there that would be worth photographing?"

"History. We're coming up on the seventy-fifth anniversary of one of the fiercest battles of World War II."

"In Alaska?"

He nodded. "Japan invaded the island in June of 1942."

I shook my head. "I never heard that story. Tell me more. Maybe there's an idea for a novel."

"Few knew about it. The government kept it a secret, not wanting people to panic. We were still reeling from Pearl Harbor."

"You said this is a freelance assignment?"

"I pitched the idea to *National Geographic* about doing a feature on the islands. A reporter and I will fly to Anchorage and then hire a bush pilot to take us to Attu."

"How long will you be gone?"

He shrugged. "A week, ten days. It depends on whether the crazy weather there cooperates."

"Well," I said, gathering up the remnants of lunch, "bring back lots of notes. Maybe I can come up with a story idea."

"You mean *we*. You and Don."

I grunted. "Whatever."

While Garrett took a power nap in his room, I tackled the project of cleaning out my walk-in closet. Items would be assigned to one of three piles: keep, which would be sparse, as the cottage was already stocked with just about everything I needed; pitch, which would probably need a dumpster; and sell, which would go to the garage. I hoped to have everything organized for a garage sale by the end of the month, which was pushing it, but with Garrett's help it was a distinct possibility. Having to travel frequently at a moment's notice had effectively honed his ability to pare down to the essentials.

When I opened the double doors and flicked on the overhead light, I almost gave in to a surge of panic. The shelves were crammed with boxes and bins stuffed with memorabilia. "The artifacts of life," as I called them, crowded every shelf and spilled over onto the carpeted floor.

Maybe I could rent one of those self-storage units. I chased that idea from my brain before it had time to take root. That's all I needed—another expense. When was the last time I'd even looked at any of this stuff? That's all it was—stuff. Life was too busy in forward motion to take time to go back. I dropped a scrapbook chronicling my high school and college years in the "pitch" pile. *What about the grandchildren? Won't they want to know about "the olden days"?* I moved it to the "keep" pile.

It would have been so much easier if I'd died first, then someone else could have decided what to do with it all. I worked methodically, ruthlessly, until I came to the last shelf on the right side. My breath caught as I read the label on the box: "Sonny." Inside were my brother's personal effects sent by the U.S. Marine Corps after the crash.

I pulled it from the shelf with both hands and slid to the floor. As I lifted the lid, hot tears blurred my vision. I knew the contents by heart. I fingered his dog tags, allowing myself to remember. The snapshots, his letters, all were neatly tucked inside the boot box that had once contained a pair of Dingo boots Sonny bought but never had the chance to wear. They were given to Goodwill with the rest of his clothes. At the bottom of the box I found his black, leather-bound Bible. I pulled it out and opened it. Garrison Joyner was printed in neat block letters on the back of the front cover.

Paul wouldn't let me name our firstborn—and only-born as it turned out—after my brother. "No kid of mine is going to be named Garrison," he'd said. "Sounds like a fort."

He approved "Garrett" though, which was as close to my brother's name as he would allow. Actually, the two words came from the same old French word, *garir*, that meant "to provide or defend." I didn't tell Paul that, of course.

Blinking back tears, I softly ran my fingers over Sonny's name. On the opposite page, in Sonny's precise handwriting, were the words of his favorite Scripture, words that had pierced my heart and seared themselves onto my soul that day thirty-three years ago:

Who shall separate us from the love of Christ? Shall trouble or hardship or persecution or famine or nakedness or danger or sword?

No, in all these things we are more than conquerors through him who loved us. For I am convinced that neither death nor life, neither angels nor demons, neither the present nor the future, nor any powers, neither height nor depth, nor anything else in all creation, will be able to separate us from the love of God that is in Christ Jesus our Lord. – Romans 8:35, 38–39

That was the day I walked away from God.

A bombshell arrived in the mail the next morning. Tossing the junk aside, I slit open the envelope with the realtor's logo and return address with my finger, read the contents, then headed straight for the phone.

"This can't be right," I told Irene when she finally came on the line. "When we took out the home equity loan, the house was appraised at three hundred thousand. Did property values go down that much in two years?"

She had my house listed at two hundred thousand. That meant, after all the wheeling and dealing, I might get a hundred fifty thousand—not enough to pay what I owed.

"Actually, property values went up," she said.

"Then why only two hundred thousand?"

"Honey, it looks to me like someone fudged the assessment on your loan."

The next two weeks were crazy. Garrett and I went through the house, room by room, working around potential buyers coming to look at the house and answering phone calls regarding the furniture. A couple who'd just built a house bought the living room, dining room, and my bedroom suites within the first week I'd placed the ads online. They wouldn't need it until they closed, so I still had a place to sleep for another month.

At least their deposit, 50 percent of the sale price, was enough for one month's mortgage payment, which I wanted to pay right away.

Gina, my foreclosure attorney, advised me to wait until I had enough to get caught up. I hoped that would be after the moving sale in October. Garrett bought the pool table for more than I was asking and offered to buy his bedroom furniture, but I told him it wasn't for sale. Eventually, he'd have a place—and a family—of his own.

The furniture in the guest room—Paul's room—wasn't sold, for which I was thankful. I still hadn't sorted through his things.

On the morning of the second day of cleaning out the garage, getting it set up for what I'd advertised as a "mega-garage sale," I found Garrett's old tackle box among the boxes of Christmas decorations in the loft.

"Guess what I just found?" I called to Garrett, who was getting ready to power wash the cement floor. "Your old tackle box."

Through high school and college, he'd been an avid fisherman, watching fishing shows and saving his money for the latest gadgets. By the time he graduated from college, he'd built up quite a collection of rods, reels, lures, and whatever else helped to make his favorite sport more fun. He'd taken most of it with him when he moved out, but ended up selling the majority of it to help pay for a new camera a few years later. Those were his "starving artist" years as he worked to build a name for himself. A couple of his favorite rods and his tackle box, however, he refused to part with.

"Put it at the top of the ladder," he called up to me. "I'll bring it down when we break for lunch."

I pushed the plastic box, at least eighteen inches long, a foot wide, and another foot high, along the plank floor. I was almost to the top of the ladder when it caught on a board on an uneven section of the floor. I gave it a shove—and it careened over the edge, bounced off the ladder, and crashed to the cement floor below, breaking open and scattering the contents.

Garrett gasped.

The scene below me spun. I couldn't breathe.

Strewn across the floor among the lures were bundles and bundles and bundles of bills, all with the picture of Benjamin Franklin.

CHAPTER NINE

"Where did all this money come from?"

Garrett's hushed voice echoed the question in my heart. Garrett had no clue, but I did.

We stared at the bundles lined up in neat rows on the kitchen table between us. Garrett's long fingers rubbed the mustard colored strap of one of the bundles we'd hurriedly snatched from the garage floor and stuffed in a plastic bin. Paul's shirts now lay heaped on the cement floor. Ten bundles lay on the kitchen table between us, each containing a hundred one-hundred dollar bills.

"A hundred thousand dollars," he whispered. "Cash."

"I can do the math." I didn't mean to sound irritated.

Garrett's green eyes probed mine. "You know where it's from." Not a question.

I pushed back from the table. "We could use some coffee."

Garrett pointed to my chair. "Later. Sit."

I opened my mouth to argue, but the look on his face gave me second thoughts. I sat.

"What aren't you telling me?"

When did this son of mine become so wise?

Picking up a bundle, I held it to my nose, thumbed through the crisp bills, then placed it neatly back on its stack.

"Look at me, Mom."

I shook my head. Avoiding his eyes, I said, "Your father was amassing money before he died."

Garrett stared at me, the creases in his forehead deepening with his puzzled frown.

"Why?"

As I gaped at the stacks of bills on the table, the suspicion I'd buried with Paul resurrected its ugly self. Blinking back hot tears, I hung my head, shame washing through me like a dirty river.

"I think . . . I suspected . . ." I took a deep breath. "He was going to leave me. There was another woman. I'm sure of it. His shirts reeked of her perfume."

"Do you know—?"

"Who she was?" I shook my head. "Only that she had expensive tastes. A Gucci bag, Chanel perfume, and yes, even the Mexican vacation were charged to one of your father's credit cards. Which I ended up paying for."

Years of restrained bitterness threatened to burst through my carefully constructed dam like a thawing river in March. I swallowed the lump that lodged in my throat. I would not cry.

"The vacation he died on," Garrett said. "I should be surprised, but I'm not."

I pulled a slightly used tissue from my pocket and blew my nose. "Your father cashed in his life insurance, withdrew all the funds from his IRA, and convinced me to take out a home equity loan to build a garage, but behind my back he borrowed more—a lot more—than the garage was worth. We figure—"

"Who's 'we'?"

"Me and Gina Rosenfield, my lawyer. And Stephanie Morley, the bank manager. We estimate he had at least a three-hundred-thousand-dollar nest egg stashed away somewhere."

Garrett patted his T-shirt pocket, then his shorts. "Do you have a tablet and a pen handy?"

"On the side of the refrigerator. The pen is in the spiral thingie on the top of the notepad."

He tossed the tablet with my grocery list on the table. "How'd you attach the magnets to the back of the steno pad?"

"Hot glue gun. Those little grocery shopping list pads with fifty sheets cost more than a steno pad with a hundred. Plus it's bigger and already has a line in the middle."

Garrett grinned. "You are the only person I know who divides up a grocery list into four sections."

"One for each store. I hate to shop. I get in and get out. As fast as possible."

I pushed myself up from the table to make the coffee. My knees weren't so watery anymore. The grocery pad discussion had calmed me down a little.

I opened the cabinet door. "Regular or hazelnut?"

"Hazelnut. Make it strong. Black."

By the time I poured the coffee, Garrett had a page full of notes. The sweet aroma of hazelnut rose from his steaming cup as I placed it on the table beside him.

"Thanks," he muttered, not even looking up from the pad. I returned to the counter. To my brew I added water to tame it down, five heaping spoonfuls of sweetener, and enough French vanilla creamer to make it light brown.

Cup in hand, I joined him at the table. "There's something else."

Garrett peered at me over his reading glasses.

"That money could be your father's gambling winnings. He didn't always lose, you know."

"Maybe he borrowed all that money to pay his gambling debts."

"I've considered that. No one's come after me for any debts he left behind. Except . . ." I shivered.

Garrett's head jerked up. "Except what?"

I told him about the grill cover at the cottage and the prowler Bertha said she saw.

"Maybe they're after this." I pointed to the stash on the table.

"I'm glad I came home early. You shouldn't be alone."

"I don't suppose there's any way to trace this cash—where it came from?"

Garrett scratched his fuzzy chin. "Looks like new bills. I think they can be traced. But they could be counterfeit."

"Counterfeit! Oh, great. How can we find out without getting ourselves into trouble?"

He picked up a bundle and sniffed it. "I don't smell anything." He dropped the bundle back on the table and tapped the pen on the tablet. "We need an expert—someone who'll be . . . discreet. Hey, how about Don? He was a state cop before he became a famous writer. I'm sure he would know someone—"

"No! We can't ask him."

"Why not?"

"Because."

He sighed. "Because why?"

"Because I said so, that's why."

Garrett's green eyes sparkled like he knew something I didn't. "You like him."

"I've only just met him."

"Uh-huh."

"Let's just say he's kinda interesting."

Garrett grinned. "Just as I thought. You like him."

The doorbell rang. I looked at Garrett in panic. I wasn't expecting anyone. A couple was coming to see the house this evening, and the garage sale wasn't slated to begin until tomorrow.

"Get that money out of sight." I grabbed the plastic storage bin from the cluttered kitchen countertop and shoved it at him. "I'll get the door."

I stopped at the hallway mirror to check my appearance, running my trembling fingers over my hair and adjusting the shoulders of my work shirt. The doorbell rang again—twice. Whoever was out there was getting impatient. Well, let them. This was my house. For now. I glanced out the window at the side of the door.

My heart pounded in my ears. Standing on the doorstep stood two people I least wanted to see—Bertha and Don.

I took a deep breath, unlocked the door, and swung it open. Before I even had a chance to utter a greeting, Bertha pushed past me. Don followed her.

"Come right on in," I said, closing the door.

"I'm so sorry," Bertha began, running nervous fingers over her chenille robe and glancing up at Don, who loomed over her with a look of sweet patience on his face. "I don't want to cause any trouble between you and your new gentleman friend. I was wrong, you see. I came over as soon as I saw him pull into your driveway."

"Wrong about what, Mrs. Rossi?" Garrett stepped into the foyer, planting himself on my left. Don stood facing Bertha on my right—so close I could smell his musky aftershave. A tingle of pleasure shot through me.

"Oh, Garrett! You dear boy! Well, young man now, I suppose. I can hardly believe you're all grown up with a beard and receding hairline and . . . At least you don't have a spare tire. Are you home for long?"

She peered at Don. "You look familiar."

Of course he looks familiar. Your eye was glued to your binoculars when he brought pizza the other day.

"Don't you know who this is?" Garrett said. "This is Don Bridges, the famous mystery writer."

Confusion flashed through her gray eyes. "I don't read mysteries, I'm afraid. I don't even read those sappy Melanie Joy stories everyone raves about."

Garrett snorted. I glanced at Don, who was biting his lower lip, no doubt to stifle a laugh.

"Is there something in particular you came here for, Mrs. Rossi?" I asked.

She frowned, probably trying to remember which excuse she had concocted this time.

"You said you were wrong about something," Garrett prompted.

A light flashed in her eyes. "Oh, yes, I remember now. Forgive me. I don't see as well as I used to, especially at night. I told Melody the other day that Don—I didn't know her new man was Don yet though—was prowling around her garage while she was gone a few weeks ago. But I distinctly recall the prowler looked and moved like a woman. I thought I saw your truck parked on the street that night, but now that I remember, it was an SUV, not a nice truck like yours. Is it new?"

Don's blue eyes gazed into mine. "You had a prowler?"

Bertha rushed on. "Oh, yes, she did. Dressed in all black like you see on those TV crime shows. I watched as she snuck around the garage until the motion light came on. Then she ran to her SUV and drove off."

"Are you sure it was an SUV?" Don shifted into cop mode.

"I think so. It was black. Shiny black. And not one of those compact ones, either."

I could tell Bertha felt important. She'd milk this until the cow was dry. I had to get her out of the house.

"Don, why don't you walk Mrs. Rossi home—she lives right across the street—and—"

"Your man doesn't have to walk me home. I'm perfectly capable—Wait!" Bertha, who'd turned to leave, whirled around to face me. "I see you're getting ready for a garage sale. The paper said it isn't supposed to start until tomorrow, but I was wondering—being your next-door neighbor and all and keeping an eye on your place when you're gone—if you'd let me in a day early? I get a little flustered in crowds, and I know you'll have lots and lots of people."

I smiled, stepped to the door, and swung it open. "I'll think about it." I glanced at the hall clock for effect. "But we really need to get back to organizing for the sale."

"Yes, well, I better let you get to it then. I imagine you must have quite a mess to clean up."

Smiling, Garrett grasped her elbow and nudged her toward the door. "We've only begun to sort through the mess. I'm sure you can appreciate . . ."

She pulled her elbow out of Garrett's grasp. "Not *that* mess. I mean the mess from whatever it was that fell and broke."

I froze. Was she watching us this morning through her binoculars? Did she see the money? Oh, Lord. A wave of dizziness swept through my head.

Her beady eyes bored into mine. I was sure she could see into my soul.

"I heard a crash," she said, "like plastic hitting concrete, and right after that, I noticed your garage door, which had been open all morning, was shut. I was on my way over to see if anyone got hurt when I saw you lugging something—looked like one of those plastic bins. Neither one of you moved like you'd been hurt, so I just turned around and went back home."

"I dropped Garrett's tackle box from the loft," I said.

"Smashed it up good." Garrett grabbed her elbow again and all but pushed her out the door. "My favorite one too. Oh, it looks like rain. We better hurry."

I shut the door after them, afraid to look at Don. I could sense his cop instincts on high alert just from the way he stood, from the way he gazed at me, from the knowing expression on his face.

"Coffee?" I gave him what I hoped was a sweet smile. My insides were quaking like Jell-O in a windstorm.

"Sure."

He followed me to the kitchen. Where was the plastic bin with the money?

"All I have made is hazelnut." I pulled a mug from the cupboard. "I can make regular if you want."

"Hazelnut is fine." He positioned himself in front of the refrigerator and watched me pour his coffee. I hoped he didn't see my fingers trembling. I glanced discreetly around the kitchen. No bin, but my grocery tablet, with Garrett's notes, lay on the table.

"Here you go." I put the mug on the table and snatched up the tablet, which I tossed onto a cluttered counter. "Creamer?"

He nodded. "I'll get it."

I almost passed out when he opened the refrigerator door. The plastic bin with the money sat on the top shelf beside the creamer.

"No!" I rushed across the floor and shoved him out of the way. "You don't want that creamer. It's old—outdated." I grabbed an unopened bottle and thrust it into his hands. "Here. I just got this one yesterday."

I slammed the refrigerator door shut. What was he doing here anyway?

He poured creamer in his coffee and then turned back to the refrigerator.

I snatched it out of his hand. "Leave it on the table. Garrett might need some." My smile trembled.

"You're awfully jumpy today."

I took a deep breath and sat down. "What do you expect? I'm only selling my whole life is all. Sit."

"Yes, ma'am." He pulled out the chair between Garrett's and mine. "Do you want me to fetch anything before I do?"

"I'm sorry. I didn't mean to sound like a shrew. I'm just tired. Please. Have a seat."

When he sat down, I poured creamer into my already over-creamered coffee. "How's Charlie?"

"She's fine."

Don looked right at home at my kitchen table, sipping his coffee, blue-jeaned legs stretched out, ankles crossed. Black socks. He must have taken his shoes off in the hall. His forest-green chamois shirt opened at the neck, revealing a few wiry stray gray hairs above the neck of his white T-shirt, sleeves loosely rolled up to his elbows. Paul never looked so at home—so *right* sitting there. And this was his house.

Something stirred deep within me. Longing? A wish to escape my loneliness? A desire to fill the empty places in my heart? No. I was a loner. I liked being alone. This was just a tumultuous time in my life. I was vulnerable. I'd let my guard down. Well, I'd just put it right back up.

I took a sip of coffee and grimaced. "Why are you here anyway? Didn't I tell you I'd be busy getting ready for the moving sale?"

He reached into his shirt pocket and dropped a USB drive on the table. "My latest manuscript. Thought you could read it and do your thing."

"Do my thing?"

"The romance thing. You're the expert."

I snorted. "Oh, I'm an expert all right. That's why I've been given the ultimatum to team up with you or else."

"I was given an ultimatum too. I tried to incorporate romance, but it didn't work. There's wisdom in 'write what you know.'" He sipped from his mug and then set it back on the table. "This is good coffee. Are you going to make more?"

"I hadn't planned on it. Garrett and I need to get back to work." I glanced at the microwave clock. "I wonder what's taking him so long. He really needs to learn when to cut Bertha off."

"There's one in every neighborhood. It can be a good thing though. People like her know when something's off. They can give you details most other folks miss."

"Yeah, like the neighborhood watchdog. I don't appreciate people like her sticking their nose in my business and then blabbing it all over town. I'm a private person, in case you haven't noticed."

I snatched Don's half-empty mug from the table and emptied it in the sink. Turning, I tried to take on a polite, but dismissive, tone.

"Thanks for stopping by, but I really don't know when I'll have time to look at your manuscript. It might be a while."

He stood up and planted his hands on his hips, a suspicious look on his face. "What are you so uptight about?"

"I told you. I'm selling my house. This is a stressful time."

Don stared at me. "You're not a very good liar."

"Tell him, Mom."

I hadn't heard Garrett come in. I shot him a stern look, the one that never failed to unnerve him when he was younger. But it failed now. I watched with dismay as he marched to the refrigerator, pulled out the container, and dumped the money on the table.

CHAPTER TEN

Don whistled. Garrett plopped in his chair. I leaned against the counter, my trembling body hot and cold at the same time.

"Mom found this in the garage loft this morning." Garrett stacked the bundles in neat piles on the table. "It was in my old tackle box."

Anger, like a black monster, rose within me. I couldn't even trust my own son. I marched to the table and swept the money back into the container.

"Garrett, this is my business. You don't even live here anymore."

Don ignored me and turned to Garrett. "Any ideas where it came from?"

"My dad probably hid it there. He had a gambling problem." Garrett looked at me. "I bet this is what your prowler was after."

Don pulled a pen and a small tablet from his shirt pocket, flipped it open, and began scribbling.

"Melody, what dates were you at your writing retreat last month?"

"You should know. You were there too."

Garrett snickered. I glared at him. "Nothing happened."

"I need the date you arrived and the date you left," Don said, his cop voice firm. "Times, too, if you remember."

"You are not getting involved in this."

"I'm already involved. What dates?"

"I don't remember."

"Check your calendar."

"Why do you need to know? Nothing was stolen. Nobody even broke in."

"Don't forget the grill cover at the cottage." This from my son, Benedict Arnold.

I shot him an I'm-going-to-kill-you look. "I probably put it on the wrong way."

Garrett shook his head. "That's not what you told me." He looked at Don. "My mom is OCD about that place."

"Garrett, it's no big deal."

Garrett glanced at the digital numbers on the microwave. "It's almost lunch time. Why don't you order a pizza? I'll pay."

"This is my life you're talking about, Garrett. And you want me to trot off and play maidservant? I think not. Don doesn't need to know our business." I put the plastic container of money back in the fridge and then turned to face Don. "I put the grill cover on wrong. My husband won the money gambling. I'll include it on my income tax return. End of story."

"You're forgetting the person snooping around the garage while you were gone," Garrett said.

"Probably some kid casing the place for something to sell for drug money."

"And driving off in a late model SUV? I doubt it." He turned to Don. "Can that money be counterfeit?"

"Let me see it again."

Garrett opened the fridge and reached for the container of money, but I grabbed it out of his hands.

"Mom, be reasonable. Don's an ex-cop. He knows how to tell counterfeit Benjamins from the genuine article. I know. I read *The Real Deal*."

I rolled my eyes. "Oh, give me a break. That's fiction, as in made up, make-believe."

"Yeah, but you have to get the details right. That's what you always told me."

Garrett grabbed the cold plastic container and dropped it on the table in front of Don, who ran his fingers over the top bill.

"From what I can tell, it's genuine. Melody, do you have a magnifying glass?"

I stomped across the kitchen, yanked open the junk drawer, and rifled through the mess until I found it.

"Here." I plunked it on top of the money. "I have a moving sale to get ready for. When you two are done playing Sherlock Holmes and Watson, put *my* money in *my* bedroom closet."

I slammed the door on my way out.

For the next hour, I worked in the garage, organizing and arranging artifacts from my life with Paul. I was debating how best to display Paul's expensive shirts when Garrett walked in.

"What do you think?" I shook out a black silk number and held it up by the shoulders. "Should I hang these on a line or stack them?"

"Hang the best ones. Stack the rest." He ran his fingers through his hair. "Do you have the keys to Dad's safe?"

"What safe?"

"The one we found in his bottom dresser drawer."

I tossed the shirt on the table. "What were you doing in his bedroom? I've only started going through his stuff."

"Looking for anything that would give us a clue about the money. You didn't know he had a safe?"

"No. He kept our insurance policies, passports, and other important papers in a safe deposit box at the bank. Whatever is in the safe is probably work related."

Garrett frowned. "Somehow I can't picture Dad bringing work home."

"He was the chief accounting officer for a growing trucking company. He had a lot of responsibility and very little help." I hung the black silk shirt on a borrowed clothes rack.

"How many people were in his department?" Don. I hadn't seen him come in.

"Three. Paul and two clerks. But I don't see what this has to do with anything. I gave everything I found in his desk that was work related to the company after Paul died. I haven't heard from them since."

I'd returned a box of files to the company a few weeks after Paul died, along with his office keys. I'd gone through and sorted the household files and Paul's personal files. Other than the financial mess he bequeathed me, there were no surprises.

"Did you find a small, gold-colored key?" Garrett asked.

"Other than his office keys, the only keys I found were his house keys, which I put in the kitchen cupboard for a spare set, and his car keys, which I returned with the car."

"Did you check all the desk drawers?" Don asked.

"Yes."

"Obviously, you didn't go through his dresser drawers."

"I'm just going through those now." I planted my hands on my hips and blew a lock of hair off my forehead. "Listen, Mr. *Ex*-state cop—"

"Jewelry box?"

I rolled my eyes. "Dress watch. Wedding band. High school class ring. Fraternity pin. No key."

"Any hidden compartments?" Garrett seemed to relish his role in this treasure hunt.

"Garrett, your father wasn't a secret agent. He was an accountant. Granted he had some secrets, but—Where are you going?"

"I have an idea," Garrett said over his shoulder.

I hurried after them to Paul's room, which looked like a crime-scene gone awry. Garrett strode over to the nightstand, where a framed photo of Garrett in his Little League uniform and Paul in his team shirt and ball cap stood. Flipping it over, Garrett twisted the holders and pulled off the back.

"Aha!"

Taped to the inside of the back was a small, gold key. Ripping it off, Garrett hurried to the desk, where a black, fireproof box about the size of a small tackle box rested. He inserted the key, turned it, and lifted the heavy lid. Inside were a set of keys on a key ring, a passport, driver's license, Social Security card, a flash drive—and five more bundles of one hundred dollar bills.

"Why would Paul have another passport?" I asked when my head stopped spinning. I snatched up the travel ID and opened it.

"This can't be right." I flashed the passport at Don and Garrett. "That's Paul's picture, but the name is Samuel D. Miller."

For the next hour we huddled around the kitchen table, studying the contents of the firebox. The money had been zipped up in a plastic bag and stashed with the cash we'd found earlier.

Both the driver's license, which had Paul's picture, and the Social Security card were issued to the fictitious Samuel D. Miller. We Googled the name but came up with no obvious connections. The only bit of information we found that might have any significance was the obituary of a Samuel D. Miller from Yoder, Kansas, who died a year before Paul did.

"Yoder is an Amish community," Don said. "Miller is a common Amish surname in the Midwest. The Amish don't use middle names, but due to increasing government paperwork, they've started to add middle initials, usually the first letter of the father's first name."

"Paul's father's name is DeWayne," I said. "I still don't understand why Paul would have a fake passport and how he could even get one."

"It's not that hard," Don said, "especially for someone with gambling ties."

"But wouldn't he get caught if someone were to check out the name with the Social Security number?" I shook my head in disbelief.

"It's not uncommon to steal the identity of someone who's passed away." Don examined the passport again. "The ideal thing is to walk through an old graveyard and get the name from the tombstone of someone who passed away, say, fifty to a hundred years ago. But even if this Samuel D. Miller had recently passed on, the name is common, especially in the Amish community. And the majority of Amish don't have Social Security numbers. They're permitted to opt out for religious reasons. All he had to do is say he was breaking ties with the Amish community and wanted a Social Security card."

"Wouldn't he have needed a birth certificate?"

Don shrugged. "He could just say he was born at home and his parents never had the birth recorded."

"So what do we know?" Don opened his notebook to a new page.

"Dad hid a hundred fifty grand here at the house," Garrett said.

Don scribbled "$150K, cash" on the page. "Why?"

"He was going to leave me," I said. "There was another woman. But why go to the trouble of faking another identity?"

Don added to his list. "Fake passport, driver's license, and SS card."

"The keys," I said. There were three on the ring. One looked like it was for another safe, and the other two appeared to be door keys.

"Wait." I snatched them from the table. "These two—" I held up the silver door keys—"look just like the keys to my writing retreat."

I scooted to the bedroom and returned with my purse. Fishing out my key ring, I held one of the keys to the patio door of my writing retreat up against one of the keys on Paul's ring. It matched. My stomach churned.

"I didn't give these to him. He hated the place and came with me only once—when we were first married, right after Dad died and Mom sold it to me for a dollar."

"And don't forget the password-protected flash drive." Garrett rubbed the back of his neck. "I've tried everything I can think of— dates, names, places—but I still can't get in."

"His laptop and cell phone were password protected too," I said.

Don added "laptop, flash drive, cell phone" to the list, marking each with the letters "PP."

"Don, with your background, surely you know someone who can hack into these," Garrett said.

Don's head jerked up, his lips stretching into a wide grin. "As a matter of fact, I do." He fished his cell phone out of his shirt pocket. "Anne Hagan. My daughter."

I wasn't too keen on bringing still another person into this growing web of intrigue, but, truthfully, the sooner we confirmed the money was genuine and legitimate, the sooner I could use it to settle my finances. I still wouldn't keep the house, but a nice condo on the Gulf coast for the winter months sounded like a good plan. I figured I'd still have half left after taxes and lawyers' fees. Maybe I'd even put some aside so I wouldn't feel so pressured to write a bestseller. And maybe I wouldn't have to team up with Don.

Although I kind of liked the guy. He was ruggedly handsome—not in a pretty boy way like Paul, but manly—a real John Wayne-type like the heroes in my romances. Definitely a family man. He'd never leave a woman alone to face the challenges of life. He was true-blue through and through.

Sighing, I chased the fantasy out of my head and tuned back in to reality.

"Anne says she'll be happy to help." Don slipped his phone back into his shirt pocket. "I'll take the laptop and flash drive—"

"No you won't." I snatched the flash drive from the table and closed my fist around it. "None of this is leaving the house. Why can't she come here?"

"Hannah's still not feeling up to par."

"Well, I'm sorry, but this stuff is not leaving the house without me. And I don't have time right now. The moving sale starts tomorrow morning at nine and—oh, I forgot! Someone's coming to see the house this evening. And thanks to you two, the place is a mess."

"I'll clean up, Mom. You go to the garage and get set up." Garrett stood and headed for his father's room.

"I'll give you a hand," Don said. "After all, I helped to make the mess."

I pointed my index finger at both of them. "And if you find anything suspicious . . ."

"We won't," Garrett said. "We've already combed through every nook and cranny of Dad's room, and you've done the rest of the house. What about the garage loft?"

I groaned. "I forgot about that. I'll never get done in time. I'll be up all night."

"I'll help with the loft," Don said. "I'm sure Garrett can take care of your husband's room."

"And when we're done, you and Mom are going to sit down for a brainstorming session." Garrett winked at me. "She just came up with a terrific story idea."

That giddy schoolgirl feeling rose in me again.

Five hours later the house sparkled, the garage was organized and ready for the big sale, and Don and I had briefly brainstormed the World War II idea over coffee. Then he left, his pocket notebook filled with ideas. We'd research separately, come up with a few plot ideas, and meet again after the moving sale.

"I didn't think we'd make it," I said, surveying the neatly stacked tables and arching my aching back.

"Without Don, we wouldn't have. He's kind of handy to have around." Garrett laid his arm across my shoulders.

I leaned my head against him. "Too bad he couldn't stay for supper."

"Tell you what," Garrett said. "Let's eat out. That way the kitchen stays nice and clean for the showing. How long will it take you to get ready?"

I checked the time on the wall clock hanging above the door to the kitchen.

"Give me thirty minutes."

I forgot all about the money.

We were seated in a booth at Angelo's enjoying our appetizers when I remembered.

"What did you do with . . ." I glanced around, lowering my voice. "You know."

Garrett placed a slice of bruschetta on his plate. "It's safe."

"Where'd you put it? We shouldn't have left. We should have postponed the showing." Spicy marinara sauce rose up in the back of my throat.

"It's fine, Mom. I took care of it."

"A hundred and fifty thousand dollars—cash? We just walked out of the house and left it." My heart hammered as I pictured the realtor leading the potential buyers through the house. "I'll go start the car. Have the waiter box this up for us."

"Calm down, Mom. It's in a safe place."

"Where?"

Garrett grinned. "Don has it."

"I specifically said I didn't want . . ." I lowered my voice. "How do you know you can trust him?"

"One, he's a former state cop with a spotless record and numerous awards. Two, he's a Christian—the real deal. Three, I've got good instincts when it comes to people, and I like him. Look, if you're that worried about it, we'll stop by his place on the way home."

"You know where he lives?"

"He's staying with his daughter, Anne, until things settle down with her little girl. Not too far from Aunt Peg's."

An hour later we pulled into the driveway of a two-story brick house and parked behind Don's Ford F-150. We followed a stone pathway to the wooden porch, which was illuminated by a single bulb hanging from the ceiling. Slivers of light framed the closed drapes in the picture window. A smoky wood scent tinged the cool fall night. A fall-themed wreath hung from the paneled front door. Garrett pushed the doorbell, and a few seconds later the door swung open and a petite, pixie-faced blonde smiled at us.

"You must be Garrett and Melody. I'm Anne. Dad is upstairs reading the girls a bedtime story. He'll be down in about five minutes. Come on in."

I stepped into the foyer, expecting Garrett to follow me. When he didn't, I turned to see why. He stood in the doorway, gaping at Anne like she was an apparition.

"Garrett, you're letting the cold air in," I said.

"Sorry. I . . . uh . . ." Garret moved forward, unable to take his eyes off Anne. The toe of his boot caught on the threshold, and down he went on the hardwood floor, flat on his crimson face.

Anne rushed to help him up. "Oh, I'm so sorry. I keep telling Dad that thing is too high. I trip over it myself at least once a week."

"What's all the racket?" Don appeared at the top of the stairs. The sound of someone coughing came from one of the bedrooms behind him. "Garrett, Melody. I'll be right down. Just have to tuck the girls in and assure them Sasquatch didn't break in."

My world-traveler son pushed himself to his feet, a sheepish grin giving him a boyish look. Anne closed the door.

"Come on into the kitchen," she said. "I just made a batch of homemade hot chocolate."

As we followed Anne down the hall, Garrett close on her heels, I couldn't hold back a grin. Sometimes you find the diamond in your own backyard.

CHAPTER ELEVEN

The aroma of cocoa and vanilla filled Anne's warm kitchen and mingled with the faint scent of wood smoke. We had passed a blazing fireplace in the family room on the way to the kitchen, which was located in the rear of the first floor. Walnut-brown cabinets and cupboards, probably the originals that had been painted, lined three walls. A doorway led to what appeared to be a mudroom, and another doorway opened into a walk-in pantry. Woven cotton rugs, softened by countless washings, added splashes of color to the yellowed linoleum floor.

"Don't mind the mess," Anne said, pointing to the glass bowls splattered with hardened chocolate and a pink mixture on the scrubbed pine table in the center of the busy room. "The girls and I made Dad cherry cordials for his birthday tomorrow."

"Tomorrow's his birthday?" I pulled out a chair, ignoring the slivers of milk chocolate and powdered sugar, and lowered myself on the stained red chair cushion.

"It's the big six-oh," Anne said, a dimpled smile adding to her sweet charm. A chocolate-splattered white bib apron tied in the front around her tiny waist covered her faded blue jeans and a Pirates T-shirt.

She swept back wisps of dark-blonde curls that had escaped her loose ponytail and opened a cabinet door. "Uh-oh. No clean mugs."

She strode across the room and retrieved a small wooden footstool from its place beside the garbage can. Plunking it on the floor in front of a cupboard, she stepped up and stretched her arm to the top shelf. But the mugs were still out of her short reach.

"That's what I get for letting Dad put away the dishes." She put a knee on the countertop.

"Wait!" In three quick strides Garrett was beside her. "I'll get it. That looks dangerous."

She laughed. "I do it all the time. They just don't design kitchens for shorties like me."

Six-foot-four, and with long arms that had made him the star player on his high school basketball team, Garrett easily reached the top shelf. "How many?"

"Four." She stepped down from the stool and ladled the hot chocolate into the mugs as Garrett handed them to her.

"Now for the secret ingredient. Real whipped cream." She dropped a dollop into each cup.

Garrett took a sip from his mug and closed his eyes, apparently savoring the taste. "This is the best hot chocolate I've ever had!" He grinned at Anne. "Where have you been all my life, angel?"

A rosy blush spread across her cheeks. I stirred my hot chocolate, watching the interchange between these two, remembering what Don had told me about this middle daughter. She was a single mother with two young daughters, one with cystic fibrosis; she had a deadbeat ex-husband who took off when the child was diagnosed; she was a computer whiz who worked out of her home so she could provide for her girls and be available for them at the same time. I'm sure life hadn't turned out the way she planned. She was only in her late twenties, but Anne had experienced enough of life's heartbreaks to sour the sweetest soul. Yet, watching her bustle around her kitchen, I detected no self-pity, no bitterness. She exuded a joy that bubbled up and spilled over on everything around her. No wonder Garrett was smitten.

He helped her clean up the table, carrying the bowls to the sink and placing them next to a stack of what I assumed to be supper dishes, while she got the soapy water running and wiped down the table. He certainly hadn't learned that from his father.

"No dishwasher?" he asked, looking around the kitchen.

Anne shook her head. "It broke down last year. I looked into getting it fixed, but it would cost almost as much to repair it as to buy a new one. I don't have the money right now. Dad wanted to buy me one, but I said no. I'm one of those women who can't stand putting a dirty dish in the dishwasher. I practically wash them first anyway, so I might as well wash them by hand. Plus Kadie helps me—one of her daily chores. It gives us some great mother-daughter time we wouldn't have otherwise."

Garrett grabbed the dish towel hanging from the oven door. "How many children do you have?" He wiped the dripping bowl she handed him and set it on the counter.

"Two girls. Kadie, short for Kadence, is eight, and Hannah is six."

Garrett surveyed the artwork and photos on the refrigerator. "That would put them in what grades?"

"Second grade and kindergarten. I homeschool them. It was so much simpler with Hannah getting sick so much. The CF always gets worse in the fall when the weather changes."

I had to smile when he grinned down at her.

"The girls are nestled, all snug in their beds—at least for now." Don dropped his large frame in the kitchen chair beside mine. He still wore the jeans and shirt he'd worn earlier in the day. He smiled at me, but his eyes betrayed his tiredness—or perhaps worry.

"Thanks, Dad," Anne said, drying her hands on her apron. "I'll finish these later. I'm sure Melody is anxious for an update."

It was already nine o'clock. She'd be doing dishes until midnight. "Finish up. I can wait."

Don and I sipped our hot chocolate in silence while Anne and Garrett finished the dishes and chatted. When they were done, Anne hung her apron on a peg by the pantry door and grabbed a notebook from the counter next to the refrigerator. Garrett held the chair across from me for Anne and then slipped into the one next to mine.

Anne flipped open the notebook to a clean page. "I haven't had a chance to boot up the laptop, but I'll need some information before I try. Dad said the laptop, flash drive, and cell phones are all password protected. People most often use names—not a good idea—and significant dates, like birthdays and anniversaries, for their passwords. Those are easiest to break."

In block letters she printed "NAMES" on the top of the page. "I'll need the names your late husband used, his legal name, nicknames, titles, as well as the names of family members."

"Paul John Harmon. Harmon spelled 'o-n.' His parents called him 'PJ' when he was growing up, but he hated it. I can't think of any other names he used or that anyone called him except for the fake passport."

"Any terms of endearment?"

"What?"

"Did you have a pet name for him? Like 'sweetie pie' or 'honey bunch'."

"Good Lord, no."

"Any high school or college nicknames?"

"I met him in college. I was a senior, so I don't know about high school. He never talked about his high school days. But his frat brothers called him Stringbean because he was so tall and thin. Sometimes it was Bean for short."

"So he just went by Paul mostly? Okay, what about names of anyone close to him? What did he call you?"

"Melody."

"Never Mel?"

"No. He hated nicknames. Said only ignorant people used them."

"Children?"

"Just Garrett. No nicknames for him either."

She gave a wry smile. "I guessed as much. How do you spell your name, Garrett?"

He obliged.

"Middle name?" she asked.

"Paul."

"Paul's parents' names?"

"DeWayne and Nanette."

"Any siblings?"

"No. I never really thought much about it, but we're a small family. Paul's family lives in West Virginia, and we visited once a year at Thanksgiving. He never mentioned cousins or aunts or uncles. My parents are both gone now. Like Paul, I was an only child. So there's not much fodder in terms of names, I'm afraid."

"What about heroes? Or favorite celebrities or sports stars?"

"He liked to watch Pitt football."

Over the next hour, I provided her with enough names and dates to fill four pages in her notebook. It was going on eleven when she finally closed her notebook.

"That should get me started," she said. "Oh, wait, I forgot— Have you had any other occupation besides writing, especially when you were first married?"

"Paul wasn't keen on my working."

She rolled her eyes. "Barefoot, pregnant, and in the kitchen, huh?"

"I liked the barefoot part, and I would have loved another child, but Paul just wanted one. I'm a disaster in the kitchen."

"I can vouch for that," Don said, teasing.

"Dad mentioned you and he are going to work together. I love romance novels, but I haven't had much time to read lately, so I'm not familiar with your name."

"She uses a pen name," Garrett said. "Melanie Joy."

"Melanie Joy!" Anne squealed. "I love Melanie Joy books!"

A fan. Finally. I loved this girl more every minute.

The next three days flew by, with the moving sale and more potential buyers roaming through the house. What didn't sell at my garage sale, Garrett and I loaded in the Explorer and donated it to Goodwill, the Salvation Army, and the local men's shelter.

"You were right to let Don take the money," I told Garrett one morning over breakfast after the moving sale. "So many people were coming and going, we were crazy busy. It would have been easy for someone to slip in and steal it. It's at Anne's, right?"

"Do you want me to go and check on it?"

"You want an excuse to see Anne again, huh?"

A faint blush spread across his cheeks.

"I've never seen you react like that. You've always been so sure of yourself."

"I've never met anyone like her. She's . . ."

I smiled. "I know."

He poured himself another cup of coffee and stared out the kitchen window at the windy morning. "So what's next?"

"Pack my stuff and move to the cottage. I really need to get up there and get ready for winter."

Garrett turned around, concern in his green eyes.

"This isn't the best time of year to be moving to the mountain. Winters are always harsher up there than here, and the place doesn't even have central heat."

"I've got the fireplace."

"Yes, but it's not like a furnace that kicks on when the temperature drops too low."

"You're forgetting the wall heaters, one downstairs and one in the loft."

"Do you have enough firewood for the winter? I could—"

"I'll be all right, Garrett. Really. Until the house sells, I don't want to leave it empty."

He shook his head. "I don't like the idea of you all alone on that mountain all winter."

"I won't be all alone. Jake will be there."

His eyebrows furrowed. "Who's Jake?"

"Jake Esau. He moved into the red-shingled cabin down the road over the summer. He visited me the last time I was there, last month, and told me about his new handyman-security business. Most of the places on the mountain are summer camps and hunting cabins and are vacant most of the time. So he'll check on them periodically, cut firewood, do maintenance and repairs. So, you see, I won't be alone and helpless."

"Where's he from?"

I shrugged. "I didn't ask."

"How old is he? What was his occupation before he moved to the mountain?"

"What's with the third degree? I don't know how old he is. I didn't ask. He's old enough to be retired."

"How old does he look?"

"I don't know—late fifties, maybe."

"Have you Googled him to find out anything more about him? I mean, he could be a con artist or a rapist or an escaped felon. Don't forget there's the state pen in Marienville and the federal pen up near Kinzua."

"Honestly, Garrett, you sound like a mother hen. I'm a big girl. I can take care of myself. Besides, if it makes you feel any better, Don bought the old farmhouse up the road."

Garrett perked up. "Really? He's going to live there?"

"I don't know about living there. He said he wanted a place for Anne to get away with the girls."

"I have a bad feeling about this, Mom. Why don't you wait until next spring? You're going up there all alone, with this Jake guy, who you know nothing about, lurking around during the worst weather of the year. You won't have any neighbors. And don't forget the hunters."

I smiled. "See? I won't be all alone. I know all the hunters who own cabins on my mountain."

"When's bear season? Right before buck season. All those bullets flying. Mom, this is not a good idea."

"Don't worry, Garrett. I'll be fine. I know that mountain."

He gave me a worried look. "I'm still not convinced you'll be safe."

I patted my son's hand. "Don't be such a worrywart. I'll be okay. Really."

"I hope so. I want you to text me every day though, and I'll be a phone call away."

"Yes, dear." I took a sip of my coffee and smiled at him. He was a good son.

CHAPTER TWELVE

"Sorry I couldn't help you with your moving sale, but that flu bug first flattened me and then your Uncle Butch. He still isn't back to his ornery self yet." Aunt Peg pulled a pan of lasagna from the oven and placed it on the ceramic cooktop. "This might be too spicy for him just yet."

Despite her bout with the virus that was making its rounds, my godmother had insisted on having Garrett and me for dinner before I moved to the mountain. I hoped they still weren't contagious. That's all I needed—the flu. She'd suggested I bring Don, too, but he'd returned to his home in Erie since things with Hannah had settled down.

We hadn't had time to get together and discuss the book idea, but I'd e-mailed Don my thoughts, mentioning we should probably wait until Garrett got back from his photo shoot. But Don e-mailed back, "We can't wait that long. The proposal is due before that. How about if I draw up our ideas and tell Cassie the sample chapters will be forthcoming after your move? You've got a lot on your plate right now."

I'd answered: "Good idea. That should give her something to work with and get her off our backs. Thanks."

"You still look a little pale," I said, slicing cucumbers for the salad. "I appreciate the dinner, but it could have waited. I'm planning to come back around Thanksgiving for the closing."

"You were lucky the house went so quickly. A lot of homes around here are on the market for months. The Gildingers are still trying to sell theirs, and they moved to Florida a year ago." She slapped a loaf of Italian bread on a wooden cutting board and plugged in the bread knife. "Did you get everything sold? I can't imagine having to pack up a lifetime, deciding what to do with all the photos, cards, the kids' drawings, and report cards. Why, I still have the letters Butch wrote me when he was in the service. I've started going through things I don't know how many times, but I get so flustered I put it all away. I want to keep everything."

She placed thick slices in a wicker breadbasket and folded a deep-red linen cloth over it.

"There." She glanced around the kitchen. "Lasagna's done, bread's sliced, cheesecake's in the fridge. Is that salad ready?"

I spread a handful of grape tomatoes over the top. "It is now."

I carried the bamboo salad bowl to the dining room and placed it on the table set for four with Aunt's Peg's favorite dinnerware, glazed terracotta with bold sunflowers painted on a deep-red background with a mustard-gold rim. A pot of mums in a riot of blazing colors sat in the middle of the table that was covered with a deep-red linen tablecloth. A matching linen napkin tucked neatly into a sunflower napkin ring rested on each plate.

"The table looks fantastic," I told Aunt Peg, who'd followed me with the breadbasket. "You make me feel special."

"Oh, honey, you *are* special." She gave me a one-armed hug before placing the breadbasket on the table beside the lazy Susan that held salt and pepper grinders, a shaker of grated cheese, and a butter dish.

"I'll get the lasagna," she said. "You get the boys. You'll probably have better luck prying them away from the ball game than I will."

I grinned. "Hopefully, it's either a blowout or the game's almost over. I'm taking my life in my hands interrupting a Steelers game."

When I stepped into the den, Garrett and Uncle Butch didn't even notice. Their eyes were glued to the flat-screen TV on the wall above the fireplace. My heart sank when I read the score: the game was tied at 21. The Steelers had the ball on the twenty-yard line in their own territory. Third down and nine. Then the quarterback fumbled the snap and the defense recovered the ball. Garret groaned. Uncle Butch yelled, "You idiot!"

Aunt Peg stood in the doorway. "Looks like I better cover the lasagna with aluminum foil and put the salad in the refrigerator."

"I'll help." She shook her head. "Sit. Relax. You've had a busy month."

I settled on the love seat and picked up the day's newspaper from the coffee table. I checked the weather before I scanned the front page. Not because I was interested in the news, but because a newspaper is a great source of ideas for novels. And Lord knows I needed to fire up the muse—or fire her and get a new one. I was about to flip to the back page when a headline toward the bottom caught my eye:

Man's Body Found on the Point

The body of a McKeesport man was found early yesterday morning floating in the water at the confluence of the Allegheny, Monongahela, and Ohio rivers. According to Pittsburgh police, a couple jogging through Point State Park at daybreak noticed an empty boat drifting on the river near the Point and then spotted the body. Police identified the man as Devon Grove, 46. Grove, whose wife said he couldn't swim, apparently drowned when he fell overboard. Police aren't saying whether they suspect foul play, pending the results of an autopsy. Grove, an accountant for Wellsboro Trucking, leaves a wife and two children.

Wellsboro Trucking? That's where Paul had worked. Did Grove work there when Paul was there? The name wasn't familiar, but Paul rarely talked about his job. I only knew the names of the company president and secretary. Shortly before he died, though, Paul had come home from work extremely upset. When I'd asked him about it, he just mumbled something about "the idiot I have to put up with every day."

Paul supervised two others who worked under him, the accounts payable manager—a woman whom Paul said was "brilliant"—and "that bumbling excuse of a clerk." He stormed into his room one night and slammed the door. A half hour later when I went to tell him supper was ready, I overheard him talking on the phone. Instead of knocking, I pressed my ear to the door. His voice was loud, clipped, the tone he used when he was trying to control his temper.

"We'll just have to pay him," he'd said.

I'd assumed he was referring to a creditor. Paul's office was responsible for invoicing clients and paying the bills. Now I wasn't so sure. I carefully tore out the article, folded the paper in half, and slipped the article into my pocket. Worth looking into.

The following Friday I moved into my writing retreat on the mountain, stopping at Aunt Peg's before I left town for good to say good-bye. She had a casserole waiting on the kitchen counter for me.

"Stuffed shells." She slipped the dish into an insulated casserole carrier. "This way you don't have to worry about supper. You can bring the dish and carrier back when you come for Thanksgiving."

"I will." I wrapped my arms around her for a long hug. "Thanks for everything. Mostly for always believing in me."

"Oh, honey, that isn't hard." Her dark-brown eyes glistened. "When is Garrett leaving?"

"He's already gone. His flight for Anchorage left an hour ago. He helped me load up the Explorer yesterday and then spent the evening with Anne."

Her face lit up. "Sounds like the most eligible bachelor is off the market," she said, a twinkle in her eyes. "And what about you? How's the situation with Don?"

"We're a writing team, Aunt Peg. That's all."

She gave me a knowing look. "Uh-huh. There's a spark in your eye that I haven't seen in years.

"Aunt Peg, a man like that wouldn't be interested in me."

Her hands, moist with strawberry-scented lotion, cupped my face. "Don't sell yourself short, sweetheart. I know what you're thinking—you're not worthy of him. I could kick that Paul's rear from here to kingdom come for doing this to you." Her gaze pierced my soul. "It's not a matter of whether or not *you're* worthy, Melody. It's whether *he* is worthy of *you*."

My heart warmed. "I love you, Aunt Peg."

"I love you too."

I glanced at the kitchen clock. "I'd better get going. I want to get to the cottage before the store closes at noon."

"Don't forget the stack of newspapers I've been saving for you. They're by the door in the mudroom. Your uncle will carry them out for you."

She gave me a worried frown. "I don't know why you don't just install a furnace or electric baseboard heating and stop fooling around with that fireplace and those propane heaters. They can be dangerous."

"Have you been talking to Garrett?" I smiled. "I'll be fine."

"You *do* have a smoke alarm, right?"

"Yes, Aunt Peg."

"Make sure you put in fresh batteries. What about a carbon monoxide detector?"

"I don't have one yet, but I'll get one after I've settled in. I promise."

"Make sure you do. When was the last time you had your chimney cleaned?"

My mind went blank.

"Just as I thought. Hire someone to clean it. Soon."

I shook my head. "You worry too much. I've been building a fire in that fireplace for twenty years. And before that, in the woodstove."

"All the more reason to have the chimney cleaned." Then she smiled softly, her eyes taking on a reminiscent gaze. "I remember your mother telling me about that thing, how quickly it produced heat and warmed up the place. What did you call it?"

"Hot Stuff."

"You're some pretty hot stuff yourself." My uncle's voice boomed through the vast kitchen.

"Uncle Butch, you are such a tease."

He opened his bear-like arms. "How about a hug for your favorite uncle?"

I stepped into his embrace, suddenly having mixed feelings about moving. Besides Garrett, Aunt Peg and Uncle Butch were the only family I had left. As much as I loved my writing retreat, here in Greensburg I had people who cared about me. Was I making a mistake? *Well,* I thought, picking up the casserole, *it's too late now.*

The weather on the mountain was relatively mild for early November, with partly cloudy skies and daytime temperatures in the mid-forties. At night, the thermometer plunged below freezing. According to The Weather Channel, the next ten days were supposed to be more of the same, with a 40 percent chance of precipitation on Tuesday that could come as snow, rain, ice, or a mix. Since I still hadn't filled the propane tank, I used the wall space heaters sparingly.

I kicked myself for not buying a couple of electric heaters when they were on sale. At this rate, my firewood supply wouldn't last another week. I could have sworn I had more firewood in the woodshed than I did.

I stared into the smoldering fire in the hearth and pulled the fleece blanket tighter around me. I'd been huddled beneath it all morning, drinking cup after cup of steaming tea, trying to get warm, resisting the urge to burn another log. I hated being cold, but I had to be frugal with what little cash I had left after catching up with the mortgage. It would be a while before my royalty checks got healthy again, if they ever did.

After reading the proposal Don had submitted, Cassie had agreed to give us an extension to get the first three chapters written. Until the complete proposal was ready to submit to publishers, though, and until we got a contract, there wouldn't even be an advance. How long would the little money from the sale last? I'd get some money after the house closed at the end of the month, but even that wouldn't last all winter.

I'd tried several times to start writing, but I couldn't seem to focus. Our discovery of Paul's cache was foremost on my mind, edging out all other thoughts. Anne still had Paul's laptop, flash drive, and cell phone but hadn't been able to break the passwords yet. Don had Paul's fake IDs and the cash, which we put in a safe deposit box at my credit union. He told Garrett we shouldn't touch the money until we'd determined the source. I was hoping the laptop and flash drive held the answer.

I sipped my tea, which was colder than my nose. This was crazy. Here I was freezing myself to death, when I had a hundred and fifty grand of Paul's gambling winnings at my disposal. As his widow, wasn't it mine? Don didn't think it was counterfeit. Who was Don to tell me what I could and couldn't do with it anyway? He was a state cop turned mystery writer. Garrett trusted him, but he was a big fan of his novels and, obviously, of his daughter. But until we closed on the house, why couldn't I use some of the money?

I set my mug on the coffee table, lifted a sleeping Rascal off my lap, and pushed the fleece blanket aside. I checked the signal on my cell phone. One bar. I called the propane company and placed an order. If I was going to be broke, I'd rather be warm and broke than cold and broke.

Willie had a list of locals who sold firewood. I checked the time on the mantel clock. Eleven thirty. Since the time change, Willie closed the store at noon. I could make it. Shoving my feet into my sneakers, which I kept loosely tied, I grabbed my purse and keys and rushed outside.

Then I saw the Explorer. The windshield glistened white with frost. The sun's rays hadn't reached the driveway yet. I hated to scrape. But I had no choice. Maybe it wouldn't take too long. The old girl could warm up while I scraped. It was five minutes before I found the scraper wedged beneath the spare tire in the back. Why hadn't I started the engine first?

I slid behind the wheel, inserted the key in the ignition, and turned. Nothing. Great. The battery was probably dead. I pushed the button for the overhead light. It didn't come on. Now what? Surely there were auto mechanics in the area.

Back in the cottage, I searched for the Marysville phone book for fifteen minutes before I found it in the loft under the bed. My fingers flipped through the yellow pages until I came to "M." No mechanics were listed, but there was a heading for "Mechanical contractors." None were listed. "See also Air Conditioning Contractors & Systems; Heating Contractors; Plumbing Contractors," I read. What else would it be under?

I flipped the flimsy pages to "Automobile Repairs & Servicing" and groaned. Two pages of listings. Where to start? I needed a map so I'd know which ones were the closest. I wished I'd renewed my AAA membership, but that was a luxury I couldn't afford. I was rooting through the Explorer looking for my Pennsylvania map when I found Jake's business card in the glove compartment.

Jake! Why didn't I think of him earlier? Even if he didn't know much about the workings of an automobile engine, he surely would be able to help me find a mechanic and get me some firewood. It would take me fifteen, twenty minutes to walk to his cabin.

I was halfway there when gray clouds rolled in and the wind picked up. I knew this mountain, and snow was on that wind. I shivered in my sweatshirt, wishing I had the sense to grab my thermal-lined, hooded Carhartt jacket and put on wool socks and hiking boots instead of the old sneakers I kept around to slip into when I had to step outside to get firewood.

But when I rushed out of the cottage, a quick trip to the store in the Explorer was all I had in mind. The sun shown brightly overhead, promising warmth for the afternoon. Maybe I should go back to the cabin, but I was already halfway there. So I trudged on, praying the clouds were just passing through. At least I'd decided to take the blacktop road rather than the trail through the woods. The road was warmer and easier to walk, and traffic was practically nonexistent.

I was almost to Jake's driveway when a pickup stopped beside me and the passenger window slid down. "Hop in," a man's voice said. The head of a furry white-and-orange dog with a pink nose leaned out. Giddiness bubbled up in me.

"Charlie!" I peered past the Brittany Spaniel to the man sitting behind the wheel. "Don. What are you doing here?"

"We need to write those chapters. I figured you should be settled in by now." His eyes roamed from my bare head to my thin sweats to my sneakered feet and back again. "Where are you headed on a day like this dressed like that, anyhow? Where's your coat? And hat? Do you know the majority of your body heat is lost through your head?"

"That," I said, pulling my hands up into my sleeves and trying to keep my teeth from chattering, "is a myth. I researched it for my last book. Studies have shown that only a small percentage of body heat is lost through the head."

He shrugged. "You're freezing. Don't deny it. I saw you shivering. Climb in before you turn into an icicle. Charlie, move over for the lady."

I pulled my hands out of my sleeves and pointed to Jake's driveway, hoping he didn't notice how badly they were shaking. "Thanks, but I don't need a ride. I'm almost there."

"Visiting the new neighbor?"

"Not a social call." I jammed my frozen fingers into the side pockets of my sweatpants. "My Explorer won't start and the phone book had two pages of listings of auto repair places and I have to get to the store because I need to buy firewood because—"

"Slow down, woman." He shifted his truck into park. "What's wrong with your SUV?"

"Dead battery, I think. The overhead light won't come on either. I should have had it checked out before I moved. She was getting harder to start. I suppose you don't know of any place I can call?"

He leaned across the seat and shoved the door open. "Get in."

I peered through the bare trees at Jake's place. His driveway was empty. No smoke rose from the chimney.

"Are you going to stand there all day and freeze your hair back to its charming natural state of frizz or are you going to get in where it's warm?"

I climbed up beside Charlie and slammed the door. "What I do with my hair is none of your business." I held my hands in front of the heating vent. "Can you turn up the blower?"

"I can." He just sat there.

I sighed. "Why do you always have to be such a smart aleck? Will you *please* turn up the blower?"

He grinned. "Do you know the origin of that phrase—smart aleck?" Don leaned toward me and flipped the fan on high. "The original smart aleck was a guy named Alec Hoag, a renowned thief, con artist, and pimp in New York City in the mid-1900s. He ran a con game so successful he was on the other side of town before his victims knew what happened. I do research too."

"What are you staring at?" I ran my hand over my hair.

He blinked his blue eyes and looked away. "I'm not staring at anything."

"Yes, you were. You were gawking at my hair. Is my frizz coming back? My hair treatment was supposed to last ten to twelve weeks."

"So that's what happened to it."

I pulled down the sun visor and snapped open the mirror. Outside of being windblown, which I liked, my hair looked smooth and silky, the way I'd always wanted it to look. I pushed up the visor. "Don't you like it?"

He stared at me for a moment and then shook his head.

"What's wrong with it?"

"Nothing," he muttered, shoving the truck in gear and checking the rearview mirror. "I just liked your frizz better."

What kind of man liked frizzy hair?

It didn't take Don more than a minute to discover why my Explorer wouldn't start.

"Battery terminals." He pointed to where the cable hooked to the battery. "See that?"

I leaned closer, brushing his shoulder, to get a better look. "You mean that white, ashy stuff? What is it?"

"Corrosion."

I groaned, mentally reviewing the bills that were due. "How much?"

He scratched his beard. "How about this: I fix it, and you go on a dinner date with me. Tonight. It *is* your birthday, you know."

"You can fix it? Great. How did you know it was my birthday?"

"Garrett. Since he couldn't be here, he asked me if I'd make sure you weren't alone on your big day."

So now my son was playing matchmaker. My new clothes were hanging in the coat closet until I cleaned out the cedar wardrobe in my loft. I hadn't organized it in years. Would the emerald green silk be too cold? Don's voice broke into my wardrobe planning.

"I need baking soda, an old toothbrush, and petroleum jelly."

Fifteen minutes later my Explorer was running smoothly.

"You need to replace this battery ASAP," he said, inspecting the engine as it ran. "When was the last time this baby had a complete service checkup?"

"Before Paul died, I think."

"I'll get you the name and number of a reputable mechanic in the area." He let the hood slam shut. "Now, about that dinner date."

He took me to Rosalia's Italian Restaurant in Marysville. I often ordered takeout—their Stromboli was to die for. I was surprised, though, how crowded the place was for a Tuesday evening. As we waited for a table to open up, I pulled out my phone and checked the weather.

"Uh-oh. This doesn't look good." Using my index finger and thumb, I enlarged the screen. "See that?"

Don leaned closer to get a better view, his forehead brushing against my hair. A tingle shot through me. I pointed to the map on the screen. "That area of white with pink and red spots means snow, sleet, and ice. It's heading this way."

The lights flashed on our pager. Don stood. "Our table's ready."

"Maybe we should go." I bit my lower lip. "It can get pretty bad on the mountain."

"We'll be fine."

"But The Weather Channel—"

Don snatched my phone out of my waving hand and closed the app. Slipping it into his shirt pocket, he grabbed my hand and pulled me to my feet.

"You worry too much. Come on. I'm hungry."

The appetizer alone—bruschetta and breaded mozzarella sticks—would have been enough for me. Don, of course, had to say grace, right in the middle of the busy restaurant. I bowed my head along with him. While he thanked the good Lord for the meal, I asked Him to hold off the snow and ice until we got back.

"I thought you said you didn't pray," Don said, spreading the stiff, black linen napkin across his lap.

"I don't."

I debated whether to do the ladylike thing and put my napkin on my lap or play it safe and use it to cover my white silk blouse. What had I been thinking? I tucked the corner of the napkin inside my V-neck collar.

"I saw your lips moving." He pulled a thick slice of bread from the basket on the table and smeared butter on it.

"If you must know, I prayed to get home safely. Not that He listens to me."

Don gave me a soft smile. "You'd be surprised." He reached across the table and pushed a stray strand of hair away from my eyes. "I apologize for the comment I made about your hair this afternoon. It does look nice, but I liked it before you did whatever you did with it."

So he wasn't the smooth-talking ladies' man I'd thought he was. Cassie's words came back to me: *Don hasn't looked at a woman since Francine died.* He was just as nervous as I was. Our gazes locked. Those blue eyes were deep tonight. My tight muscles relaxed as my resistance to this man cracked like an ice cube dropped in hot water.

The waiter placed steaming soup bowls on the table. I fumbled for my soup spoon, which slipped out of my grasp and plopped into my soup, splashing hot broth on the napkin draped over my blouse. For an instant I cringed, waiting for the ridicule. But the man across from me wasn't Paul. Instead, he chuckled. Instead of the usual mortification, laughter bubbled up from inside me.

"Now that I got that out of the way," I said, fishing the spoon out with my fork, "let's eat."

The wedding soup was the best I'd ever tasted, the chicken Parmesan was crisp on the outside and succulent on the inside, and the spaghetti neither overcooked nor undercooked. I ate half of everything and requested a take-home container for the rest.

"This meal could feed me for a week," I told Don, who'd cleaned up his plate pretty good.

"Why don't we order cheesecake and have it back at your place?" he said, watching me scrape spaghetti into a Styrofoam take-home box. "I'll build a fire while you put on the coffee."

My cell phone rang once, the wind chimes ring indicating a voice mail message. I reached into my purse then remembered it was still in Don's shirt pocket. I held out my hand.

"It's from Irene, the realtor who sold my house. She sent it this afternoon, and I'm only getting it now." I rolled my eyes. "Such is reception on the mountain."

"Melody?" Irene's tone told me the news wasn't good. "We have a problem. The buyers backed out."

CHAPTER THIRTEEN

"How can they back out?" I asked Irene, who'd been waiting for me to call back. "We signed a contract."

"The husband got laid off from his job unexpectedly, and with the loss of half of their income, the mortgage company turned them down."

"They can do that?"

Irene sighed. "The contract you all signed was a binder's agreement, which, if you remember, contains a contingency clause that states conditions under which the agreement can be broken: if the house doesn't pass inspection, if the seller doesn't maintain the property properly until the purchase is finalized, if any liens against the property are discovered, if the title isn't clear. Those conditions, of course, are the responsibility of the seller, and you met all of them."

I exhaled a breath I didn't realize I was holding. "I was worried that a lien had been placed against it because the mortgage payments were in arrears."

"You showed good faith when you caught up with the payments."

"I *was* caught up. I still need to come up with this month's payment." I'd have to dip into the living expenses fund or the money we found that Paul had hidden.

"Hello? Melody, are you still there?" Irene's voice jerked me off my train of thought.

"Sorry. I was thinking. What did you say?"

"I said that you met all the conditions, and I admire you for your honesty and wanting to do the right thing. Others would have left the account in arrears, expecting the purchase price to cover the delinquent payments. There was only one stipulation for the buyer in the contract."

"To come up with the money." I ran my hand through my hair. "What about the down payment?"

"The earnest money, which is different from the down payment due at closing, was put in an escrow account, remember, to be used toward the purchase price at the closing. Since they were the ones to back out of the deal, the money is yours."

"How much is it?"

"I'd have to check the paperwork. Usually in binder agreements like this, five hundred dollars or 1 percent of the purchase price. Hold on. I'll check."

Because I didn't want the house on the market for long, I'd agreed to lower the asking price from two hundred thousand to a hundred fifty thousand. I couldn't remember the exact amount of the earnest money. It wouldn't belong to me anyway at closing. It would go to the bank that held my mortgage.

"Here it is," Irene said. "Fifteen hundred."

I pictured the couple going through the house. I'd been there at the time. They were in their early thirties, like Paul and I were when we first plunked down our down payment to build the place. We'd had stars in our eyes too. So many hopes and dreams. The couple's young son, who was in kindergarten, bounced from room to room. Children don't even try to contain their excitement, their joy. I swallowed, closing my eyes against the dreams that had died and the tears that threatened.

"Give it back to them," I said.

Irene paused. "Are you sure?"

"Yes. They need it more than I do."

Irene told me she'd already replaced the "Sale Pending" sign with the "For Sale" sign and had re-posted the advertisements online, as well as in the newspapers.

"There was a lot of interest when it first went on the market," she said. "I feel confident it'll sell before the end of the year."

Before the end of the year? That meant two more payments.

I suppressed a groan. "Thanks, Irene. I'll talk to you later."

I clicked off and dropped my cell phone in my purse. Elbows on the table, I leaned my face into my hands, holding back the scream rising from my chest. I needed to get outside, somewhere I could shake my fist in heaven's face. I wanted to get back to my cottage, where I could scream at the unfairness of it all and weep with abandon. I was so tired of holding up so everyone would say how brave Melody was. Tired of holding in the anger, the rage.

Not saying a word to Don, I slid out of the booth, nearly knocking over the waiter bringing the check. Shoving the heavy oak door outward, I stepped onto the wooden deck. Frigid air slapped my cheeks. Snow flew sideways across the parking lot, driven by a wild wind that tore at my blouse and right through me. My coat. I'd left it in the restaurant. Don's truck, parked in front of the building, mere steps away, was locked.

I took a deep breath, closed my eyes, and began counting. One thousand one, one thousand two, one thousand three . . . inhaling and exhaling slowly and deeply with every count. That's what the anger management brochures Paul brought home from the one and only session he attended said to do. Force out the bad thoughts. Focus on something pleasant.

Don's face, lined with concern and kindness, appeared in my mind's eye. The sparkle in his sky blue eyes. The way the gray swept through his trimmed beard, giving him a dignified look. Charlie's affectionate nuzzle when I'd climbed into the truck today. The flood of emotions pushing against the dam abated. What if I lost my writing retreat? My bravado dissolved.

"I will not crumble with every setback," I said to myself. "Within every problem is the seed to the solution."

The door behind me swooshed open and a current of warm air enveloped my bare legs. Why had I chosen the emerald green silk capris? And shiny dress sandals with heels? I was usually so practical, checking The Weather Channel before deciding what to wear. But tonight I acted like a giddy schoolgirl getting ready for her first date. Don draped my winter-white wool coat over my shoulders, stepped around to face me, and gently slid the buttons through the buttonholes.

"I'm sorry," I began, dropping my gaze. A tear trickled down my face.

His hands grasped my shoulders. "Melody. Look at me."

I shook my head. His cupped hand slid under my chin. A gentle lift and my eyes met his.

"Stop apologizing for everything," he said. "You say you're sorry for things that are someone else's doing. You probably apologize to a chair when you bump into it."

I forced my lips into a smile. "Actually, I've done that."

His eyes swept my face with a tender glance that sent sparks through my soul. The musky, manly scent of his aftershave, like invisible fingers, lured my nose to nestle in the crook of his neck. He leaned forward, and I raised my head ever so slightly and closed my eyes. But his lips brushed against my forehead instead. He pulled the hood of my coat over my head.

"You don't want your hair to get frizzy." He handed me my purse and then reached down and lifted a white plastic bag from the glistening wood deck.

"Your take-home box. And dessert. Let's go back to your place and get a fire going. Nothing better than strawberry cheesecake on a blustery winter night in front of a blazing fireplace."

"Sounds good to me." I slipped my arm through his as we started down the steps. *But the fire's already started.*

It took twice as long to get back to the cottage as it had to get to the restaurant. The roads were a sheet of ice, making maneuvering them tricky even in a four-wheel drive. But then a four-wheel drive wasn't much better on ice than a two-wheel drive. The snow, the first accumulation of the season, came down not in soft flakes, but in tiny, hail-like pellets that melted on the warm blacktop and then refroze.

I breathed a sigh of relief when we turned off the main road into my driveway. Snow I didn't mind driving in, mostly because of my trusty Explorer with Trac control, but I refused to go anywhere if there was even a chance of ice. Rain could turn to freezing rain without warning. It all depended on the temperature. And the forecasters weren't all that accurate with the predictions. It was a different world up here on the mountain.

My relief at getting back in one piece, however, was short-lived. The porch light, which I'd turned on before we left, was out, and the cabin was dark inside. I always left a small lamp burning in the living room.

"Uh-oh," I said as Don eased up behind my Explorer. "The power's out. I'm not surprised. With virtually no one living up here year-round, trimming back the trees isn't a priority. And the wind looks like it's picking up too."

I'd seen nasty snowstorms on this mountain before, but I didn't figure on one so early in the season. I wasn't ready for it. The trees were already coated with glistening ice. The ones I worried about during a storm like this were the evergreens. By November, the oaks, maples, birches, and quaking aspens were bare, but heavy, wet snow and ice could bring down the sturdiest pine. And white pines and hemlocks surrounded my place.

"I'll get the fire started then go up to the farmhouse and get Charlie," Don said. "You mentioned you needed firewood. How much do you have?"

I pictured the nearly empty woodshed. "Enough for tonight and tomorrow, I think. But if the power is out for longer than that . . . One time it was out for a week after a storm like this."

"I'll bring a load with me."

"You have firewood?"

"There was a pile in the barn when I bought the place, and I added to it last month."

Don stepped around the truck to get me. Opening the door, he put out his hand to help me down. I put my sandal on the running board.

"Hold it." He pushed me back in the truck and stared at my feet in the light of the cab. "For a woman who's such as weather freak—"

"I know." I felt so foolish. "I should have worn more practical shoes. What was I thinking?"

I was thinking how much I wanted to look nice for you. I fumbled in my purse for my keys, which I shoved into his outstretched hand. "Here. My hiking boots are on the mat by the back door. There's a pair of socks stuffed in them."

He jammed the keys into his coat pocket, grabbed the plastic bag with our cheesecake, pulled me over his shoulder, and carried me, fireman style, through the blizzard to the cabin. The inside was as cold as the outside. The fire had died out late in the morning, and I'd used the wall heater—on low to conserve what little propane I had—to warm up the place while I got ready for our dinner date. Although I'd had the place insulated, a wind like the one blowing outside now felt like it came straight through the walls. I shrugged my coat off and draped it over the coat tree. My flannel jammies were calling me.

Fortunately, I'd lugged in a few armfuls of firewood and filled the wooden barrel with dry kindling after breakfast. So while Don got the fire going, I slipped out of my silky dress clothes and into red-plaid flannel pjs and then pulled on a pair of wool-blend socks over my frozen feet.

When I returned to the living room, smoke belched from smoldering logs in the hearth, filling the room with its acrid smell. Don knelt on the stone floor, waving a newspaper.

"I thought you knew how to build a fire." I covered my nose and mouth with my sleeve. My eyes burned.

"Downdraft. And a cold chimney that doesn't want to draw the smoke up. The wind out there isn't helping either."

"When that happens to me, I use a box fan to force air up the chimney." I grabbed another newspaper. "A lot of good it'll do now without electricity."

It took a good half hour before we got the fire going. By then it was nearly eleven o'clock, and I was yawning. We'd opened both front and back patio doors a foot to let the smoke clear out, but the acrid smell remained. I was too tired to care. I just wanted to curl up on the sofa under my fleece blanket and go to sleep.

"Too tired for dessert, huh?" Don stretched and yawned. "I guess I'd better head on up the road, then—unless you want some company. That's a nasty storm out there."

I shook my head. "I've stayed here in worse storms. I'll be fine."

He grabbed his coat, which he'd tossed on the reclining chair, and thrust his arms through the sleeves. "You have my cell phone number, right? Call if you need anything."

"I'll text. The signal here isn't strong enough for voice calls."

"Where's your woodshed?"

"Out back."

"I'll start my truck and bring in a few armloads of firewood while it de-ices."

I yawned. "Thanks, Don. For everything."

By the time he pulled out of my driveway, I didn't have to worry about going out in the ice storm for firewood. He'd brought in enough to fill the box and stacked more just outside the back door and covered it with a tarp from his truck. As I watched the taillights of his truck disappear into the blizzard, I wished I had let him stay.

I usually loved a good snowstorm. I'd never been afraid of the wind or the weather on this mountain. And while I respected nature in its fury, I never feared it. But tonight I did. The wind howled, and ice pellets spitting against the glass sounded like a million BBs hitting the windows. The forest screamed like a woman in labor, branches waving wildly in the winds, limbs cracking and tumbling through the night to the glistening ground beneath.

The hair on the back of my neck prickled. Goosebumps, not from the cold, sprouted on my arms. The air in the cabin was thick with a sense of foreboding. Rascal sensed it too. She'd been underfoot since I got back. Now, as I stood at the back patio door watching the storm unleash its fury, she wrapped herself around my legs, rubbing up against me. I lifted her, pressed her to my chest, and rubbed my cheek against her soft fur. Her claws dug into my sweatshirt.

"It's all right, baby." I ran my hand over her back. "We're safe and sound inside."

Was Don safe and sound inside his farmhouse? I shook the image of him hunched over the steering wheel, his truck in a ditch. One thing about storms—they sure fire up the imagination.

Running my fingers through Rascal's gray-and-white fur, I carried her into the living room and settled on the sofa, pulling the fleece blanket over us both. I stared into the flickering flames, praying that Don was safe. Praying that the house would sell soon. Praying . . . I was almost asleep when I felt, then heard it—a thunderous crack, a sound like a giant broom sweeping the back porch roof, followed by an earthshaking thud. Rascal shot off my lap as I threw the blanket aside and rushed to the back patio door. Pressing my face against the icy glass, I peered out. A gigantic shadow lay across the backyard, its roots swaying in the wind, its boughs coated with snow and ice.

My dreaming tree.

CHAPTER FOURTEEN

I awoke the next morning to someone rapping on the front door. I peeked out from under the fleece blanket. The mantel clock showed 8:00 a.m. The fire was out. Whoever was out there—probably Don— was impatient, as the rapping against the glass resumed, louder and more insistent.

"I'm coming, I'm coming." I nudged Rascal off the sofa and pushed the blanket aside. My bleary eyes blinked against the snow-reflected light pouring in through the windows as I shuffled to the door and peered through the slats of the vertical blind. Someone dressed in a blaze-orange hunting coat and brown duck pants stood on the snow-covered front deck, getting ready to rap on the window again. The folded back edge of his orange knit hat rested above his thick eyebrows. Tiny icicles hung from his shaggy black beard. Not Don. The mountain man, maybe? Through the glass his piercing dark eyes met mine. An escaped con? My heart leapt to my throat.

"Melody?"

He knew my name. Maybe Willie sent someone to check on me.

"Are you all right? It's me, Jake."

Jake! I pulled the chain to open the blinds. Straight white teeth— none missing, no pieces of tobacco leaves stuck between them— grinned at me through the double-insulated glass. I slid the door open just enough to put my head out. Rascal scooted out.

"Jake! You scared me! I thought you were that crazy mountain man or an escaped con. I didn't recognize you with your beard."

White clouds of vapor puffed from his mouth as he threw back his head and laughed. "Do I look that scary?"

"Not really. I just have an active imagination." I opened the door wider. "Come in, please."

He shook his head. "Thanks, but I just came to see if you're all right, if you need anything. I saw your Explorer in the driveway. I was surprised. I didn't expect you to be here this time of the year."

"I sold my house in the city." An icy draft blew in the open door. I shivered. "Are you sure you don't want to come in? I could make you some tea or hot chocolate or coffee. I have instant."

"Power's still out, and from the looks of all the trees down on the road and on the power lines, it's going to be awhile before it's restored. I can drive you to a motel in Marysville, if you want."

"I'll be fine. I have a propane stove, so I won't starve, and a fireplace, which reminds me, I need a cord of wood for the winter. Can you get me some?"

He gave me a blank stare for a second or two and then blinked. "Uh, sure. How soon do you need it?"

I grinned. "Yesterday."

He frowned. "That soon, huh?"

"The move was kind of sudden. I can pay you."

"I . . . sold the last of it a few days ago. To a guy who owns one of the hunting camps up here. I planned to cut more, but it's back in the woods a ways. Down in a ravine. My truck—" he jerked his thumb toward a beat-up, red Dodge Ram parked behind my SUV "—isn't all that great in snow. I'll have to wait until this stuff melts to get to it. Wait!" He tapped his leather work gloves against his thigh and pointed to the backyard. "I don't know if you noticed, but a huge tree is down in your backyard. I can—"

"No."

"But it's perfect. That monster will give you enough firewood to get you through the winter and spring—longer even. And I don't have to fight the forest to get to it."

"No."

"It won't cost you as much. I'll just charge you for labor and gas for my chain saw."

"I. Said. No."

He looked puzzled. "Why not?"

"It was my dreaming tree. I used to climb it when I was a girl and dream of a great and glorious future."

He gave me a blank look and shrugged. "Well, it won't do you any good now."

I sighed. "Look, I'm getting cold. If you don't mind, I'd like to shut the door and keep what warmth I have in the cottage inside."

"Okay, then. I can probably cut you some firewood next week. In the meantime, how about I clean out your woodshed?"

"Thanks, but I can do that myself for free."

He shrugged and turned to go. "Suit yourself."

I closed the door and watched him back up in the turnaround and then slip and slide up the driveway. The back end of his truck fishtailed as he pulled onto the main road a bit too fast for the icy conditions.

Freezing, I hopped back on the sofa under the fleece blanket and wondered what Don was doing. I thought about calling him, but he probably took the advice he gave me and turned off his cell phone to conserve the battery.

I fished my phone out of the front pouch of my hoodie, and turned it on. Wonder of wonders—I had service. There were three text messages from Garrett and one from Cassie. She probably wanted to know how Don and I were coming along with the book. I'd get back to her later. I checked the messages from Garrett—progress reports on his travel.

"In Anchorage. Leaving 4 Attu when fog clears." The next message was from Sunday. "Up & away. TTYL. Love u." I'd text him later and let him know I was settled in. I wouldn't tell him about the house sale falling through until he got back. Maybe by then we'd have another buyer.

On the upside of this downturn, Garrett would have a place to stay for another month or so. But I knew he was anxious to find his own place and settle down. And I was sure that, wherever it was, it wouldn't be far from Anne.

I slipped the phone into the side pocket of my sweatpants, threw off the blanket, and padded into the kitchen. Now for a cup of tea and a bowl of hot oatmeal. I headed to the sink to fill the kettle, but then remembered the power was out. Without electricity, the water pump wouldn't run. I'd forgotten about that when I went to the bathroom in the middle of the night and flushed the commode. Now the holding tank was probably empty. I sighed.

I'd have to use the outhouse, which Garrett called the "poogie house." If I trudged through the woods to my well house, I could hand pump water from the old, hand-dug well I used before I had the deep well drilled. It was only about fifty feet from the cabin in the back, but it would be tricky footing with the snow and ice and who knows what debris hidden beneath.

I did have a pitcher of drinking water in the refrigerator I could use to make tea and oatmeal. Maybe I should forego the oatmeal—it was steel-cut and took longer to cook than regular oatmeal—and have cold cereal instead. Although I could still use the stove when the power was out, I didn't know how much propane was in the tank or when they'd be able to make it up the mountain to deliver my order. But tea would warm me up. I filled the kettle with water from the pitcher for my tea, struck a match, and lit the burner.

Once I had the water on, I turned to the second order of business— heat. The coals from last night's fire weren't hot enough to ignite the kindling, so I knelt on the stone hearth and began rolling and twisting folded sheets from the stack of old newspapers Aunt Peg had given me. I was almost done when a front-page headline caught my eye. The paper was dated the day before I moved.

McKeesport Man's Death Ruled a Homicide

The death of a McKeesport man whose body was found last week floating on the water at the confluence of the Allegheny, Monongahela, and Ohio rivers has been ruled a homicide.

An autopsy revealed Devon Grove, 46, had been hit over the head with a blunt object, then either was pushed or fell into the water. The official cause of death was by drowning.

Police say witnesses reported seeing a woman on the boat with Grove the evening before his body was discovered by a couple who were jogging through Point State Park.

One source close to the investigation, speaking on the condition of anonymity, said that Grove, who worked as an accountant for Wellsboro Trucking, is suspected of being involved in an embezzling ring. A recent audit of the trucking company's financial records revealed the loss of several million dollars over the past five years. An investigation continues.

The past five years? Paul had been the chief accounting officer up until his death twenty months ago. Could he have known . . . A cold, hard lump settled in the pit of my stomach. The money. Maybe it wasn't his gambling winnings.

Hatred, like a red, hot poker, stabbed my heart. I hated Paul. I hated the addiction that drove us apart. Hated that he loved gambling more than me. Hated that he upped and died and left me with his debts.

"If you weren't dead already, Paul John Harmon, I'd kill you!" I shouted, shaking my fist at the beamed ceiling.

Maybe Devon Grove embezzled the money and set it up to look like Paul did it. Or that "brilliant" accountant woman who worked with him. I shook my head. Paul would have picked up on the missing money. He was too much of a control freak. He had to know everything about everything. That's why he'd been so good at his job. Too good.

Maybe Don knew the money we found had been embezzled. That's why he insisted on his being one of the two signatures to access the safe deposit box. Maybe he was part of the embezzling ring and was using me to find the rest of the money. My cell phone buzzed. I pulled it out of my pocket and glanced at the number on the screen. Don.

"Hey, Don." I hoped my voice didn't betray my suspicions. I wanted to ask him about the money to see if his reaction would tell me whether he knew anything about the embezzling case or not. Deep down, I hoped he was what he said he was—an ex-cop turned writer. I wanted to trust him. But I had a feeling Don knew more than what he'd told me.

"I'm going into town and called to see if you needed anything," he said.

I shook my head.

"Well?"

Of course. He couldn't hear my head shake. "Uh, no, I don't think so. Wait. Maybe some candles and a lighter thingie."

"What's that I hear?"

Good lord. My tea.

"Gotta run. My whistle's kettling."

I got to the kitchen just in time to turn off the stove.

After breakfast, I decided to sweep the outhouse and clean up the woodshed. Once the snow and ice melted, I'd scour the woods for dead limbs that the storm blew down. If I was lucky, I'd find a tree or two. Storms like the one last night were good for knocking down deadwood.

As I swept wood chips from the shed floor, I thought about Jake wanting to cut up my dreaming tree for firewood. It was bad enough it was gone, but I wasn't going to watch it go up in smoke. Something niggled in my brain. Something about Jake. It had to do with my dreaming tree. I was separating some of the logs I'd cut over the summer—they were greener and needed to dry more before I burned them—when it hit me. Even if I'd consented to let Jake cut up my dreaming tree for firewood, I couldn't have burned it for a year at least. Green wood wasn't good to burn.

Jake should have known that. What kind of a handyman was he anyway?

By the time Don showed up around three, with the bed of his truck filled with firewood, the outhouse had been swept and stocked with two rolls of toilet paper, the shed had been cleaned and organized, and I was searching the cabin for my favorite hammer. It was missing from my toolbox in the shop where I usually kept it.

I answered his knock at the front door. "Where did all that firewood come from? I hope that's not from your stockpile."

He shrugged. "I have plenty. Here." He thrust a bulging white plastic grocery bag at me. "Supper. Just needs reheated. I'll pull around back and unload the firewood."

I put the bag on the counter and pulled on my Carhartt jacket and work boots. By the time I joined him out back, he already had the truck backed up to the woodshed and was staring at my fallen tree.

"Whoa!" He gave a low whistle. "You were lucky."

"That was my favorite tree." I pulled on my leather work gloves.

"That monster came mighty close to falling on—and probably crashing through—your cabin roof. See?" He pointed to a dent in the metal porch roof. "It caught the edge of the roof."

"I don't feel very lucky. That was my dreaming tree. When I was a girl, I'd climb . . . never mind."

Sympathy flashed in his eyes. "I'm sorry."

"Jake wanted to cut it up for firewood, but I said no way."

"Jake was here?"

"To see if I needed anything. Where's Charlie? Didn't you bring her?"

He glanced around and whistled. Charlie came bounding from behind the outhouse with what looked like a rag between her teeth.

"What do you have there, girl?" He pulled the cloth from her mouth and shook it out.

"That's one of my old college T-shirts. One hundred percent cotton. They make the best rags. But how did it get in the woods behind the poogie house?"

Charlie seemed excited about something. Her stumpy tail wagged like a metronome gone wild, drool dripping from her pink tongue. She raced partway to the outhouse then stopped, panting, and looked back, as if to say, "Aren't you coming?"

"I'd better go see what she found," Don said.

I followed him. Behind the outhouse, Charlie stood over a small hole she apparently had just dug. I peered past the snow and wet dead leaves.

"What's that?"

"Looks like a hammer."

I leaned closer. My hammer! "I've been looking for that thing for the past hour. How did it get back here?"

I reached for it, but Don's hand clamped down on my forearm. "Don't touch it."

I stared at him in confusion. "Why not?"

His eyes probed mine. "Because it might have been used to kill someone."

CHAPTER FIFTEEN

I gaped at him. "And you know this how?"

Don pulled his cell phone from his shirt pocket and grimaced. "No signal. I have to take a short walk." He shot me a warning look. "Do *not* touch that hammer or anything close to it. It would probably be a good idea for you to go back to the cabin."

My stare turned into a glare. "You're not retired, are you?"

He pressed his lips together.

"You lied to me! You said you were retired."

"I didn't lie to you, Melody. I *am* retired. I was reactivated when they called me in for this investigation."

Investigation. What was he investigating? The article about the embezzlement at Paul's company flashed through my mind.

"I thought you were retired. Finished with the force. Kaput. You let me believe that." I took a deep breath. "Letting someone believe something that isn't true is called deceit. You can lie without using words. And you call yourself a Christian." Bile burned my throat. "You make me sick."

I turned to leave.

"Melody, wait!" Don grabbed my arm, pulling me to him. His eyes begged me to understand. Suddenly it was Paul's eyes searching mine, imploring me to forgive him one more time. Pleading promises he never intended to keep. I'd been down this road before. I pressed my hands against Don's chest and shoved.

"Don't. I have nothing to say to you." I fought the urge to scream at him, but instead lowered my voice. "And there's nothing—I repeat, nothing—you can say to me to make me believe you're anything but a lying, cheating, selfish, heartless . . ." I blinked back tears. "And I almost believed you were different. But you're just like the rest of them."

I spun on my heel and marched back to the cabin, where I slid the back patio door shut so hard it bounced open again. I closed it, pushed the lock, and pulled the blinds shut. Then I repeated the process with the front door. Turning around, I spied the white plastic bag on the breakfast bar—the supper Don brought. I snatched the bag, opened the back door, and tossed it out. Broth and meatballs splattered across the snow. Wedding soup.

Around four o'clock, Don's backup arrived. At the sound of an engine shutting off, I peeked out the vertical blinds to see a black SUV pulled behind my Explorer. I couldn't see the driver. Don, who had been in the backyard unloading the firewood that I determined I would *not* burn, hurried to the vehicle. Puffs of white vapor spewed from his mouth as he gestured toward the outhouse and consulted his notebook. He glanced at the cabin. I eased the blind shut and stepped back from the door. I placed another log on the fire and headed to the bathroom. Then I remembered. The power was still out. I'd have to use the poogie house.

I waited for another fifteen minutes before grabbing my jacket and trudging through the snow to the outhouse, a small wooden structure built with rough, whitewashed lumber and a slanted metal roof. Don and his colleague were behind the building. I imagined yellow crime scene tape strung through the trees.

"Hey," I called. "Am I allowed to use the outhouse?"

"Go ahead," Don said.

"Thanks."

What was I thanking him for? This was my property, my poogie house. I slammed the door shut. "That'll show him," I muttered.

"I heard that."

"Good."

I took my dear old time, eavesdropping, hoping to hear something that made sense. Why my hammer—my *favorite* hammer—had been wrapped in one of my old T-shirts and buried behind the outhouse. But apparently they were done. I heard nothing other than snow crunching under their footfalls.

When I got back to the cabin, they were waiting for me on the front deck. A petite, middle-aged woman holding a black plastic case and a sealed, transparent plastic bag that contained my hammer stood beside Don. She wore a black, down-filled vest over a yellow turtleneck jersey and blue jeans. Wisps of strawberry blond hair peeked from under her black-and-gold knit hat.

"Melody," Don said, pointing to her with a file folder, "this is Sergeant Virelle Reddick of the Pennsylvania State Police."

I nodded toward her. Her solemn expression reflected the seriousness of the business at hand, but behind her glasses were the kindest eyes I'd ever seen.

"May I see your badges?" I said, feeling my anger subside—a little. I was still furious with Don for his deceit, but Sgt. Reddick was just doing her job. She put the case down and showed me her identification. I looked at Don. "Where's yours?"

He sighed, shoved the folder under his arm, and pulled his wallet from the rear pocket of his jeans. His ID card identified him as Captain Donald Marcus Bridges.

"The date this was issued was two years ago. I thought you were a policeman longer than that."

"I told you. I retired. I'm just helping with the investigation."

I looked him straight in the eye. "What, exactly, are you investigating?"

"Let's go inside."

I swallowed. This couldn't be good.

Don and Sgt. Reddick settled on the sofa while I lit the kerosene lamp from the mantel and set it on the coffee table. I chose the recliner. Rascal jumped up on my lap as I pulled my legs up under me. My fingers absentmindedly stroked her soft fur. Don ran his hand through his hair. I'd noticed he tended to do that when he was uncomfortable or nervous. Sgt. Reddick held up the plastic bag.

"Do you recognize this?"

"Yes. That's the hammer my dad gave me."

"Are you sure?"

I held out my hand. "May I see it?"

"Don't take it out of the bag." She passed it to Don, who gave it to me.

I turned it over, examining it through the plastic in the glow of the fire, hoping it wasn't mine. But it was.

"See that?" I pointed to letters carved deeply in the worn wooden handle. "My initials—MLJ—Melody Louise Joyner, my maiden name. My dad gave this to me when I was around ten. I wanted to help him with remodeling the cabin, and he got tired of me taking his hammer and smashing my fingers. So he bought me a smaller one."

I handed the bag back to Don.

"When was the last time you saw it?" Sgt. Reddick asked after she wrote in her pocket-sized notebook.

"Let me think . . . one of the nails in my footstool was coming out when I was here in September. I used the hammer to pound it back in."

"What did you do with it when you were done?"

"I put it back in the shop. The building out back was my father's woodshop. He was a carpenter."

"Where did you put it?" she asked.

"In the toolbox."

"Could someone have taken it?" Don asked.

"When? I keep the shop locked when I'm not here. I didn't see any signs that someone broke in. If anyone had taken it, it would have been when I was here. And no one else was on this mountain when I was here in September. Except Jake."

If anyone would have taken it. Smart, Melody. Like that was a possibility. Someone did take it. Someone did bury it behind the outhouse. And that someone wasn't me.

"Who's Jake?" Sgt. Reddick asked.

I told her. "But why would he take it? I would think he has his own tools."

"Do you know that for a fact?"

I squirmed. "No. But he has a handyman business. One can't have a handyman business if one doesn't have tools, now, could one?" That sounded stupid.

I waited while she scribbled in her notebook. The mantel clock ticked. A burning log popped, spewing sparks on the stone hearth and making me jump.

"I have his business card here somewhere," I offered. "He left one at every cabin on the mountain. At least I think he did. You got one, didn't you, Don?"

He shook his head no. Sgt. Reddick opened the file folder, pulled out a picture, and handed it to me.

"Do you recognize this man?"

I inspected the color photo of a middle-aged man with a thin face, receding hairline, and big ears.

"No." I handed it back to her. "Who is it?"

"A man by the name of Devon Grove."

I gasped. "Devon Grove? Isn't he the guy that was found in the river at the Point? I saw an article in the paper about it."

Murdered, the police said. Hit over the head with a blunt object. That explained the hullaballoo over the hammer. A sick feeling punched my stomach.

"He worked for the same company that my late husband Paul worked for. In the same office. Paul was in charge of the accounting department."

"You knew Devon Grove?"

"No. I never met anyone Paul worked with. Except the owner and one of the secretaries. But that was at a Christmas party when Paul was first hired."

"When was that?"

I shrugged. "Twenty-five years ago."

I wouldn't go into why I never accompanied him to any more company parties. It was none of their business anyway.

"Tell us about Paul."

"He's dead. What else is there to tell?"

She reviewed what she knew about him: that he was the company controller for Wellsboro Trucking for twenty-five years, hired just when the company was getting off the ground, and growing with them. That he had a gambling addiction.

"And don't forget his *paramour*," I said, trying unsuccessfully to keep the bitterness out of my voice. "The one he sent flowers to and took on a vacation to Mexico."

Don grimaced.

"We know about her," she said.

"Oh, then you know who she is . . . was."

"Yes."

"Who?"

"Melody, do you really want to know?" This from Don.

"Yes. No. I don't know. I pretended for so long . . ." I'd always wonder. "I guess it's truth time. Knowing couldn't hurt more than it did when he was alive."

Don and Sgt. Reddick exchanged glances. "Her name is Stephanie Keith." Sgt. Reddick handed me another photo. "She was the accounts payable manager in Paul's office."

I wasn't surprised. "The brilliant one. That's how Paul described her."

I studied the photo, which had obviously been taken from a distance. She was sitting at a table in a restaurant, her dark-brown hair cascading in soft curls just below her shoulders. Her gaze was fixed on her companion, whose back was to the camera but who I would have recognized anywhere. Paul. I held the photo closer. There was something familiar about her. Maybe she'd been at the memorial service. I handed the photo back to Don.

"How did your husband die?" Sgt. Reddick asked.

"You should know. You know everything else."

"Melody . . ."

"I know, Don, you have to be thorough. But your thoroughness is dredging up a lot of pain. Pain I tried to bury with Paul. Pain I hid and denied for most of our married life."

Don hung his head, his elbows perched on his knees, his hands clasped together in front of him.

I sighed. "He fell off an eighth-floor balcony at a resort in Playa del Carmen."

"Did you have a viewing?"

"No. Just a short memorial service a month after it happened. It took a little time to cut through the Mexican red tape."

"You have a death certificate, right?"

"Do I look like a complete idiot, Don? Of course I have a death certificate. But it's in Spanish—a document that was essentially useless because it wasn't accepted by the bank and insurance companies here in the good ol' USA. I finally received an English Certificate of Death Abroad through the consulate."

"Who got the death certificate for you?"

"The funeral director." I hated that I sounded sarcastic.

"What about an autopsy report?"

"That was in Spanish, too, as was the police report. I have them filed in the bank deposit box. I gave up trying to get them in English."

Sgt. Reddick stepped back into the conversation. For the first time in the interview—the *interrogation*—she stumbled over her words. "Did you at any time see his . . . remains?"

"No. I couldn't afford to have his body shipped from Mexico. Do you know how much they want to ship bodies, especially over the border? All the expenses came out of my own pocket. Why do you think I had to sell my house and move to the mountain?"

"His remains?" Sgt. Reddick prompted.

"Oh, sorry. You've opened up a can of worms. He was cremated and his ashes shipped home. The Mexican funeral director in Playa del Carmen took care of it all. Paul's parents had a fit. Said they'd never forgive me. But they didn't offer me a cent to bring him home."

"What did you do with his ashes?" she probed.

"His parents have them. They were mad enough about the cremation, but when they found out the urn was opened and inspected at the airport, Nanette—that's Paul's mother—went ballistic."

"I see." Sgt. Reddick flipped through her notebook. "You said, and I quote, 'Pain I tried to *bury* with Paul.'"

Maybe they didn't know everything. "I was speaking metaphorically." A shiver shot through me.

"Do you remember the name of the funeral home that took care of the cremation?"

I shook my head. "I'll have to check. I have a file folder with all the stuff related to Paul's death. The funeral directors—the one in Mexico and the one in Greensburg, where we had the memorial service—took care of everything. It made it a lot easier. No picking out a casket, no having to decide what suit to bury him in. No standing all day, greeting people I didn't know, pretending . . ." My voice choked. I sat up. "Where are you going with this? Why are you asking these questions?"

"Melody, what were you doing the night of Friday, October 25?" Sgt. Reddick asked.

"Why?"

I thought back to the dates the articles were printed. Wasn't that the night Devon Grove was murdered? The article said a woman had been seen on his boat. Did they think it was me?

"Melody, answer the question," Don said.

"What was that date again?"

"Friday, October 25."

That was the Friday night before Aunt Peg's dinner. Garrett had gone to Anne's for the evening, and, feeling restless, I drove across town for pizza. When I got to Pizza Palace, I decided to dine in.

"I don't remember," I lied.

They exchanged glances.

I squirmed and looked at Don. "Is this an interrogation? Wait! You think the money we found was embezzled." Fear slithered through my veins. "You think Paul embezzled it. And I helped him."

"Melody, you're putting the cart before the horse."

"A cliché, Don? From you?" I swallowed hard. "I refuse to answer any more questions without my lawyer present."

"Melody, please," Don said.

"Where was your son?" Sgt. Reddick asked. What didn't she know about my life? I felt violated.

"What part of 'I refuse to answer any more questions without my lawyer present' don't you understand?"

Don rubbed the back of his neck. "Melody, not answering makes it look like you have something to hide."

"Garrett went out for the evening. He had a date." I glared at Don. "With Anne."

"What time did he come home?" Sgt. Reddick asked.

I stroked Rascal, sleeping soundly on my lap. "I don't know. Sometime after I went to bed."

"So you were home alone, all evening?"

"Yes."

I was digging myself deeper and deeper into a hole. All they had to do was check my credit card statement and they'd see a charge for pizza on that day and time. Or they could ask Bertha. She'd be able to tell them what time I left and what time I returned. Long enough to commit murder? This Sgt. Reddick had kind eyes, but she was a tiger when it came to her job. And her job was to ferret out the truth.

I looked at Don. "Has Anne been able to get into Paul's laptop and flash drive?"

"Why do you want to know?" Sgt. Reddick said.

"I wasn't asking you, Sergeant." I pointed to Don. "I was asking Mr. Retired Ex-Cop-Turned-Writer-Turned-Liar here. What about that fake passport? Paul had one. I didn't. Mine is legit. So is my driver's license."

"Melody," Don said, "we have to explore all possibilities. You know that."

"No, I don't know that. But you think one of those possibilities is that I was part of an embezzling ring and murdered Devon Grove."

What a fool I'd been, thinking we had something going between us. Maybe that's what he wanted me to believe so he could get close to me—use me to get information. His new badge was issued six months before Paul died.

I glared at Don. "Cassie never told you about the farmhouse, did she? You already knew about it because you were following me. I was a suspect in your precious investigation before I even met you." A well of sorrow opened up deep inside me. It had never been real. Tears stung the back of my eyes.

Sgt. Reddick opened the black case.

"What's that?" I dreaded her answer.

"We need to fingerprint you."

Oh, dear Lord, no. Please no. I put my hands under my thighs. My fingerprints were all over that hammer.

I shook my head. "You can't fingerprint me without my lawyer present."

Don nodded. "Yes, Melody, we can." Was that sadness I saw in his eyes? Pity? Regret? Or disappointment?

"What if I refuse?"

"Look, Melody, we don't have your prints on file and won't be able to distinguish them from anyone else's on the hammer."

"Oh, don't tell me," I said, pulling my hands out from beneath my thighs. "You have my best interests at heart."

After taking my fingerprints, Sgt. Reddick left. Don walked her out to her SUV and then returned to the cabin.

"Melody." He stood by the recliner where I sat, stunned. "You don't know how hard this is for me."

I stared into the fire. "Seriously? How hard it is for *you*? Give me a break."

"I told you, we have to consider all options. You understand, don't you? I couldn't—and I still can't—tell you anything. I'm sorry if you thought I lied."

"Was Cassie in on it too?"

"Why would she be?"

"The whole team-up-with-Don-so-you-can-resurrect-your-pathetic-writing-career scenario. It was all a setup from the get-go, wasn't it?"

He squatted in front of me, his hands on the arms of the recliner. "No. That was all Cassie, or should I say, our publisher. She doesn't know anything about the investigation."

I swiped a tear from my face. "Once we met in person, we could have collaborated through the Internet. You didn't have to buy the farmhouse."

"I bought it because of Anne and the kids. And because I've always wanted a getaway place. And because I wanted to be close to you."

I held back a sob. "I was foolish to think you were really interested in me. All the time you were using me to get evidence for your precious investigation. Well, you got it. Now leave."

He paused, as though debating with himself. "Melody, close to five million dollars was stolen. Granted, some was spent, but Paul's fake passport and driver's license indicate he was getting ready to run. But the time wasn't right, and he didn't expect to fall off a balcony and die. I'm telling you more than I should here, but I want you to understand. I think he and his . . . he went to Mexico to check things out and get things ready for the great escape." He gazed into my eyes. "There's a lot more money somewhere. If you're not involved, you could be in danger."

If I wasn't involved. Hot tears blurred my vision and tracked down my cheeks.

"Leave." I swallowed. "Now."

CHAPTER SIXTEEN

After Don left, I locked both doors and curled up on the sofa, Rascal curling up contently beside me. Once they found out I'd lied about being home the night Devon Grove was murdered, they wouldn't believe anything I said. Not only was I in danger of being falsely accused of murder and spending the rest of my life in jail, but the person who *had* murdered Devon Grove was out there somewhere.

What would the forensics report show? My fingerprints for sure. Maybe someone was just playing a cruel joke. How could my hammer have been used in a murder that had taken place in Pittsburgh a hundred miles away?

The sound of the refrigerator clicking on broke into my thoughts. I blinked against the glare of a suddenly, too-bright room. I'd turned on every light in the place so I'd know when the power came back on. Nudging Rascal off the sofa, I turned down the wick on the kerosene lamp until it went out and added a log to the fire. Then I switched off all the lights except the pendant lanterns hanging over the breakfast bar. Those I dimmed enough so a soft glow filled the kitchen and the living room.

The dusky light filtering in through the windows told me it was after five. With the loss of the sun, the cabin was colder. I'd call the propane company the first thing in the morning to see when to expect my delivery. Hopefully, it would be tomorrow. Until then I didn't want to use the wall heaters. Thanks to Don, I had enough firewood beside the fireplace and on the back deck right outside the door to last me a couple of days.

I peered out the front door. The deepening shadows seemed threatening, not soothing like they usually did. I should have replaced the bulb in the pole light. Maybe I'd splurge and buy some of those solar-powered path lights. And an old-fashioned gas lantern.

Night descended quickly in the forest, and without streetlights or any other cabins within shouting distance, the darkness here on the mountaintop was deep. I couldn't see my hand in front of my face. I know. I tried once. When I was thirteen. The power had gone out during an evening thunderstorm one summer and hadn't come back on until morning. I huddled in my bunk, eyes wide open, peering into the blackness, unable to discern anything. No shadows, no shapes, nothing. The blackness wrapped around me like a python, squeezing so tight my breath came in short gasps.

The claustrophobia lessened when I turned on the little flashlight I used for midnight reading, threw the covers over my head, and shut my eyes, forcing myself to breathe deep. I still kept a flashlight in the nightstand drawer and made sure the batteries were fresh.

I peered through the glass of the front patio door into the dusky yard, still covered with a white glaze. The snow and ice from last night's storm had partially melted in the afternoon sun and then refroze into a glacier that covered everything in sight. At least the snow and the waning moon would keep the blackness at bay. Nevertheless, I flipped the switch and light flooded the front deck, spilling over into the yard.

I plugged in my laptop and let it boot up. I reached into my sweat pants pocket for my cell phone, but it wasn't there. When was the last time I used it? I was sure I put it in my pocket. Maybe it fell out when I went out to help Don unload the wood. I pulled on my Carhartt jacket and grabbed my flashlight. Careful not to slip and fall on the treacherous ice, I traced my steps to the hole behind the outhouse. If I'd dropped my phone here, Don or his partner would have found it. I was sure it wasn't in the cabin.

Could it have slipped out when I used the poogie? *Please, dear God, no.* I opened the door, flipped on the light switch, and shone my flashlight down the hole. Something shiny reflected back at me. My cell phone. Six feet down. Great. Now what? I studied it, trying to figure out a way to retrieve the thing without lowering myself in the hole—a close, dark space.

My heart hammered against my ribs. My chest tightened. Sweat broke out on my forehead. *Breathe deep, Melody. Breathe deep and slow. One-thousand-one, one thousand-two.* I could tear up the seat. The hole was dry, and I'd dumped in a bag of lime on Saturday. When had I last used the poogie before this afternoon? In the spring when the power was out. The phone was probably just a little wet. I could handle that. It *was* cold. Did pee freeze? I shivered.

I fetched my crowbar, work gloves, and my headlamp from the shop and got to work. I just had to pry off the top of the box seat. Then I could lower the stepladder into the hole. The 100-watt bulb screwed in the white porcelain ceiling socket would give me plenty of light. I inserted the crowbar into the seam and leaned. Five minutes later I had the top loose. I shoved my gloved fingers into the crack and lifted the front edge of the plywood board. I leaned it against the back wall and turned to get the ladder. But something caught my eye.

A bulging camouflage backpack hung from the side wall just below the top edge of the seat. I lifted it from the nail and placed it on the floor. I unzipped it and peered inside. It was filled with bundles of cash, all bound with the familiar mustard-colored currency strap. My head spun. With trembling hands I lifted them out, one by one. When the backpack was empty, thirty bundles of one-hundred dollar bills lay on the floor beside me. Three hundred thousand dollars.

I was sure this was some of the embezzled money. If Paul was responsible, when could he have hidden it here? Paul wasn't unskilled when it came to carpentry. His woodworking hobby was one of the things that had attracted me to him. Paul had come to the cabin with me a couple of months before he died. But he couldn't have done it then. I'd been on deadline and hadn't wanted him to come. But he insisted. Maybe he was scouting a place to hide the cash.

"Well, Paul," I said, shoving the bundles back into the pack, "hiding your cache in the outhouse was just brilliant."

If I hadn't dropped my phone down the hole, it wouldn't have been found until the outhouse either fell apart or was torn down. Pulling my gloves up tighter, I lowered the aluminum stepladder into the hole. A half hour later, the seat had been nailed back down, the ladder and crowbar put back in the shop, and my cell phone was zipped up in a plastic storage bag filled with rice. The phone hadn't been wet when I plucked it up, but after cleaning it with Lysol, I decided it wouldn't hurt to let the rice draw out any moisture. The backpack I put in the clothes dryer until I could figure out what to do with it.

I should have called Don, but I was afraid to turn on the phone until it had a chance to dry out. That was my excuse, anyway. I could have e-mailed him, but what would I say?

"Don, come quick. I found another three hundred grand in the poogie house."

Would he even believe me? I shouldn't have nailed the top back on so he could see the nail the backpack was hanging on. But how could I prove I didn't put it there?

Then there was the matter of the money. Wasn't there such a thing as a finder's fee? Ten percent or something like that? Ten percent of four hundred fifty grand. I used my finger to do the math in the air. Too many zeroes. Just move the decimal point to the left, Paul had told me when I tried to balance the checkbook. Forty-five thousand would be a nice windfall. Even if the finder's fee was 1 percent—one more decimal point to the left—more air math—forty-five hundred would still be better than zilch.

I shook my head. What was the matter with me? If I kept back part of the cash, would I be any better than Paul, who'd stolen the money to begin with? Besides, I was probably a suspect.

I was too upset to even think about supper, so I made myself a cup of peppermint tea and carried it to the loft. I still needed to get my bedroom organized. I'd had a four-foot closet built onto one of the three walls of the loft, and into that I'd shoved the clothes I brought from home. So now my city clothes were jammed in with my mountain clothes. I should have made the closet bigger.

Was that something Jake could do? He never did say what profession he retired from. Since he was starting a handyman business, I assumed he knew something about carpentry. I snatched a pen and notebook from the top of the nightstand beside Sonny's Bible, sat cross-legged on the bed, and began a list of things I would ask Jake to do: build an addition to the closet, install outside lighting, change the bulb in the pole light, mount my new 29-inch flat screen TV, a gift from Garrett, on one of the cabin walls. Garrett had secretly packed it in the Explorer and then covered it with a stack of clothes still on hangers. On the accompanying card, which he'd taped to the box, he'd written that he'd also foot the bill for satellite TV service. I'd texted him my thanks.

After making my list for Jake, I put the notebook beside the Bible.

"What should I do, Sonny?" I whispered, running my fingers over the soft black leather. "I want to trust Don, but I'm afraid to."

I so longed for someone to talk to, someone in my corner. I could call Aunt Peg, but she'd just worry, and there wasn't much she could do except lend a listening ear and offer a comforting shoulder to cry on. I was beginning to have second thoughts about moving so far from the only family I had left. What was I thinking?

I glanced around the bedroom. My eyes were drawn to the wall above the headboard where I'd hung the framed cross-stitch my mother had given me as a wedding present: "To love and be loved is the greatest joy on earth." That had always been my dream. Was that kind of love even possible?

I lifted the Bible and reverently opened the cover to where Sonny had written what he called his life verse and read, once again, the words that were burned in my memory:

Who shall separate us from the love of Christ? Shall trouble or hardship or persecution or famine or nakedness or danger or sword?

No, in all these things we are more than conquerors through him who loved us. For I am convinced that neither death nor life, neither angels nor demons, neither the present nor the future, nor any powers, neither height nor depth, nor anything else in all creation, will be able to separate us from the love of God that is in Christ Jesus our Lord.— Romans 8:35, 38–39

I needed that kind of love. "God," I whispered. Tears dripped onto the Bible in my lap. "I want a faith like Sonny's."

How long I sat there, perched on the edge of my bed, hugging that Bible, I don't know. But eventually the tears stopped flowing. I looked around for a box of tissues, but it was on my desk across the room. My sleeve would have to do. I checked the time on the bedside clock. It was already after nine. I still wasn't hungry. Or tired.

A movie would be just the thing to get my mind off the unsettling events of the past two days. The ultra-slim television, which was also a DVD player, was still in the original carton downstairs in the storage room—Garrett's bedroom at one time. I had also stored my box of DVDs in there. I snatched up the notebook, flipped to a clean page, and started another list—things to do, beginning with "buy or have Jake build DVD cabinet."

Placing the notebook back on the nightstand, I scanned the loft. Where could I put the television? I wanted it where I could see it from the bed. Until I talked to Jake, I'd have to set it up myself, but that wasn't a problem. Fortunately it was a free-standing model as well as one that could be mounted on a wall. I could have it set up and be curled up beneath my cozy-warm, quilted comforter watching *The Sound of Music* before midnight. I wasn't going to get much sleep tonight anyway, so why not a midnight movie marathon?

Somehow I managed to lug the bulky but surprisingly light box with the television up the circular stairway. I stationed the TV across from my bed, against the railing, and ran an extension cord to one of the wall outlets. I added "find TV stand" to my to-do list. I hauled the box of DVDs to the loft and decided it was time for a tea break.

Downstairs, I filled the kettle and put it on the burner. Then I rooted through my tea bin, found an old kettle I'd left on the burner too long, and chose an herbal blend of lavender and rose and dropped it in my glass mug.

While the water was heating, I climbed to the loft and turned my attention to organizing the cedar wardrobe. It had been one of the few things I kept from my parents' house. Mom had used it to store her good dresses and her fake fur coat, as well as Dad's one suit. My wedding gown and Mom's was still hanging inside, zipped securely in a thick white clothing bag. I'd never have a daughter to wear it.

Opening the doors, which extended only halfway down the five-and-a-half-foot armoire, I paused to savor the sweet woodsy scent of the red cedar, its fragrance stirring memories of happier times. Like trying on Mom's wedding gown and discovering it was a perfect fit. I carefully lifted the ivory padded hanger and draped the gown over the railing. Then I pushed together all the remaining clothes hanging on the wooden rod, tugged them out, and dumped them on the bed. Then out came the zippered plastic bag with my grandmother's handmade quilt and several shoe boxes filled with photos and mementos. I laid them on the braided rug beside the bed.

That should be it, I thought, running my hand across the bottom. Something wasn't right. It wasn't wood that met my fingertips, but something softer, like leather. Leaning into the wardrobe, I lifted out a scuffed-up, black briefcase with the initials "PJH" engraved on a brass plate on the front. I'd given this to Paul for our first Christmas. My stomach clenched. Paul. I knew what was in it.

Trembling, I pushed the latches. They popped up with a click. I opened the briefcase and gasped. More Benjamins. I counted another thirty bundles. Another three hundred thousand. Making that seven hundred fifty thousand dollars total, counting what we found in the garage. I had over a half million dollars in cash in my cottage. My blood turned to ice. Did I lock the doors? I pressed my palms against my temples in a vain effort to stop the room from spinning. Then . . . I fainted.

CHAPTER SEVENTEEN

The odor of hot metal filled my nostrils. Where was I? My head throbbed. My cheek, wet with drool, lay in a pile of paper. I blinked. The face of Benjamin Franklin stared up at me. It sluggishly came back to me: cleaning out the wardrobe, finding Paul's briefcase.

I sniffed. What stunk? And what was that awful, high-pitched racket? The kettle! I needed to get downstairs before the cabin burned down. I tried to get to my feet, but I was too woozy. *God. Please. I don't have fire insurance.* I took a deep breath, pushed myself to a kneeling position, and then stood. The room whirled around me. I maneuvered down the circular stairway, clinging to the railing, and stumbled to the kitchen.

Pulling the neckline of my sweatshirt over my nose, I snatched a potholder from the countertop, wrapped it around the handle of the kettle, and lifted. It wouldn't budge. It was melted to the burner. I turned off the flame. Another kettle ruined.

When the trembling stopped, I replaced the herbal tea bag with Earl Grey, filled the glass mug with water, and slid it in the microwave, setting the time for three minutes. I added a couple more logs to the fire, remembering what I had upstairs and in the dryer. I rushed to both doors to make sure they were locked. The next time I could afford to visit the doctor, I needed to have my blood pressure checked.

When the microwave dinged, I carried my mug to the living room and curled up on the sofa, pulling the fleece blanket over me. Rascal nosed her way onto my lap.

"What should I do with the money, girl? Hide it, spend it, or give it to Don?"

Her eyes closed. Oh, to be a cat and not have any worries except what to eat and where to sleep. I was sure Devon Grove was killed because of the money. I didn't want to be next. Orange flames licked the logs and stretched up the chimney.

Stephanie Keith was involved, I was sure of it. Could she have been the prowler Bertha saw? The one who had tampered with the grill cover? I scratched Rascal's head and took another sip of tea, my mind wrapping around the way Stephanie gazed at Paul in that picture. Why had she looked so familiar? Something niggled in my brain. Something about that picture wasn't right.

I pulled Rascal onto my chest, rubbing my cheek in her soft fur.

"They suspect me of being Paul's accomplice, Rascal. Isn't that ridiculous? I couldn't deceive someone if my life depended on it. I'm sure 'big fat lie' was written all over my face this afternoon. I'll probably get arrested for obstruction of justice, tampering with an investigation, and who knows what else?"

Rascal adjusted her position on my chest, her sharp claws piercing through my shirt. I laid her back on the blanket in my lap.

"You never liked Paul, did you, girl? You saw things, heard things I didn't. Remember the time you peed on his pant leg? He was livid! It was all I could do to keep a straight face."

I stroked her curled back softly. "You knew he was planning to run off with her, but then he died." I shut my eyes, forcing the picture of Stephanie gazing at Paul out of my mind. "I wish I could run away. Take the six hundred grand and disappear. I could dye my hair—"

My eyes flew open. That's what wasn't right about Stephanie's picture. The hair was wrong. I remembered where I'd seen her. I shot up so fast, Rascal flew off my lap and scampered up the stairs. Fishing my cell phone from the bag of rice, I turned it on. One bar. If I didn't move an inch. But one bar was enough to send a text message. I punched in the numbers I already knew by heart.

Not five minutes later Don stood outside my front door, hair tousled, in a red-plaid flannel shirt that hung crooked, tail half in, half out, buttons misaligned with the buttonholes. Bare ankles peeked out between the bottom of his jeans and the tops of his brown moccasins.

"You have something you want to talk to me about?" He sounded grumpy. Not my problem.

"Come in. Hurry." I grabbed his sleeve and yanked him into the cabin, peering into the darkness behind him. Satisfied he was alone, I locked the door and made sure the blinds were closed tight before turning to face him.

His eyes, those blue eyes I could swim in, searched mine. "Before you say anything, there's something I need to tell you." His voice was husky with emotion. I couldn't read his face. A mixture of emotions warred in every crease around his eyes, his mouth. Sadness, determination, tenderness. "I'm taking myself off the case."

"Why?"

"Because I can no longer be objective."

"Why not?"

"Because . . ." He took a deep breath. "I have feelings for you."

"Well, that's just great."

He picked up on my sarcasm. "I thought . . . well, I thought you kind of liked me too."

"I do kind of like you, Don. It's just . . ." I took a breath. "I found something. Now that you're off the case, I don't know what to do with it. Well, I do, but I don't want to throw myself at her mercy, kind eyes or not."

He raised his eyebrows. "Who? Sgt. Reddick? She's a pro. The best. I wouldn't come out of retirement to work with just anyone. What did you find?"

"I have to show you. Come on."

He followed me into the laundry room. I tugged open the dryer door and pointed to the backpack inside.

"What's in it?"

"Open it and see."

He grunted. "I have to get something out of the truck. Be right back."

He returned slightly out of breath, pulling on a pair of latex gloves—the kind they wore on those crime scene shows. A digital camera hung around his neck.

"You locked the door, didn't you?" I said.

"Yes. And made sure the blinds were closed tight." He nodded at the backpack. "I suppose that has your fingerprints all over it."

I grinned. "Actually, it doesn't."

I told him about losing my cell phone and prying off the poogie seat to get to it and discovering the pack hanging on a nail. "A job like that—you better believe I had my leather work gloves on."

He snapped some pictures and then pulled the bag out of the dryer, unzipped it, and peered inside.

"How much?" he asked. More flashes from the camera.

"Three hundred grand. And that's not all."

His eyebrows rose. "There's more?"

I nodded. "Upstairs. But put that back in the dryer first."

He carefully zipped the backpack closed and placed it in the dryer before following me up the circular stairway.

"I found that—" I pointed to the bundles scattered on the loft floor "in the bottom of the wardrobe, hidden under a bunch of stuff. Another three hundred thousand. It was in Paul's old briefcase. And, no, I didn't have gloves on, so my prints are all over it, as well as my drool. I fainted."

He whistled, surveying the scene, and snapped more pictures.

"I thought you were off the case."

He shook his head. "I just changed my mind."

A tingle of joy shot through me. "What are we going to do with the money?"

"I'll take it up to the farmhouse and when Virelle gets back, she'll take it as evidence."

"I have an idea."

He arched his eyebrows. "Do I want to hear this?"

"Probably not. Why not leave the money here?"

"It's not safe, Melody. Those people are killers."

"The money has been hidden here all along. They haven't found it."

"Yet."

"Are you hungry? I am. I haven't eaten all day. How about pizza? Frozen, of course."

"Don't change the subject."

"You want to catch them red-handed, don't you? How can you do that if you take the money they're after?"

He stopped for a moment and looked at me. "No, Melody. It's too dangerous."

"Think about it. It makes sense."

He sighed. "All right. I'll think about it. Now go put that pizza in the oven. I'm starved."

While Don snapped pictures and scribbled in his notebook, I put a frozen pizza—stuffed crust, of course—in the oven and put milk in a pan for hot chocolate. I was out of instant packets, but there was a recipe on the back of the cocoa can. I was rooting around in the spice cupboard for vanilla when Don came downstairs.

"I need to get pictures of the outhouse, where you found the backpack."

"Do you really have to take pictures of the inside of my poogie house?" I sighed, imagining crime scene tape strung up all over the place, preventing me from accessing it should the power go out again. "Of course you do."

I checked the time left for the pizza and turned off the flame under the pan. "I'll get my boots on and meet you at the outhouse." I giggled. "There's the title for our book, Don—*Meet Me at the Outhouse*. Or better, *Meet Me at the Poogie.*"

I giggled again. And giggled. And giggled. Until my giggles turned to hysterical laughter.

"I'm sorry," I said, when the laughing fit spent itself. "I laugh at the craziest times. I was in an accident once. We were coming home from college for the holidays and hit a patch of ice on the interstate. When we stopped spinning and hitting guardrails, I burst out laughing. No one was hurt, but the car—this small, foreign convertible—was totaled. Everyone was mad at me for laughing."

Compassion, not ridicule, filled his eyes. "It's a coping mechanism—a way to release tension and fear. I understand."

"You do?" I dried my eyes on my sleeve. "I'll meet you—" I swallowed a giggle "—outside. You'll need my crowbar."

"Thanks for not blocking off my outhouse with crime scene tape." We were sitting side by side on the sofa. A fire blazed in the hearth. "What took you so long, anyway?"

He helped himself to another slice of pizza. "I talked to Virelle."

"And?"

He paused. "She surprised me and agreed with you—to leave the money here. We'll set up surveillance cameras and monitor them. But I don't like it."

We'd hidden all the money in the bottom of the cedar wardrobe in my bedroom. It would take a while for Paul's accomplices to find it. We didn't want to make it too easy, but we wanted them to find it.

"I'll be fine."

He stood. "It's late. I really should be going."

"Wait!" I grabbed his arm. "I almost forgot. What I called you for in the first place. The picture of that woman with Paul you showed me this afternoon? She looked different in the picture—her hair was darker. But that's the bank manager I spoke with about my mortgage. Stephanie Morley."

He sank back down and pulled his notebook out of his pocket. "Are you sure?"

"Yes." I explained about going to the bank to see about the foreclosure. "Paul's bank, not mine. I have an account with my credit union. She wanted me to give her my account and routing numbers, along with the passwords. Something didn't quite set right, so I refused."

"She was probably trying to find the money. Even if they spent a million, there's still at least another million out there somewhere. I suspect your husband was the ringleader. He'd make up fake invoices, and she'd write the checks. Most of them were made out to the owner of a truck parts company. He's disappeared too."

"Too?"

"Stephanie left Wellsboro Trucking after your husband passed away," Don said, slipping his notebook into his shirt pocket. "She just vanished."

"She was part of the embezzling ring."

"As the accounts payable manager, she wrote the checks for the fake invoices."

"How could she get a job in a bank? Wouldn't they run a background check?"

He shrugged. "Apparently, the same person who manufactured Paul's fake ID and passport made one for her. These people are good at what they do."

"Why did she keep her first name? Wouldn't that give her away?"

"When you're not used to switching identities, it takes a while to respond when someone uses your fake first name when talking to you. They probably didn't want to take the chance of being found out. Besides, how many people use their real first name when taking on a new identity?"

"Aren't you telling me more than I should know?" I asked. "I thought I was a suspect. That's probably why Virelle agreed to leaving the money here. So she can catch *me* red-handed, absconding with the cash."

Don's thumb gently traced my jawline. "Melody, you're an open book. You don't have a dishonest bone in your body."

"And how would you know? We haven't spent that much time together."

"I was a cop for thirty years. You learn to read people. Instinct."

I leaned my face into his hand. "And what do your instincts tell you about me?"

He lifted my chin and gazed into my eyes. "That what you see is what you get. You aren't afraid to be who you are." He smiled, a tender smile that melted my insides. "That's why I love that crazy hair of yours and those baggy old sweats you wear. You're comfortable in your own skin."

"I let myself go after Paul died. No, before that. I allowed him to cow me into thinking I wasn't worth anything because I didn't have a job outside the home. My writing embarrassed him. That's why I wrote under a pseudonym." A lump lodged in my throat.

"But he didn't succeed. You kept right on writing."

"But I stopped believing in myself. The romance in my fiction fizzled. That's why I need a writing partner if I ever want to write again."

"You survived, Melody. You'll write again. And you won't need me or anyone else as a partner. Because it's here." He tapped my temple and then laid his hand over my heart. "And here."

I smiled. "I'm glad *someone* believes in me."

"I'm not the only one. Cassie does, and so does your son—*and* my daughter Anne."

I nodded. "And Aunt Peg and Uncle Butch." I looked up at him. "But not Virelle. I could tell in her eyes—the way she spoke to me. She thinks I was in on it."

Don shook his head. "She's focused on doing her job."

"Was Devon Grove part of the ring? Was that why he was killed?"

Don shook his head. "We don't think so. We think he found something in the books and was blackmailing them."

A shiver ran through me.

"They don't know where the money is, Melody. Your husband paid off Stephanie and Frank Nooley, the owner of the truck parts company, for their part in the scheme and kept the lion's share for himself. He suspected the net was closing in and was making arrangements to leave the country permanently."

He grasped my shoulders. "His accomplices will do anything to get their hands on that money. That's why you're not safe. They think you know where it is."

CHAPTER EIGHTEEN

"Hey, lady, I can't fill your tank with that humongous tree in the way."

The deliveryman from Pete's Propane, whose name was Vince, according to the patch on his too-short uniform jacket, stood at my front door, scribbling on a pad. Behind him a dirty white tanker truck idled loudly in the driveway. What day was it? What *time* was it?

"I didn't expect you this early." I tightened the belt of my white fleece robe.

"Early? It's almost noon. Just getting' outta bed, huh?" He snorted. "You city folks."

Wisps of dirty blond hair shagged out of his coffee-colored knit hat with a Pete's Propane patch on the front. Brown insulated coveralls, stained at the knees, were stuffed into his five-buckle, black-rubber boots, which dripped a mixture of mud, melting snow, and road cinders on my deck. I was about to explain I'd had a late, crisis-filled night, but decided I didn't owe him any explanation.

"I'm sorry."

"Yeah, so am I. I come all the way from Marysville for nothin'. You're my only delivery on this godforsaken mountain." He ripped out a pink slip and shoved it at me. "I hope you ain't outta propane."

"Can we move the tree?" I asked. "I can help you."

"What do I look like? Paul Bunyan? Heh-heh. And you shore don't look like Wonder Woman. Sorry, lady, I'm just the delivery guy. And even if I was allowed to move your tree, I ain't got time. I got a bunch of deliveries up north I gotta get done by five."

"Can you come tomorrow?" I'd have to call Jake. I wasn't happy about losing my dreaming tree, but what was I to do? I needed the LP. "I'll take care of the tree today."

"No can do, lady. We ain't open Saturdays." He pronounced it *Sat-dies*. "You'll have to call the office and schedule another delivery. The number's on the slip."

I scanned the bill and gasped. "A hundred dollars? But you didn't put anything in my tank."

He shrugged. "I gotta charge you for the trip. You shoulda called us."

I sighed. "Okay. Thanks anyway. I'll call and reschedule."

"Make sure you have that thing moved first."

"I will."

He stood there watching me with an expectant look on his shaggy face.

"Is there anything else, Vince?"

"Yeah. The hundred bucks. Read the bill." He pointed to the bottom of the slip. "See? It says 'all accounts due upon delivery'."

"But you didn't deliver anything."

"Policy, lady."

"I'll get my checkbook," I mumbled.

"No, lady, cash only."

I scrutinized the bill. "I don't see that anywhere on here."

He shrugged. "New policy. Just changed it."

I stared at him a moment and then shook my head. "No can do. No propane, no payment."

Surprise washed over his face. "But—"

"You heard me. Furthermore, there are other companies that would be more than happy to take my order." I nodded to his truck. "And I'll just bet their trucks have long enough hoses to reach the tank, tree or no tree."

His mouth gaped open, his face blood-red.

I ripped the invoice in half. "Fill the tank, Vince, and write up another bill of sale."

"But—"

I raised my eyebrows. "Before I call your employer and tell him you tried to rook me."

He swallowed. "Yes, ma'am."

I got my tank filled, a new bill of sale, and his copies of the old one. He even agreed when I said I'd mail a check to the office. City folk. Yep.

After Vince left, I tried calling Jake but didn't have a strong enough signal. I was about to text him when a red Dodge Ram pulled in my driveway, its bed loaded with firewood. Jake, dressed in blue jeans and a fleece-lined, blue-jean jacket, bounded up the front steps.

"Hey, Mel, I brought you some firewood. With all the trees down from the storm, I got enough to last me through spring. Thought you might need some too. No charge." He grinned. "Where do you want me to put it? In the woodshed?"

"Actually, my woodshed's full. A friend brought me a load yesterday afternoon and unloaded it before I knew what he was doing."

"So you don't want the firewood?"

"Yes, I do. I've moved to the mountain, you know, and will need as much as I can to get through the winter. Why don't you stack it on the side of the woodshed?"

"This side?" He indicated the side toward the poogie. His eyebrows creased together. "What are all those tracks? Looks like they go behind the outhouse."

I was about to say something about having diarrhea when Don's truck pulled in behind Jake's. *Thank You, Lord, for keeping me from uttering untruths.*

Jake stiffened. The truck door opened and Charlie jumped out, racing across the slush to me.

"Charlie! How's my girl?" I caressed her ears, putting my face next to hers. Her rough tongue lapped my cheek.

"I'll just stack the wood by the deck," Jake said.

"What kind of wood is that?" Don asked. "I might need some myself." He stuck out his hand. "Don Bridges. I just moved into the farmhouse up the road."

Jake shook the offered hand. "Jake Esau."

"The guy who bought the red-shingled cabin?"

Jake nodded. "Retired. Wanted to get out of the city."

"I know what you mean," Don said. "What city? I'm from Erie, and the noise just drives me nuts. So when this place came up for sale, I jumped on it."

What was with Don? He wasn't usually so chatty.

"Pittsburgh," Jake said.

Don shook his head, as if commiserating with him. "Man, that's worse than Erie. Melody says you're starting a security-handyman type business."

"Yeah, I need something to supplement my pension."

"Where'd you retire from, anyway?"

"Steel mill."

"Do you have a business card on you? I want to do some remodeling before Christmas, and I might need some help."

Jake patted his pockets. "Sorry. I left them back at the cabin." He pushed up his sleeve and glanced at his watch. "I didn't realize what time it was. I have an appointment to see about a remodeling job. In the village. One of those old houses. I forgot all about it."

"I guess I better move my truck so you can get out," Don said. "Charlie. Stay."

She sat, leaning against my leg.

Jake gave me a pleading look. "I'm sorry, Mel. I'll bring your firewood tonight."

I watched Don as he backed up and pulled beside Jake's truck.

Grocery shopping was on my to-do list for the afternoon—I wanted to get a new whistling kettle—and I wasn't sure if I'd be back by the time Jake came back. I really didn't want him here when I wasn't, good deed or no. But neither did I want to hurt his feelings. You never know when you might need a friend on the mountain.

"I'm not sure I'll be here. Why don't you call me before you come? I can help you unload."

"What was that all about?" I asked Don after Jake left. We sat touching shoulders on the sofa, enjoying a cup of tea and the warmth of the fire. I was still in my robe.

"Just pumping him for information and didn't want to sound like a cop."

"You don't trust anyone, do you?"

He tucked a stray strand of my hair behind my ear. "I trust you."

"Why don't you trust Jake? He seems like a nice enough guy."

He shrugged. "I've learned to follow my instincts."

I looked at him. "There's more to it than that. I had a funny, weird feeling when I first met him too. But I was wrong. He's turned out to be a pretty nice person. He checked on me yesterday and brought me some firewood today."

"What do you know about him?"

"That he's retired. That he bought the red-shingled hunting camp down the road. That he's started a handyman-security business."

"Then why hasn't anyone heard about it? You said he left a business card and flyer at all the places up here on the mountain, yet I never got one. I checked all the other camps. Nothing. Not even Willie knew about it until you told him. You'd think if he was serious about this, he'd let Willie know and post something in his store."

I squirmed. "Willie told me in September about him buying the camp. When you showed up and shot that rattler, I thought you were Jake." I thought about what I knew about Jake. Not much. "I guess I really don't know anything about him. He never offered information, and stupid me never asked. Paul was right. I'm too trusting, too naïve—"

His fingers pressed against my lips. "Hush. You are far from stupid. And there's nothing wrong with trusting people. That's what's wrong with the world. Everybody distrusts everybody else. Everyone thinks the other person has an ulterior motive."

"Are you saying I should trust *everyone*?"

"No. You have to be wise as a serpent and innocent as a dove."

I cocked my head to the side. "That sounds familiar. Where have I heard it before?"

He grinned. "Matthew 10:16."

"Just what I need—a Bible-spouting cop." I giggled.

"*Ex*-cop. And speaking of the Bible, would you like to go to church with me on Sunday? I know you and God have had some issues, but—"

"I'd love to."

"You would?"

I studied his surprised face. "Yes, I would. Where are we going? What should I wear?"

"Pine Ridge Christian Church. It's—"

"I know where it is. My parents used to take us there. I remember one Easter it snowed. Easter was late that year. I still insisted on wearing my frilly dress and Mary Janes. I learned an important lesson that day."

"What was that?"

"Dress for the weather."

He grinned and tugged the ends of the belt on my robe. "Speaking of which, when are you going to get out of that robe and get dressed, woman? It's already two o'clock."

I shrugged out of my robe and grinned. "I'm already dressed. I put the robe over my sweats because the fire was out when I got up. The cabin was freezing. I was starting a fire when the propane guy showed up."

"The propane guy?"

I grinned and told him the story. "Not bad for a naïve city girl, huh?"

"Not bad at all." He chuckled. Then his face got serious and his eyes probed mine. "Something's changed. You're different. In a good way."

"Romans 8:35 to 39," I whispered, blinking back sudden tears. "That's what happened to me."

His eyes gazed into mine for a moment, and then he leaned toward me. I closed my eyes and lifted my face to receive his kiss—just as his cell phone buzzed. He fished it out of his shirt pocket and glanced at the screen.

"It's Virelle," he said. "We'll continue this . . . conversation . . . later."

I ran my finger down his bearded jawline. "Promise?"

While Don went home—he got a better signal at the farmhouse than I got at the cottage—I took advantage of the warmth from the afternoon sun and the blazing fireplace and took a shower. Charlie lay on the hardwood floor just outside the bathroom door, her face on her front paws. Don came in, jabbering, after I was dressed and still drying my hair.

Upset was written all over his handsome face.

I shut off the dryer. "What did you say?"

"Why weren't the doors locked? I walked right in, and you never heard me."

His facial muscles twitched, his lips pressed together in a white line.

"You're angry."

"Melody," he said with a sigh, "please lock the doors. At all times. Promise me."

"I promise." I wrapped the hair dryer cord around the handle. "I forgot to check them before I got in the shower. Why are you so upset?" I looked up at him. "What did Virelle say?"

He grabbed my hand and led me to the sofa. A cardboard box sat on the coffee table.

"What's that?" I leaned down to read the lettering.

"One of the surveillance cameras."

"One? How many do you have?"

"Four."

"I'm not a suspect any longer, am I?"

"You never were, Melody."

"Then why—"

"Virelle and I have been doing some digging."

"Oh, so you were the ones who planted the hammer behind the outhouse?"

"Melody, get serious."

I made a straight face. "Okay, I'm serious." I plopped down on the sofa. It was hard to be somber when my insides were leaping about like a fawn in a hayfield.

He sat beside me.

"Stephanie Keith, a.k.a. Stephanie Morley, quit her job at the bank. We lost her trail."

He pulled up a picture on his phone and handed it to me. "Do you recognize him?"

I studied the photo, but didn't recognize the clean-shaven, heavy-jowled man with a buzz cut. "No. Who is it?"

"Look closer. Look at the eyes."

I stared at the screen. "Jake! But he looks so different."

"That's a picture of Frank Nooley, the third member of the embezzling ring."

"But how can someone change his appearance so drastically?" I handed the phone back to Don.

"A beard, change of hairstyle and dress, facial expression, weight, posture, even the way a person walks. Look at how different Stephanie looked as the bank manager."

"The eyes," I said. "A person can change everything but their eyes."

"Eye color can be changed with colored contact lenses, but you're right. If you look close enough—the eyes are the windows to the soul. There's no such person by the name of Jake or Jacob Esau. Jake Esau is Frank Nooley."

"Then why don't you just arrest him?"

"Because we're hoping he'll lead us to Stephanie."

"And the rest of the money."

The fawns stopped leaping inside me. Suddenly, I wasn't so keen on being the bait.

CHAPTER NINETEEN

Since Jake said he'd be back in the evening, Don set up four surveillance cameras, one on each side of the cottage, and camouflaged them well. Even I couldn't see them tucked up under the eaves. I felt safe knowing that whatever or whoever was outside my place, day or night, would be recorded by the all-seeing eye and transmitted via Internet, courtesy of my WiFi, to Don's and Virelle's computers, which had the camera software installed. It was like having my own private ADT home security system, except for the fact it wouldn't call 9-1-1 if there was a break-in.

Don wasn't too keen about leaving me on my own, but I'd insisted. Frank would surely suspect something was up if Don was hanging around all the time. Sure I was a little nervous—putting it mildly—but I was also angry about being set up. Besides, I told him, we could get some fodder for our romantic suspense novel.

It was nearly seven when Jake-Frank knocked on the glass of the front patio door.

"Why don't you have a doorbell?" he asked when I slid open the door. "All this knocking can't be good for that glass."

"I didn't plan to have so much company. Besides, it would take a sledge hammer to break that glass. It's triple pane."

"I brought your firewood."

I grabbed my hooded Carhartt jacket from the coat tree. "I'll help you unload it."

"Nah. You stay in here where it's warm. It'll only take a few minutes. But I'll take a cup of hot coffee when I'm done."

"All I have is hazelnut."

He grimaced. "What about beer?"

I shook my head. "Tea? I've got lots of flavors."

"Do I look like a tea-guy? Sorry, Mel, but tea's a woman's drink. I have a six-pack in my truck. It's nice and cold." He winked at me. "I'll share."

I suppressed a shudder. How could I have thought he was such a nice guy?

"Thanks, but no thanks," I shoved my arms in the thermal-lined sleeves. "I'll help you."

My cell phone buzzed, indicating I had a text message. I pulled it out of my sweatpants pocket and glanced at the screen, holding it close to my face so Frank-Jake wouldn't see who the caller was.

"I'd better take this," I said. "I'll be right out as soon as I return this call. "Thanks, Fr . . . er, for the firewood."

Oh, great. I almost called him Frank. How was I going to do this? I opened Don's text.

Let him unload the firewood by himself so I can watch him.

Don had probably heard every word of the conversation with Jake-Frank. He'd installed a couple of listening devices hidden in the smoke detector and the carbon monoxide detector. He'd wanted to wire me, but I said no way. I'd watched too many crime scene shows where the bugging backfired and the wired person got killed as a result.

The one in the carbon monoxide detector hung on the wall between the kitchen and the living room, and the one in the smoke detector was on the ceiling in my bedroom. I'd protested the one in the bedroom on the grounds that I'd never let Frank—*Jake*—upstairs, but Don told me the devices picked up all sounds, not just voices. Which gave me no small measure of comfort, imagining a killer sneaking up on me while I slept soundly, snuggled under my cozy, warm quilt.

"Can't you just leave Charlie here?" I'd asked Don. I loved Rascal, but let's face it, cats just aren't good protectors of the home front. They will arch their backs, get their hackles up, and hiss. But that wouldn't scare anyone.

I walked to the wall between the kitchen and the living room. "I got your message," I whispered at the smoke detector. "Frank is outside unloading the firewood. I suppose you know that. And are watching him. Roger and out . . . ten-four . . . whatever."

My cell phone buzzed again. *J-A-K-E is outside unloading firewood, not Frank.*

"Oops," I said to the smoke detector.

I erased both messages, slipped the phone in my pocket, and pulled a boxed pizza out of the freezer. My assignment was to keep Frank—Jake—busy for an hour or so while Virelle and Don searched his cabin.

Don had his laptop with him so he could watch the surveillance feed and listen to what went on in the cabin. My hands shook as I struck the match to light the oven pilot light. How on earth was I going to pull this off? Crime shows were my second favorite programs, next to romantic comedies, but being a fan and actually doing the job were worlds apart.

When the oven was preheated, I placed the baking stone with the pizza on the middle rack. Then I put another log on the fire, settled on the sofa, and opened my laptop. Writing, getting lost in another world, a world I created and controlled myself, always calmed me. And I needed all the calm I could get. If I didn't settle down, this was never going to work.

Jake rapped on the glass at the front of the cabin just as I pulled the pizza out of the oven.

"Come in, Jake."

I'd heard somewhere that repeating a person's name frequently, especially aloud, helped you to remember it. I breathed a silent prayer as the door opened and closed. Lights. Camera. Action! Ready or not, I was knee-deep in this drama. I carried the pizza into the living room and placed it on the coffee table that I'd covered with a thick bath towel.

"Sorry it took so long," Jake said, putting a six-pack of beer on the floor beside him. He pulled off his cowboy boots and dropped them on the mat by the door. I wondered how he managed to stay off his backside wearing those fancy things. More show than go.

"I backed the truck up to the porch and then couldn't get it back out. Not even in four-wheel drive."

"The ice out there is terrible, Jake."

He shook his fleece-lined denim jacket off his shoulder and draped it over the coat tree. "I just might have to spend the night."

He grinned, and chills raced up my spine. Not in this lifetime.

I snapped my fingers. "Weight. You need weight in the back end, Jake. You took all that firewood out of the bed. Now it's too light."

He leered at me. "Like I said—"

"I have a big flashlight. It isn't supposed to snow tonight. You can walk. Your place isn't that far, Jake."

He sighed. Loud. "I take that as a no. Why do you keep saying my name like that?"

"Like what?" I took a deep breath. *One-thousand-one, one-thousand-two.* "Look, Jake. I'm still not over my husband's death, and it's going on two years." *God, forgive me for lying.*

He gave me a look of fake sympathy. "Aw, that's a shame. You must have loved him very much."

I hung my head so he wouldn't see my eyes. I wasn't a good liar. I wasn't even good at evading the truth gracefully.

"Aw, Mel . . ." In two quick strides he was across the room and wrapping his arms around me. It was all I could do not to shove him away. "I'm so sorry. He must have been some guy."

I nodded. Paul was some guy, all right. I leaned my head on Jake's shoulder for a moment, playing the part of the bereaved widow, and then stepped back. Was Don listening?

I snapped my fingers. "Kitty litter."

His face screwed up. "Kitty litter? What does that have to do with Paul?"

I wanted to ask him how he knew my husband's name was Paul, but I was afraid it would blow my cover. I mean, I knew how he knew, but he didn't know I knew.

"Haven't you seen that commercial on TV?" I pantomimed shaking a bag of kitty litter on the floor. "Where the guy dumps a bag of kitty litter under the wheel of a car stuck on ice? It provides traction." I pointed my thumb over my shoulder. "I have a bag in the utility room. I'll go get it."

He plopped on the sofa and patted the cushion next to him. "We can try that later. Now let's dig into that pizza. Grab me a beer, will you?"

It was going to be a long hour. I plopped a slice of pizza on a cardboard plate and sat in the recliner. "Help yourself."

Two beers and an eternity later, Jake nodded toward my laptop, which I'd set on the floor beneath the coffee table when the timer went off for the pizza. "What are you working on?"

For the past hour and a half, we'd made small talk, lying through our teeth to each other. It was all I could do not to keep from pulling my cell phone out to see if Don had texted me to let me know he and Virelle were done. It hadn't vibrated, so I was stuck entertaining a man who might very well be a murderer.

Don't think about that, Melody.

"I'm brainstorming some ideas. My publisher wants me and Don to team up to write a romantic suspense. Don's a mystery writer, and I write romances. Under a pseudonym. Melanie Joy. The market hasn't been all that great, and they think . . ."

I was babbling. Surely he saw how scared I was. I took a slow breath. *One-thousand-one, one-thousand-two.*

I smiled. "I'm sorry, it's just that I'm so excited about the idea we have for the book. That's why Don's up here. On the mountain. To work on the novel together. We have to submit the first three chapters by the end of the month. That's in three weeks. Neither one of us has ever—"

My pocket vibrated. Relief flooded through my tense muscles. "Sorry, I have to take this." I pulled the phone from my pocket and glanced at the screen. "It's my agent. Getting back to me. About the idea I texted her. Yep, that's who it's from."

I clicked opened the text message. *Back at the farmhouse. I heard everything. You can get rid of him now.*

"Oh, dear." I tried not to sound relieved. "The publisher wants the chapters by Thanksgiving. You better leave." I nodded to the laptop on the floor. "I have to get back to work. Deadlines."

He ran his napkin across his mouth and tossed it on his plate, which he placed on the empty pizza stone. Wordlessly, he crossed the hardwood floor to the door and pulled on his boots and jacket. I went and got the bag of kitty litter.

"Do you want me to help you?"

"Nah, that's all right. I'll put a few logs in the back over the wheels and pull out slow in four-wheel drive. I should be all right."

I nodded, feeling awkward, like a teenager saying good night to a date she didn't like and was glad to see go but didn't want him to see it.

"Do you want me to come back tomorrow and take care of that tree? I noticed it's still lying in the backyard."

"Thanks, but no. I haven't decided what I'm going to do with it yet."

"Well, then, good night, Mel." His lips brushed my forehead. I bit my bottom lip so hard, I thought I drew blood.

"Good night, Jake. Wait. Don't forget this." I handed him the remaining four cans of the six-pack still attached by the plastic thingie.

"Thanks," he mumbled. "I'll stop by tomorrow to see if you need anything. Thanks for the pizza."

"You're welcome." *Will you go already?*

"Hey! How about I take you out for supper tomorrow? As a thanks for the pizza?"

I shook my head. "I can't. The book, remember? I have to get up early and write all day."

"You'll need a break by evening. Come on. I'll pick you up at six."

"I don't—" My pocket vibrated. I sighed. "My agent again."

I hurried and clicked it open. *Say yes.* I erased the message and smiled at Jake.

"You're right. I'll need a break." I held up the phone. "Push, push, push—that's all she does. I'll see you tomorrow at six."

He didn't seem to have any trouble getting out the driveway. As his taillights disappeared into the night, my phone vibrated again. Now what? I opened Don's text message.

Good girl.

CHAPTER TWENTY

I awoke Saturday morning around seven with Rascal nestled next to me on top of the covers. I poked my nose out from beneath the down-filled comforter. The air in the cottage was frigid. Snuggled in my warm flannel pj's, I'd actually slept through the night. The fire had gone out.

Although I had filled my propane tank, I didn't like the wall heaters fired up at night while I slept. Although the unit came with a sensor that would automatically shut off the heater should the oxygen drop below a certain level, I still worried about leaks and fires and carbon monoxide poisoning. And I'd never spent the winter here. I usually closed up the place around Thanksgiving and opened it again in the spring around St. Patrick's Day. If we got a mild spell, I'd make the trip from Greensburg to check on things and spend a few days on the mountain.

I wasn't prepared to winter here. I should have taken more time getting things ready, but I'd been so focused on selling the house, I'd neglected to adequately prepare. And I'd been in such a hurry to move. I hadn't figured winter would set in so early. I thought I'd have at least a month before it got bad.

Shoving the covers aside, I forced myself out of my cozy cocoon, hoping some warm embers remained in the hearth so I wouldn't have to start a fire from scratch.

An hour later, I sat before a crackling blaze, a cup of mint tea on the lamp table beside me, my computer in my lap. I'd wanted to write a chapter for our proposed novel and e-mail it to Don before noon, but after several false starts, I still stared at a blank screen. How on earth was I going to do this? I couldn't write in the middle of a crime investigation.

I clicked on the desktop weather icon to check the forecast for the afternoon. I planned to clean up the mess in the backyard where my dreaming tree lay. I still hadn't decided what to do with it. I couldn't bear the thought of it chopped up and burned, yet it couldn't remain where it was. My plan was to hack off the limbs with my chainsaw and drag them into the woods behind the outhouse. I'd have to call a tree service to haul away the trunk. It was at least three feet in diameter and a good forty feet in length—more than my little chainsaw could handle.

Unable to concentrate on writing, I decided it wasn't too cold to get started on the tree now. I dressed for working outside on a frigid morning: thermal underwear, turtleneck jersey, quilt-lined bib overalls, sweatshirt, and wool-blend socks. After I laced up my work boots, I pulled a thick knit headband over my ears and zipped up my Carhartt hoodie. As I worked and warmed up, I'd shed the layers.

The temperature on the outdoor thermometer read twenty degrees as I swept last night's snow from the back deck and steps. In the shop, I gassed up the chainsaw, grabbed my leather work gloves and goggles from the bench, and headed to the backyard. It seemed a shame to disrupt the quiet of the pristine morning, so I set the saw down on the snow-covered ground.

Closing my eyes, I lifted my face to the sunlight filtering through skeleton branches and inhaled the heady scent of pine boughs and wood smoke. My mind spun around a tune I'd heard my mom sing often: "Oh, build me just a cabin . . . la-da-da-da-da-da-da."

Somewhere a woodpecker tapped for his breakfast. The spell punctured, I took a breath, bent down to the saw, and yanked the cord. The engine sputtered, coughing plumes of blue smoke into the frosty air, and roared to life. I pulled my goggles down over my eyes and got to work.

I'd only been working maybe a half hour when the chainsaw quit. Surely it wasn't out of gas. I sighed. Maybe it needed a new filter. Another thing on the "should-have-done" list: have chainsaw serviced. Upset with myself, I hauled it back to the shop, where I plunked it down on the workbench.

"What in tarnation do you think you're doing, woman? Do you know what time it is?"

I spun around. Don stood in the doorway, arms folded across his chest. A blue knit hat looked as though it had been jammed on his head in a hurry. He wore a plain gray sweatshirt over jeans and untied sneakers. No socks. No jacket.

"Well, good morning to you too." I pushed up my goggles so they rested on top of my head and pointed my thumb over my shoulder. "The chain saw quit on me."

He grunted. "It's probably protesting going to work so early. It's a good thing it isn't bear or deer season yet. You would've ticked off a lot of hunters with the racket."

I glanced at the wall clock above the door frame. "Quarter to nine. Just getting out of bed, are you?"

"I've been up since six. Writing."

I gave him an apologetic smile. "I tried. I wasted an hour this morning trying to wring words out of a muddled brain." I shrugged. "Writer's block."

"No such thing."

"Well, the muse went AWOL. I don't know how you expect me to write with everything that's going on." I turned back to the bench. "Do you know anything about chain saws?"

The rubber soles of his sneakers squeaked as he crossed the rough wood floor to stand beside me. He studied the saw, frowning. "If I did, I wouldn't tell you." He put his bare hand over my gloved one. "We can take care of this later. Hop in the truck. I made a pot of coffee. Hazelnut."

I'd never been inside the farmhouse, although Ginny and Harvey Campbell had been my and Sonny's playmates when their chores were done. As Don pulled into the driveway, I noticed a new bow window, energy sticker still on the glass, on the side of the house that faced the expansive backyard and the wood line about fifty feet away.

Inside, the aroma of sweet cinnamon filled the expansive kitchen.

"I like the window." I took off my gloves, stuffed them in my pockets, and hung my jacket on the wall hooks by the door. "I always wanted one, but Paul didn't. He never said why. I think it was because I wanted it so badly. He could be contrary like that."

Don poured two mugs of steaming coffee and placed them on the scrubbed pine table beside a pan covered with aluminum foil. He peeled back the foil.

"Have a cinnamon roll. Fresh baked this morning."

I pulled a warm, sticky roll from the pan. "I'm impressed," I said, licking my fingers. "You are a man of many talents."

A slight blush spread across his cheekbones above his beard. He held up an empty cardboard tube. "Lest you get the wrong idea."

"Ah, the three C's—cardboard, can, and carry-out—the extent of my kitchen skills. But then, you know all about that. You've seen my kitchen after one of my attempts at making something from scratch. Except oatmeal. And slow cooker chili. Oh, and I can slap a sandwich together, as long as it's not too complicated."

He laughed. "You're the only woman I know who can wield a chainsaw yet burn water."

"That's not fair. I fainted."

He grinned. "True. But I've seen several recycled kettles around your place. I thought it was a decorative theme or something, but now I know better. You scorched them all."

I pulled a strip of roll off the bun and pushed it in my mouth. "Mm . . . this is excellent. I've made these, but I manage to leave them in the oven too long. I see you're putting up a bird feeder."

"The girls are coming up for Thanksgiving, and they love bird-watching, especially Hannah. When they first moved to Greensburg, I put up a feeder in their yard and gave them a *National Geographic* field guide to birds in Pennsylvania. With Hannah having to miss so much because of her illness, I figured it would keep her mind occupied." He smiled. "She can recognize and name every bird that comes to that feeder."

"Proud grandpa, aren't you?"

"What are your plans for Thanksgiving? Why don't you and Garrett join us? He'll be home by then, won't he?"

"He's flying in Monday. I'll check with him. Aunt Peg invited us to her place, but my guess is he'll jump at the chance to be with Anne." I paused. "You know he's got a thing for her, don't you?"

"He's a fine young man, Melody." He shook his head. "But I'm a little protective of Anne. If she'd listened to me when she brought Wade around . . . but she's stubborn. And was in love. Or so she said. What does an eighteen-year-old know about love, anyway?"

"More than you think, but you're a man. Men see things differently than women."

He lifted his coffee mug to his lips and held it there, his eyes seeming to go back in time. After a short moment, he nodded. "That's why I don't do romance. In my books, I mean."

I took a breath. "You loved once. Anne's mother. Cassie told me you raised the girls by yourself."

I didn't know how much to say. Everything about this man told me he was Semper Fi to the core.

"Cassie also told me you haven't even looked at a woman since Francine died."

He pressed his lips together and stared out the window. I watched his Adam's apple bob up and down and then saw him blink.

"I'm sorry. It's none of my business."

He nodded, his face set firm. "You're right. It's none of your business."

I pushed away from the table. "Thanks for the coffee and rolls. I needed a break." I took my empty mug to the sink and rinsed it. "I need to get back to that tree."

I shoved my feet into my boots, looped the leather laces around the black hooks, winding them around my ankles, and tied them in a double knot in front. I grabbed my jacket from the coat tree and flung it over my arm. Charlie, who'd been lying under the table, got up, stretched, and sauntered over to me.

"Where are my gloves?" I asked, petting her behind her soft ears.

"Forget it," Don said in a voice that startled me.

"I can't. They're my best work gloves. Maybe I left them in your truck."

Don stood. "No, forget the tree. I'll take care of it. Next week."

I shook my head. "I want it out of there today. I don't want to look at it anymore."

He sighed, gulped the rest of his coffee, and patted his mouth with his wrist.

"All right." He nodded. "I'll take care of it today, but don't forget your date tonight."

I groaned. "I wish I could. Why do you want me to go out with Frank anyway? He's—"

"Jake."

I grimaced. "Oh, right. Jake. I don't like being alone with him. He's always leering and drooling."

"That doesn't surprise me. You're an attractive woman." He waved at my head and gave a slight smile. "It's starting to get curly again."

I ran my hand over my hair. It did feel a little wiry. "Must be the dampness. The treatment lasts ten to twelve weeks, and it's been . . ." I counted on my fingers. "Let's see . . . I had it done in the middle of September—"

"Eight weeks."

"Stop changing the subject. Why am I supposed to go out with Fr—Jake tonight? I thought you said he was dangerous."

"We're hoping with you being gone from the cabin for the evening, Stephanie will show up. He's not going to hurt you unless there's no other way to get the money. Right now he thinks you're clueless."

I took a sharp breath. "This is the last time I play your cop-and-robber game. I'm not cut out for this cloak-and-dagger stuff. I'll go out with Frank tonight, then I'm done. Understood?"

He looked at me with concern. "Jake. You're going out with *Jake*. If you call him Frank . . ." He shook his head. "You're right. I've expected too much from you. Call him and cancel."

"No. I said I would do this, and I will. I don't go back on my word. But maybe your partner can tail us? I'd feel a lot safer."

"She's in Mexico."

"What's she doing in Mexico?"

"Checking something out."

Something clicked. My mouth went dry.

"Paul. Those weren't his ashes, were they? Oh, dear Lord . . ." I gazed out the door window. "I assumed . . . I never thought . . ." I swallowed. *One-thousand-one, one-thousand-two . . .*

"Melody, look at me."

I stared at the linoleum floor. *One-thousand-three, one-thousand-four . . .* The blue blurred with the white. Don's hand cupped my chin and lifted.

"DNA," I blurted. "I'll get the ashes from his parents. I'll tell them . . . I want some of them. For Garrett. I'll—"

"DNA is destroyed during the cremation process."

"Then how will we know if those ashes are really Paul's?" Panic swept through me. *Breathe! One-thousand-five, one-thousand-six . . . I'm going to faint. Or throw up.*

He grasped my shoulders. "Listen to me. Virelle will find out. You can be sure of that."

"How?"

"She'll talk to the Mexican police, the hotel staff, and the funeral director."

A million what if's bombarded my brain. "But what if they lie? What if they're part of the cover-up?"

"Melody, calm down."

"Don't tell me to calm down! If those aren't Paul's ashes, whose are they? And where is Paul?"

"Those ashes are probably Paul's. We're just covering all the bases."

"But what—"

He pulled me to him—not gently, either—and pressed his lips to mine. To shut me up? To calm me down? But, oh, this *wasn't* calming me down. *Au-contraire.*

"Don . . ." I pulled out of his arms, my heart beating a million times a second. "I need to . . . think . . ." I stepped to the door. "I'm going to walk back to my cottage. It's not far. Less than a mile. It'll help me settle down."

"Melody, I didn't mean—"

I held up my hand. "Please don't say you didn't mean to kiss me. Look, I understand that you don't want to talk about Francine. I understand if you don't want to commit yourself to a relationship. I understand. Really, I do."

"I didn't say that I didn't want to commit myself to a relationship." He ran his fingers through his hair. "I have a job to do, and you're not helping."

"Not helping? Then why am I going out with Frank tonight? Why did I even tell you about the money? Why should I trust you?" I swallowed a sudden lump in my throat. "I need to think. I'll see you . . . whenever."

I slammed the door on my way out.

As I walked on the blacktop back to my place, my mind was like a computer with a thousand tabs open. What would Virelle discover? What if Paul was still alive, and it was all a scheme? Then why'd he leave the money? And why were Frank and Stephanie looking for it, if they were in on it? And if Paul was still alive, someone had to have died in his place.

I tried to remember back to the time I received the news of Paul's death. He was supposed to have been at a conference in Phoenix. That's what he told me, and I never questioned him. Deep inside I knew he wasn't at a conference. But I liked it when he was away. There was less tension in the house. And I could write without feeling guilty. No comments like, "Why don't you get a real job and contribute something to maintaining this place?"

When the hotel manager called and told me in accented English that Paul had fallen to his death, I was too stunned to think. Looking back now, I realized I shouldn't have taken their word for it. I should have flown to Mexico and identified the body myself, not left it up to the police, who had gotten his identification and my contact information from Paul's wallet, which had been in his back pocket.

I had tried to reach Garrett, but he was somewhere in the Ukraine on assignment, with no cell phone service. I'd called his boss, using the business card Garrett had given me for emergencies. But by the time my son was able to contact me, the arrangements had already been made.

I'd already contacted the funeral director recommended by the hotel manager, and when I learned how much it would cost to have his body shipped back to Pennsylvania, I told the guy to cremate him and ship the ashes. Paul's mother, of course, had been furious. They had the money to have his body shipped home. But they didn't offer, and I wasn't going to ask. It was all I could do to call and tell them their only child had died.

"Want a lift?"

I jerked back to reality. A red Dodge pickup idled on the road beside me, spewing acrid diesel fumes in the crisp midday air.

"Fr— For goodness sake, Jake! You scared me!"

He gave me a puzzled look. "Aren't you supposed to be writing?"

I shrugged. "Writer's block. I thought a brisk walk in the fresh mountain air might help get the words flowing. I was so absorbed in my story I didn't hear you drive up."

He shifted into park. "That so? I went over to your place to ask you what time you wanted me to pick you up tonight. I keep forgetting to get your cell number. When you didn't answer the door, I checked around, but no sign of you. Your SUV was parked in the driveway. I saw tracks of another vehicle. So I drove up the road to see if you were at that writer guy's place."

I bristled. "I'm a big girl, Jake. There was no need to—" I was going to say "check up on me," but decided against it. "—worry about me. I'm fine, see?"

He nodded, tapping the steering wheel with his thumbs. "I thought I heard a chain saw over at your place. Early. Around eight-thirty or so. Kind of early for a tree service crew."

"Yes, well, that was me."

His brows rose. "You?"

"Yes, me. Don't look so surprised."

He shook his head and gave a low whistle. "You're some woman, you know that?"

I forced a smile. "So I'm told. If you don't mind, I really need to get back to thinking."

"What time do you want me to pick you up? I thought we'd go to The Village Pump over by Vowinckel. Best wings around."

"I thought we'd decided on six?"

"That's right. Too early. How about seven?"

"Six-thirty. I don't want to be out too late. I have to get up early for church tomorrow morning."

"Church?" he sputtered. "I didn't take you for the churchy type."

I folded my arms and squared my jaw. "And exactly what type did you take me for?"

The muscles in his cheek twitched as he punched the passenger window button. "See you at seven, Melsy."

He shoved the truck in gear and sped away, tires spitting gravel and ash. I waited until the taillights disappeared over the crest of the hill before I let loose.

"It's *Melody*, you jerk," I shouted.

CHAPTER TWENTY-ONE

I didn't make it to church on Sunday morning. I woke up before dawn with the chills and was too sick to get out of bed and turn on the wall heaters. The fire, of course, was out. Shivering beneath the down comforter, I wished I hadn't replaced Hot Stuff, that old black woodstove with its fire-brick interior. It retained heat long after the fire went out. The fireplace was cozier but not as practical. I had the old stove stored in a corner of the workshop for sentimental reasons.

When Don came to pick me up around nine, I was still huddled in bed in the loft. He rapped on the glass, calling my name. I tried to answer, but all I managed was a croak. My throat felt like a thousand sharp knives going down every time I swallowed. He rapped against the glass again. I tried to get up but fell back against the pillows, my head spinning, my stomach churning. I closed my eyes.

The next thing I knew, Don was perched at the edge of the bed, the back of his hand against my forehead.

"You're burning up," he said. "How long have you been sick like this?"

I tried to open my eyes, but squeezed them shut against the light coming in the French doors of the loft.

"Close . . . blinds," I croaked. "Hurts."

The drapes rustled. The next thing I knew, something cool and wet was pressed against my forehead. I tried to get up, but the wooziness and nausea hit me like a lightning strike. I groaned.

"Just lie still. We need to get that fever down. Do you have any aspirin?"

I turned my head ever so slightly to the right. My neck hurt too.

"I take that as a no. Ibuprofen? Acetaminophen?"

I edged my chin to my chest.

"I take that as a yes. Where is it? In the medicine cabinet?"

"Purse . . . hurts . . ."

"In your purse? I saw it downstairs when I came in. Be right back."

The next thing I knew his arm was behind my shoulders, lifting me gently.

"Here. Open up."

Something cold and metallic pressed against my mouth. I opened my blistered lips and let him place a small spoonful of ice chips on my tongue.

"Thanks," I mouthed, melted ice running down my cheek. The inside of my mouth felt blistered. He eased me back on the pillows. A rattling sound told me gel caps were being shaken out of a plastic bottle.

"Holy moly! These things look like horse pills. No way you'll get one of these down. If you have what I think you have, you probably can't even swallow."

I heard him mumbling under his breath.

"Can you hear me?"

I blinked.

"Good. I'm going to get the wall heaters going and start a fire in the fireplace. It's freezing in here. Looks like you've got that nasty flu bug that's going around. If it's the same thing Anne had last week, you won't be able to swallow a pill. I'll drive to Marysville and get you some liquid medicine. I'll pick up some broth and chicken stock and make you a batch of Don's famous chicken soup."

I raised my head slightly. "How . . ." I wanted to ask him how he got in. But all that came out was a pitiful croak. I'd made sure both doors were locked and checked all the windows when I came in last night after my "dinner date" with what's-his-name. My head spun. "Door?"

"I'll lock the door when I leave. You shouldn't leave your keys on the counter. Anyone could come in and take them."

"How . . . did . . . you . . . get . . . in?" It took some time, but I got it out.

"I'm a former cop, remember?"

He picked the lock. I shivered, both from fever and from fear. If he could pick the lock, Frank could, too, or Paul or . . . Another wave of dizziness and nausea hit. I must have fallen asleep because the next thing I knew, lips were brushing against my forehead.

"Here. Take this."

Don lifted my shoulders and pressed a small plastic cup against my lips. I winced when I swallowed the cherry-tasting medicine. He eased me back on the pillows and put a cool, damp washrag on my forehead.

"Thank you," I whispered. I wanted to pull my hand from beneath the covers and touch his, but everything hurt.

"Get some rest." He chuckled. "That was a stupid thing to say. You can't do anything else. I'm not leaving until you're back on your feet."

A sweet peace filled me. I tried to smile, but my cheek muscles hurt too much. I leaned back into the pillows and succumbed to the dizziness.

Don stayed at the cabin, taking care of me, bringing me chicken and vegetable broth, tea, and water. I could only sip a little at a time; otherwise, I'd heave everything back up. At one point, he threatened to take me to the emergency room because I'd thrown up so much.

"You're getting dehydrated," he said.

By then I was able to do a little more than croak.

"One more day," I whispered. "If I still have the fever tomorrow, I'll go."

I promised to sip more water. He brought me everything, even broth, in a plastic water bottle that came with a wide, chunky straw. I had a hunch he bought it when he went to town on Sunday to get medicine and the fixings for soup. He'd also bought a thermometer—one of those digital ones that he only had to wave over my forehead, and presto, it gave a reading.

"Will you leave me alone already?" I croaked when he'd taken my temperature for the umpteenth time that day. I think it was Monday. Or Tuesday. Since I'd gotten sick, the days had melded together.

"A hundred and four degrees. Your temperature hasn't gone below a hundred and two for two days."

"I have the flu. I'm supposed to have a fever." I rolled away from him.

It seemed like only a minute later when I sensed him waving his new toy over my forehead again.

"Will you leave me alone?" I moaned. "You were just here."

"Two hours ago."

"Oh."

"Here, take your medicine." He lifted my upper body with gentle hands. It hurt to move.

"Go away."

He pressed the plastic medicine cup to my lips. I let it trickle down my throat. It still felt like daggers going down when I swallowed. I closed my eyes and leaned back.

It was dark outside when I awoke again. My small, bedside lamp was turned on low. The flame in the propane heater cast flickering shadows around the room. I tried to sit up, but dizziness and nausea forced me back on the pillows. Something nudged my arm. A light weight on the edge of the bed. I turned my head slowly.

"Charlie," I murmured.

I pulled my hand out from under the covers and ran my fingers over her silky head, which rested on the bed. There was another weight pressing against my leg. I glanced down. Rascal lay curled up next to me. My heart smiled. I closed my eyes.

When I opened them again, it was still dark, but Don was sitting at my computer desk, his back to me. I couldn't see the screen. He must have sensed I was awake because he swiveled around to face me.

"How are you feeling?" He rose from my office chair, crossed the room, and stood over me—with the thermometer.

I groaned. "Not again."

He waved the thing over my forehead. "One hundred and one point seven. It's coming down."

I blinked. "What time is it?"

"One o'clock in the morning."

"What day?"

"Tuesday."

I tried to sit up. "I want to use the bathroom."

"That's a good sign. I've really been worried, Melody. I was going to take you to the hospital in the morning."

I grimaced. "I really have to go, and I don't want to use the bucket I've been using for the past few days. Not that I'm ungrateful, but . . . Will you help me? I'm still pretty woozy."

When I got back to bed, I wondered what I'd been thinking when I put in the circular stairway.

My fever finally broke in the wee hours of Wednesday. By noon I was able to get some of the soft, soup vegetables down without cringing. My throat was definitely better, although fever blisters lined the inside of my mouth, spilling down my throat.

"This is really good soup," I told Don when he came up to take my temperature—again.

"Then why don't you finish it? I didn't put that much in the bowl. Here." He held a spoonful of soup to my mouth. "Open wide."

I shook my head. "My stomach is still a bit queasy."

He took my temperature. "Ninety-eight point six. Finally."

"How much did you pay for that thing?"

He shrugged. "Not that much. I needed one anyway. For when the girls come."

"When the girls come?"

"Anne's bringing Kadie and Hannah for Thanksgiving—I told you, remember? They're coming a week early to bake Christmas cookies to send to the troops."

I frowned. "What day is today?"

"Wednesday."

Something niggled in my brain. "Garrett. He was supposed to come home Monday."

Don sat at the edge of the bed and tucked my hair behind my ears. "He got in yesterday. One of his flights was delayed, and he missed the connecting flight. He's coming up with Anne on Sunday."

I smiled. Garrett and Anne. I wondered if she felt the same way for him as he did for her. I'd find out soon enough.

"Oh, no," I said.

"What's the matter?"

"You've been here the whole time I've been sick?"

He nodded.

"I hope you don't get sick. The girls . . . Hannah . . ."

"I won't get it. I got a flu shot. I'm guessing you didn't."

I made a face. "I hate needles. I've never gotten a flu shot. I never get the flu."

"I can see that."

I pushed back the covers and dangled my legs over the edge of the bed. "I think," I said, grabbing his hands and pulling myself to my feet. "I'd like to take a shower now."

An hour later, exhausted, I climbed back into bed. Wearing clean pajamas.

"Need anything?" Don asked.

"Just some sleep."

"I'll be downstairs. Ring the bell if you need me."

I frowned. What bell? He picked up a small brass bell with a red satin ribbon from the nightstand and shook it. "This one. It's been here since Sunday. I told you about it, but you probably don't remember."

"I don't. But thanks."

He tucked the comforter around me. "Sweet dreams."

I watched him cross the room and disappear down the stairs. Then I closed my eyes and snuggled under the covers. I was almost asleep before I realized the sheets on the bed were fresh. I smiled to myself. It was nice having someone to take care of me.

Don insisted on staying with me until the weekend or until I got my strength back, whichever came last, he said. I wasn't in a hurry for him to leave. But I was in a hurry to get well. It was getting boring lying around all day. I started a couple of games of Scrabble with some Facebook friends. I downloaded Words with Friends on my Kindle and began a few games there too. But none of my opponents were online all day like I was. That was probably for the best because thinking wore me out. Between games and soup, I slept a lot. By Friday, I was getting antsy and driving Don nuts with my whining.

"Here." Don handed me my laptop and a flash drive. I was ensconced on the sofa, where I'd spent the past two days. "I've written the first three chapters. Read them over and weave your magic."

"Magic." I snorted. "If I ever had any, it's gone now."

"We all go through dry spells, Melody. Just keep believing in yourself. You've had a traumatic couple of years."

I opened the laptop and keyed in my password.

"Just so you know. I did try." I opened my Work-In-Progress folder, clicked on a Word document, and turned the screen so Don could see.

"This is the stupidest story," he read. "How can I even think I'm a writer? I'm kidding myself!" He lowered himself beside me. "That's it? Three sentences?"

I shrugged. "They say when you've hit The Wall to write anything that comes to mind. I did." I turned the screen my way, highlighted my inspiring words, and punched the Delete key. Then I plugged in the flash drive.

"I'll see what I can do." I opened the folder marked "Melody to read." I clicked on "Chapter 1" and began reading. "Don't you have something to do besides dance attendance on me?"

He grinned and pushed himself to his feet. "I'm going up to the farmhouse for a bit. I'll be back at noon to make lunch. That'll give you a couple of hours."

He snatched his jacket from the coat tree and thrust his arms through the sleeve. Charlie pranced between the sofa and the door, her stubby tail wagging away, overjoyed to be going outside.

"Wait," I said as he slid open the front door. "Can you get me a tablet and pen? The ones on my work desk. Upstairs."

"Yes, dear." He took the circular stairs two at a time.

I was scribbling notes on chapter two when someone rapped on the door. I looked up and saw a man with a dark beard and knit hat peering through the glass. Don had left the blinds open. My heart jumped into my throat until I recognized the piercing eyes. Frank! Er . . . Jake. When was I going to get the name right? I placed the laptop on the coffee table and flung the blanket aside.

"Haven't seen you out and about since Saturday night." He stepped into the living room. "The weather's been nice, and I see your Explorer hasn't been moved."

He was as bad as Bertha, but her motives were purely nosey. *Jake* was keeping tabs on me for more nefarious reasons. He gave me the creeps. "I've been sick," I said, suddenly feeling weak. "I'm still not up to par. Mind if I sit down?"

He leaned toward me and studied my face. "You do look peaked." His eyes scanned me from head to bare toes and back to my face. "Looks like you must have had it bad. Your clothes are hanging off you."

I made my way back to the sofa and eased myself onto the cushions. Jake followed me and lowered himself beside me.

"You didn't feel good Saturday night when I dropped you off. I could tell. The way you brushed me off when I tried to kiss you good night. Your face looked a little flushed even then." He stretched out his legs, his boots dripping snow on the braided rug beneath the coffee table.

"Come to think of it, I was feeling a bit queasy, but I thought it was the hamburger." Just thinking of the grease unsettled my stomach.

"Yeah, I came to check on you late Sunday afternoon, but that Don guy's truck was parked in your driveway. I didn't want to bother you. I figured you were writing."

Was I supposed to correct him? He was fishing for information. Did he think I was stupid not to notice? Well, let him fish all he wanted. He wasn't going to get even a nibble. I blinked at him innocently and forced a smile.

"Thanks so much. You are a dear. It's nice to know someone's looking out for me."

"I'm not the only one. That guy's truck never left your driveway all week, night or day." He smirked. "I figured you two must be having one heck of a session."

I stiffened. He wasn't just fishing. He was letting me know he had been watching me.

"Oh, yeah, it was just great, if you want to call puking your guts out and having a temperature of a hundred and four degrees for three days straight fun." I eyed him with fake concern. "You *did* get your flu shot, didn't you?" I pointed to the used tissues lying in a pile on the coffee table beside my laptop. "I'm still contagious, you know."

He shifted away from me. "No, you're not. You're only contagious the first day or so. You look like you're on the mend."

He didn't sound so sure.

"I looked it up." My voice was still hoarse. "I research everything. A person is contagious a day before symptoms appear—and you were with me Saturday night—and up to a week after becoming sick. It hasn't been a week."

Shortly after that, he left. In rather a hurry, I thought.

CHAPTER TWENTY-TWO

When I told Don about Frank's visit, he agreed with me. "He's letting you know you're being watched. I don't like this."

"What did you find when you searched his cabin Saturday night?"

We were sitting at the breakfast bar, enjoying a late lunch. He munched on a chicken salad sandwich, while I sipped tea and nibbled on toast.

"Nothing besides the usual stuff. He hides his tracks well."

"What about the property around the cabin?"

"Struck out there too."

"How on earth were you able to search his cabin without leaving tracks in the snow?"

He smiled. "That's classified."

"It is not. Come on, tell me."

He tapped my forehead. "Think, Melody. How would you do it?"

He'd been trying to get me to think like a mystery writer, but I was proving to be a slow learner.

"You roped down from the trees?"

He shook his head and laughed. "You watch too much TV."

Now it was my turn to shake my head. "I don't watch TV. I got sick of the programming years ago. I just watch movies now. The Hallmark Channel. And NCIS. And baseball."

"Then you watch TV."

"Not as much as I used to. And not at all since I moved up here. I've yet to subscribe to a satellite service. That's the only option on this mountain, except an old-fashioned antenna. Now there's an idea. I've got a new TV. Garrett bought it for me. And I read in *Consumer Reports* that new TVs—how can I say this so it makes sense? I can

214 · MICHELE HUEY

use an antenna with a new TV and save money on a television service provider. But I don't know if I'd be able to get The Weather Channel. I've missed it."

He sighed. "Melody, you're trying to sidetrack me."

I nodded.

"How would you not leave tracks?" he probed.

I thought. And thought. Then shrugged. "By stepping in his tracks and the tire tracks?"

He grinned. "Bingo."

"That's not very imaginative. Or exciting."

"But it was effective."

"Wait! What if he has surveillance cameras like you put up here?"

"He doesn't."

"Are you sure?"

He raised his eyebrows and gave me a do-I-look-like-I-don't-know-what-I'm-doing look.

I sighed. "Are you sure Jake is Frank Nooley?"

"Yes. The prints checked out."

"Did you find any other prints? I mean, besides those of the previous owners? I mean, anything pertaining to the case?"

He grinned. "Now you sound like a cop. Good girl. Actually, yes. Stephanie's. Why the confused look?"

"Have they ever been arrested or anything? No? Then how were you able to identify their prints?"

"We have our ways."

"In other words, 'think like a cop, Melody.' All right, I'm thinking."

I reached down to take a bite of my toast but discovered my plate was empty. I put two more slices of bread in the toaster oven and set the timer.

"You're getting your appetite back. Good."

"You could have gotten their prints from their vehicles, or places of work, or places of residence." The timer dinged. I slathered real butter on the hot toast and sprinkled on cinnamon sugar. "It could have been any one of a million and one ways. Like you said, you cops have your methods."

"By the way, Stephanie was working at the bank as a part-time trainee when you and your husband took out the home equity loan."

"I'll bet it was Stephanie who fudged the estimated value of the house. I can see Paul orchestrating that, giving her time off from the trucking company so she could get her foot in the door at the bank."

"Why didn't you recognize her then?"

"I didn't go to the bank when we took out the loan. Paul brought all the papers home and told me where to sign." I held up my hand. "Stupid. Naïve. I know. But I was on deadline, and he knew that when I was in the middle of writing a book, I lived in the world I created. You know about that."

A sudden fear struck me. "What if they know you're still a cop? They know you're an ex-cop because it's right on the dust jackets of your books in your bio and on your website. What if they suspect you're hanging close to me so you can catch them?"

The kettle whistled. I opened the tea tin, which I kept on the breakfast bar, and blindly grabbed a bag and plunked it in my cup, avoiding Don's eyes.

"Is that what you think?" he asked softly. I felt his gaze on me.

My cheeks burned. "That just popped out."

I slid off the stool but tripped over Rascal, who'd been lying at my feet. Don reached out and caught me before I fell. His arms slipped around me, pulling me close. The musky scent of his cologne sent a thrill through me. I didn't care if that was the only reason he was staying close to me. As long as he stayed close. I rested my head on his shoulder. The kettle screamed.

"It doesn't matter." I slipped my arms around his waist.

He cupped his forefinger under my chin. My eyes met his.

"Doesn't it?" he whispered.

"No. Yes." I pushed away from him. "The whistle's kettling. I don't want to burn another kettle dry."

With trembling hands I poured my tea and put the kettle back on the burner. Would my emotions ever settle down? Skirting Don, I carried my cup into the living room and sank onto the sofa. A low fire burned in the hearth.

Don followed me and knelt before me, his deep blue eyes probing mine. He's not Paul, I told myself. Paul never took care of me when I was sick. Paul took off and let me suffer through it. Don never left my side, cleaned up my puke, swabbed my fevered forehead, fed me ice chips, emptied the bucket. That's going far beyond the call of duty. I desperately wanted to believe in the goodness of this man. I *needed* to believe.

"Don," I said, dipping the tea bag in the steaming water and burning my fingers. "I'm thankful you've been here this past week. You've taken good care of me." I turned my head so he wouldn't see me blinking back tears. "We were supposed to be a writing team. That's all. You said yourself Cassie told you the publisher wanted us to work together. It was just a coincidence that you were investigating my husband. Right?"

When Don didn't say anything, I turned to him. The expression on his face was awful. Like there was something he had to say but didn't want to say it.

"Melody," he began, softly.

My heart sunk. The toast I'd eaten suddenly turned into a cold, hard lump in my stomach. The room spun. My fists clenched. My heart stopped for a nanosecond. I inhaled sharply.

I held up my hand. "Don't. Don't say it. Please."

He pulled my hand down, clasping it in both of his, caressing it with his thumbs.

"I was the one who arranged for the publisher to team us up. For the very reason you stated. To get close to you to find the money. And catch the embezzlers. Cassie knew nothing about it."

I yanked my hand back. "Go away. Leave me alone."

"I can't."

"I can take care of myself. You don't have to be my shadow. You can keep an eye on things from the farmhouse." Bitter tears coursed down my cheeks. "Just stay away from me."

"I can't stay away from you."

"Because I'm a suspect?"

"No." He framed my face with his hands, his thumbs caressing my cheeks. "Because I've fallen in love with you."

I should have known. Should have seen it. I wrote scenarios like this, for crying out loud! Yet I couldn't see it in my own life. Couldn't believe it was true. I was ready to swoon in his arms, as per my romance scenes, but his phone decided it was the right time to buzz. He took the call in the kitchen. All I heard were a few grunts and an "Okay, thanks."

"That was Virelle, wasn't it? Is she back from Mexico?" I asked when he returned and sat down beside me on the sofa. "What did she find out?"

He twiddled with the phone and then slipped it into his shirt pocket.

"According to the police and the funeral director, the man who fell to his death from the balcony and the body that was cremated *was* Paul."

"How can you be sure?"

"Virelle talked to several people at the resort, but no one remembers Paul. And the identification on the body was Paul's."

"Didn't they compare the information on his driver's license with the body? Picture, eye color, height?"

"They had no reason to. And . . . he hit the pavement face down."

My stomach lurched. "So there wasn't much left to identify him with."

"I'm sorry, Melody."

"Too bad they didn't run a DNA test."

"Again, they had no reason to. It wasn't a suspicious death."

"Speaking of DNA, have you gotten the results from the hammer? Was Devon Grove's DNA on it?"

"We're hoping it comes back next week."

"Why is it taking so long?"

"Because our labs are backlogged months. We're lucky they're rushing this one through."

I snorted. "You call a month rushing."

"Yes. Sadly."

I wanted to get back to the "I've fallen in love with you," but the magic of the moment was gone. Suddenly, I felt drained. I stood and headed for the stairs.

"I'm going to take a nap. You don't have to stay. I know you have things to do at the farmhouse. I'll be all right." A vision of Frank's piercing eyes passed through my mind. I shuddered. "Lock the door behind you. I'm sure you had an extra key made."

"Yes, I did. But I'm not leaving."

I put my foot on the first step and gripped the handrail, hoping I had the energy to climb the stairs. All I wanted was to crawl into my bed, pull the comforter over my head, and escape into sleep.

"Melody?"

I stopped.

"Ring the bell if you need anything."

Could I really believe in this man? I wanted to. Oh, how I wanted to.

It was dark when I awoke. The bedside lamp cast a soft glow through the loft. The wall heater was burning. I sniffed. Supper wasn't chicken soup. I smelled something tomatoey. Not spicy. I rolled on my side, blinking the sleep out of my eyes. What time was it? I glanced at the numbers glowing red on the alarm clock on the nightstand. Eight o'clock! I'd slept six hours. The last thing I remembered was looking at the time, telling myself I'd get up in an hour, no more than two. I shoved the covers aside. I didn't want to get up. I was still tired. But I was hungry. And whatever Don was cooking smelled good. Really good.

I pushed my feet into my moccasins and stood. Well, tried to stand. A wave of dizziness swept over me, and I plopped back down on the pillows. Don. Something churned in my stomach. Pieces of memory surfaced, hazy, just out of reach. I squeezed my eyes shut, trying to remember. What was it? Relax, I told myself. Don't try to think. Let it surface on its own.

Then I remembered: Don said he loved me. Warm honey coursed through me. But on its heels came dread. Unbelief. Distrust. The flotsam and jetsam of the wreckage of my life with Paul.

Oh, God, I created some of that wreckage when I turned my back on you. I'm sorry. I want to believe Don. But I can't just yet. Help me. Please.

I lay there with my eyes closed, listening to the fire crackling in the hearth downstairs, Charlie lapping water from her bowl, Don tapping at his laptop's keyboard. Sounds of a home—a contented, settled life.

Who can separate us from the love of Christ?

Why did that particular verse pop into my mind? I reached for Sonny's Bible, which I kept on the nightstand, and opened it to the verse he'd written there so many years ago. To the words I'd read so many times that I knew them by heart. Words that gave me the answer I needed. I was loved. By God. And by the man downstairs. Believing was a choice. And I chose to believe that Don loved me.

And I knew, as I'd known from the moment I opened my eyes to Camo Man that first day, I loved him too.

I tried to stand again, but the room whirled around me. Lowering myself to the bed, I reached for the nightstand and rang the bell.

Supper consisted of homemade tomato soup and doodles, a dumpling-like concoction Don made from eggs and flour and dropped in the simmering soup, and grilled cheese sandwiches.

"I can't believe you made this delicious soup from tomato juice." The blisters inside my mouth had just about healed, and I was ready to expand my menu from chicken soup and vegetable broth and toast.

We ate in comfortable silence, the words spoken earlier riding a silent current between us. He'd said he loved me. Why would he tell me that if it weren't true? When I knew he'd set the whole thing up, I was ready to throw him out. But how would I have found out if he hadn't told me? And the look in his eyes . . . Was I seeing what I wanted to see or was it really there? When he helped me downstairs I thought I knew for sure he loved me. But I'd just been very sick. I was still fatigued. This wasn't the time to try to figure things out.

"I want to go to town tomorrow for some groceries," I said when we settled on the sofa with our after-dinner tea.

He looked at me. "I'll take you."

"No. I need to go by myself. I need some space, Don. I'm not used to having someone around 24-7. I'm used to spending my time alone."

"Then I'll go home tomorrow."

I inhaled sharply. "Home? To Erie?" I wanted him out from under foot, but not that far.

"The farmhouse is home now."

"Did you sell your place in Erie?"

"Not yet."

We watched the fire lick the logs in the hearth.

"What I said about wanting to be alone. I didn't mean—"

"Don't worry about it. I understand." He gathered up the teacups and stood. "Why don't you get ready for bed? I'll clean up and bunk on your sofa again tonight. I'll go home in the morning. Anne and the girls will be up Sunday afternoon. I need to get the farmhouse ready."

Sadness seeped through me. I wanted him to stay. Forever.

CHAPTER TWENTY-THREE

The raucous buzzing of a chain saw woke me up on Saturday morning. I slipped out of bed and padded to the French doors. The condensation on the bottom of each of the panes of glass had frozen, but using my hand, I cleared a section of window and peered out over the porch roof. Someone was cutting up my dreaming tree! I grabbed my robe and hustled down the stairs.

"What do you think you're doing?" I yelled out the back door.

The man wielding the saw didn't hear me over the racket, so I thrust my feet into a pair of boots by the back door and hurried out. The morning was frigid, the sky clear as I stomped through the frosty grass of the backyard. While I'd been sick, the weather had warmed up enough to melt the snow and ice.

I stopped about six feet from him and waved my arms. "Hey! You! Hey!"

He straightened up, turned the saw off, and peered at me through his safety goggles.

"What are you doing?"

"What does it look like I'm doing? I'm getting rid of this tree."

"Who gave you permission?"

A puzzled look crossed his face. "This is the Harmon place, right?"

"I'm Melody Harmon, and this is my property. That's my tree you're cutting up. And I didn't give you permission."

He put the saw down, yanked off his leather gloves, and pulled a folded paper out of the breast pocket of his brown, insulated coveralls. An orange patch above the pocket read "Buggsy's Tree Service."

"I got orders to haul this thing out of here." He pulled down his goggles, letting them dangle around his neck.

"Well, you didn't get them from me. Let me see that."

He pulled the paper away from my outstretched hands. "Says here a Don Bridges called and asked for it to be removed. Wanted the limbs cut off and stacked in the woods behind the outhouse, and the trunk left intact."

"He can't do that! That's my property. What's your name?"

"Buggsy."

"Take a coffee break, Buggsy. I'll be right back."

I stomped into the cottage and punched speed dial. No service. Great. I went back outside. Don was talking to Buggsy.

"Mr. Bridges," I said, storming up to them. "A word with you, please. Now."

Don held up his index finger in a just-a-minute gesture. He didn't even look at me.

"I'm freezing out here," I said.

"Then go inside."

I stomped my boot on the hard ground. "Just who do you think you are, ordering my tree to be removed? You had no right. You—"

He looked at me then, a soft mellow look in his eyes. "Melody, I've got this covered. Go inside before you turn into the abominable snow woman."

"But—"

He pointed to the back door. "I'll be in in a minute and explain."

"You better." I huffed off.

Inside, I yanked my boots off and dropped them on the mat. Tea. I needed a cup of tea. My favorite mug was on the breakfast bar with a Plantation Mint tea bag and a slip of paper beside it. I snatched up the note.

"Good morning, love," I read. "Breakfast casserole on the stove. Enjoy. Will be back around nine with a surprise for you."

Some surprise. I pulled back the aluminum foil from the top of the casserole dish, allowing the aroma of cheddar cheese and sausage to escape. My stomach rumbled, finally a healthy hungry. The kettle was still warm, so I made my tea then helped myself to two squares of the casserole. I'd just settled myself on the sofa with my plate when I heard the back door slide open and then close. The chain saw started back up again, reigniting my anger. I put the plate on the coffee table and charged into the kitchen.

"Just what do you think you're doing? Stop him!"

"Melody, sit down."

"Don't order me around. That's my tree, my dreaming tree. And you ordered it cut up."

"No, I didn't. They're not going to cut it up, only the limbs. Which was what you were trying to do last Saturday. What were you planning to do with it?"

I sank onto the sofa, blinking back tears. "I don't know."

"Did you read the instructions I gave them?"

I nodded numbly.

"Then you know I want the trunk left intact."

"Why? What good is it now?"

He sat beside me, putting his arms around me.

"You'd be surprised."

I buried my face in his soft green chamois shirt, mourning the loss of my tree and all it meant. He rocked me gently, his chin on the top of my head.

"What are they going to do with it?" I asked when I trusted my voice not to quiver.

"Do you trust me?"

I stared into the fire. "What kind of question is that?"

He cupped my face in his hands and turned my head gently. His eyes searched mine.

"Do you trust me?" he repeated.

Did I trust him?

"A simple yes or no will do," he whispered.

I shook my head. "It's not simple."

"No, it's not," he agreed. "But either you do or you don't. There's no middle ground. And you can't sit on the fence."

Did I trust him?

"Yes," I said, looking into the depths of those blue eyes. "I trust you."

But don't let me down. Don't betray that trust.

I left to buy some groceries in Marysville before Buggsy was done. I didn't want to watch or hear him hauling my tree away. Don had started my Explorer and let it warm up while he scraped the windshield and side windows.

"You'd better get a new battery for that thing," he told me as I was finalizing my shopping list.

"Can't that one last another month or so?" Until my house sold, I could barely afford the essentials, like groceries and electricity. Filling the propane tank had eaten up a big chunk of my funds.

"Only if you don't plan to use it too much. I'll be just up the road most of the time. So you can call me if you need me."

Oh, I need you.

"*Most* of the time? I'm sorry. I don't mean to sound like a clinging vine. It's just that I've gotten used to you being around, and I kind of like it."

"You're no clinging vine, Melody. You're an independent woman who's fought tooth and nail to survive. Besides, I like being around. I'm the clinging vine."

He pulled me close and brushed his lips against my forehead. I melted. *I've fallen in love with you.* I wanted to hear the words again.

"Don . . ."

Then his phone chirped. Again.

"Don't answer it," I said. "Kiss me instead."

He pulled the phone from his pocket and tossed it onto the sofa. The kiss was all I'd dreamed it would be. And more.

I stopped at Willie's to pick up my mail on the way home. I had a street address—12100 Getaway Mountain Road—but couldn't see the expense of a rural mailbox, so I hadn't signed up for mail delivery. Besides, I'd reasoned, it would get me out of the cottage.

Camp St. Jude, as my mom had called my writing retreat before it *was* my writing retreat, was a place to get away from the world. Even my dad carried a poem in his wallet he'd cut out from a newspaper about a cabin in the mountains "where I go when things perplex me, where I seek to understand. . . ." When he died, I took the tattered, yellowed paper and slipped it into my own wallet.

"Melody Joyner, you look like death warmed over!" Willie bellowed when I stepped into the store.

"I just got over a really nasty flu bug. It knocked the stuffing out of me. I was down almost a week."

"I wondered why you hadn't picked up your mail. I figured you'd be in right after the storm. I know you aren't afraid of bad weather. Except ice."

"You got that right." I inserted my key into my PO box, which was stuffed full.

"It didn't take long for the junk mail to catch up with me." I rifled through the stack, separating the postal sheep from the goats. Into the trash bin, ripped in half, went all but the electric bill, an envelope from the credit union, a couple of magazines, a card from Aunt Peg, a postcard from Garrett, a reminder of my hair appointment this coming Tuesday, a thick envelope from the realtor, and a security-tint envelope with my name and address scrawled across the front and no return address. Those I stuffed into my tote bag.

The bell on the door rang as an elderly woman stepped in. I recognized her as one of the resident villagers, Mabel Barnes.

"Weren't you just in here this morning, Mabel?" Willie asked her.

"Did you hear about that big storm coming?" She sounded out of breath. "They're saying it's going to be a bad one—worse than the one we got last week."

"Can't say I have," Willie answered. "When's it supposed to hit?"

"The Weather Channel says Wednesday or Thursday, but they don't always get it right. At any rate, I thought you'd want to know so you can stock up on stuff."

Another storm? I made a mental pre-storm things-to-do list.

"Oh, Melody, dear!" Mabel chortled. "I hear you've become a year-round resident."

I smiled. "Yes, I have, Mrs. Barnes."

"Oh, call me Mabel, dear. I do hope this means another book is forthcoming. I loved your last one, *Love Me Forever*. Or was it *Never Say Die*? No matter." She waved her wrinkled hand in front of her thin, creased face. "I've read both of them. In fact, I've read all of your books. I'm a big fan, you know."

"Thank you, Mabel. That means a lot to me."

So, not everyone thought my writing had descended into writer's purgatory. Maybe I didn't need Don to resurrect my career.

"Except the last couple," Mabel said with a frown. "The writing hasn't been your usual. But what you've been through, with your husband's sudden death and all. No wonder."

"Is there anything I can get for you, Mabel?" Willie asked.

She gave him a puzzled look. "Get for me? What did I come here for? Oh, yes, the storm. I came to tell you about the winter storm."

"Thank you, my dear," Willie said. "I don't know what I'd do without you. I'll be sure to stock up."

"Oh, I almost fergot," Willie said after Mabel left. "There's a package come for you yesterday that didn't fit in your box with all the other stuff. I put it in the back. Let me go get it."

While Willie fetched my package, I checked the weather forecast on my cell phone.

"Here it is." Willie plunked a thick, white, Priority Mail envelope on the counter. I didn't recognize the handwriting, but I did the return address—my house in Greensburg. It had been postmarked on Thursday. Maybe Anne had sent Paul's flash drive. But why would she use my house address as the return address? Curious, I pulled the flap up and peered inside. What I saw made my head spin.

"Melody, you okay? Your face is whiter than a bleached undershirt."

I stuffed the envelope into my tote bag and forced a smile. "I'm fine, Willie. It's just been a long day shopping, and I'm still getting over the flu."

He nodded. "Ain't up to snuff yet. I understand. But here—" he reached beneath the counter and pressed two chocolate bars with almonds into my hands—"Don't want to forget your treat."

Don wasn't at the cabin when I backed up to the front deck. I breathed a sigh of relief. I hadn't decided what to do about the package. Then again, it would be nice to have someone else to haul the groceries in. I hated shopping, and I especially hated unloading groceries. I sometimes pulled around to the back deck because it was closer to the kitchen.

But after a day of above freezing temperatures, the ground was sure to be too soft. I didn't like leaving ruts in the yard. Which reminded me—was Buggsy able to haul the tree away? I stepped around to the back of the cabin. It was gone. Sorrow—intense, pervading—filled my soul. Gone. Like the dreams I'd dreamed sitting in its branches.

"Need some help unloading those groceries?"

I jumped. "Fr—Jake. I didn't hear you."

"I was out for a walk in the woods and decided to stop in and see how you're doing. You looked peaked the last time I saw you." He leaned toward me. "You still do."

"I probably overdid it today. Cabin fever, I guess, after the storm and being sick all week. I just had to get out."

"You look like you could use a hand. Come on, I'll haul your bags into the kitchen while you make yourself a cup of tea."

A shiver ran up my spine. I didn't want this character within six feet of me. I took a deep breath and smiled at him.

"Sure," I said, "why not?"

I hoped Don was still monitoring the bugs he'd planted in my cottage.

By the time Frank-Jake left, I was wiped out. I probably should have given myself an extra couple of days to recover. But more than that, the tension of watching my every word, my every move, when Frank was around was draining. I'd never think of him as Jake, and more than once I found "Frank" on the tip of my tongue. Not smart.

He'd offered to help me put away the groceries, but I'd declined, citing my exhaustion. And I didn't have to fake that. I wasn't cut out for this cloak and dagger stuff. I locked the door behind him and watched as he disappeared up the road into the early winter darkness. I stepped to the smoke detector.

"Don? Are you there? I . . . just wanted to tell you I miss you."

And I'm afraid to stay here alone tonight.

"I'm going to put away the groceries, build up the fire, take a shower, heat up some of that wonderful chicken soup, and go to bed."

I love you.

I closed my eyes and pictured him listening. "Ten-four and over and out and . . ." I swallowed, then whispered, "I love you."

When I settled on the sofa with my soup, I pulled out my cell phone to check my messages. The screen was black. I'd forgotten to recharge the battery. I plugged it in, but the battery was completely dead. I'd have to wait until it recharged some before I could use it. By then, I figured, I'd be too tired.

I ate my soup and then put the kettle on for tea. I was reaching for my tea tin when I spied the tote bag on the chair. The envelope. I felt the blood drain from my face. I checked to make sure all the blinds were closed then pulled the Priority Mail envelope out. Knowing what was inside made my insides quiver.

I took the envelope to the living room and sank onto the sofa. With trembling fingers, I pulled out the single bundle of one-hundred dollar bills. My head swam. With it was a folded piece of paper and a snapshot. I glanced at the photo and then opened the note.

You have until the 22nd to get the money—ALL of it—or something tragic will happen. Do not tell your boyfriend anything. We are watching.

I held the picture closer. My breath caught. I recognized the blonde woman and the two little girls playing in the front yard of a two-story brick home. I'd seen photos of the girls on Don's refrigerator. The picture was of Anne, Kadie, and Hannah.

A sharp rapping on the front door made me jump. "Who is it?" I croaked, stuffing the money, the snapshot, and the note back into the envelope and shoving it beneath the sofa cushion.

"Who do you think?" Don's voice came through the glass.

I stumbled to the door, unlocked it, and slid it open. He stood there, hands jammed in his jeans pockets, hair tousled, eyes searching mine.

"Just checking to make sure you're okay. I could stay another night, if you want."

I shook my head. "I . . . I'm fine. Just really tired. In fact, I'm just going up to bed."

He leaned in and gave me a kiss. "Are you sure?"

I swallowed. "Yes, I'm sure."

CHAPTER TWENTY-FOUR

I had less than a week. How much money did they expect? Did they—I was sure Frank and Stephanie were the "we" in the note—know about the money I'd already found? Maybe I should tell Don. He'd know what to do. But could I risk anything happening to Anne and the girls?

They had to know how much Paul embezzled. After all, they'd helped him to steal it. How much of it had he spent or gambled away? They'd murdered Devon Grove. They wouldn't hesitate to kill again. But why had they waited almost two years after Paul's death to come after the money?

Think.

Don's investigation. He was getting close, and they knew it was a matter of time before they'd be arrested. Could I somehow get back the money I'd turned over? How? I couldn't tell Don. But how would they know if I did? *We are watching.* I shivered. Don said there were no cameras but the ones he'd put up. But about bugs? A tiny microphone could be hidden anywhere. Like in a smoke detector. What if they'd taken out the ones Don had put in? I shook my head. Don would know, and he'd come to check to see why they weren't working.

I had less than a week. And with a winter storm coming. I doubted if the money, if indeed there was more, was hidden here at the cottage or the house in Greensburg. Don had searched thoroughly, and he knew what to look for. My thoughts swirled and swirled around like a merry-go-round out of control. Where would Paul have hidden the money? Where? I couldn't think. All I could see in my mind was the snapshot of Anne and the girls.

I threw back the covers. I'd call Garrett. No. I didn't have a strong enough cell signal for a voice call. I'd text him. I glanced at the time. After three a.m.! He'd be sleeping and wouldn't get my message until morning. What if they had my phone tapped?

This was ridiculous. I was being paranoid. Frank and Stephanie were human beings—outlaws. They didn't have the resources Don and the state police did. They weren't omniscient and they weren't omnipresent. But they wanted me to think so.

I rolled over and spotted Sonny's Bible. Frank and Stephanie were neither omnipresent nor omniscient, but I knew someone who was. I grasped the leather-bound book and pulled it to me, holding it close to my heart under the covers and mouthing the verses I knew by heart:

If God is for us, who can be against us? . . . Who shall separate us from the love of Christ? Shall trouble or hardship or persecution or famine or nakedness or danger or sword? . . . No, in all these things we are more than conquerors through him who loved us. For I am convinced that neither death nor life, neither angels nor demons, neither the present nor the future, nor any powers, neither height nor depth, nor anything else in all creation, will be able to separate us from the love of God that is in Christ Jesus our Lord.

"In *all* these things," I whispered to myself. "I am *more* than a conqueror! *More* than a conqueror. With Your help, Lord, I will overcome."

Exhaustion finally took over, and I closed my eyes.

My sleep was so long and so deep I didn't even hear Don come and go on Sunday morning. I'd planned to go to church with him today, since we'd both missed last Sunday because I was sick. I lay in bed for several minutes. Slowly pieces of yesterday replayed in my mind like a kaleidoscope: the chainsaw hacking up my dreaming tree, Frank-Jake popping up to help me unload groceries, the Priority Mail package.

In my mind I saw the mustard-yellow strap, Benjamin Franklin's face, the sloppily scrawled note, the picture of Anne and the girls. I'd fallen asleep with the threat heavy on my mind and heart. It was no lighter this morning. Friday. I had until Friday, or they would hurt Anne or one of the girls, or all of them. How much did they know about them? Did they know about Hannah's CF? I had no doubt they would kidnap one of the girls to hold as ransom until they got what they wanted.

If they knew Don took the cash we'd already found—three-quarters of a million dollars—they wouldn't hesitate to use Don's love against him. I don't think they cared about Hannah's illness or what it could mean. No, wait, if they knew, they could use that as leverage: Kidnapping Hannah would bring about the quickest results. I had to warn them. Tell them to go into hiding.

Did Frank and Stephanie know Anne was working on getting into Paul's laptop and flash drive? Paul was obsessive about keeping accurate records of everything, our possessions, serial numbers, pictures of our stuff for the insurance company in case of fire or natural disaster . . . I could still hear him lecturing me about not keeping a file of such data for my "business-related expenses."

"It's just stuff, Paul. It can be replaced."

"That's right," he answered, "with the money we get from the insurance company when we prove our losses."

I knew better than to argue with him. Paul was always right. So I let him snap away to his heart's content. That probably was on the flash drive—proof of our prosperity.

Goal-oriented, meticulous Paul. He was smart, planned ahead, hid his addiction, but in the end it all came to nothing. Because he hadn't planned on dying before he could finish what he'd started.

Where would he hide bundles of money?

This was driving me crazy. So was Rascal, who knew I was awake and was chewing on my hair—her way of telling me to get out of bed and fill her food and water bowls. I threw back the covers to a warm loft. The propane wall heaters weren't on. Don knew I didn't like to run them when I was here by myself sleeping, so he must have used his key to get in and get a fire going in the fireplace.

Downstairs, I found a note on the breakfast bar. *Sleep, my love. I'll be back after church. With lunch. Don.*

I put the kettle on for tea and reheated a small piece of leftover breakfast casserole. But my stomach protested the slight spicy smell when I went to take that first bite. I had to eat. I needed energy. The BRAT diet—bananas, rice, applesauce, and toast—would satisfy a hungry, but slightly nauseated stomach. Good thing I'd bought bananas, unsweetened applesauce, and instant brown rice yesterday. I smiled in spite of everything. I was going to cook myself some breakfast. If I didn't burn the water first.

After breakfast I checked my text messages, my phone battery now completely recharged after being plugged in all night. Three from Garrett, two from Don, one from Cassie, one from Irene, and one from an "unknown caller."

Garrett had flown to DC and planned to be back on Monday, and then he'd drive to the cabin. Don wanted to know if I was up yet at 8:00 a.m. and to text him when I awoke. Cassie complained that I didn't answer my e-mails anymore and wanted to know the progress of the book.

Irene had a buyer interested, but only if the mortgage payments were caught up. Catch-22. I couldn't make the payments until I sold the house, and I couldn't sell the house until I made the payments.

There was ten thousand in cash under the sofa cushion. No one, except whoever sent it to me, knew I had it. If the winter storm held off until Wednesday, I could drive to Greensburg tomorrow, deposit the money in my credit union account, make the delinquent mortgage payments, and get back to the cabin before the first flake or ice pellet. I hit Reply. *Working on it. TTY 2morrow. In person.*

I clicked on the message from the unknown caller—and wish I hadn't. *Six days.*

I think better when I'm in motion, so I cleaned up the kitchen, made the bed, ran the vacuum, threw in a load of laundry, and scrubbed a clean bathroom. I was swabbing out the commode when I remembered where Paul had hidden the key to the first firebox. He'd been here at the cabin to hide the two stashes of cash. If he had another firebox hidden somewhere, he'd have hidden the key and would have felt safe concealing it in a picture frame. I rushed up the stairs to the loft, where I kept two framed photos: Garrett's high school graduation portrait and an eight-by-ten of Sonny in his dress blues. They hung on the wall above the log headboard on either side of the framed cross-stitch.

I hopped on the bed and pulled them off the wall. I'd used the adhesive picture-hanging strips rather than nails. I plopped on the bed and took apart Garrett's picture first. Nothing. Then Sonny's. Nothing. I blew out a breath. I'd thought for sure once Paul found a clever hiding place, he'd use it again. Maybe I missed something.

I checked both frames again, running my fingers along the inside of the wooden borders and the cardboard mounts. Nothing. I was putting the frames back together when my eye caught the cross-stitch: *To love and be loved is the greatest joy on earth.* Surely Paul wouldn't have hidden anything there. He hated it, mocked it for being corny and naïve—"Just like you, Melody. When are you going to stop living in that romantic world you make up? It's not real, you know." When had he become so cynical?

I reached for the cross-stitch. And found what I was looking for.

I stared at the silver key. It didn't look like the one for the lockbox we'd found in Garrett's baseball picture. It looked familiar. My wondering was interrupted by the sound of a motor shutting off, truck doors slamming, and voices. I glanced at the time. After one. Three dismantled frames were scattered across the top of my bed. Footsteps coming up the front steps. What to do? Boots stomping on the deck. I shoved the key between the pages of Sonny's Bible. A key turned in the front door lock. I gathered the frames and pictures in my arms.

What to do? The front door slid open. I yanked down the comforter and dumped the mess on the mattress.

"Melody?" Don's voice. "Sh! Girls. She's probably sleeping. Still getting over the flu. I told her not to do too much too soon, but you know women."

They giggled.

"Don't be too hard on her, Dad. It takes a lot to get a good woman down."

I already liked Anne, but I liked her even more now. The aroma of pizza wafted up to the loft. Lunch. I stood, bunching up the comforter over the dismantled frames. I'd take care of it later. I tousled my hair to make it look like I'd just gotten out of bed and headed for the stairs. Time to see if I could lie to Don and get away with it.

"You must have worn yourself out with all that cleaning this morning," Don said, helping himself to another two slices of pizza. We sat around the coffee table, Don and me on the sofa, Anne in the recliner, and the girls on the floor with Charlie.

"We walk in and see the vacuum cleaner left out, the bathroom lights all on, a pile of clothes in the laundry basket . . . I was beginning to think you were raptured and we were left behind."

The girls giggled.

"Grandpa!" Hannah said. "Be nice to Miss Melody. She's Garrett's mom."

"Thank you, Hannah." She was a slender child, with a shy smile, innocent blue eyes, and wispy blond hair held back in a ponytail with a bright-blue scrunchie. The whisper of dimples in her pale cheeks added to the charm of this sweet-natured, soft-spoken, six-year-old.

"When's he coming back?" Kadie asked. She was an older, heavier version of Hannah, but with darker, thicker blond hair, which tumbled about her shoulders in waves.

I glanced at Anne, whose cheeks were a rosy blush. I had the feeling both girls spoke their minds, Hannah in her soft-spoken way and Kadie in her outspoken one.

I was about to answer, but Anne beat me to it. "Tomorrow." So they were keeping in touch. This was good. Very good.

"We're baking cookies tomorrow, right, Grandpa?" Kadie said. "You promised."

"If your mom brought all the ingredients." Don raised his eyebrows at Anne, who nodded.

"I wouldn't dare forget," she said with a grin. "They've been pestering me all week."

"What kind are you baking?" I asked.

"You mean *kinds*, plural." Don laughed.

"That's right," Hannah piped up. "It's a family tradition. We always bake cookies the week before the week before Thanksgiving."

"To send to the troops," Kadie added. "Of course we have to save some for Grandpa and for ourselves."

"Wow," I said. "You must bake a lot of cookies."

"Uh-huh." Kadie's head bobbed up and down. "Chocolate chip— that's my favorite; oatmeal raisin—that's Grandpa's favorite, and sugar cookies—those are Hannah's favorite because she likes to make a mess."

Anne laughed. "Kadie's baking style is throw, mix, and plop— throw in the ingredients, mix it together, and plop it by heaping spoonsful on cookie sheets. That's why she's in charge of the oatmeal raisin and chocolate chips. Hannah's the artist in the family and loves cutting out different shapes and then designing them with different colored icing and sprinkles."

"What's your favorite kind of cookie to make, Miss Melody?" Hannah asked.

"I don't bake, honey."

"She burns water," Don said.

"Grandpa! You're teasing us again!" Kadie giggled.

Don shook his head. "I'm not pulling your leg." He nodded toward me. "Ask Miss Melody."

All four pairs of blue eyes focused on me.

I nodded. "I'm afraid that's true. I'm a kitchen klutz."

The girls giggled again. "What's a klutz?" Hannah asked.

"Someone who isn't very coordinated," Anne said. "But I'm sure that's an exaggeration."

Don told them about my most recent kettle-burning incident.

"Oh, my, Miss Melody, you're downright dangerous," a wide-eyed Hannah said.

"So that's why Garrett knows how to cook so well," Kadie said with confidence. "He would have starved if he didn't."

We all laughed.

"Honey," I said, "that's not far from the truth."

They wanted me to come to the farmhouse and help with the cookie-baking, but I begged off, citing my recent bout with the flu.

"I'm afraid I've used up my energy quota for the day," I told them.

"Take a nap," Don said before he left. "I'll be down this evening. With some cookies. What kind is your favorite?"

"Pumpkin cookies. My Aunt Peg makes them from pumpkin she grows in her garden. I used to help her."

His eyebrows rose. "She was taking a risk."

I smiled at the warm memory. "Aunt Peg loves taking risks. But I'd hardly call sprinkling in chocolate chips, raisins, and walnuts in batter a risk."

His lips brushed my forehead. "Sleep well, love. See you in a couple of hours."

I watched them drive away, love mingling with a growing fear and dread. I locked the door, closed the blinds, and went to the sofa to pull out the envelope with its deadly contents. But my fingers found nothing but crumbs. I yanked off the cushions, panic racing through me.

The bundle of money, the picture, the note, even the envelope, were all gone.

CHAPTER TWENTY-FIVE

I sank to the floor, bent over, and peered under the sofa. I couldn't tell if there was anything there, so I pushed it back. If there was anything under the sofa, it might be wedged between the floor and the black muslin that lined the bottom of the sofa. Lifting the sofa, one end at a time, I moved the furniture back—pens, highlighters, popcorn, crumbs, cat hair, a long-missing crochet hook, a penny, but no bundle of money, note, picture, or envelope.

Who could have taken it and when? I didn't dream it, did I? No, I distinctly recalled Willie plunking the envelope on the counter and me shoving it in my tote bag. Maybe I *thought* I stuffed it under the cushions and had put it in my tote bag instead. Or maybe I took it out from the sofa and put it somewhere safe. I didn't remember doing anything but shoving it under the cushions.

Where did I put my tote bag anyway? I thought I'd left it on the breakfast bar or hanging from one of the counter stools last night. Was it there this morning when I got up? I squeezed my eyes shut and tried to picture the scene when I came down the stairs. Yes, the brown-and-black bag, crafted of thick upholstery material as a gift from a Melanie Joy fan, had been hanging from the chair. It wasn't there now.

The cleaning spree. I must have hung it on the coat tree or shoved it in the closet in the spare room or taken it up to the loft. I only used it when I went shopping or to a book signing. I didn't do much of either lately.

I found the bag in the first place I looked—on the coat tree—its handles looped over my fleece moose coat. It was empty. I closed my eyes again, trying to remember if I'd cleaned it out before I hung it up. *I must be going crazy.* At least I would be by the time this was all over, either that or dead. My cell phone buzzed, indicating a missed call or text message. I pulled it out of my sweatpants pocket. Two text messages. One was from Don, the other from Garrett. I opened Garrett's first.

Will b home 2morrow. Flying into Latrobe, then driving 2 cabin. Good. He'd beat the storm. Which reminded me. I had to go online to The Weather Channel and check the updated forecast. But first, I clicked on Don's message. *What's all the racket? Ur supposed to be napping.* The bugs. Of course. How could I have forgotten? At least I knew they were still working and Frank and Stephanie hadn't found them. I texted back. *Lost something under sofa.* Not a lie. *Moved it back. What a mess! Will vacuum, then go 2 bed. Promise.* I added "XOXO" for good measure. Then I ran the vacuum.

Upstairs, I checked to make sure the key was still in the Bible—it was. I'd planned to reassemble the picture frames and hang them back up, and then do some research online, which included checking an updated weather forecast. But I was afraid the racket, even the noise of my fingers tapping on the keyboard, would incite another text from Don, asking me why I wasn't sleeping. So I popped in one of my favorite CDs, *The Sounds of the Rocky Mountains*, and turned it up so the music, which incorporated thunder, an elk bugling, a stream trickling down a mountainside, would drown out what I was really doing.

I reassembled the frames and hung them back up. Then I sifted through my jewelry box as quietly as I could, looking for the silver chain from the pendant watch Paul had given me on one of our first Christmases. He'd presented me with a wristwatch, but it went kerflooey, either gaining or losing time, when I wore it. The problem wasn't the watch—it was me. I'd never been able to wear wristwatches. I'd told him this when we were dating, but apparently he hadn't heard me, wasn't listening, or forgot. So he returned the wristwatch, telling them it was defective (when it was I who was defective, he told me), and brought home the pendant watch.

I slid the watch off the chain and slipped the key on, then hung it around my neck, tucking it beneath my top. *If anyone wants this key they'll have to kill me first.* When Don came later, I'd ask him if the surveillance cameras picked up anyone coming to my cabin when I was asleep last night.

Who could have taken the envelope? Who was able to get into my cabin? Don had a key. Paul had had a key, but Don changed the locks. I had keys to the new locks and hadn't put a spare in my outside hiding place. So if it hadn't been Don, it had to have been someone who could pick locks. Or stole one of the keys from my purse. Someone who knew when I'd be asleep. But I'd tossed and turned all night before falling asleep around three. So it had to have been between three a.m. and whenever I got up around ten. It could have been Don when he came to get me for church. Or Frank or Stephanie, but they'd come while it was still dark, before 7:00 a.m.

Or maybe one of the girls found it when they were playing with Rascal in the living room before we all sat down for pizza. No, they would have said something. And if it *had* been Don, why didn't he say something? Why hadn't I told Don?

This was driving me crazy. Who could I talk to? Who could I trust? I trusted Don but couldn't tell him anything because I didn't want to endanger his family.

I could trust Aunt Peg. And Garrett. But I couldn't call them. Besides the cell signal being too weak for voice calls, Don was listening, and so, I had a feeling, were Frank and Stephanie. I could, however, make the drive to Greensburg and back in a day. But I'd have to do it tomorrow if I wanted to get back before the storm hit. I was afraid, with my post-influenza energy level, the round trip would be too much. The three-hour drive *one-way* would be too much.

I checked the weather forecast. A winter storm watch was posted for Tuesday evening through Wednesday. A nasty system had paralyzed the Midwest, including New Mexico and Texas. It was now heading east, while another low-pressure system was sweeping down from Canada.

According to The Weather Channel, two scenarios were possible: The two systems would merge into one monster storm with snow, sleet, and freezing rain, or they would remain separate, both eventually tracking off the coast. The forecasters were leaning toward the systems merging.

How much snow? And how much ice? And exactly when?

I checked the time. I could drive to Greensburg tonight and stay at Aunt Peg's. I'd call Garrett from Aunt Peg's landline and tell him I had some important business to tend to. I had a hunch about the key around my neck.

I set the CD player to Repeat All and turned up the volume just a smidgeon. As I quietly packed my tote bag for an overnighter, I wondered when Don would realize he'd been duped. That I, Melody Harmon, a.k.a. Melanie Joy, the naïve, reclusive romance novelist whom he was trying to forge into a mystery writer, had given him the slip. I felt guilty, but I had to do this.

I left a note on the breakfast bar—a red herring, so to speak. *Don, Feeling antsy, so am making a quick run to Clarion for some things I need before the storm hits on Tuesday.* I checked the time. *It's almost four now. Should be back by eight. I didn't text you because I need some time alone. Love, M.*

Lord, forgive me for lying.

I backed out of the driveway onto the hardtop road and headed down the mountain. It was for Don I was doing this. To save Anne and Hannah and Kadie.

I'd shut off my cell phone before I left the cabin and had no intention of turning it on again. I had no idea whether Don or Frank or whoever was out to get me could track me through it. I pulled into Aunt Peg's driveway a little before seven.

She opened the door. "Melody! What on earth are you doing here?"

"Can I pull my Explorer into your barn?" I said, stepping in quickly.

Dressed in gray-polyester slacks and a soft-blue cashmere sweater, Aunt Peg nodded, but not before giving me a puzzled look.

I returned to a pot of hot tea and a bowl of steaming chicken soup waiting for me on the kitchen table. Exhausted after the drive and the tension of the past week, the past month, the past year, I plunked myself down, said grace, and then plunged my spoon into the broth, brimming with vegetables and chicken and noodles. Aunt Peg was not stingy when it came to making chicken soup. Or anything else for that matter.

She sat at the table across from me, studying me and sipping tea. "Have you been sick? You look like a skeleton."

"Remember that flu bug you and Uncle Butch had? It put me down for a week."

"I wish I could have been there to take care of you. To make you chicken soup. Instead you were all alone."

I smiled. "No, I wasn't. Remember Don Bridges?"

Her eyes widened. A trace of a grin tugged at her lips.

"He bought the farmhouse up the road. He's getting it ready for when his daughter and her two girls come for Thanksgiving. Since we're working on a novel together . . . we're . . . spending time together. When I got sick, he took care of me. His homemade chicken soup is good. Really good. But not as good as yours, of course."

"Of course." She leaned her elbows on the table, hands clasped together under her chin. "Going above and beyond the call of duty, I see."

Time to change the subject. "Where's Uncle Butch?" I slathered another slice of homemade bread with Aunt Peg's apple butter.

"At a hunting camp in Tionesta with a few of his hunting buddies. Bear season starts on Friday, and they wanted to have a few days to work on the cabin and scout the area." She poured more tea in my cup. "So what are you doing here? No phone call, no warning. You just show up at my door and ask to hide your SUV. Something's up."

Should I tell her? It sure would be nice to let someone else help shoulder the burden, the worry about what would happen if . . . a shiver ran through me. No, telling her might put her at risk too.

"You're still sick."

I shook my head. "I'm still a bit on the weak side."

"Then why didn't you stay at the cabin? It must be pretty important for you to make the long drive. How long are you staying?"

"Until tomorrow. There's a winter storm moving in—"

"I know. Remember? I'm a weather freak too." She tapped her thumbs against her teacup and studied me. "And I know you wouldn't have come without a good reason."

I put my soup spoon down. "Aunt Peg, I want to tell you, but . . . I can't. It would just . . . be best."

She nodded and patted my hand, keeping her warm one on my still cold one. "Whatever it is, Melody, know that I believe in you."

My eyes filled. I tried thank her, but the words wouldn't squeeze past the lump in my throat.

"Now," she said, gathering up the dirty dishes, "go up and take a nice, hot bubble bath. There's an aromatherapy candle in the guest bathroom and eucalyptus bubble bath. Eucalyptus relieves stress, you know. Then go to bed and get a good night's sleep. Oh, and there's eucalyptus pillow spray by the bed. Holler if you need anything. Or if you want to talk."

"Your landline. I have to call Garrett."

Her white brows arched. "This gets more intriguing by the minute."

But she didn't press me for details. *I believe in you.* I crossed the kitchen and gave her a hug. "You're the best, Aunt Peg. I don't know what I'd do without you."

I had Garrett's phone number in my address book, so I didn't have to turn on my phone to get it.

He answered right away. "Aunt Peg? What's up?"

"Garrett, it's me, Mom. Listen. I'm at Aunt Peg's. I have some business to tend to tomorrow. I should be done tomorrow afternoon. I'll meet you at the cabin. Don changed the locks, and I forgot to leave a key hidden, so you'll have to go to Don's if you get there before me. Anne and the kids are there."

"I know."

I smiled to myself.

"Do you want me to come to Aunt Peg's? Do you need me for anything?"

Yes, I want you to come to Aunt Peg's. And, yes, I need you. I'm so tired of being alone. But I couldn't risk it.

"No, I'm good. I'll see you tomorrow night. I'll come to Don's."

"Sounds good. See you then. Love you, Mom."

"I love you, too, Garrett."

Chalk up another person who believed in Melody. He didn't even ask why I was using Aunt Peg's phone, and he didn't probe me for details.

After a long soak in the claw-foot tub, I toweled off, slipped into my flannel jammies, and headed for bed. The room was the one I'd always stayed in—a spacious bedroom with a high ceiling and a brick fireplace. But instead of a hearth for burning wood, a gas fireplace had been installed and burned with a predictable flame. No cracking and popping or the smell of smoke.

The quilted comforter on the double four-poster bed, complete with a country-style canopy, had been turned down. A bar of chocolate with almonds lay on the pillow. On the nightstand was a cup of hot chocolate with whipped cream, a set of keys, and a note:

Melody, use my car tomorrow for your running around. Going to the church tomorrow to make nut roll. Will probably be gone when you get up. You know where everything is. Love you, Aunt Peg.

I loved Aunt Peg's nut roll. She and a group of ladies usually took orders and made them around the middle of November to raise money for missions. I sipped the hot chocolate, feeling warm and loved. Then I turned out the light and let my damp hair sink into the thick, soft, down pillow. The next thing I knew, it was morning.

Feeling rested and refreshed, I dressed, packed my stuff, and went downstairs. The aroma of cinnamon and fresh bread filled the kitchen. Freshly baked cinnamon rolls waited in an aluminum foil-covered pan. I chose a hazelnut pod and popped it in the coffeemaker, where a mug already awaited the hot java.

Over a cinnamon roll and coffee, I planned my day. First the credit union. I fingered the key hanging from the chain around my neck. It looked exactly like the one to my safe deposit box. Hiding the money where I—or anyone else—would never think to look was brilliant. Paul had hated my credit union and let me know in no uncertain terms he thought it beneath him to do business with anything but a real bank.

Until now I'd never thought about the fee that had been automatically deducted from my account. I just assumed the fee for my own box had gone up, when it had been for two boxes. But how could he have done it without my signature? Unless he forged it.

Then I remembered. Paul had given me the paper to sign when I was in the middle of a writing session, deadline breathing down my neck. He knew I was too busy to look at what I was signing. I forget what he told me it was. But he didn't have an account at the credit union and I did, so it was simpler to have the fee deducted from my account than to open up a new one. Diabolical and clever.

After breakfast, I opened my laptop and checked the weather. The storm was headed toward the mountain as predicted, and the first phase—freezing rain—was supposed to start sometime tomorrow. I planned to be back at the cabin tonight. Then I checked my e-mail and opened the one from Garrett, which was sent last night after I'd talked to him.

Mom, Anne got into the flash drive. I've attached the two documents that were on it. See what you make of them. Will talk tonight when you get back. Love you.

One was an Excel document and another a .pdf file. I opened the Excel document, which appeared to be a spreadsheet. I saved them to both my computer in a "Misc." file and to my Dropbox account and Cloud drive. I didn't have time to examine either one since I was already running behind schedule.

At the credit union, I didn't have any trouble accessing Paul's safe deposit box. I presented a copy of our marriage certificate and a copy of the English Certificate of Death Abroad, which were in my safe deposit box. I followed the teller, a young woman wearing black slacks and a purple, cowl-neck sweater, back into the vault, where, using my key, she pulled out the three-foot long drawer, carried it to a private room, put it on the table, and left, closing the door behind her.

I scanned the room for a security camera. I didn't see any. I didn't think there would be any in this room, but you never know anymore. I took the key from around my neck and inserted it. Taking a deep breath, I lifted the lid.

More bundles of Benjamins.

CHAPTER TWENTY-SIX

I counted fifty bundles. Half a million dollars. I stacked them in the rolling briefcase Paul had gotten me for my birthday the year I sold my fifth book. By then he was starting to take notice. On an impulse I'd unearthed it from the piles of stuff I had stacked in the spare room at the cabin before I left.

See, Don? I'm learning to trust my instincts.

Before closing the box and putting it back in its place, I scanned it once more. A small, white envelope was taped to the bottom. I peeled it off and opened it. Another key. Once again, it could be for anything, but my gut was telling me another safe deposit box. But where? Maybe the spreadsheet would tell me. I hadn't had time to examine the document closely, but it would be just like Paul to record where he stashed his cache on a password-protected flash drive. Who knew he had such a criminal mind?

Nodding to the teller on my way out, I strode out of the credit union like a model on a runway. No one would ever have guessed how I was shaking inside or that my hands were sweating. I stashed the case in the trunk with my tote bag and pulled out my laptop.

Slipping into the driver's seat and locking the door, I keyed in my password and made my way to the file Garrett had sent to me. As I studied the spreadsheet, it appeared that Paul had listed where he'd stashed the money and how much. He'd even listed how much he'd taken from the company, the date, how much Stephanie and Frank's cuts were, and how much he'd paid Devon Grove and when.

Some of the first few entries were marked in a "Paid Back" column. Did he actually pay back some of the money he stole? He'd even kept track of his gambling winnings and losses, as well as what he spent the money on. I didn't want to read those entries. Not yet, anyway.

I pored through the document, eliminating the caches we'd already found. Only one left. At the OmniBank & Trust in Wheeling, West Virginia. Paul's hometown. Paul's parents' bank, no doubt. This would not be a walk in the park. Paul's parents hated me.

Before I left for Wheeling—it would take me about an hour and a half on the interstate—I stopped by my realtor's office. Irene was surprised to see me, even though I'd texted her I'd be in.

"I didn't expect to see you until Thanksgiving," she said, pointing to the guest chair in front of her cluttered desk. "Have a seat."

I sank onto the red leather chair. "Didn't you get my text message?"

"No, but I haven't had time to check. Let me finish this paperwork first, and then we'll talk."

I pulled my cell phone from a pocket in my purse to check that the message I sent her did, indeed, go through. I was about to turn it on when I remembered I could be tracked that way. Sighing, I slipped it back into my purse.

I felt like twiddling my thumbs. Whenever I had a free moment, I usually read and sent text messages, not to mention checking the most updated weather forecast. I scanned the office. Only two of the five desks scattered throughout the room were occupied. I supposed that Monday mornings in a real estate office were like slow news days at a newspaper.

"All done," Irene said, closing a file folder and dropping it in a desk tray. She pulled out another file folder labeled "Harmon, Melody" from a wire-folder rack on her desk and flipped it open.

"We do have someone interested in the property, but they don't want to commit unless the loan payments are caught up. They don't like that the bank was about to foreclose last month." She peered at me over her reading glasses. "What is the status of your payments?"

"All caught up."

"What about next month's payment? When's it due?"

I squirmed and let out a sharp breath. "The first of the month. Two weeks from today. I thought we'd be closing at the end of this month, so I didn't plan to make any more payments. I have some money set aside for living expenses, but I don't want to dip into that." I thought about where I could cut more from the budget. "I don't see how I can come up with the payment for December without depleting the funds I've set aside to live on."

"You don't have any other resources? These people will put in a bid only if they are assured the December payment won't be missed and there are no pending liens against the property."

I thought about the half million in the trunk of Aunt Peg's car. No one knew about it. Yet. I shook my head. "I'll just have to take the payment from my living fund and then hope the house sells soon. I don't know how I could come up with January's payment."

"What about the income from your writing?"

"Not much there, and what does come in is already earmarked."

"No advances in the wings?"

I thought about the book Don and I were supposed to be working on. "No."

She studied my face for a moment. "It's up to you. What do you want me to tell these people?"

I shot up a quick, silent prayer. . . . *In all these things we are more than conquerors through him who loved us.* What choice did I have? If I didn't make the payment, I was back to the foreclosure scenario for sure. If I did make the payment, there was a chance these people would buy the house, and even if they didn't, I had another month to sell the place.

"Tell them not to worry," I said. "I'll make the payment early. Today."

When I got back to the car, I was unable to access the Internet using the realtor's WiFi, so I drove to the mall and parked outside

JCPenney and accessed theirs. After transferring money from my saving account to my checking account, I made the December mortgage payment via EFT. Then I e-mailed Irene. "Good until January."

Eleven thirty. It would take an hour and a half to get to Wheeling. I Googled "OmniBank & Trust plus Wheeling, WV" and clicked on its webpage. Three branch offices in the Wheeling area. Great. Which one? With the storm coming, I didn't have time to ditty-bop around Wheeling, looking for the right branch office. I minimized the webpage and opened Paul's spreadsheet. I scrolled down to the entry. Nothing except the name of the bank. Paul knew which branch and knew whoever might try to get into the box wouldn't.

I could pay a visit to Paul's parents, who would most likely be uncooperative. And that would take more time. I checked the map again for the locations of the branches. A plan formed in my mind. I smiled softly. It just might work.

It was around one thirty when I pulled into the parking lot of the main branch office. I freshened my makeup and ran a lift comb through my hair, which was slowly reverting back to frizz. Don would like that. A warmth infused me. Don. What had been his reaction when he read my note? The warmth coursing through me suddenly turned to ice. What if my plan didn't work? It had to. It just had to.

Help me, Lord.

I checked my purse for the documents I'd need: identification, marriage certificate, death certificate, and a copy of Paul's will, in which I'd been named the executor. We'd both drawn up wills shortly after Garrett was born, naming each other as executors. Paul had made an appointment with his attorney to discuss updating the will, his attorney told me later, but died before he was able to keep the appointment. So I remained the executor of Paul's estate and was legally allowed to access his safe deposit box . . . *if* only his name was on the box. How had the fees for the box been paid after Paul's death?

If they hadn't, what had happened to the contents of the box? What if someone else's name was on the box?

I felt woozy and tired and hungry. I should have stopped for lunch. Or at least at a Starbucks for some coffee. I still had the hour-and-a-half drive back to Greensburg, where I'd exchange Aunt Peg's Audi/AWD for my Explorer and then another three hours to the cottage. I'd get back home no earlier than seven. I was still feeling the effects of the flu. Maybe I should stay at Aunt Peg's tonight and head back early tomorrow morning before the storm. But time was of the essence. Once Don and Frank figured out where I was, it was only a matter of time before they'd catch up with me. If my plan was to work, I had to get back to the cottage tonight.

One step at a time, Melody. One step at a time.

I gave myself another look in the mirror and then snapped up the visor, popped the trunk lid, and eased out of the car. I put my laptop in the trunk and extracted the rolling briefcase.

"Here we go, Melody," I told myself as I headed to the building. "Piece of cake. Just like the last time."

I waited in the line for the next available teller, my stomach in knots. All I wanted to do was retrieve the money, get back to the mountain, and be done with this whole sordid affair. And sleep. It wasn't even two, and I was exhausted. After a five-minute wait, I stepped to the window.

"I've only recently learned that my late husband, Paul, rented a safe deposit box in this bank," I told the teller, whose nameplate identified her as Gwen Clarkson. "I'm not sure if the box is in this branch or in one of the others. I do have the key." I plunked it on the counter, along with the folder with the wedding and death certificates, and a copy of Paul's will. "And copies of all the documents you need. I am the executor of his estate."

She scanned through the papers. "Identification, please?"

I handed her my driver's license, which she examined.

"Is this your current address? Greensburg, Pennsylvania?"

I shook my head. "I just moved at the beginning of the month and haven't had time to change the address on my license yet. I'm still in Pennsylvania, though, and I still own the house at that address."

She handed my license back to me and tapped her keyboard. My heart pounded in my ears as she studied the monitor.

"Our records show the fee is three months delinquent. The money was automatically withdrawn from Paul Harmon's account, but when there were no deposits made for eighteen months, the funds ran out. We sent a registered letter, which was returned to us for lack of a signature."

"When did you send it?"

She scanned her monitor. "November 1. We're getting ready to declare the box abandoned and turn over the contents to the state as unclaimed property."

"What do I need to do to access the box?"

"Pay the overdue fee, plus late fees."

"That's it?"

She blinked. "You've already given me the proper documentation and identification."

I reached into my purse and fumbled for my wallet, trying not to think about the half million in cash that was in my briefcase.

"How much is it?"

"Three hundred dollars."

I inhaled sharply. "Does that include the late fee and anything else?"

"Three hundred dollars will cover all that's owed."

I fished my checkbook out of my purse. "I'll need a receipt."

Alone in the private room, I stared at the ten-by-ten box on the table in front of me. I swallowed before opening the lid.

It was empty!

Stunned, I ran my hand across the bottom. Nothing. A million questions whirled in my mind. Who? When? How? According to Paul's spreadsheet, this box was to have contained another half a million, and Paul had not taken it out, unless he didn't record it. But that wasn't like Paul. I wondered if the bank had a record of who had accessed the box.

I shut the lid and left the empty box on the table.

I waited another five minutes until Ms. Clarkson was available again.

"Is there a problem?"

"Yes, there's a problem. The box is empty. According to my late husband's records, there should have been valuables in that box. Has the bank already turned the contents over to the state?"

She tapped the keyboard again and studied the monitor.

"No, ma'am. By law we have to wait thirty days after we send the registered letter to declare the box abandoned. It's only been eighteen."

"Can you tell me when the box was last accessed and by whom?"

She stared at me a moment, as if determining whether or not it was proper procedure to give me this information. Then she blinked and tapped her keyboard. I exhaled a breath I didn't realize I was holding.

"According to our records, the box was last accessed on February 20, 2014, by Paul Harmon of 435 Oak Tree Circle, Greensburg, Pennsylvania."

A month before his Mexican vacation—and death.

I had two recourses and didn't know which was worse: head back to the mountain and hope that Frank and Stephanie would believe me when I told them the box was empty or pay a visit to Paul's parents.

DeWayne and Nanette Harmon lived in a one-story, off-white, vinyl-sided house in Cobblestone Court, a relatively new housing development just off the fairways of the Oak Haven Country Club. After Paul died, they'd decided the house where they raised their only child held too many memories. I wouldn't have known of the move had Garrett, their only grandchild, not told me.

I pulled onto the cement driveway and parked in front of the brown-paneled garage door. A curtain framing the front room bow window fluttered. She wouldn't expect me to show up in an Audi, so maybe I had a chance. I strode up the sidewalk to the front door, my stomach tied in knots, and muttered a quick, "Help me, Lord," as I rang the doorbell. And waited. Rang it again. And waited.

"Nanette, are you going to get that?" DeWayne's voice filtered through the door. A fall-themed wreath, with gourds and berries artfully crafted among the boughs, hung on the beveled glass.

A moment later the door swung open.

"What do *you* want?"

Nanette hadn't changed much since I'd last seen her at Paul's memorial service. Except the bitter lines around her mouth and eyes had deepened. She stood, all four-feet-nine-inches of her, holding the door partway open, scowling at me. Her short, blue-gray hair was perfectly coiffed. Behind fashionable glasses, her steel-blue eyes glared at me. Her cobalt-blue velour pullover, shoulder seams sagging, hung loosely over blue jeans that looked to be a size too big.

I took a breath. "May I come in?"

"What for?"

"Please, Nanette." She'd never wanted me to call her "Mother" or "Mom" or "Mom Harmon" or anything like that. "Mrs. Harmon" was what she'd preferred, but DeWayne said that was too formal for family. She still bristled when I called her by her first name.

"Let her in, Nan." DeWayne came up behind her and opened the door wider. "Melody, it's been too long. Come in."

Nanette stood frozen in place, glaring at me and blocking my way.

"Sweetheart, please," DeWayne said in a soft voice. Her chest heaved, and she leaned back against him, giving me room to pass.

"Thank you." I stepped over the threshold.

"Nanette, why don't you go put some water on for tea," DeWayne said, as I pulled my suede boots off and placed them on the throw rug by the door.

As Nanette huffed off to the kitchen, I followed DeWayne into the living room, furnished with an oatmeal-colored fabric sectional and glass-topped, chrome tables on plush white carpeting. A scent of apple cider and cinnamon spiced the air. I lowered myself onto the thick cushions of the sectional.

DeWayne settled himself in the matching recliner opposite me.

"Whatever it is, it must be important," he said, studying my face.

"It is."

I'd gone over and over in my mind on the fifteen-minute drive from the bank what I'd say to them. How to break it to them that their only son was a scoundrel and thief. Of course, I wouldn't use those words. But they had to know. Better to come from me than reading it in the paper or hearing it on the news.

We made small talk, mostly about Garrett, while Nanette got the tea ready in the kitchen. When she appeared at the doorway carrying a tray, DeWayne stood, took it from her, and placed it on the glass-topped coffee table. As she poured the tea from a bone china teapot decorated with red roses into matching cups, I noticed how her hands trembled.

"Here, sweetheart, let me do that," DeWayne said.

It was then I noticed how ravaged he looked. His shoulders hunched forward. Lines had etched themselves into his face over the twenty months since I'd seen him at Paul's memorial service. Grief haunted his eyes. Her eyes. Sorrow and regret washed through me. I'd lost a husband whose love for me had grown cold. They'd lost their only child. I couldn't imagine losing Garrett.

"A parent should never have to bury a child," I'd heard a pastor once say.

As I accepted the cup from Nanette, suddenly all the years of pain, the memories of Nanette's slights and thinly veiled insults melted away. It didn't matter anymore.

I put my cup down and wrapped my hands around Nanette's. I wanted to say, "I forgive you," but somehow I felt it would just start another argument. Instead I said, "I'm sorry."

She looked at me with startled eyes before pulling her hand out of my grasp. But at least she hadn't jerked it away. DeWayne had settled on the end of the sectional, and Nanette sat beside him. She looked up at him, a question in her eyes. He nodded. And she turned to me.

"I suppose you're here about the money."

CHAPTER TWENTY-SEVEN

My jaw dropped.

"Yes," I said, setting my cup down on the tray. "I am. But I didn't expect—"

"Us to know about it?" Nanette said.

I nodded. "How much do you know?"

Nanette looked at DeWayne. "You tell her. I . . . can't."

"We knew Paul had a gambling problem. It started in high school. At first we thought it was harmless, a passing fancy. But when . . ." DeWayne shook his head and sighed. "I'll cut to the chase here. We bailed him out, time and again. He'd promised us he'd get help."

"I was the one who gave him the money," Nanette said. "I didn't tell DeWayne. I lied when he asked me where all the household money was going."

She pulled a tissue from the box on the end table and dabbed her eyes. "I was wrong. I know that now."

"A month before he passed, Paul stopped by and left a briefcase. We lived at the old house then," Dewayne said. "He said he had some old college papers in it that he wanted to leave with the rest of his memorabilia in his room."

"We believed him." Nanette's voice broke. "I thought he made the trip just to see us and brought this old stuff he wanted to leave at home. We found the case when we were getting ready to move. When we opened it and saw all the money, we knew the only purpose of that visit was to hide it."

"It was locked—*locked*!" Dewayne said, his voice brimming with hurt and anger. "I was insulted. We're . . . we *were* his parents."

It didn't surprise me that they'd pried open their son's locked briefcase, but it did that Paul had left it with them. He must have been getting desperate.

Nanette reached over and grasped DeWayne's hand.

"We figured he hit it big," DeWayne said.

"He did, didn't he?" Nanette's eyes were wide, pleading.

I took a deep breath. *Lord, help me.*

"I'm so sorry to have to be the one to tell you." Then I told them everything. When I was done, they stared at me, eyes wide in shock.

"Embezzled?" Nanette whispered. "I never thought . . ."

"Where's the money now?" I asked.

"It's gone." DeWayne whispered. "I'm so sorry."

My mouth went dry. "What do you mean, 'gone'?"

"We spent it," DeWayne said. "We were so happy not to have to mortgage this place. We paid cash for the furniture. For the first time in our lives, we had no debt. We figured it was payback for all the times we bailed him out."

"We did invest some after we went on the cruise, though," Nanette said. "Didn't we, DeWayne?"

Cruise. They went on a cruise.

"We can cash in what we invested," DeWayne said. "But that will take more time than Melody has."

"Can't we just write her a check?" Nanette asked.

"For half a million dollars?"

"Oh."

"Yes—oh." DeWayne ran his fingers through his thick white hair.

"Did you know anything about his safe deposit box at the OmniBank & Trust?"

"No, why?" Nanette asked.

"According to Paul's records, there was supposed to be another five hundred grand in it, but it was empty. Bank records show Paul had accessed it a month before he went on his last trip."

DeWayne nodded. "That was about when he left the briefcase with us. But there was $450,000 in it, not $500,000."

"He probably took fifty thousand for his trip," I said.

Or maybe it was a payoff, since most of the trip expenses were on the credit card that I paid off. I didn't tell DeWayne and Nanette that though. They'd had enough shock for one day.

I checked the time. Four o'clock. I had to get back to Greensburg, exchange vehicles, and head to the mountain.

"Don't worry about it," I said, pushing myself up from my comfortable seat. "I'll figure something out. Thank you for your time."

"We'll pay back the money," DeWayne said. "Every penny. It belonged to Paul's employer, and he stole it."

Tears filled my eyes. How would they ever be able to pay it back? They'd lose everything they had. Here were two more wrecked lives in Paul's wake. Anger—at Paul, at Frank, at Stephanie—mingled with sorrow and pity.

"I have to go. I . . . I'll pray for you."

"Melody . . ." DeWayne stepped to me and wrapped his arms around me. "Take care of yourself."

Nanette, tears streaming down her face, nodded. "I never hated you, you know," she whispered. "I was blind. He was my baby boy. I thought you weren't good enough for him. But now I know it was the other way around. You were too good for him. Can you ever forgive me?"

I knelt before her and put my arms around her. "Yes, I forgive you."

By the time I got back to Aunt Peg's I was beyond exhaustion. I'd spent the entire drive trying to figure out what to tell Frank and Stephanie. I stumbled into the kitchen and slumped into a chair.

"I'll make tea," was all Aunt Peg said. Four nut rolls, encased in plastic bags, sat on the counter. She took one, sliced it up, and arranged the slices on a plate, which she placed on the table.

"This will hold you until supper. You're staying. I made Chicken Parmesan."

Over dinner we made small talk, but Aunt Peg wisely waited until we cut into another nut roll and refreshed our tea to broach the subject.

"Garrett called." She squeezed honey into her tea. "Three times."

I broke a slice of nut roll in half and bit into it. The sweetness melted in my mouth.

"Is your cell phone battery dead?" she persisted.

I never could lie to anyone, let alone Aunt Peg. "No."

"I see." She stirred her tea, her face thoughtful. Then she frowned. "No, I don't see. Why do you have your phone turned off?"

"I don't want you involved in this."

"In what?"

"I can't say."

"Can't or won't? Listen, Melody sweetheart, I told you I don't have to know what's going on, but that isn't true. I do have to know what's going on."

"You said you believed in me."

"I do. Oh, dear, this isn't coming out right." She took a breath. "I'm worried. This isn't like you. Taking off without telling anyone, including your son, where you're going. Hiding your SUV." She hitched her eyebrows and looked me in the eye. "Who or what are you running from?"

I stirred my tea and stared at the swirls in the cup, my heart pounding in my throat.

"Garrett's frantic," Aunt Peg prodded.

"I'm going back tonight."

"That's lame. You're avoiding the question."

I sighed. "I know. But it's the best I can do under the circumstances."

"Don called too."

"How . . . he doesn't have your number."

"He does now. Both my landline and my cell phone numbers." She shrugged. "He must have gotten them from Garrett. Do you want to hear the messages he left?"

I could imagine. "No. I'll get an earful when I get back, I'm sure."

"He's frantic too."

Poor Don.

"I'm doing this for him," I said.

"Doing what? You might as well tell me, Melody. I'll keep prodding until you do."

My eyes scanned the kitchen. "Do you have a home alarm system?"

"Yes."

"These people are dangerous. They've already killed one man and have threatened . . ." I took a deep breath. "They've threatened Don's family, particularly Anne and the girls, if they don't get what they want."

"What do they want?"

"The money they helped Paul embezzle."

She snorted. "Paul again. Why am I not surprised? And they think you know where this money is."

"I found over a million dollars in cash—bundles of one hundred dollar bills—stashed in out-of-the-way places. A hundred fifty thousand was hidden at the house, and I found another six hundred thousand at the cabin. We also found some other things."

I told her about the fake ID, passport, and flash drive.

"Anne—she's a computer whiz—was able to get into the flash drive," I said. "Paul kept meticulous records. There were two more places he'd stashed money—in a safe deposit box in my credit union and supposedly in one in the bank in Wheeling, his hometown."

"Supposedly?"

I nodded. "I found half a million in the one in the credit union, but the one in Wheeling was empty. There was supposed to be another half million in that one."

I told her about the visit to Paul's parents.

"You know, I always thought she hated me. I mean, she didn't act like the mother-in-law I wanted. I was pregnant before the wedding. She never forgave me. I overheard her talking to DeWayne one time. She said I'd trapped Paul into marriage. She'd wanted Paul to marry into money. Even had someone picked out. But I ruined all that."

"Oh, honey, you didn't ruin anything. Paul loved you. Even I saw that. Even in the end. But he couldn't break the chains of his addictions. They were stronger than his love for you and Garrett. And about Nanette . . . she's . . . how can I say this gracefully? Oh, I'll just say it. She comes across as a snob. But then, I've learned that people who act superior actually feel inferior. The snootiness is just a cover-up to mask how very insecure they really are."

I nodded. "I see that now, hindsight being twenty-twenty. I thought about it all the way back from Wheeling. Since Sonny died, I'd viewed the world with my own pain-colored glasses. I felt God betrayed me when He let Sonny die, then all my dreams for a happily-ever-after marriage came crashing down with Paul's first affair, then all his broken promises. To survive, I insulated myself in a dream world I created for my fiction. I cast Nanette as a villain and didn't bother to look too closely at the image I'd created."

"Did DeWayne and Nanette know anything about the money that was supposed to be in the safe deposit box?"

I sighed. "They spent it."

Aunt Peg gasped. "Half a million dollars?"

I told her about how they'd found the money when they were moving.

"They thought Paul won it gambling, and since Paul was dead, it was finders keepers. I didn't know until they told me today how much they'd spent over the years, bailing him out of trouble."

"Do Frank and this other person know how much money Paul had hidden?"

"Stephanie." I shrugged. "I'm not sure. I think they have an idea, since they helped him and got a cut. They just don't know where Paul hid it. He was preparing to leave."

Aunt Peg nodded thoughtfully. "That's obvious, with the fake ID and passport. I don't understand how Don fits into this."

"He's not just a mystery writer. And he's not an *ex*-cop. He's undercover, investigating the embezzling ring and murder. They murdered the guy who was blackmailing them. With my hammer, it appears. And planted the so-called evidence at the cabin."

"Oh, dear. You must feel betrayed again."

"Funny, but I don't. Don went above and beyond the call of duty when he took care of me when I was sick."

Aunt Peg studied me, a soft smile playing on her lips. "You're falling for him."

Warmth gushed through me, and I couldn't deny it.

"From what you tell me, Don seems like the kind of person who won't let his personal feelings get in the way of his professional duty. You can learn a lot about a person by reading what they write, even if it's fiction. Have you been cleared of this murder?"

"I think so. My prints were the only ones found on the hammer. The DNA analysis hasn't come back yet. But Don knows I didn't kill Devon Grove."

"Yes, but if the evidence points to you, there's not much he can do. Do you have an alibi?"

I shook my head. "I lied. I told them I was home all evening, but actually I went out for pizza. It could have been long enough to slip on the boat, whack him over the head with the hammer, shove him into the water, and get back home."

"Have you told Don the truth yet?"

I sighed. "No."

We sat in silence for a while, the apple clock ticking on the wall above the sink.

"You're not going to go along with this, are you?" Aunt Peg said. "You're not going to meet those thugs' demands and hand over the money."

I shook my head. "They think I am. But I have a plan."

It was nearly seven when I went to the barn to get my Explorer and head back to the mountain. The updated forecast called for the storm to begin with an icy mix late tonight. Aunt Peg wanted me to call Garrett and Don and let them know I was on the way, but I was too afraid this would tip off Frank and Stephanie. My strategy depended on the element of surprise.

"How about if I call Garrett and just tell him I heard from you, and that you're okay?" Aunt Peg said. "I won't tell them you were here or that you're on your way."

We stood on the rough, wooden, barn floor, an icy wind whistling through the cracks of the weathered-board siding. I'd packed my stuff, including the briefcase with the half million, on the floor behind the driver's seat.

"Aunt Peg, you're going to do that anyway."

A sheepish grin spread across her worried face.

I wrapped my arms around her. "I love you, Aunt Peg. I'll be fine."

"Call me when you get there."

"I can't. I don't have a strong enough signal for voice mail. I'll text you or send you an e-mail."

She pursed her lips together. A shiver ran through her.

"You're cold. Hop in. I'll drop you off at the house."

I turned the key. Nothing but a groan. I pumped the gas pedal and tried again. Same thing.

"Battery's dead. I should have listened to Don and bought a new one."

"Then you'll stay the night? Honey, you look beyond tired. And you're still getting over that flu."

I shook my head. "I have jumper cables. And I know how to use them."

She sighed. "I'll get my car."

By the time I pulled into my driveway, it was after eleven. Freezing rain, dim headlights thanks to age-clouded lenses, and my fatigue combined to make it a harrowing drive. The cabin was so cold I could see my breath. I turned on the wall heaters, put on a kettle of water for tea, and then headed for the poogie house with the briefcase. I'd just put it on the floor until tomorrow. I was too tired to find the crowbar and hang the bag where I'd found the backpack.

I figured I had a few minutes before Don and Garrett came barging in, demanding an explanation for my impromptu trip. I carried the bag over the slippery ground, which by this time tomorrow if the forecast was right, would be covered with six- to eight-inches of snow. And by this time tomorrow, if my plan worked, Frank and Stephanie would be behind bars.

But tonight, all I wanted to do was hide the money, take a hot shower, enjoy a cup of Dreamtime tea, and go to bed. And text Aunt Peg, Garrett, and Don. I'd just tell them I was back and that I was going straight to bed. I'd talk to them in the morning. And I'd wire myself up in the morning. And call Frank. But not tonight.

I swung open the door to the outhouse and went to put the briefcase on the floor beside the door, but the briefcase hit against something. Something that shouldn't have been there. I flicked on the flashlight and shined the beam inside.

My blood turned to ice. Propped against the seat, staring at me with unseeing eyes, was Virelle. Dried blood tracked down the side of her face from where someone had bashed the side of her head in. And on the floor beside her body was a bloodstained crowbar—*my* crowbar.

CHAPTER TWENTY-EIGHT

I doubled over, spewing the contents of my stomach all over poor Virelle. Stomach acid burned my throat. When I was done heaving, I slammed the door shut and jammed down the wooden latch. Grabbing the briefcase from the frozen ground, I slipped and stumbled back to the cabin and turned on my cell phone. Ignoring the text messages, I speed dialed Don. Nothing. Why couldn't I ever get a signal here? I tossed the briefcase in the spare room amid the clutter, shut the door, and snatched my keys from the breakfast bar.

The freezing rain had turned the road into a sheet of ice, making the short drive to Don's treacherous and long. Don's porch lights were the only lights on at his place, except for a small light over the kitchen sink, which reflected off the ice-covered back deck, and the pole light in the driveway. One car was parked beneath it, which I recognized as Anne's. It was almost midnight. Where was everyone? I checked my cell phone. No bars, but it wasn't showing "No Service." Don's phone went straight to voice mail.

"Don, come quick!" I tried not to shout. "There's a dead body in my outhouse!"

Then I called Garrett. He answered on the first ring.

"Mom? Where are you?" Garrett's voice sounded urgent.

"I'm at Don's. I just got back and—"

"Haven't you read or listened to any of your messages?"

"I haven't had time. There's a—"

"Hannah was life-flighted to Children's Hospital in Pittsburgh. She couldn't breathe."

"When?"

"Around suppertime. Don called an ambulance, but they decided when they got her to the ER at Clarion to send her to Pittsburgh. Her doctors are here. Don and Anne drove down."

The freezing rain had turned into a sleety mix, covering my windshield wipers with a heavy coat of slush. Ice pellets plinked and plunked against the hood and roof. I turned down the noisy fan and wrapped my jacket tighter around me.

"How is Hannah?" I asked.

"She has pneumonia. They've admitted her. She'll be here a few days."

"Did you drive down? Your car isn't here."

"I never . . . to . . . cabin. . . . flight late."

"You're breaking up, Garrett. I must be losing the signal. Did you say you never got to the cabin?"

". . . halfway there . . . Anne called . . . turned around . . . came down."

"So you're all in Pittsburgh?"

"Virelle's . . . Kadie . . . farmhouse. . ."

"Wait!" I couldn't breathe. "Kadie . . . Oh, dear Lord . . ."

"Mom?" The spotty transmission didn't mask the alarm in Garrett's voice. ". . . wrong?"

"That's what I was calling about. It's Virelle. She's dead. In the outhouse."

My heart was in my throat.

"Garrett? Did you hear what I said? Virelle's dead, Garrett. I think they have Kadie."

Silence. I checked the signal. No bars. I tried calling back, but it didn't go through. I could only hope he'd heard me before the call was dropped. As I backed into the turnaround, the pole light went out. I looked at the house, which was all dark now. No electric. I shivered. I was alone on the mountain with a killer. Who had Kadie.

Back at the cabin, I shut off the burner under a bone-dry kettle and checked the doors and windows to make sure they were all locked. Then I went through the cabin, room by room. I aimed the flashlight beam in every nook and cranny. Everything was just as I had left it. Either Frank couldn't get into my cabin or . . . the surveillance cameras! I could go outside, stand in front of one, and wave my arms, jump up and down. Wait. No I couldn't. The power was out. No WiFi.

But the power didn't go out until a few minutes ago. Wouldn't the cameras have picked up Frank and Virelle? How did Frank overpower Virelle? She was a trained cop. Maybe he took her by surprise. Where? If I understood Garrett correctly, Virelle was staying with Kadie at the farmhouse while Don and Anne went to the hospital with Hannah. Did Don have his laptop with him? Even if he did, I doubted in the emergency that he was monitoring the surveillance camera feed. That would have been Virelle's job.

I wondered if the bugs were still working. They were hidden in the smoke and carbon monoxide detectors. Both ran on battery. I checked them. Both had green lights, which indicated they were working. I wished I'd listened to Don when he explained how the bugs worked instead of tuning him out, which is what I tend to do when something goes over my head.

Standing in front of the wall between the kitchen and the living room, I spoke to the carbon monoxide detector.

"Don, I don't know if you can hear me. Virelle's dead. I don't know where Kadie is. Before I left, I got a note threatening Anne and the girls if I didn't give Frank the money. I assumed it was Frank. Or Stephanie. Who else would it be?"

I took a breath. *Lord, please let him hear me.*

"I have—*had* a plan, but now, well, I have to figure out plan B." What if Frank was listening to me right now? *Oh, Lord, help me.*

I took a deep breath.

The first thing was to find Kadie. If Frank had her, she might be at his cabin. I pictured the girls at my cabin on Sunday. How much fun they had with Rascal. Wait! Where *was* Rascal? I'd forgotten all about her. When I left Sunday, I'd planned to be gone only a day, so I'd filled up her water bowl and food dish. Even if I'd taken longer, I was sure the girls would take care of Rascal in my absence. But when I'd checked the cabin tonight, there was no sign of her. Surely Frank wouldn't . . . That made no sense. Rascal could take care of herself, even if she was outside in the ice storm. Kadie. I had to focus on finding Kadie.

A cup of tea would calm me down and help me to think. Trying to do things with one hand while holding the flashlight in the other was a pain, so I found my headlamp and pulled it on. The kettle was ruined, so I poured some water into a saucepan and lit the burner, thanking God my propane stove didn't need electric to work and that I'd filled some water containers after the last storm to keep on hand. While the water was heating up, I sat at the counter with my notebook and pen, scribbling the thoughts as they came to me.

Number one: Find Kadie. The first place to check would be Frank's cabin. He'd given me until Friday to come up with the money, so he probably didn't know I was back. Unless he had Virelle's laptop and was watching the surveillance camera feeds before the power went out. But maybe he couldn't get into the laptop. I was sure it would be password protected. I wrote IF in big block letters. So many ifs . . . IF Frank had the laptop. IF he was able to use it and watch the surveillance feeds. IF he had Kadie. IF he was listening to me right now and had heard everything I told the carbon monoxide detector.

I had to assume the worst.

The water was boiling, so I poured my tea and took it into the living room, which was now cozy warm, thanks to the wall heater.

The first place to check would be Frank's cabin. I'd have to hide the Explorer, though, in case he didn't know I'd returned. Don's barn would be the perfect place. If the storm panned out to be all it was forecast to be, the snow would cover my tracks fast. But I had to get it up there soon, before the snow got too deep.

Then I'd walk to his cabin. I knew the way through the woods, even in the dark. That was one big advantage I had over Frank and Stephanie if she was with him. I knew this mountain. They didn't. Frank's cabin had once been owned by the parents of my first boyfriend, Robbie. I met him when I was nine, and he gave me my first kiss the summer before I turned fifteen. Over the years, we'd made a trail through the woods. Although it was overgrown now, I still knew it well. We used to joke that we could walk it blindfolded.

Using the trail through the woods would be better because the ice and snow wouldn't be as thick on the ground, and I didn't have to worry too much about tracks yet. The trail led to the back of the cabin, behind the woodpile.

If Kadie was there, how would I rescue her? How would we escape the other two?

I shook my head. I couldn't think about that now. It would come to me. But first I had to find Kadie.

I finished my tea, poured a packet of hot chocolate in a thermos, and put more water on to boil. In the bathroom, behind a closed door—I was fairly sure the bugs couldn't pick up any noises made here—I dressed for the hike: thermal underwear, jeans, hooded sweatshirt, wool socks, work boots, and fleece jacket under my Carhartt jacket.

I thought about donning my rain poncho but decided it would be too noisy. I put my compass in my pocket just in case. By then the water for the hot chocolate was boiling. I poured it into the thermos. Tucking my leather mittens under my arm, I pulled on my ski mask and headlamp and left.

The storm was still in the sleet stage, and the road to Don's iced over. I drove my four-wheel-drive carefully in the lowest gear so I wouldn't have to use the brake. Fortunately, the dirt road leading into Don's barn was behind the house, and I knew the snow would soon cover my tracks. Closing the barn door, I thought I saw a light in the house. I peered into the sleety night, but when I saw nothing but darkness in the house, I decided it was just my imagination.

Then I headed for Frank's cabin. A full moon behind snow-laden clouds gave me enough light to walk in the woods beside the road without my headlamp. Just past my driveway, I turned right, following a deer trail that intersected with the old path between the cabins. Twice I stopped to get my bearings, turning on the headlamp to read the compass. The forest floor was only a little slippery under the canopy of naked hardwood trees and thick pine branches, which caught the freezing rain and sleet.

After about fifteen minutes, the smell of wood smoke told me I was getting close. I stopped and peered into the night. Through the trees, I could see the shape of Frank's small cabin. I gingerly stepped closer, careful not to make any noise. A light shone from a side window, casting a yellow flickering beam on the glistening ground. The sleet had turned to snow, which would muffle my steps. I crept up to the back of the cabin and then around to the side, where I peeked in the window that was open an inch. A faint odor of propane reached my nostrils. I crouched down.

Frank was talking to someone. I leaned closer.

"Don't argue with me. I know what I'm doing."

"How do you know she knows where the money is?" A woman's voice. "Paul covered his tracks well."

"If she don't, she'll find it to save the kids."

"But we don't have the kids."

"She don't know that."

"Of course she does. She and that cop have a thing going. Don't tell me she hasn't been in contact with him in spite of what you wrote on that stupid note."

"Her cell phone's turned off. I been calling her. It goes straight to voice mail. She knows he can track her with the phone on. She's no dummy."

"You could have fooled me."

"You're just jealous."

"And why should I be jealous?"

"Because, in spite of everything, she still had Paul's heart. You knew that. That's why you want her dead."

Paul still loved me? After all he did? I swallowed a sob. My knee shifted on the ice, and I brushed against the shingle siding to catch myself.

"What was that?" Stephanie said.

"What?"

"Sh! Listen."

I held my breath and prayed I wouldn't slip on the ice again.

"You're a bundle of nerves, woman. That's sleet hitting the windows."

"Are you sure? I thought I heard something else. What if someone's out there?"

"Who'd be out there on a night like this? The cop and his daughter went to the hospital with the sick kid. The other kid, well, you blew it."

"You were the one who blew it," Stephanie said.

"How did I blow it? I followed that female cop to Melody's cabin. You were supposed to snatch the kid."

"I tried, and look what it got me. That kid's got sharp claws. My face is a mess."

Frank's mean laugh pierced the night. "It'll heal."

Good for you, Kadie.

"So what's your plan now, genius?"

"This."

"What's that?" Stephanie said.

"A warrant for the arrest of one Melody Harmon for the murder of one Devon Grove. I took it from the cop." I could imagine his sick grin. "Guess the results of the DNA test on the hammer came back."

"But she didn't arrest Melody, because you bashed her head in."

He sniggered. "With Melody's crowbar."

My head spun. Not only was I wanted for murdering Paul's blackmailer, but I'd also been framed for Virelle's murder. Footsteps came to the window. I huddled closer to the cabin. The screech of wood against wood filled the air as someone jiggled with the sash to raise it higher.

"Hey, you're letting the cold in." Frank cursed. "Shut the blame window."

"That thing stinks. I'll asphyxiate. Don't you have a battery-operated lantern?"

"Why waste batteries? We might need them."

The floor creaked as Stephanie turned and stepped away from the window. "I should have stayed in Greensburg instead of listening to you and driving up here. At least I'd be warm. And breathing clean air."

"There was nothing more you could do. You lost her. Admit it. She gave you the slip."

So my paranoid weaving in and out of traffic, taking all the side roads and alleys I knew of, had paid off.

"I thought she'd go to her aunt's, but her SUV wasn't there. I checked her house, but nothing. I even stopped at that nosy neighbor's, pretending I was interested in buying Paul's house, but she hadn't seen her. And, believe me, if anyone knew if Melody had stopped at the house, it would have been her."

"She has to come back here eventually. And when she does, we'll have two million dollars to split."

Two million? I'd found 1.25 million. Paul's parents spent half a million minus fifty thousand. That meant there was three-quarters of a million dollars somewhere. The good news was they didn't have Kadie. I had to find Kadie before Frank and Stephanie did.

CHAPTER TWENTY-NINE

"Kadie," I whispered loudly, knocking on the back door of the farmhouse.

Inside, Charlie barked.

I'd left Frank and Stephanie arguing, slipping away from the cabin undetected. I took the path partway then cut through the woods to save time. If Kadie was still in the farmhouse, we'd be safe until morning. No way were Frank and Stephanie coming out in this. Besides, they thought I was still in Greensburg.

"Kadie!" Still I whispered. I couldn't be too careful. I opened the storm door and rapped on the steel door. Charlie barked and jumped up against the door. "It's me, Melody! If you're in there, open up."

I eased the storm door shut and stepped to the kitchen window. Peering at me through the glass were a pair of green eyes—cat's eyes. Relief flooded through me.

"Rascal!"

I rapped on the window. "Kadie!"

"Melody?"

"Yes. Open up."

Arms wrapped around my waist as soon as I stepped into the kitchen.

"Melody! I'm so glad you're here! I had to make sure it was you. Gramps told me not to let anyone in unless it was you."

I knelt down and wrapped my arms around her. She wore an insulated winter coat. Charlie's wet nose poked my face, and her rough tongue licked my nose.

"Oh, honey, I'm so glad to see you."

"Sgt. Reddick left and never came back. And then that other lady came, sneaking around the house. She tried all the doors. Then she pounded on the back door and yelled that she knew I was in here. I thought you were her coming back for me. But when you said Rascal's name, I knew it was you."

"You're a very smart and very brave girl," I said, giving her one more squeeze before releasing her.

"Can you turn that light off? It hurts my eyes." She held her hand up in front of her face.

I reached up and switched off my headlamp. The farmhouse was cold. It didn't take long for a drafty old place like this to lose heat after the power went out.

"I have to text Gramps and tell him you're here." She pulled out a cell phone from her coat pocket.

"You have a cell phone?"

"It's Mom's." She punched in a number. "They're worried about you, you know."

"Yes, sweetheart, I know. But it couldn't be helped."

While she texted Don, I thought about where to hide. The farmhouse was too cold, and I wasn't familiar with its fireplaces. Besides, the smoke from the chimney would give us away. The barn would be way too cold. The roads were too icy to risk taking her to a motel. That left my place. Which would work. Frank and Stephanie didn't know I was back, and we could stay warm, with just the wall heaters going. In the morning, I could always turn them off and light the oven.

"Come on, honey," I said when she was done texting. "We're going to my place."

"Can Rascal and Charlie come?"

I held her face in my hands. "We'll take Rascal, but we'll have to leave Charlie here. We'll make sure she has enough food and water. We have to be really, really quiet. Just like here."

"Because of the bad guys?"

"Yes, sweetheart. Because of the bad guys. Now, where are your boots?"

After I got Kadie settled in my bed beneath the down comforter, with Rascal curled up beside her on top of the bed, I made myself a cup of tea. We'd lost the cell signal about halfway between the farmhouse and my cabin, so I didn't know if Don had responded to Kadie's text. I had to come up with a plan, but my brain refused to work. It was almost 3:00 a.m., and I'd been on the go for two days, pushing myself beyond endurance.

I was exhausted, and now that I'd allowed myself to relax a little, I felt it in every ounce of my body. I was afraid to fall asleep, though, in case Frank or Stephanie came and I didn't hear them. I was sure they'd check the cabin in the morning, just in case I showed up. But maybe when they saw my Explorer wasn't in the driveway, they'd figure I was still in the city.

It didn't get light until after seven. I was sure they wouldn't come until at least nine. If they came. I could—I *should*—get some sleep. I needed my wits about me.

I checked Kadie—she was sound asleep—and turned down both wall heaters. Then I snuggled beneath my fleece blanket on the sofa and closed my eyes.

It was after eight when Rascal woke me, prancing on my pillow and chewing my hair. She was used to her bowls being filled when I got up to visit the bathroom around five, so she was well beyond her patience. Throwing back the fleece blanket, I pushed myself to a sitting position. And groaned. My body ached all over. At first my groggy brain didn't register why. I felt like I did when I spent the day getting firewood or going on a long, challenging hike.

I leaned back and closed my eyes. Rascal hopped on my lap, biting my fingers.

"In a minute, Rascal." I stroked her soft fur.

Yesterday's events, like scattered puzzle pieces, floated through my mind. The long drive. The storm. The money. My eyes flew open. What day was it? Wednesday. I didn't have all the money. Would they believe Paul's parents had spent half a million of it?

Tea. I needed a cup of tea. But first I wanted to check on Kadie. I went upstairs but she wasn't there. The bed was empty, the covers thrown back.

"Kadie!" I called, my breath white vapor puffs. "Kadie, where are you?"

Nothing but the steady ticking of the battery-operated wall clock. I shivered—from the ice water running through my veins and from the frigid air around me. *Why is it so cold?* The wall heater in the bedroom wasn't burning. I peered over the railing downstairs. Neither was the one in the living room.

Had the propane run out? It shouldn't have. I'd just had the tank filled. I didn't smell the sickeningly sweet gas, but then my heaters shut off automatically when the fire, for any reason, went out. I shut off the valve to the propane line then did the same for the one downstairs. I tried to light my stove. Nothing. Maybe something was clogging the line outside at the tank. I opened the back door and trudged through the knee-high snow to the tank to shut off the valve there.

That's odd. It's already off. Frank must have shut it off. But why? There were no tracks around the tank, but then the way it was snowing, they'd be covered in an hour. I turned it back on then went back inside. I checked the bathroom, the spare room, the kitchen for signs of Kadie. My legal pad, neat printing across the top page, lay on the breakfast bar, an ink pen beside it.

"I went to check on Charlie," I read. "I didn't want to wake you. You looked so tired last night. Don't worry. I'll be OK. I dressed warm. Kadie."

Relief mingled with fear. If Frank had seen her . . . When had she left? I peered out the blinds on the front patio door. One set of tracks plowed through at least a foot of wet, heavy snow that blanketed the front deck, and it was still coming down. She couldn't have left more than a half an hour ago. How long would it take her to slough through that without snowshoes to get to the farmhouse? I was glad I had her wear her boots instead of her sneakers last night. I didn't see any other tracks, just hers weaving through the front yard, then disappearing up the driveway. Maybe the storm had given us a reprieve from the bad guys.

I had to go to the bathroom, and when the power was out, I didn't use the indoor toilet. I'd forgotten to tell Kadie, so the tank was probably empty. I'd have to use the outhouse. Oh, gravy! No, I couldn't. Not with what I knew was in there. I wished I'd had the time last night to fill the tub so I'd have water to flush the commode. I used it anyway.

I checked the time: 8:35 a.m. I had to go after her. I could wait and use the farmhouse bathroom. Slipping out of my wet sweatpants, I tugged on a pair of dry ones I plucked from the hamper. I opened the door to the spare room, where I kept my winter hiking gear. A shiver ran through me. It was even colder in here than it was in the main part of the cottage. I grabbed my waterproof, bib snow pants and matching hooded jacket. Several sets of snowshoes hung from the wall. I chose the mountain terrain shoes. With the type of crampons and bindings, they'd be best on the ice and deep snow. I grabbed the pair of kid's snowshoes that Garrett had worn when he was about Kadie's age and stuffed them in an oversized backpack, which I kept packed with emergency supplies. Then I snatched four snowshoe poles, thankful I hadn't sold Garrett's poles and shoes.

I strapped on the shoes and stepped out the door, locking it behind me. Even with snowshoes and poles, it was slow going, with the wet snow kicking up on the back of my legs with every labored step. The wind was picking up and ice pellets mixed with the heavy flakes. I got as far as the paved road, which hadn't been plowed yet, then her tracks disappeared. The only tracks in the snow on the road were tire tracks. It looked as though she'd stepped into a vehicle. Had Don come back?

I peered up and down the road. Which direction did it go? I headed to the farmhouse, following the tire tracks. When I got there, I plucked the spare key from the porch light and let a frantic Charlie out. While she did her business, I did mine. I filled her water bowl with the jug of water Don kept under the sink for emergencies and dropped a couple of scoopfuls of dry dog food in her dish. Before I'd closed the bag, she was at the door, wanting in.

"I wouldn't want to be out in that any more than I have to either," I told her, wiping her wet fur off with a dishtowel. She sat obediently while I lifted each paw and dabbed it, checking for ice wedged between her claws.

"Good girl," I said when I was done. She cocked her head to one side, a question in her eyes.

"I wish I could take you, but that snow is too deep. Don't you worry, though, I'll find Kadie."

Charlie's rough tongue licked my cheek and then she stepped to her breakfast. I stood and began to pull on my gloves. That's when I saw the note on the table. My heart sank when I read the words written in big, block letters: "YOU CAN HAVE THE GIRL WHEN I GET THE MONEY."

They had Kadie!

The plans I had to catch them had gone south when I returned to find my backup crew gone—Virelle dead and Kadie alone. I couldn't catch them by myself, and I had no bargaining chip. They did. I'd wanted to catch them without having to turn over the money, which I'd planned to restore to Paul's former employer. But now I'd have to give them the money in exchange for Kadie's life. I hated this feeling of helplessness, of failure. It had been familiar territory when Paul was around. But ever since Don, I'd begun to believe in myself . . . and God.

"Now what, Lord?" I whispered, snatching the note from the table and studying it. Something about the printing niggled in my brain. This didn't look like a woman's script. I'd done some research on handwriting for one of my novels. This writing was bold, angry, threatening, strong—done by an angry or stressed-out man.

I stuffed the note in my jacket pocket. I had to come up with a plan to save Kadie—and me. I highly doubted they would let us live. They'd already murdered two people, one of them a trained police detective.

Call upon me in the day of trouble; I will deliver you.

One of the Bible verses from Psalms that I'd helped Garrett memorize when he was in Bible club so many years ago popped into my mind. I shook my head. I wanted to believe it, but where was God when Paul was cheating on me, slapping me around, putting me down? Where was God when I lost my house? My career?

For I know the plans I have for you, plans to prosper you and not to harm you, plans to give you hope and a future.

Was all this part of His plan for me?

All the days ordained for me were written in your book before one of them came to be.

"All right, Lord," I whispered. "I get it. This is a day of trouble, that's for sure. I'm calling on You, asking You to help me. Save Kadie. Don't let Frank and Stephanie get away with the evil they've done, the evil they have planned. I believe You are in control. Show me what to do."

I glanced out the kitchen window. The snow was still coming down, but I didn't see any ice mixing with it. I'd drive my Explorer to the cottage and get the money, then head to Frank's cabin on foot through the forest. Locking the door behind me, I headed to the barn, where I'd hidden the Explorer—had it only been the night before? Fortunately, the doors slid sideways to open or close, and I didn't have to shovel wet, heavy snow to get them open. I had to coax my old Explorer to start, though, but she did eventually fire up. I let her run while I checked out how deep the snow was I'd have to back into. Thank goodness it wasn't as deep on that side of the barn.

Making sure she was in four-wheel drive, I put her in reverse and pushed the throttle to the floor. Snow flew out of my way as I plowed backward down the slope and to the main road. I twisted the wheel and straightened out. Putting her in low gear, I eased forward, gradually increasing my speed. I made it all the way down my driveway with only a few minor slips. Four-wheel-drive is a big plus in snow but can be tricky on ice. I'd driven my Explorer in all kinds of winter weather. While the ice made me somewhat nervous, I knew I could drive in it. I didn't know about Frank though.

A plan formed in my mind. Neither Frank nor Stephanie knew this mountain. I did—and in every mood she was in. If I could somehow get Kadie, I knew I could drive down off this mountain—with the money. I doubted that either one of them could.

At the cottage, I stuffed the money in my backpack—all 1.1 million dollars of it. Then I picked it up. Good grief! How was I going to make my way over the snow with a twenty-plus-pound pack on my back? I'd hiked with a heavy pack before, but never on snow this deep. I knew I needed a wider, larger shoe to spread the extra weight over the surface of the snow, but my mountain terrain shoes were still the best bet to get me through the woods. The snow wouldn't be as deep in the woods.

I didn't know what I was going to do when I got there yet, but I needed to be as quiet as possible. When we were in the village, I'd call Don. I rooted through my purse for my cell phone and finally found it in the pocket of the coat I'd worn last night. I pushed the button to turn it on—nothing. Dead battery. I should have turned it off last night when the power went out. I slipped the phone in my jacket pocket. I had a charger in the Explorer. I couldn't risk a dead battery in my escape vehicle, so I'd wait to plug it in until we were on our way.

Then I headed to Frank's place, praying that God would answer my prayer.

A half an hour and several stops later to adjust the pack, the cabin came into view. I stopped, wanting to observe the place before I made my move. It was curiously quiet. Too quiet. No smoke curled from the chimney pipe. Frank's truck and Stephanie's luxury car were parked in the driveway under a foot of snow and ice, so I knew they were still here. No tracks marked the pristine snow around the cabin. Not even to the outhouse. Loosening the straps, I slipped the cumbersome pack onto the snow and crept forward. I pressed my ear to the window where I'd eavesdropped the night before. Nothing. It was as still as death.

I scratched the window lightly. Last night Stephanie had jumped at every sound. Surely she'd hear this. I kept my head below the glass pane. Nothing. I ran my fingernail across the glass again, tapping it lightly, but there was no reaction from inside. Were they even there? Maybe they'd left before the roads got too bad. But how? There hadn't been a third vehicle in the driveway last night. Was there another partner—someone who picked them up?

There was only one way to find out—go inside. They were probably expecting me anyway. So I went in. And gagged.

The heat was suffocating. A portable propane heater was going full blast. Frank and Stephanie were there all right. Dead. Their staring eyes told me that. From the stiffness of their bodies, I estimated they'd died no more than twelve hours earlier. Rigor mortis, I knew, begins to dissipate after that time.

A beer bottle lay on its side on the linoleum floor beside the recliner, inches from Frank's dangling fingers. An empty wine glass sat on a small table beside Stephanie, who was sprawled sideways on the sofa. A half-eaten pizza lay in an open box beside an open wine bottle on the coffee table. There was no blood, no bruises on their bodies, no sign of struggle. It was as though they'd simply fallen asleep. Sweat poured down my face. My insides were quivering. I unzipped my jacket with trembling fingers, getting the zipper stuck halfway. Gosh, it was hot!

The propane heater! Covering my mouth and nose with my gloved hand I rushed outside. On the snow-covered porch, I exhaled and inhaled deeply, hoping the carbon monoxide that probably had killed the pair inside hadn't begun to affect me. I took a deep breath, then, holding it, went back inside, where I shut off the heater and the valve to the propane supply line. Hadn't they known that running an unvented propane heater in a cabin this small would spew the colorless, odorless poison?

I went back to the doorway and took another deep breath. The open door admitted fresh, cold air, but still I was afraid to breathe while I was inside. I checked the cabin for signs of Kadie, but I knew she wasn't here. She couldn't be. Frank and Stephanie were long gone before she disappeared.

Then who had her? Who had left the note? I pulled it out of my pocket and read it again. "YOU CAN HAVE THE GIRL WHEN I GET THE MONEY." When *I* get the money, not when *we* get the money.

Who was "I"? And where was Kadie?

When I got back to my cottage I slogged up the driveway and along the road, hoping I'd find signs of Kadie. A white Dodge Ram extended cab with Wyoming plates sat in my driveway behind my Explorer. Tracks led from the truck to the front door, which slid open as I approached. A man wearing hunting camo stepped out, pointing a pistol at me.

"It's about time you showed up," he said, a familiar sneer in his voice.

He cocked his head to the door. "Get inside."

"Where's Kadie?"

"She's fine. For now. But if you don't get your fat butt in here pronto, she isn't going to be."

That voice. "Fat butt"—I'd been called that before. My heart stopped.

"Paul."

CHAPTER THIRTY

"In the flesh."

"You better not have hurt her," I said, hurrying up the steps as fast as I could with snowshoes and a backpack stuffed with over a million dollars and a pair of kids snowshoes strapped on the back of that. At the door, I slipped the pack off and set it down, then loosened the bindings on my snowshoes and pulled them off.

Kadie was huddled on the sofa beneath my fleece blanket when I stepped into the cottage. When she saw me, she threw off the blanket and rushed to me, wrapping her arms around my waist and burying her face in my down jacket.

"Oh, Melody! I'm so sorry." Her shoulders heaved with her sobs. "I shouldn't have left."

I stroked her hair. "It's all right, honey."

I glanced at the man I was still married to, who stood by the door, a stoic expression creasing his once-handsome features. His thinning hair, salt-and-pepper like his trim beard, was pulled back in a ponytail.

"Surprised to see me, sweetheart?" His voice dripped with sarcasm.

"Don't call me *sweetheart*." I unzipped my jacket and spread it across the back of the sofa.

"I'll call you whatever I want."

"You haven't changed a bit." I unlaced my boots and then undid the clasp on my bib snow pants and stepped out of them, dropping them on the hardwood floor behind the sofa. "You can muscle up, grow a beard, dye your hair, but you can't change what you are inside, Paul. Only God can do that."

He rolled his eyes. "Oh, spare me. When did you get religion? Oh, I get it. When that Don guy came around. Oh, yeah, I know all about your new boyfriend. He's supposed to be a Christian." He spat out the word. "So you pretend to be one too."

"He isn't my boyfriend."

"You think he is. Getting all dolled up for him. You never did that for me."

"Yes, I did. You never noticed, so after a while I figured why bother."

"You think God is going to help you out of this? Think again. He never helped you before. Why should He now? Even if He exists, why should He care about you?" He snorted. "You're a nothing. A nobody."

I smiled. "He specializes in nothings and nobodies, Paul. You should give Him a try."

He forced a laugh. "Sit down and shut up."

I sank to the sofa beside Kadie, wrapping my arms around her.

"Were you cold this morning, Melody?"

I stared at him. "You! You turned off the propane. Why? So I'd be cold? You always did think your main purpose in life was to make me miserable. Really, Paul, the length your hatred takes you surprises me."

"Don't give yourself so much credit. I wouldn't waste hatred on you. I had to flush you out of your cozy little den, so I turned off the propane."

"I didn't see your tracks."

"I shut it off last night, figuring you'd wake up cold and go outside to check the valve. By then the snow would have covered my tracks." He smirked. "I was right, but by then it didn't matter. I already had the girl."

"You killed Virelle."

A satisfied—chilling—smile spread across his face. "And Frank and Stephanie. And that snitch . . . with your hammer. Pretty brilliant if I may say so myself. All I had to do is slip a little something in their drinks to help them fall asleep—fast—then turn up the heater. Stupid Frank had no idea that an unvented propane heater in such a small space sucks up the oxygen, not to mention the carbon monoxide it gives off. When they're found, it'll look like accidental carbon monoxide poisoning."

I stared at this man to whom I'd been married for thirty-two years. I didn't count the year and a half I was a "widow." When did he become such a monster?

"You murdered your own partners."

He shrugged. "I had to. They were blackmailing me. What I paid them wasn't enough. No honor among thieves, I guess."

"You're sick." I tightened my grip on Kadie. "Who was the man who fell off the balcony?"

His eyes lit up. "That was pure coincidence—serendipity, if you will. Steph noticed how much the guy looked like me when he checked into the resort. On a business trip. You see, there really was a conference, my sweet."

He lowered himself to the leather recliner beside the fireplace, keeping the gun trained on me.

"It didn't take much for Steph to get him up to our room and dead drunk. We switched wallets and passports and arranged for his . . . accident. Of course, I had to sit through a boring three-day conference as . . . whatever his name was."

Whatever his name was. He didn't even remember the name of the man he'd murdered and then assumed his identity.

I held up my hand. "Don't tell me anymore."

"I don't think you realize what a brilliant man you're married to."

"*Was* married to."

"Oh, did you divorce me in my absence?" He sneered. "I'm also a very rich man, as you've figured out with the help of your boyfriend—"

"And son."

His face slackened. "Garrett. My only regret in all this."

"It's not too late to do the right thing. Turn yourself in. Show your son you can be a man—"

"Too late. I've come too far to quit now." He stood and pointed the gun at Kadie. "I want my money, and I want it now. Or—"

"You can put that thing down." I rubbed Kadie's arms through the fleece blanket. "I'll give you the money."

His mouth twisted in a wicked grin. "All of it? You have it here?"

I nodded, miserable. This wasn't panning out the way I'd planned. He was going to get away with it. And there wasn't a thing I could do about it.

"Where all did you find my caches?"

I told him.

He shook his head, frowned, and pointed the gun at Kadie's head. "You're lying. You left one place out. Purposely."

I stood, placing myself between Kadie and the gun. "I'm not lying. But I did leave out one thing. I don't have all of it. Your parents . . ." I took a deep breath. "Your parents found what you left with them and spent it."

His jaw dropped. "They *spent* it? Nearly half a million dollars?" He swore. "What did they spend it on?"

"A new house. New furniture. A cruise. They figured it was payback for all they did for you—bailing you out time and time again. You should be ashamed of yourself. You used your own parents." Red-hot anger melted the icy fear that had been growing. "I'll get your filthy money. Take it and go."

He snorted. "And leave witnesses? I don't think so. Everyone thinks I'm dead, and everyone who knew I'm alive is dead." He narrowed his eyes, an evil gleam piercing the slits. "Except you two."

"You'll never get away with it."

I knew he would, but I wanted to plant that seed of doubt in his mind.

"Stop talking, fat butt, and get me my money."

"It isn't your money. It belongs to your former employer. A loser like you could never win that much gambling."

He leapt from the chair and backhanded me across my face. Pain shot through my face. I staggered but stayed on my feet. Kadie cried out.

"I'm fine, Kadie." I stared into Paul's demon-like eyes. "He can slap me around all he wants, but he'll never—*never*—get to me again."

He raised his arm to strike me again then dropped it. "So, my little mouse has finally found her voice." He laughed. "The mouse that roared. Too bad it's too late. You might have made something of yourself if you'd roared sooner."

"I might be a mouse," I hissed, "but I'm not yours."

His mouth twisted in a grotesque sneer. "What? You think that Don guy has a thing for you? Think again, sweetheart. He only wants one thing from you. And you're too blind too see and too stupid not to give it to him." He snorted. "You probably already have."

"That," I said, my gaze locking on his, "shows how little you know me."

Surprise flashed in his dark eyes. I was surprised myself at how well I was handling the fear. Oh, I was afraid all right, but the anger—at Paul, at his deception, at his callousness toward human life, at his greed—trumped the fear. I was more afraid for Kadie. He could do what he wanted with me. He could hurt me physically, but he would never inflict damage on my spirit again. His words would never again plant themselves in my mind and twist my thinking.

"Let her go," I said. "This is between the two of us."

"No can do, sweetheart. She knows."

"I'm not your sweetheart."

He slapped me again. This time I tasted blood in my mouth.

"Stop hurting her!" Kadie screamed. "I'll tell you where the money is."

"No, Kadie." I wiped my swelling lip with my sleeve. "Don't tell him."

She didn't know where it was. She was bluffing, buying time. Her blue eyes, sparked with determination, met mine. "He's hurting you. No amount of money is worth that."

"Oh, sweetheart." I dropped on the sofa beside her and pulled her to me. Salty tears dripped off my face and onto the blanket.

"Where?" Paul shouted. "Where is it, kid?"

"It's up at the farmhouse. In the barn."

He stared at her for several long seconds. "No, it isn't. You're lying."

She shook her head. "I'm not lying." I could feel her trembling beneath the blanket.

"Yes, you are. The money is right here in this cabin." He grabbed Kadie, pulled her to her feet, and shoved the gun to her temple. The terror that flashed from her eyes shot through my heart.

"Let her go. I'll give it to you."

"The money first. Then I'll let her go."

I shook my head. "No. Release her. Now."

"Get the money now or I pull the trigger."

"It's on the front deck," I said. "In the backpack."

"All of it? You're lying. No way two million dollars can fit in there."

"I'm not lying. It's all in there. All except what your parents spent."

"Get it."

I couldn't see the point in arguing anymore, stalling for time, hoping that somehow Don and Garrett would show up. I retrieved the backpack from the front deck and dropped it at his feet.

"There," I said. "Take it and go." I kicked the pack toward him.

He stared at it for a moment and then pressed the muzzle against Kadie's temple. "Put on your coat and boots."

I did what I was told.

"Now pick up the backpack and put it in my truck while girlie here puts her coat and boots on."

I looked at Kadie and nodded. "Do as he says, honey."

"See, little girl?" Paul jeered. "All a man has to do to get a stubborn woman to submit to him is to cuff her around. Let that be a lesson to you."

"Don't call me little girl," Kadie said, pushing past him to the coat tree, where her coat and boots were.

"Get moving," Paul said, waving the gun. "I don't want to stay on this godforsaken mountain any longer than I have to."

"The roads haven't been plowed. There's nothing but ice under all that snow. How do you expect to get down off this mountain? If you go into a slide, there are no guardrails or trees to stop you. That's a sheer drop."

He sneered. "Honey, I didn't spend all last winter working on a dude ranch in Wyoming for nothing." He puffed his chest out. "I got myself in shape, and I learned how to drive on snowy mountain roads."

"Don't be so sure of yourself. Wyoming isn't Pennsylvania."

"No. It's worse. Now quit stalling. Your new boyfriend isn't going to get here in time to rescue you."

He grabbed Kadie, who was zipping up her coat, by the arm and pushed the patio door open. Snow was falling in thick, heavy flakes. I shoved the bag of money behind the driver's seat and turned to face Paul.

"Get in your vehicle," he said. "Take the kid with you."

"You're going to let us go?" Kadie said.

He laughed—an evil laugh that sent shivers up my spine. "You can say that."

I nodded at Kadie. "Do as he says, sweetheart."

"Now what?" Once Kadie was buckled in her seat, I closed the door.

He held out his hand, palm up. "Cell phone. And don't tell me you don't have it."

"I don't. It's in my purse in the cottage."

His fist slammed against my cheekbone. I fell against the Explorer.

"Get it. And bring your purse. Nice try—leaving your purse behind. You were hoping when they found you, they'd think it suspicious that you ran off without it."

I staggered to the cottage, fighting dizziness and nausea, and brought out my purse. Reaching in, I fished around until I felt my phone. I shoved it at Paul. "It's dead."

"The kid. She have one?"

"I don't think so."

He reached past me, opened the driver's door of my Explorer, and pointed the gun at Kadie. "Give me your cell phone, kid."

God love her, she didn't even blink. "I don't have one."

"You're lying. Don't tell me your mother would leave you alone on top of this godforsaken mountain without a cell phone."

"Why do you think everybody's always lying to you? My mother had other things on her mind—like my sister who couldn't breathe. And besides, I wasn't supposed to be alone. Virelle was with me. You killed her—remember?"

Her bottom lip quivered.

"Leave her alone. She doesn't have a phone."

He tossed my phone in the air like a clay pigeon and shot it. The report from the shot echoed across the mountaintop, making me jump. The acrid smell of gunpowder reached my nostrils.

"See? I learned some other things on that dude ranch." He snickered. "You and the kid are going to have a little accident. Remember that drop-off you told me about?"

So that was his plan—push us off the road and over the cliff. By the time anyone found us, his tracks would be long gone. And if they weren't, they could belong to anyone. No one would see us down in the ravine. If the crash didn't kill us, hypothermia would.

"Get your scraper and scrape just enough so you can see out. Not the whole thing. You're in a hurry, see, and figure it'll defrost soon enough." His mirthless laugh pierced the frosty air. "Another contributing factor to your demise."

Helplessness welled up in me. As usual, he was the one in control. He knew my every vulnerable point. And now I had an extra one—Kadie.

"That's enough," he said when I'd scraped a peephole. "Get in and drive. Head to the village—where that stupid store you like is. I'll follow you." He waved his gun and grinned. "With this."

CHAPTER THIRTY-ONE

Slipping in behind the wheel of my Explorer, I reached across the seat and squeezed Kadie's hand, giving her a smile I hoped conveyed a bravery I didn't feel.

"We'll be just fine, sweetheart," I whispered, my breath in a white vapor. "God's got this."

She nodded, blinking back tears. Her hand trembled in mine.

"Let me start the engine." My bottom lip was swollen and throbbing, blood still seeping from where Paul had whacked me, making it painful to talk. "We'll say a little prayer while it warms up."

"Won't he be mad?"

"Probably. But we're going nowhere if this thing stalls out—or doesn't start. He knows that. There's nothing he can do about it."

"Except shoot us."

"Well, that too."

I turned the key and pumped the gas pedal. It took several tries—with me trying to flood the engine. If the old girl didn't start—and Paul knew how cantankerous my Explorer could be—maybe he'd give up and just leave without killing us. But that would be a first-class miracle.

To my surprise and utter disappointment, she started on the fourth try. Paul had already backed out of the driveway and waited on the road, passenger window down and, I had no doubt, his gun pointed at us. I glanced at Kadie. Her head was bowed, her eyes closed, and her lips were moving.

"Dear God," she prayed, "You said in Your Word that You give angels charge over us. We need an angel now. Please send one. Thank you. Amen."

"Amen." *Lord, I second that. Even if I don't get out of this alive, please spare Kadie. And don't let Paul get away with this.*

"Here we go," I said, putting the Explorer in reverse. Kadie kept her head bowed and her hands clasped together.

A foot of snow covered the road—there were no tracks—so I drove slowly toward the village, using the lowest gear. The snow had changed to freezing rain, leaving a crust of ice that glistened in the headlights. Although it was mid-morning, the heavy skies gave the mountain a dusky look.

I glanced in the rearview mirror as often as I dared to take my eyes off the road—one eye, that is. My left eye was swollen shut from when Paul punched me. I knew this road well, and even with one eye, I could anticipate every curve, every hill—unlike Paul. Even when he came to the cottage with me, I was the one who drove. I had that to my advantage, but how to use it . . .

Paul followed us, hugging my back bumper. How could I keep him from pushing us off the road? One nudge with that big, fancy truck of his and we'd tumble down the side of the mountain.

When we got to the top of the big hill, he edged closer, bumping us from behind. It was all I could do to keep the Explorer on the road. The noisy fan and still-cold engine did little to defrost the windshield.

He bumped us again, sending us into a slide. Bile, bitter and sudden, rose in my throat. Kadie let out a little cry. Keeping my foot off the brake, I turned into the slide and managed to straighten us out again. Then Paul pushed us with his bumper, steering his truck so that we edged closer and closer to the drop-off on the left. My quaking hands tightened on the wheel, my heart slamming inside my chest.

Just then an enormous black bear charged out of the woods and ran directly in front of us. I twisted the wheel to avoid hitting it. Kadie screamed. The Explorer spun on the icy road, finally coming to rest front first against the embankment on the right. My mouth slammed against the steering wheel—right where Paul had slapped me. I opened my eye. The sickeningly sweet odor of antifreeze filled the air.

I reached for Kadie. "Are you all right?"

Kadie nodded, her face drained of all color. "But I don't think your car is." She pointed out the windshield.

Steam spewed from under the hood. Oh, great. The impact had damaged the radiator. If I kept the motor running, it would overheat. I turned off the engine.

"Where is he?" Kadie asked.

I peered out the driver's door window through the icy rain. There was no sign of the bear. "We must have missed him. He probably ran off into the woods."

"Why would he run off into the woods?"

"He was probably more scared than we were."

Kadie frowned. "Scared? That horrible man? I don't think so."

"Wait a minute. You mean Paul?"

She nodded.

"Didn't you see it?"

"See what?"

"That bear."

"What bear?"

I frowned. "Didn't you see a big black bear come charging out of the woods right in front of us? That's why I swerved—to avoid hitting him."

Kadie gave me a puzzled look. "I didn't see any bear."

"Well, you wouldn't, I guess. You had your eyes closed."

"No, I didn't. I opened them the first time he hit us. Where is he?"

I twisted around, looking for Paul's truck. We were the only vehicle on the road.

"I don't know. Maybe he gave up and drove off."

Kadie shook her head. "No, he didn't. Look."

Tire tracks led off the road and over the cliff. Just then an explosion rocked the Explorer, followed by a flash from the ravine. Paul! Had he gotten out in time?

"Stay here," I told Kadie, picturing the inferno in the ravine.

I crossed the slippery road and peered over the edge of the cliff. Flames shot up through naked trees and hemlocks. Thick, black smoke roiled from the blazing, crumpled heap that was Paul's truck. It lay on its side, passenger side down. Through the smoke and flames, I saw that the driver's door was smashed in, the window shattered. It must have hit a tree on the way down. A lump lodged in my throat.

"Is he dead?"

Kadie stood beside me, shivering. I slipped my arm around her.

"I don't see how he could have gotten out."

But he'd fooled us once before. I knew I wouldn't rest easy until a body was found in that truck and an autopsy confirmed it was Paul.

"Your lip is bleeding." Kadie bent down and scooped up a handful of snow. "Here, put this on it. It'll take the swelling down and stop the bleeding. That's what Mommy said when I busted my lip riding my sled last year."

I took the snow from her and pressed it against my throbbing lip. It came away bloody. Blood had dripped onto the front of my jacket. Kadie handed me another scoop of snow. The skies still spit freezing rain, covering my Explorer with a solid glaze. Kadie wrapped her arms around her shivering body.

"We need to get out of this weather." I headed for my Explorer. "Stay here. I'm going to try to back it out of there."

After several tries, though, the engine refused to turn over. She wasn't going anywhere without the help of a tow truck. I rejoined Kadie on the road.

"Looks like we'll have to walk back. Are you up to it?"

"There wasn't a bear," she said.

"Yes, there was. I saw it."

She shook her head. "No, there wasn't. See? No tracks."

I stared at the road. The only tracks besides our footprints were tire tracks. No bear tracks.

"I saw a bear. I know I did."

Kadie beamed. "It was the angel God sent to protect us."

I was about to say that maybe I imagined it, with my left eye swollen shut and the windshield still frosted up, but that would be lying. I saw a bear, tracks or no tracks. It was there. And it was the reason I swerved the Explorer and ended up against the embankment instead of over the cliff. Paul, who'd been riding my bumper, hadn't had time to react and met the fate he'd intended for us. I shuddered.

Maybe Kadie was right. Who's to say what form angels take?

We walked the two miles back to the cottage, where I made hot chocolate for Kadie and a cup of Soothing Nerve tea for myself, heating the water on a two-burner propane camping stove I dug out of the storage shed out back. While the water heated, I got a fire going in the fireplace, and Kadie tried to text Don on her cell phone. There was still no signal.

"Better turn it off to conserve the battery," I told her.

After I washed my face—patting the bruises lightly, we snuggled side-by-side on the sofa, watching the flames lick the logs. Would I ever be able to enjoy a fireplace again without remembering Paul's fiery death?

After a while, Kadie nodded off. I covered her with the fleece blanket and moved to the recliner to boot up my laptop. I had to write what happened—every little detail—while it was still fresh. Hard to tell how long the electric would be out and the roads closed.

Meanwhile, there were dead bodies all over the mountaintop—one in the outhouse, two in the old cabin, and one in the charred vehicle in the ravine. I took a sip of tea through a straw and began typing.

I finished my account just as Kadie stirred. We made peanut butter and jelly sandwiches and ramen noodle soup for lunch and then trekked to the farmhouse to bring Charlie back to the cottage. Rascal didn't like that too much. Her hackles rose and she hissed at the dog before scooting up the circular stairway to hide under my bed.

After lunch, we tried the cell phone again, but there was still no signal, so we played Go Fish with a deck of I Spy cards I found in the junk drawer.

"Garrett and I used to play this game all the time when we came to the cottage." I smiled at the memory.

"I like him," Kadie said. "So does Mommy."

I wondered how Hannah was. The precipitation had finally stopped around midafternoon, but the temperature hovered just below freezing. How long before the road was plowed? I had no way of getting off this mountain—unless I borrowed Frank's truck. Stephanie's luxury car would be useless in this.

We played several games, and then I went outside for more firewood. I was glad I'd covered my woodpile with a heavy tarp. After I brought in several armloads and stacked them by the fireplace, I felt as though I'd tumbled down the mountainside. Everything hurt. I swallowed a couple of ibuprofen. Kadie sat on the floor beside Charlie, who was stretched out on the hearth.

"Sweetheart, will you be okay for a little while? I need to lie down."

Kadie nodded. "I can read my book."

I turned up the setting on the battery-operated lantern. "What are you reading?"

She pulled a book from her backpack and held it up. "*Murder on the Mountain*. My grandpa wrote it."

I smiled. "Well, he just might have a sequel."

"What's a sequel?"

"A story that follows another story." I snuggled under the blanket. "Wake me up if you need anything. And don't open the door for anyone."

I was fairly certain there were no villains left on the mountain, but you couldn't be too careful.

I dreamed of chicken soup—homemade chicken soup with lots of vegetables and fine noodles—just the way I liked it. My stomach was growling when I awoke. The fire was crackling—Kadie must have put a couple of logs on not too long ago. I pushed the blanket aside and slowly sat up, muscles and joints and face protesting. From the kitchen came the sound of silverware clinking. The aroma of chicken soup teased my nostrils. Chicken soup? Either that was a vivid dream or . . .

I hobbled to the kitchen. The breakfast bar had been set with two bowls and soup spoons. Kadie held her face above a steaming pot I didn't recognize.

"Kadie? What are you doing? What's in the pot?"

She placed the lid back on the pot and grinned. "Chicken soup. *Homemade* chicken soup. My favorite."

"Where did it come from?"

"That man—you know—the old man of the mountain."

"The mountain man? I thought I told you not to open the door for anyone."

"He said to tell you not to worry about anything. He's got your back."

"He said that?"

"Well, not in those exact words, but that was what he meant. He said he thought the chicken soup would be easy for you to eat with your swollen mouth and all."

"How did he know about that?"

She shrugged. "He's an angel."

"You think?"

Dimples punctuated her wide grin. "I know. Can we eat now? I'm hungry."

I was a little leery at first. What if the mountain man was the fourth partner in Paul's embezzling ring and the soup was laced with poison? But my hunger trumped my fear.

The soup was delicious—the best I'd ever tasted. I enjoyed two heaping bowls of it. We rinsed the dishes with water I'd had jugged up and set them in the sink to wash in the morning. After letting Charlie out for a bit, we settled on the sofa, Kadie with her book. I wasn't going to try to read with one eye, so I gazed at the fire, thanking God for saving us. I squeezed Kadie's shoulders, and she looked up at me.

"Oh, I forgot to tell you," Kadie said. "The mountain man said he checked the propane lines, and everything's good."

I hadn't thought to check the lines. Maybe he was an angel.

Before I nodded off, I put Kadie to bed upstairs, turned on the wall heater in the bedroom, and padded down the staircase in my socks. After adding a couple of logs to the fire, I snuggled under the blanket on the sofa. I was asleep before my head hit the pillow.

Sharp rapping on the glass patio door jarred me awake.

"Melody? Kadie? Are you in there?"

Charlie pranced back and forth in front of the door, wagging her stubby tail.

Don rapped on the door again, louder. "Kadie? Melody?"

"Just a second," I yelled. The cottage was dark except for the glow from the dying embers in the fireplace. What time was it? I peered at the wall clock. Ten o'clock! We'd been asleep for three hours. I shuffled to the door and peered out. Don stood there, a worried look on his face. I unlocked the door.

"Kadie—"

"Upstairs sleeping. We're okay."

"You don't look okay." His hands cupped my face, his thumbs gently caressing my bruises.

"Grandpa!" Kadie scrambled down the stairs and jumped into Don's arms. He squeezed her close. A tear escaped his eye and trickled into his beard.

"Oh, Grandpa! I'm so glad you're here. That man tried to kill us. Look what he did to Melody."

Don planted a kiss on Kadie's cheek and set her down. "Slow down, Kemosabe. What man?" He looked at me, his eyes filled with questions.

"He was awful. I can't believe Melody was married to such a monster."

She then launched into a detailed account of the past twenty-four hours. When she finished—a little out of breath—Don knelt down and swept her into his arms again, holding her close and tight.

"Oh, honey. Sweet Kadie. We shouldn't have left you."

"It's all right, Grandpa. God sent His angels to save us."

Don raised his eyebrows at me.

I nodded. "How's Hannah?"

"Stable. She's on IV antibiotics for pneumonia. They gave her a breathing treatment, and she's breathing much better."

"When's she coming home?" Kadie asked.

"Not for a few days."

I knew Don wanted more details but wouldn't ask any more questions in front of Kadie. She'd had enough trauma for a while.

"I'll put on some water for hot chocolate. Meanwhile, Don, there's a file on my laptop you might be interested in reading."

After our late-night snack, Don carried Kadie upstairs and tucked her in. Settling beside me on the sofa, he took me in his arms.

"Sweetheart, I'm so sorry I wasn't here—"

"Don't be. You were where you were supposed to be."

He kissed my forehead and then each of my bruises. "You're one brave woman, Melody Harmon. When I found out Paul was still alive, I got here as fast as I could."

"Wait! You knew?"

He sighed. "It was the last text Virelle sent me. Just as the storm hit and her service went out—or before . . ." He swallowed, his Adam's apple bobbing. "I didn't get it until a few hours ago. She had a hunch, so she kept digging." He stared into the fire, his eyes glistening. "She was a good cop."

I blinked against the image of her staring eyes and lifeless body. "Yes, she was."

"When I saw your Explorer in the ditch and blood on the snow, I didn't know what to think." He tightened his arms around me. "If I'd lost you . . ."

"What about Paul? I suppose it was too dark to see down in the ravine. We'll just have to wait until daylight and—"

"There was a body—a man's body—in the truck. I climbed down to check."

I gasped. "You climbed down that steep cliff with all the snow and ice? In the dark? How did you know the truck went into the ravine? You can't see it from the road."

"The damage to the trees where he went off the cliff. I had my spotlight. I had to make sure you weren't in there. At the time I didn't know Kadie was with you. I assumed—I *hoped*—she was still at the farmhouse. I didn't know she was with you until I got here."

"I can't imagine what you felt—what you thought—when you couldn't reach Kadie. The storm knocked out—"

"Shh . . ." He put his index finger on my sore lip. "We'll sort it out in the morning. I radioed in what I found in the ravine. The crime-scene crew will take care of the rest. That reminds me—I need to report in." He stood. "I'll tell them to let Garrett and Anne know you and Kadie are okay."

I pushed myself to my feet, wincing at the pain of my stiffening body. "You probably haven't had supper yet. I'll heat you up some chicken soup—*homemade* chicken soup."

His eyebrows arched.

"I didn't make it," I said. "The mountain man did."

"The old man of the mountain? You mean he's real? He was here?"

I nodded. "And he makes the best chicken soup ever."

CHAPTER THIRTY-TWO

Aunt Peg and Uncle Butch joined us for Thanksgiving dinner at Anne's place near Greensburg. Don made the turkey, Anne—with Garrett's help—made the fixings, and Aunt Peg brought homemade dinner rolls and her famous pumpkin pie. I surprised everyone and brought candied yams—made from scratch.

After dinner was cleaned up and a new dishwasher humming in the kitchen, we sat around the gas fireplace in the living room.

"Aunt Peg, this is the best pumpkin pie I've ever tasted!" Anne said, savoring another bite. "You must give me the recipe."

Aunt Peg arched her eyebrows. "I don't know. . . .That recipe has been passed down for generations and is supposed to stay in the family." She tried to hold back a smile.

Garrett put his arm around a blushing Anne and pulled her to him. "You can give her the recipe, Aunt Peg. Anne's going to be a part of this family. Soon."

A chorus of congratulations erupted. Don's eyes met mine. I felt my face get warm.

"We were going to wait until Christmas to announce it," Garrett said, gazing into Anne's eyes, "but why wait?"

"Do you have a date picked out?" Aunt Peg asked.

"December 22."

"Wait!" I said. "That's three days *before* Christmas! You said you were going to announce your engagement on Christmas."

Garrett's face turned crimson. "I didn't say what we were going to announce. We were thinking of eloping but decided we'd be cheating the family—especially you, Mom. You've waited so long for me to find the right one. I couldn't deny you the pleasure of watching me say 'I do.'"

"Where will you live?"

Garrett had been renting a house in Ligonier. I'd stayed at the cottage. In spite of all that happened, I still felt safe at my getaway place. It was home. Of course, it helped that Don was just up the road from me.

"We're going to live here in Anne's house—but it'll be *our* house. Anne and the girls love it here—and so do I."

"What about your house here in Greensburg, Melody?" Aunt Peg asked. "Has it sold yet?"

"Not yet, but Irene has several showings scheduled. Keep your fingers crossed."

"What did you do with that last cache of cash you found?" Aunt Peg asked.

Garrett had been working at my house, digging out the dead shrubs on the side of the garage to make it look more presentable to potential buyers, when his shovel hit something hard. Turned out it was PVC pipe stuffed with plastic bags of cash—one hundred bundles of one hundred dollar bills—one million dollars.

This was the cache Paul referred to when he accused me of not giving him all the money. In the shock of learning his parents had found and spent the half million he'd left at their place, he forgot about it. And he was in a hurry to get the cash he set me up to collect for him and make his getaway. He probably planned to dig it up himself once he got rid of me.

I took a breath. "According to Paul's gambling records—the last file on the flash drive that Anne was finally able to get into—it was legitimate winnings. The money was all his. He wouldn't have to share it with his partners. They didn't even know about it. He didn't report it on his income taxes. He didn't have to, since he gambled under a false name, and the IRS wasn't on to him."

"So as his widow, the money is all yours?" Aunt Peg asked.

I winced at the word "widow." I'd considered myself a widow since Paul disappeared the first time. We'd thought it was he who fell to his death off that balcony in Mexico. But now I was truly a widow. Autopsy reports confirmed it was Paul's body in the truck that plunged into the ravine.

"Yes."

"I hear the 'but' in your voice," Aunt Peg said. "But what?"

"Since Paul didn't pay taxes on it, to avoid hassles with the IRS, I've instructed my attorney to pay them."

"There probably wasn't much left after that," Uncle Butch said.

"She's giving some to Grandma and Grandpa Harmon," Garrett said.

Aunt Peg gasped. "What? Why would you do that?"

"They felt guilty about spending the half million they found that Paul had left with them. They knew Paul had a gambling problem and thought it was money he'd won. They were going to sell their new house to reimburse Paul's employer when they learned the money they bought the house with was really money he embezzled from the company."

"You're a better woman than I am, Melody Harmon," Aunt Peg said. "The way they treated you was shameful."

I shrugged. "Bitterness is a heavy burden to carry. It's like an acid—it does more damage to the vessel in which it's stored than the thing on which it's poured. I feel free. Finally and totally free."

"Is there any money left?" Aunt Peg asked. "All the cash you turned over to Paul burned with the truck, right?"

I nodded, fighting a wave of nausea. To my dying day, the scene of the burning truck would be scorched on my memory. Don pulled me closer.

"Melody didn't want to have anything to do with what money was left," Don said, his thumb caressing my upper arm and sending tingles through me. "So she donated half of it to the Cystic Fibrosis Foundation and the other half to the Tom Siple Foundation."

"Tom Siple Foundation? What's that?" Aunt Peg asked.

"It's kind of like Make-A-Wish," Garrett answered. "It raises money to provide terminally ill men, women, and children with outdoor experiences. Children who are fighting chronic illnesses like cystic fibrosis also qualify. In fact, Hannah . . ." His voice choked up.

"Hannah will be going on a fishing trip this spring," Anne finished softly. "They're providing enough for the entire family to go."

My cell phone vibrated. I'd gotten a new one—one that was a lot nicer—after Paul shot up my old one. I pulled it out of my jeans pocket and glanced at the screen. Cassie! Why was my agent calling me on Thanksgiving? She'd been patient after I'd told her about the murders on the mountain, saying she'd give me some time and space to recover from my "traumatic experience." She'd been true to her word—for two weeks.

"I have to take this," I said, standing. "It's my agent. I'll be right back."

I headed for the kitchen. Don on my heels.

"Do you have this on speaker?" Cassie's voice sang. "Put it on speaker."

I obliged.

"Happy Thanksgiving, Melody and Don!" Her voice echoed through the kitchen.

"Happy Thanksgiving, Cassie," we said in unison.

"Have you started the novel yet?"

Cassie wasn't one to beat around the bush—even on a holiday—especially on a holiday.

"The three chapters are written—sort of—and we have a list of ideas for the rest of the plot." I leaned against Don, loving the smell and the feel of him.

"Great! And when will I have the final draft? By Christmas?"

I laughed. "You're kidding, right? We haven't even decided which idea to pursue, if any of them."

"Well, hole yourselves up in that writing retreat and start writing. Pick any idea. Just start writing."

I smiled. The idea of holing up on top of the mountain with Don sent a thrill through me.

"And don't procrastinate. Don, take the lead on this. She's a great writer, but she puts off her projects until the last possible minute. Gives me an anxiety attack every time. Now listen, if they like this novel, they want to sign a multi-book contract. I'm negotiating for a big advance. After all the publicity you two got with breaking the embezzling ring—"

Don pulled the phone from my grasp. "Happy Thanksgiving, Cassie. And Merry Christmas. We'll talk to you after the first of the year."

He disconnected the call and placed the phone on the countertop. Then he pulled me to him.

"I've got a great idea!" I said. "How about a series about a former cop and a dead-end romance writer who team up to solve mysteries?"

"That," he murmured as his lips met mine, "sounds like a winning combination."

ABOUT THE AUTHOR

Michele Huey writes a weekly award-winning newspaper column, *God, Me & a Cup of Tea.* Her published books include three compilations of her devotional columns and two Christian novels, *The Heart Remembers* and *Before I Die.* She is an inspirational speaker, teaches at writing conferences, and serves as the lay pastor for a small congregation that she calls "her little flock." This mother of three, grandmother of five, and wife of one lives in western Pennsylvania—her favorite setting for her fiction. She loves hiking, camping, swimming, and reading, and is an avid (and sometime rabid) Pittsburgh Pirates fan. Visit Michele online at michelehuey.wordpress.com.

Ghost Mountain
PennWoods Mystery Book 2

Life is anything but a sweet plot for romance novelist Melody Harmon. Not only is she under contract to work with ex-cop-turned-suspense writer Don Bridges, but he's also her on-again, off-again boyfriend—currently off again.

But when cast members of the local production of *The Hound of the Baskervilles* turn up missing, the director asks them to solve the disappearances discreetly. According to legend, the old sawmill-turned-playhouse is haunted—by ghosts known to abduct a human or two on occasion. Then the director's mauled body is found in the woods surrounding the mountaintop theater, and Don's granddaughter Kadie, a junior member of the cast, vanishes without a trace.

Police say wild dogs killed the director and Kadie ran away. "It's only a legend," they insist. But is it? Melody and Don must put aside their differences, defy the police's orders to back off the case, and find Kadie before it's too late.

Office of Divine Intervention
Book 1 of the "Almost" Angel series

All Grace wanted to do when she got to heaven was to sing in the everlasting choir and to find Bruce, her beloved husband who was killed in Vietnam early in their marriage. But when no heavenly task panned out, she was assigned to the "Almost" Angel Corps, regenerated human believers, who, contrary to popular belief, do not become angels when they die. Instead they are sent to earth with a new name, a new body, and a special mission: to help designated humans help themselves. But where Grace is, trouble abounds. To the chagrin of Michael, her AAC mentor, she breaks every rule in the AAC handbook. Will Grace fulfill her assignment, find her beloved, and live happily every after? Or will she spend eternity searching for a place to fit in and the only person who will fill the void in her heart?

BOOKS BY MICHELE HUEY

FICTION

The Heart Remembers
Before I Die
"Gracie's Gift" Fifth Wheel Vol. 1
"Christmas Chaos," Fifth Wheel Vol. 3

DEVOTIONAL

Minute Meditations: Meeting God in Everyday Experiences
I Lift Up My Eyes: Minute Meditations Vol. 2
God, Me & a Cup of Tea

PRAISE FOR MICHELE HUEY'S BOOKS

THE HEART REMEMBERS

"Romance, heartbreak, laughter, and suspense, all rolled up in a book that will keep you turning pages into the wee hours of the morning."—Kathleen Bolduc

"Michele has created a compelling story about the power and persistence of true love. It kept me turning pages long into the night. It's been decades since I was willing to forego sleep to see how a story ended. Yet I simply couldn't put it down. And the ending was well worth it. A beautiful reminder that God's plans are perfect and so often more than we could ask or imagine. I can't wait for Michele's next book!"—Barb Schall

"Wow! What an enthralling story by a most talented writer. The author's retelling of the Vietnam era is so surreal, I felt like I was there. I even covered my head and ducked as the bombs exploded. The story is filled with suspense, compassion, and inbounding love. It is hard to find another read that is so engrossing as this one. It is one that you do not want to miss."—Debra Hancock

"I hadn't gotten far into it before I was gulping back my astonishment at the quality of writing and the emotional contact of the story. I found myself sinking into the events, remembering the tales related by my friends, seeing and feeling what the characters saw and felt. Wow. Just wow. On a scale of one to five, I'd give it a six!"—Anne Baxter Campbell

"Every time I thought I had it all figured out, this book delivered yet another twist. *The Heart Remembers* kept me on the edge of my seat until the very end. It delivers a powerful emotional experience and offers, to everyone whose life has taken a detour from the dreams of youth, a message of hope and redemption."—Patty Kyrlach

"Heart wrenching and heartwarming at the same time. Can't wait for more novels by this author!"—Jaime Hansen

"Michele Huey is a new novelist to love. Her books speak of real women in real life situations. Her debut novel, *The Heart Remembers*, is a compelling witness to the power of love and a God who never forgets our deepest longings. This story takes root and grows true faith. I will never forget Vangie's quest."—Virelle Kidder, author and conference speaker

"Deeply moving and thought-provoking, *The Heart Remembers* takes readers on a journey of the heart that will be with them long after they put the book down. With characters you can't help but care about, Michele Huey weaves a story of intrigue, faith, and—most importantly—love. A delightful read."—Robyn Whitlock

"This is an incredible novel. I couldn't put it down. What an engaging story of redemption, the rewards of letting go, the healing God gives to His faithful ones. I will be pondering so much for a while! Fantastic story!"—Heidi Cressley

"I loved everything about this book, as it was true to life and showed how God intervenes in our daily lives to make everything work out for our good."—Sybil Nichol

BEFORE I DIE

"I LOVED IT! I LOVED IT! I LOVED IT! My eyes were filled with tears at the end. You had the courage to write about the secrets of women our age—that longing to be loved and not just taken for granted—or to feel like we're stuck with each other now, so let's just make the best of it. I saw my own self in Linda. Thank you for writing this story. May God bless it and cut it loose to touch the lives of many others."—Kerin Mesanko

"I really enjoyed Michele's debut novel and downloaded this one as soon as it was available. I was not disappointed. This book paints such a clear picture of how a couple can get so caught up in life and all of its distractions and lose focus on what a marriage should be. It is also a touching story of how there are second chances for finding happiness in a marriage and making that marriage what God intends it be."—Ann Ellison

"I was captured from the first page through to the last. Michele, you owe me several hours of writing time and a few more of sleep! I couldn't put the story down."—Janice L. Dick

"I enjoyed *Before I Die* and was hard put to put it down before I finished it. Michele has a way of drawing you into the stories and identifying with the characters of her books. So many emotions that are true to life pop up in this book and make you realize you have gone through that too or felt that way too."—Amazon review from Grandma Four Eyes

"I feel like I know these people. The characters in this book are so real and well-rounded. They could be my neighbors. I can totally relate to Linda—so many women can!—Rachel Malcolm

"What an awesome book! Once again Michele Huey captured me from the beginning. I couldn't put it down!"—Anna F. Hildebrand

"I was really drawn into the story and could not put it down."—Karen A. Getty

CONTACT INFORMATION

Email: michelehueybooks@gmail.com

Website: michelehuey.wordpress.com

Blog: godmetea.wordpress.com

Dear Reader,

I hope you enjoyed *Getaway* Mountain. Please consider submitting a review and/or rating on Amazon and on Goodreads (goodreads.com/michelehuey). Your feedback is greatly appreciated.

Blessings,
Michele

43976685R00183

Made in the USA
Middletown, DE
03 May 2019